T0301097

The White Lie

Also by J.G. Kelly:

The Silent Child

J.G. KELLY

The White Lie

HODDER &
STOUGHTON

First published in Great Britain in 2023 by Hodder & Stoughton
An Hachette UK company

1

Copyright © J Kelly 2023

The right of James Kelly to be identified as the Author of the Work has been
asserted by him in accordance with the Copyright, Designs and Patents Act
1988.

A CIP catalogue record for this title is available from the British Library

Hardback ISBN 978 1 529 35783 7
Trade Paperback ISBN 978 1 529 35784 4
eBook ISBN 978 1 529 35785 1

Typeset in Plantin by Manipal Technologies Limited

Printed and bound in Great Britain by Clays Ltd, Elcograf S.p.A.

Hodder & Stoughton policy is to use papers that are natural, renewable
and recyclable products and made from wood grown in sustainable forests.
The logging and manufacturing processes are expected to conform to the
environmental regulations of the country of origin.

Hodder & Stoughton Ltd
Carmelite House
50 Victoria Embankment
London EC4Y 0DZ

www.hodder.co.uk

This book is dedicated to the glorious dead: Robert Falcon Scott and his four final companions - Henry 'Birdie' Bowers, Edward Wilson, Lawrence Oates, and Edgar 'Taffy' Evans. Every nation has its stories, and this is perhaps Britain's best. *The White Lie* is also dedicated to the American astronauts who died on the test pad in 1967: Gus Grissom, Edward White and Roger Chaffee. Their deaths prompted changes to the spacecraft, which they had christened Apollo, and ultimately led to Neil Armstrong's first step on the moon in 1969.

Author's Note

This book is fiction, but its roots lie in these two great journeys into desolate worlds. The story I wanted to tell – about a child orphaned by war and inspired by heroes - is founded in history, but I have altered, or invented, elements of the past freely in terms of place, time, and character, but always in the interests of drama, clarity and pace. The overriding consideration is to allow the reader *to be there* – at the moment of defeat, and the moment of triumph. For those of us who have not been to the moon, or the South Pole, I hope the book provides two, unforgettable, journeys of the mind.

DRAMATIS PERSONAE
1912

THE FINAL PARTY FOR THE POLE

Robert Falcon Scott – *The Owner* – captain, RN
Edward Wilson – *Uncle Bill* – chief scientist, doctor
Lawrence Oates – *Soldier, Titus* – captain, Inniskilling Guards
Edgar Evans – *Taffy* – petty officer, RN
Henry Bowers – *Birdie* – lieutenant, RIMS

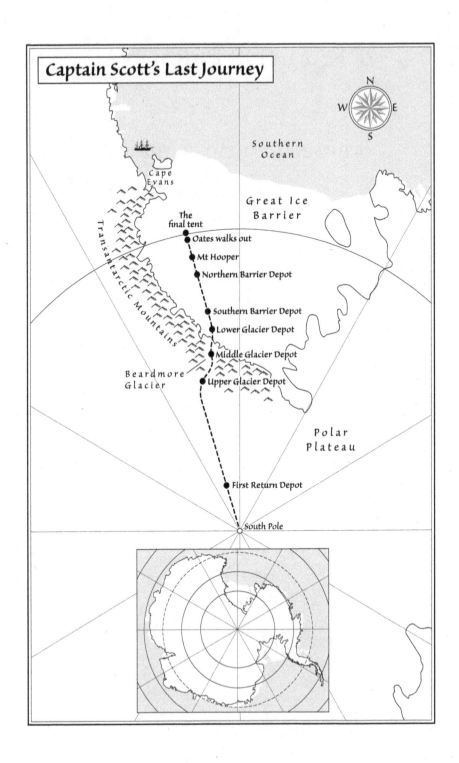

Prologue

November 10, 1912, ten miles south of One Ton Depot on the Great Ice Barrier, Antarctica.

Twelve men had set out to find the dead, fittingly, as they were all in some way apostles.

Under their feet was the sea ice, which shuddered and groaned, as if the bones of a giant were flexing with the arrival of spring. Each crash and boom of shearing ice became the plaything of echo, the thunder of gunfire.

Apsley Cherry-Garrard – Cherry to all – felt as if they were marching too late to join a lost battle.

With the others he pulled a sledge along the well-trodden path south, an arrow's flight, marked by cairns, and depots, and the makeshift graves of ponies and dogs. Unless a blizzard had blown them off course, or they'd died in the glassy depths of a glacier, Scott and his men lay ahead, in their own tomb.

Since they'd last been seen alive, dragging their sledge away into an infinity of white, six months of polar night had come and gone. The depthless hush of the Barrier's winter had fallen over them. They could not be alive.

Cherry looked at his boots, hauling, the miles passing. He thought about what lay ahead: the five dead men. He didn't think about the life he'd once had: the family estate, tradesmen's bills, lawyers, dinner tables, tea parties, church towers, chalk streams, distant views of the Hertfordshire hills. This white world was simpler, a reduction, a blank page on which stories could be written.

The only thing that mattered was character. Which made him fear all the more what might lie ahead for him: if they found what he suspected they'd find he'd be revealed as a coward, damned, disgraced.

Then, just ten and three-quarter miles beyond One Ton, according to the sledgeometer, Silas Wright, one of the scientists, said the four words that stopped Cherry's heart for a beat.

'It is the tent.'

It was a hundred yards east of the path. A mound of snow, a shadow lengthening as the day died.

Atkinson – who was their leader now – approached. Then Gran – the ski expert – brushed aside the snow at the summit and revealed the green fabric.

Cherry, immobile, felt the ice rising, seeking his heart.

He'd been sent out to meet Scott and his men at One Ton Depot eight months earlier. There had been no sign of them, but he hadn't waited long, hadn't risked another twenty miles. Bowed by the first storm of winter, he'd turned for home.

If they'd died here while he'd stood peering – short-sighted – into that tumbling blizzard the world would know he might have saved their lives. That would be his place in history: the man who'd let Scott die.

It wasn't by design, but the others stood back, Cherry apart – the accused before a jury of his equals.

Atkinson began to move snow from the entrance – a short tunnel that provided an airlock of sorts to retain heat and repel ice.

As he worked, a silence deepened. The sun was about 20 degrees above the horizon, edging west, accompanied by a pair of parhelion – 'mock suns' – which shone to left and right, each a smudge of light, refracted through ice crystals, scraps of rainbow. But the men looking on saw, for the first and last time on that continent, a third parhelion, above the sun, so that a cross shimmered in the sky, driven into the ice.

Cherry looked away, his poor weak eyes glazed with tears, hidden behind his snow goggles.

Atkinson called for help. There was only one shovel. Gwynne, the stoic Cornishman, stepped forward with the rolling gait of the fisherman, made the sign of the cross, then began to dig.

Metal cut through ice, jarring and visceral.

Atkinson got down on his knees and disappeared inside the tent.

They all bowed their heads.

When he came out they knew the truth. His shoulders slumped and a hand rose to remove his cap.

'It's them,' he said, his words set against a perfect stillness. 'Three – The Owner and two others. I can't see their faces.'

Scott was always The Owner to his men.

Atkinson beckoned. 'Cherry. I need you here.'

He walked to the tent, took off his goggles and, kneeling down, followed Atkinson along the short tunnel.

It was the moment he felt that his whole life might be a failure.

It was a grave, but it did not smell of the grave. It was a metallic empty void, full of the iron of rock and the salt of the air and the thin, lifeless reek of dead ice.

'There's no hint of decay,' said Atkinson, half standing in the green gloom.

The low tent was touching their heads, and they had to clutch each other to keep upright.

As their eyes got used to the light, Atkinson crossed himself.

Cherry looked down: three bodies, but only one face visible, that of Scott in the middle.

Edging forward Atkinson undid the sleeping-bags to reveal Bowers to the left, and Wilson to the right.

'God, the skin,' said Cherry.

The bodies were yellow, and slightly desiccated, but the flesh looked pliable and not at all mummified. Their eyes were milky and had – a little – fallen away.

In one hand Scott held a slim blood-red notebook, while with the other he'd pulled open his jacket to expose the shirt beneath, the hand coming to rest on Wilson's arm.

'What's he doing?' asked Atkinson.

'He's daring death to take him,' said Cherry. 'I think he was alone, Atch. At the end. And death didn't come – he hastened it, and it took him. He knew we'd find him. It's a message for us. That he led to the end.'

Atkinson, kneeling, pointed at the notebook.

The cover carried a message: 'For Cherry's eyes only'.

Atkinson tried to prise the notebook from Scott's grip. There was a crack – like a pistol shot – and the hand was free. The arm, brittle with ice, had shattered at the bone.

Cherry was sickened by the noise, an audible glimpse of the hell into which he felt he was about to fall.

'I'll get the men to pitch camp. Take as long as you want,' said Atkinson, bending forward to retrieve from under Scott's shoulder the document bag, which would hold the dead men's diaries.

'Atch – wait. Please.'

They stood, eyes meeting.

'Can you check the last date in the diary, Atch? When did they get here? When did they die?'

Atkinson's fingers were stiff from the cold and it took a tumbling minute for him to open the satchel and retrieve Scott's diary, which he held as if it was a holy book. He turned the pages, searching for the last entry. 'They got here on March the twenty-first. Last entry March the twenty-ninth.' Atkinson managed a thin smile: 'They didn't get this far until eleven days after you left One Ton for home, Cherry – you couldn't have helped.'

He flicked back to 10 March, the day Cherry had turned away, back towards the ship at Cape Evans. 'They were sixty miles south,' he said, putting a hand on Cherry's shoulder, then slipping out of the tent on hands and knees.

Alone, Cherry wept, because it was not the worst. But if he'd gone further, he could have laid stores. Perhaps they would have lived longer. No blame – no public blame – would fall on him. He'd done the right thing, but he knew he hadn't done the glorious thing. And even now this small grain of guilt was growing, blooming, taking shape.

In the green light he opened the notebook. The first page held only a message.

Cherry,

There's no time for sentimentality, but I hope you'll understand me when I say I wished you'd been with us on the final push. This notebook is for you. I trust you. We all trust you. Read it, keep it secret. If the truth is known now it could bring war. Hand a copy – in person – to Sir Edward Whyte at the Foreign Office. The diaries in the bag tell the truth, but not the whole truth. The world will clamour for our story. Give them the diaries.

I was warned before we sailed, Cherry. We've been hunted down. Murdered, in the coldest of blood.

Vengeance – we lived for it, until we could live no more.

Keep the original safe.

For God's sake find the truth.

Robert Falcon Scott

ONE

NORTH

I

February 1947: Lamer House, Hertfordshire

Blossom, the grey pony, delivered her foal at dusk on the night of the great party.

Mr Potts, the groom, ran with the news from the stables to the house through a thickening blizzard, thudding against the kitchen door, bursting into the fug of heat and firelight, a cloud of steam rising from the range. Candles stood on every surface. The cook kept her wide back turned, attending to pans, while two girls – brought in from the village for the night – sat peeling vegetables.

'It's a colt,' he announced, breathless, taking off his cap. All ponies, and all dogs, were named by order of the lord of the manor, so that each animal was – at least to him – a living reminder of former companions, who now lay in shallow icy graves in the Antarctic wastes, despatched by a gunshot wound to the skull. A typed list of designated names, in order, was nailed to the post of the foaling stall.

'Mr Cherry will want the news,' he said, to a boy standing by the fire in short trousers and stockinged feet. 'Go and find Barton, Falcon. Tell him Blossom is well and the colt's name is Bones.'

Falcon was afraid of Barton, largely because it was said the master now insisted the butler slept with a gun under his pillow, his appointed night-time role being watchman at Lamer House.

Falcon looked down at the holes in his socks. Mr Potts walked over and ruffled his hair. 'Jump to it – there might be sixpence in it. You'll probably find Barton in the dining room - he'll tell the master.'

Six steps took Falcon up to the corridor, which led past the brewhouse, through the green baize door, and into the hallway, where the Christmas tree had stood only a few weeks before. There was a large chandelier, with electric bulbs, that now hung useless, its intricate branches deep in shadow.

He moved silently over the black-and-white tiles to the open doors of the dining room, where light flickered.

He had not been heard, so he took off his cap, and Barton caught the slight noise in the quiet room.

'I'm busy. It'll have to wait,' he said, pinging a crystal glass with his index finger.

He'd fought in the Great War, and at church parade wore a line of medals. Falcon always imagined him on sentry duty, trudging along a trench, untroubled by bullets overhead. 'Blossom's had her foal,' he said. 'Mr Potts said the master wanted to know when the time came.'

Barton had moved on to examine his reflection in a fish knife.

'It's a colt called Bones,' said Falcon, doggedly.

A sudden squall of icy snow rattled the sash windows and all the candles fidgeted. Barton froze, the knife an inch above the linen, as if waiting for another sound. The electric lights came on, and they heard a muffled cheer from the kitchen. Then they flickered out again.

'Mr Attlee's government has decreed that light must be rationed, like everything else,' added Barton. 'It's put us all behind the clock tonight. If we don't get electricity I fear we'll struggle to keep up appearances. We've got ten for dinner – eleven if *he* makes an appearance, which he won't. The first car's gone down to the station.'

It was the third week of what the wireless called the Great Freeze, and power cuts had left them with no electricity for hours and gas lights that guttered and failed. Falcon often listened to adult conversations, and they had begun to follow a predictable path: this was, they all agreed, 'worse than the war'.

'Ten years ago half the village was in service at Lamer. Now look at us,' Barton said. He surveyed the room as if he could see the glittering past.

Falcon had heard the stories of Lamer's glorious years many times.

The master was an explorer, who'd gone with Captain Scott to conquer the South Pole. He'd come home to write a book about his adventures, and famous people came to see him: politicians, and writers, and other explorers.

Barton gave the boy a candle in a pewter dish.

'You can run an errand – even in your socks. Off you go. Through the drawing room, third door on the left. He doesn't bite.'

Falcon crossed the hallway and gently pushed open the drawing-room door. The flickering candle caught several mirrors, which reflected the flame, and his own half-lit image: a six-year-old boy, with unruly hair and pale hands, clutching pewter and cap. Clocks, poorly wound (lack of staff again), fell into line behind their master in the hallway, striking seven.

Beyond the far door was a panelled corridor, which reeked of wet dog. The master kept Labradors. The current pair were Deek and Hohol. Falcon was fascinated by the way in which the master commanded their loyalty but never seemed to show them affection. They simply dogged his heels, always in his wake, edging closer if he sat on a stile, or a wicker chair on the lawn.

The interior of the house – beyond the servants' wing and the cellars – was a hidden place, only glimpsed through French windows, or beyond a slowly closing door. There was just one occasion when the kitchen and stable staff were

allowed above stairs. On Christmas Eve all the servants gathered in the hallway under the chandelier as presents were,
by tradition, given out by the master, although this year Mr
Cherry was 'under the weather' – Falcon noted that this
news was received with sly looks.

He put his ear to the third door along the corridor and
listened.

Mr Cherry-Garrard had been ill since late autumn. The
true nature of this 'illness' was never openly discussed, certainly not in the stables, although Falcon had witnessed
several whispered conversations peter out at his arrival. A
police constable had been called on one occasion when it
was reported the master had seen German parachutists in
the park – a startling concept several months after the village
party that had celebrated VE Day. There had been other,
frenzied, periods in which the house was searched from attic
to wine cellar, while the young mistress – always *Lady* Angela
– took herself out for long walks. Mr Cherry abandoned his
usual pursuits: foxhunting, shooting and the church. Sudden
journeys were undertaken to their new flat in London. The
servants' hall was full of whispers about a place called Harley
Street. And then the master returned, looking older, startled
by familiar faces. Doctors from London called, and lawyers,
and even one man in a top hat.

Then, one day before Christmas, Mr and Mrs George
Bernard Shaw arrived from Ayot, walking up the path of
poplar trees. (Falcon always wondered why a woman would
be called George, let alone Bernard.) Mr Shaw was famous,
and Falcon had seen his picture in the paper one day
because Mr Potts had torn out the page and left it for his
wife to read. Mr Shaw had written a play called *Pygmalion*
and it was to be 'revived' in the West End – whatever that
meant. He asked Mr Potts what the play was about and was
simply told it illustrated the virtues of speaking properly.

For a while the Shaws visited almost every day. The master was never seen, but a Bath chair arrived from Harrods (a detail provided by Cook), and a bed was moved downstairs into the library.

The intervention of the Shaws, or possibly the retreat of the men in suits from London, seemed to coincide with the passing of some kind of crisis in the master's mind. Nevertheless, Barton told everyone that peace and quiet had been prescribed and must be maintained.

So, Falcon didn't knock, but edged open the door.

The room was warm, foetid and medicinal. There was a fire in the grate but no other light. Dimly, Falcon could see that the walls were covered with books. There was a camp bed, the counterpane taut, unruffled. There was a draught, but not from the door. It seemed to be slipping in through a large bay window, obscured by heavy curtains. Beside the fire was a wing-backed chair, and Falcon could just see a foot in a slipper on the edge of the hearth. And then a hand appeared, holding a cigarette, and rested on the arm, and a plume of smoke filled the air above, like a ghost.

'Sir,' said Falcon, as he'd been taught.

The dogs padded out of the shadows and nuzzled his knees. 'What is it?'

The boy had seen the master often, usually at a distance, but he'd heard him many times, because he called to the dogs, and the gardeners, and if they had guests in summer everyone else kept quiet so that he could speak. His voice was familiar, a voice of authority certainly, but kind, and intermittently uncertain, and even youthful – at least to Falcon's ear.

This was the same voice, but it seemed to come from a different place.

He walked up to the fire and turned to deliver the news. The shock of seeing Mr Cherry's face made him take a step back because for a few tumbling heartbeats he thought it was an impostor. His skin was puffy and blotched. His eyes were still pale blue, but the whites were rheumy and pink. His jaw had slumped, revealing his teeth, which had often signalled a white, sudden smile when he waved to his wife. But now they were yellow, and cracked, and Falcon could see that wires had been inserted to hold them together.

There was a glass of whisky on a small table and Mr Cherry's unseen hand emerged, moving towards it, then retreated quickly.

'It's Falcon, isn't it?' he asked.

It occurred to the boy then that when he'd been born in the stable cottage there'd been a list of names on hand for the doctor, as there had been for the vet.

'Yes, sir.'

The invalid closed his eyes then, and Falcon sensed this was because of the effort expended in asking the question and processing the answer. Mr Cherry was wrapped in a soft blanket, but it was clear his posture was rigid, as if he'd been bound to the chair with iron rings.

'Blossom had her foal, sir. It's called Bones.'

Mr Cherry's eyes opened, and he let out a gasp, as if suddenly coming up for air.

'Shall I get the mistress?' said Falcon, turning on his heels.

Cherry shook his head: 'No. I was asleep. Stay, please.'

This time his hand encircled the glass and he sipped the whisky, resting the tumbler on his chest. The 'please' had confused Falcon, who was used to doing as he was told.

'It's a colt, then?'

'Yes. Sir.'

'Have they found you a bed yet, young Falcon Grey?' asked Cherry.

'In the cottage, sir. The box.'

'I bet the tack room was more fun.'

Falcon was lost for words. It had never occurred to him that Mr Cherry knew anything about him. The master closed his eyes again, so Falcon simply sat down on the hearthrug by the dogs. He felt certain that, as he had not been dismissed, he should stay, in case there was a message to take.

Mr Cherry was right, of course. The tackle room *had* been fun. Falcon's mother, heavily pregnant, had been evacuated to Lamer in the first weeks of the war. The estate had taken several families and space was scarce, so they'd been given the old tackle room below the hayloft at Home Farm. Falcon had been born in October, at dusk, just in time to greet the first winter snow. At night they'd stood silently with the rest of the staff watching the red sky flicker over the East End of London. His mother helped in the kitchen (her London specialities were a regular source of wonder – especially bubble and squeak), and his father picked up work as a farm hand. Later, looking back, the simple word 'Lamer' was always the cue for reminiscence and anecdotes. He remembered two scenes at first-hand – remarkably both from his second birthday: he was sitting on one of Mr Cherry's ponies, and remembered seeing the world between the small, furry ears of Snippets. Later there'd been a cake and he remembered sitting, possibly for the first time, at the long servants' table. The cake was Simnel, with marzipan balls.

The idyll couldn't last. His father was a clerk at one of the breweries off The Cut at Waterloo, and farm labouring on the Lamer estate was poorly paid. The German air raids had subsided, so they'd returned to the house in New Cross. His sister, Edie, was born a year later. The family had a one-bedroom flat in a tall Victorian house on Pepys Road, which ran down to the busy thoroughfare of the London to Dover highway, or up to the green fields of Nunhead and Telegraph Hill. At the foot of the hill a bookshop was run by Uncle Pat, who wasn't an uncle at all but one of his father's 'comrades'.

Their entire flat would have fitted into Lamer's dining room. His parents slept with Edie, while he had a bed set up each night in the kitchen by the fire. His mother was a cleaner at the posh school on Telegraph Hill. Edie and Falcon were looked after by a neighbour called Aunty May, who wasn't an aunty either. The war was exciting, memories of Lamer faded, and when the rocket attacks began he plotted them on a Tube map of London pinned up in the kitchen. He even heard one – a doodle-bug – flying over the river. That was the trick of it: if you could hear the engine you were safe. When it cut out you had to run for your life. The rocket was called a V1, and their teacher said that the V stood for Victory, but Falcon's father – a great reader of newspapers – said that was nonsense: the V was for Vengeance.

Then the V2s started. These travelled faster than the sound they made, so they struck in silence, the only warning being the rush of wind they pushed ahead of the nose cone. Then came the shock-wave – which was what really did the damage, because the rocket was as tall as a house and crashed at thousands of miles an hour. In the playground the boys never stopped talking about the rockets. They said that when doctors opened up the victims – who were untouched on the outside – they found their insides destroyed, like butcher's offal. Falcon tried not to think about the reality of this, that something could kill you and you'd be gone before you knew the end of your life was approaching. It seemed unfair, cruel, as if the rocket could steal your life. His father had the right word: 'underhand'.

The Germans couldn't really aim the rockets – the target was London, and they even missed that. Then one came down on the other side of Lewisham – half a mile away - and the shock left cracks in the ceiling of the bedroom. The woman across the road, who was deaf, screamed for an hour. And the cat, Midnight, disappeared but came back after a week. The picture in the paper showed the crater, full of water from a burst main. It was like the Blitz, and people wanted to go back to the countryside where it was safe. At school there were more and more empty desks. One evening his father sat down at the table and wrote a letter to Mr Potts asking him to enquire on the family's behalf if they could return to Lamer for what they all now called the Duration. This time his father would stay behind. He'd send money, keep an eye on the flat, and feed the cat. At weekends he'd get the train to Hertford, and then the bus. That was the plan.

The next morning was a Saturday and Falcon remembered his mother singing at the sink. His father, who was on shift work, came home at eleven, had his lunch of toast and dripping, and went to bed for a nap. His mother went too, taking the baby, and Falcon was sent out to post the letter to Lamer. His mother gave him a threepenny bit for a stamp – and said he could spend the ha'penny change on sweets. He was told not to dawdle, because his father didn't want to sleep too long. Falcon promised: in return his mother said that they'd all go to the park for a treat. As he left the house Falcon could smell a bread pudding baking in the oven – which must have used a month's worth of their coupons from their ration book – so they might take that to the park and eat it from the warm tin on a blanket. As he took his cap from the peg on the door he looked at the clock on the mantelpiece: it was eleven twenty-five. If he ran they'd be in the park by just after noon, and the tea hut would be open.

Looking back, that day was a jigsaw puzzle with pieces missing. The last thing he remembered before the first blank was running down the stairs, jumping half the last flight and landing with a crash on the bare boards. This was forbidden, and he regretted it immediately, because his family were all in bed trying to have a nap. He sat on the floor listening to the silence, expecting to hear his father call him back for a reprimand. His father never hit him, but the dressing-downs were relentless and often made him cry. But nobody called out that last Saturday morning. He'd sat there, clutching his knees, hoping he wouldn't hear their voices.

He'd wanted silence – he'd wished for it.

He didn't recall going down Pepys Road at all, which was odd. Then, without any memories in between, he was in the post office at New Cross at the back of a short queue for a stamp. He posted the letter in one of the copper letterboxes in the wall outside, briefly checking the name and address in his father's neat copperplate hand:

Mr William Potts
C/o Lamer House,
Wheathampstead,
Hertfordshire.

The High Road was busy, so he ran in the gutter, because the pavements were full. He passed the New Cross Tavern and saw through the etched window a bar full of Millwall fans, decked out in scarves. It had begun to rain, which made the pavements smell like Lamer, fresh and green. He remembered his shoes slapping on the ground as he ran across the road, jumping the tram lines.

The sweet shop was called Tapton's. It had a bell attached to the door and it always took the shop assistant, the owner's grown-up daughter, a minute to appear. She came through the hanging bead curtain and he was going to ask for a Milky Way but his ears popped and he saw the girl saying something he didn't hear: pocket money then? He often wondered, later, how far above his head the V2 rocket was at that moment. It was falling, a deadweight, so perhaps a hundred feet. He thought if he'd been out in the street he might have looked up and seen it – they said they were blue and white, with fins and a silver nose.

Instead, he saw the window flex, the street scene outside – a bus passing, two delivery boys on bicycles, a line of cars – shifting slightly left to right. There was a dray horse on the far side of the road and he remembered it was spooked, its head madly shaking, its front hoofs off the ground. The shop was opposite Woolworth's and the next thing was the impact, which he heard through his bones, and which threw him against the back wall.

The normal laws of nature stopped working: he was dazed, but conscious, and pinned against the wall, but his feet weren't on the ground, which was impossible. The soundtrack caught up: he heard the scream of the rocket accelerating towards the ground, then the explosion, and then the visceral rumble of the shock-wave. Over the road the four-storey façade of Woolworth's was collapsing in slow motion, the blast travelling out, destroying the Co-op next door and buckling the surface of the road. He actually saw this, just for a moment, the road turning itself into a twisting ribbon of tar, like a skipping-rope. The smell of gas was very bad, and there was water in the air too – gushing out of the road, flying out of a wall opposite – a stream, full of silver light. Bells were ringing, and rubble falling, but with each passing second a silence was gathering itself up to cover everything.

Two cars, trundling, crashed head-on in the middle of the High Road, and both drivers fled, but in opposite directions. Fires were burning in the ruins of Woolworth's. One blazed with a livid blue light and a hiss. What sounds there were seemed to be fading away, as if his head had been plunged below the waterline in the tin bath at home. The pressure on his ears was painful, and he could feel something warm trickling out of his nose and into his mouth. He was on his feet now, but his legs gave way and he knelt down in the broken glass.

The air in the shop had been blown away, and replaced with a soupy mist laden with debris, flowing very slowly, murky and studded with brick dust and glass and splintered wood, all of it drifting out into the street through the shattered windows. It was taking him with the current, as if he'd been embedded, a piece of flotsam. He felt calm, detached, and even recalled being relieved that he'd posted the letter before the rocket struck.

Then there was another gap in his memory, because he was suddenly outside the town hall, a hundred yards up the road, standing by a lamppost that had been bent backwards, like a slingshot ready to be fired. He remembered looking up at the town-hall clock and seeing that the hands were twisted but had stopped at twelve twenty-five. Which couldn't be right. He'd lost nearly an hour of his life. Where had he been? What had he done?

His five-year-old body had begun to betray him: his knees shook, and his shorts were wet. Out on the pavement an ARP warden looked at him, then turned and jogged away, each stride leaving him airborne for longer than possible. In the shop everything had been muddy – all the colours muted – but in the street everything was vivid, and he saw now that his hands were red with blood, but he wasn't sure it was his blood. He remembered thinking he should go back to the shop, go behind the counter and help Miss Tapton, but it was too late.

A few people were dead, lying in the rubble, their arms and legs set at impossible angles. He wove a path through them, keeping his distance. He saw pieces of meat on the pavement and knew what they really were but he didn't let the words form in his head. Some people weren't dead or alive at all – they'd just come to a full stop. A bus – the number 12 to London Bridge – had hit a drinking fountain on the pavement. It was full of Saturday shoppers and they were still all in their seats, with their hats on, sitting up nicely. Falcon walked up to the side of the bus and a man was looking out of the window, a cigarette in his mouth, the smoke trickling over his face, which was perfectly com- posed – even amused – but his eyes were open with a fixed stare. The woman who sat beside him was crying into her hands, but he didn't move, or even turn to her.

Everything was happening too quickly, but in slow motion. Sound came back in a rush, and the air was full of sirens and bells, and the fall of masonry, which prompted clouds of dust that billowed out suddenly, obscuring the view east towards Greenwich. He could see for nearly half a mile along the road. All the traffic had stopped, and people were standing around, or looking up into the sky. A nurse wrapped a bandage around Falcon's head and asked where he lived, which seemed to unlock something inside him, and he started to run home, although there were shouts for him to come back. A man in overalls tried to catch hold of him, but he skipped past, nearly out of breath, ran up the High Road and then into Pepys Road. All he wanted to do was tell his father what had happened. He'd demand details, facts, observations. He might be a brewery worker, but he had what he called 'an interest in the wider world'. Twice a week he attended the Workers' Educational Settlement – an old house beyond the cemetery where he took classes in politics and literature. He told Falcon that it was his duty – even aged five – to understand 'the times we live in', not to let them slip past. The thought that he could recount the rocket attack to the family partly offset the guilt he felt at being late.

He could see that the first few houses in Pepys Road were gone, just the basements left, the bricks and windows and roof tiles blown across the street. As he looked up the road he saw the façade of one house slump into its small front garden, then break, like a wave, over the wall and spill across the street. When he got to number 14 the damage didn't seem too bad, although the front door was missing, and Edie's pram was out in the street, blown there from the front step, yellow flames gently playing within it. There were small fires everywhere, and ash was falling, pieces of paper alight and twisting. A woman opposite, who took in washing, was standing at her gate crying into a dishcloth. A man in an old suit carrying a milk can was wandering along the pavement on the far side whistling, but Falcon could see his trouser was torn, and his leg bloody.

He pushed open the front door and ran up the stairs – noting that while the carpet was unmarked the brass runners, which kept each step in place, had been pulled out, the nails scattered. There was a big crack in the wall and somewhere water was running freely. He fell over on the landing and when he got up he realised the house was on a tilt, leaning downhill. His parents' bedroom was at the front and he'd seen from the street that the window was still in place, but because it was a rule of the house he knocked three times, and then he used his voice for the first time since the blast.

'Mum?'

He heard the word inside his head but had no idea if it had come out of his mouth.

He opened the door and there they were, his mother on her side, always the right, by the alarm clock, his father on the left, and Edie between them, lying on a pillow. His mother was staring at the clock, his father the ceiling. Edie had such small eyes he couldn't tell what had caught her attention in that last second – but it was probably the sunlight, jittering, when the plane tree outside blew in the wind of the blast. He didn't feel a lot. The emotion he remembered was a stubborn sadness, which he knew would never go away – sadness at being left behind. It was as if they'd all simply gone out – the promised outing to the park perhaps – and forgotten to take him along.

He heard his own voice, and knew what he was going to say, even though he knew it was a mistake.

'I'm sorry I'm late.'

There was no echo in the room, but something about the ring of his voice made him go cold.

'I lost the time.' This was a phrase his mother often used, which reminded him he'd broken his promise.

He just wanted to lie down, to curl up at the foot of the bed. He didn't think about what had happened, but about a school outing, to Greenwich, where they'd had a picnic on the grass slope below the Observatory. They'd walked along the Meridian, which is where time begins. Falcon was pretty sure he couldn't make time go backwards, except in memories, but he finally fell asleep hoping that when he woke up his mother would be making up the coke fire.

Some neighbours and a fireman found him at dusk. He couldn't speak, and even now, more than a year later, he still felt left behind.

3

'So it's Bones, is it?' asked Cherry, waking up, but pretending he'd been resting his eyes.

'Sir. Mr Potts looked at the list.'

'Did he, now?' Cherry raised a hand and pointed at a framed picture above the fire, which showed a group of men with ski poles, a sledge piled high with boxes, and a line of ponies. The master's fingers were much younger than his face, graceful and slender, reminding Falcon of the sketches he made at the fete at a shilling a time for the church fund – 'vignettes' was the word, the lines very slender and buoyant, like kite strings.

'That's Bones, third from the right. Poor old Bones. Christopher ate his goggles,' said Cherry, sitting forward and smiling, his face animated by the flames. 'We'd made them for the ponies out of leather to save them from snow blindness – but the beasts were desperate for food, they'd eat anything, so they ate each other's goggles. Those poor ponies.'

One detail Falcon noted: the framed picture was hinged at the right edge, allowing it to open like a cupboard, and it was half an inch out from the closed position. In the half-light he thought he could see the grey metallic edge of a wall safe. (He was familiar with the world of hidden wall safes thanks to an addiction to the adventures of the Famous Five.)

Cherry stared into the fire and Falcon could see that he was living in what Mrs Potts would have called a 'brown study', an expression she'd never bothered to explain so that he carried a picture in his head of the room itself, booklined, with a mean fire, the windows draped, and a sepia tint to the wallpaper.

He noticed for the first time an old, thin, blood-red note-book on Mr Cherry's lap. There was something about the way it was precisely aligned, as if by ruler, to sit squarely, that made him think it was important, even precious.

'What's that?' asked Falcon. He took a step back. 'Sir.'

Cherry stared at the book for a full ten seconds.

'I didn't mean to ask,' said Falcon, thinking he'd crossed one of the invisible lines that seemed to define the adult world.

'It's just a notebook,' said Cherry, at last, splaying his hand on the cover.

The master's blue eyes narrowed, and it felt to Falcon that a decision was being made that might affect his young life. He was grateful for Mr Cherry's charity in taking him in – the posted letter had survived the attack – but the burden of being at everyone's beck and call was crippling. He owed his life to others.

Cherry must have caught the look of distress in the boy's face. 'I can show you a little,' he said. 'But you must never talk of this to anyone else. Do you understand, Falcon?'

'Sir.'

'You see, I have to keep this little book a secret. There are people who would take it if they could, if they knew it was here. I don't want to scare you. You're safe enough. Just don't gossip. Is that all right?' he said, manufacturing a smile.

Falcon, petrified, nodded.

Cherry opened the book and Falcon could see that it was a kind of diary, with dates.

'Can you read the writing? It's difficult.'

The script was so crabbed as to appear like code. As Falcon edged closer his hand touched the master's arm, or at least the heavy tweed of his jacket.

'Is it English?' asked Falcon.

Cherry nodded. 'Yes. It's in Scott's hand. Robert *Falcon* Scott,' he said.

'The night you were born your father came to tell me and asked if he could use the name. He had a copy of my book with him – I think he'd been swotting up. I said it wasn't mine to give but that it was a fine name and fitting. There was a snowstorm then too, of course.'

'Why is it a secret?' asked Falcon. 'At school they said Captain Scott's diary was in Cambridge and that if we ever went we could go and see it.'

'Yes, you're right. Sometimes people keep two diaries. One to be read by everyone. One full of secrets. This is the second kind of diary. One day I'll tell you all about it.'

'Is it priceless?' asked Falcon.

'Yes. It is. I try to keep it safe. But perhaps I should try harder.'

He closed the book and his sudden good spirits were gone. Outside there was the sound of snow sliding off the roof, and Cherry started, looking towards the draped French windows.

He coughed, straightening his jacket: 'I'm sorry about your family,' he said. 'I hope everyone has been kind?'

Falcon clutched his cap and found he couldn't speak. It had never occurred to him that his physical inability to answer questions about how he felt was in any way unusual – let alone a medical condition. But now he felt sick, as if the wooden parquet floor under the old rug had fallen away, and that a pit had opened up. It was just like that moment when you wake up in a half-sleep and have to put out a foot to stop yourself falling.

He couldn't talk about himself.

He must have looked pale because Cherry had a stick by the armchair and he used the shepherd's crook to snare a stool and drag it into the firelight spilling out on the rug. 'Sit, the fire's making you dizzy. You know you mustn't blame yourself – for what happened at New Cross? Mrs Potts says you feel that in some way you caused the tragedy. But that makes no sense, does it? The Germans made the rocket, fired it, and it fell. She said you were late home – and you couldn't remember why. That's shock. You were a victim too, you see. It's what we call the fog of war. If you'd been on time many other things might have happened. You might all have gone to the shops – and then you'd have died too.'

Falcon looked up and wondered if Mr Cherry knew what he was thinking: that he wished it *had* happened that way.

'In some ways you're still in shock. I've seen it, Falcon. In the Great War – in the last – in the south, too. It was a great ordeal for you – and so young. Your brain is still trying to work it all out. Time's the great healer.

'Anyway. Thank goodness you posted that letter. I hope you think of Lamer as home?'

Falcon nodded, his eyes full of tears.

There was an awkward silence in which the master seemed to be having a conversation with himself. His thin lips were moving, and his head dipped and turned, but his eyes were shut. Falcon guessed he was trying to apologise for upsetting him, rehearsing lines he'd never deliver.

Falcon felt the familiar urge to divert attention. 'Mr Bannister, the teacher at school, reads your book out loud.' That was how he knew Cherry's story, but only in random fragments.

The King wanted to see the Union Flag flying at the South Pole. Captain Scott set sail in a ship called the *Terra Nova*, which meant 'new land'. They went halfway round the world and picked up ponies on the way. When they got there they built a hut at a place called Cape Evans, while the ship sailed away in case it got caught in the ice. Mr Bannister had a globe on top of the book cupboard, which he took down and tilted towards the class, pointing out the North Pole, and then upended to show the South Pole.

It was eight hundred miles to the Pole from the hut. There was no way a small group of men could get there carrying all the food and fuel they needed, so lots of them set out together, laying depots for food and fuel to use on the way home. As they went south, groups began to turn back – the *returning parties* – allowing the others to carry on with the supplies they had left. Finally, about a hundred miles from the Pole, Scott was left with just four men he'd chosen for the final leg. Falcon could never recall their real names but he knew their nicknames: Scott was The Owner, then there was Uncle Bill, who was the doctor, then Birdie, who had a big nose, then the Soldier, who was a hero, and finally Taffy, who was Welsh.

But when Scott and his men got to the Pole they found they'd been beaten by a Norwegian called Amundsen, who had cheated by taking dogs and knowing how to ski. Scott and his men tried to retrace their steps back to the hut. Taffy died first, after a fall, then the Soldier, who was a 'Very Gallant Gentleman', walked out into a snowstorm because he had rotten feet and was holding them up. The next spring a rescue party found the last three men dead in their tent, with all their diaries. Scott blamed the cold, lack of fuel, poor rations, and bad luck for their deaths. The King came to a memorial service at St Paul's Cathedral.

Before they'd set off for the Pole, Cherry had had an adventure of his own in the Antarctic winter: three of them set off to collect penguin eggs. In the winter you never see the sun. It's always dark. A storm blew their tent away and they lay under the aurora australis and thought they'd be dead by morning. Mr Bannister put that in the weekly spelling test – 'aurora australis', as well as 'Antarctic', and 'Norwegian'. Falcon got full marks.

Mr Bannister said the book Mr Cherry wrote was called *The Worst Journey in the World* and it was a 'classic'.

There were stories in Mr Cherry's book that didn't get read out. One Easter, when everyone else was on a half-day off, Fletcher – who helped in the stables – took Falcon aside and gave him what he called 'the low-down' as he dug out last year's manure from Baker's Yard.

'He dropped one of the bloody penguin eggs,' said Fletcher. 'Blind as a bat.

'And o' course he could have saved Scott but he made a botch of that too. They sent him out to help 'em home but he gave up too quick and came back empty-handed. He stood about for a week instead of pressing on.

'He was only ten miles away from where they found 'em all dead. Then it was back off to the ship for brandy and beef. No wonder he's not right in the 'ead. That's guilt that is.

'It's in his book, all right. I didn't say it wasn't. But toffs stick together. They blamed the cold, and the short rations, and the ponies, and Uncle Tom Cobley. They said old Cherry got his orders and he followed them to the letter. Still, Scott's dead, and there's no way they can sweep *that* under the table.'

Fletcher was 'let go' that winter and never came back.

The library fire had died down.

Falcon kept wondering if Mr Cherry was going to put on another log. The master kept consulting a pocket watch, and Falcon felt he was trying to decide if he could face the party for dinner.

Falcon was still interested in the fabled sixpence, and decided he'd better keep talking. 'Did you keep one of the penguin eggs?' he asked. He thought this was what the disgraced Fletcher would have called 'a sure-fire winner'.

The mention of the word 'penguin' cheered Cherry. He took up the bottle of whisky from the floor and refilled his glass. 'Over by the bay window there's a glass case on the ledge with a piece of damask over it, in the shadows. Draw the curtain back and have a look, if you like. Be careful – there's no hurry.'

It was extremely cold as soon as Falcon left the glow of the fire. He parted the curtains and found the cloth, pulling it aside to reveal a glass bell-jar with a large yellowed egg underneath. There was nothing else to see, but he felt duty bound to examine it for a minute.

By the time he got back Cherry had rearranged himself. The blanket had been discarded, and the diary had gone, and he was lighting a fresh cigarette, tapping the packet of Pall Mall on his knee.

Falcon noticed that the hinged picture above the fire had been shut. 'I'd like to be an explorer too,' he said. 'But Mr Potts says I'd get lost straight off 'cause of my eyes. I can't see the blackboard at school so I have to learn from books.'

He peered at Mr Cherry as if to prove his point.

'They're promising glasses on the National Health Service,' said Cherry. 'It would be a comfort to think that all the taxes I pay have some useful outcome.'

'Mr Potts says you can't believe a word they say.'

'He's probably right. I can't see a thing without these . . .' He produced a pair of spectacles from his top pocket.

'We muddled through,' he said, and again the blue eyes focused on a lost horizon.

Falcon thought of a question. 'When you went to find the penguin egg, sir, it was winter?'

Cherry was letting the fumes from the whisky rise to his nose. 'That's right.'

'But if the sun never rises how could you see where to go?'

'The moon, boy. Sometimes it's in the sky all day – and then it disappears. We have to rely on our tables to time our adventures – do you see? But even in the winter the moon was with us, a great friend, a bone-white Chinese lantern, or all possible colours when the aurora blazed, green and blue and yellow. And sometimes the moon and the planets were so different to the eye you would not recognise them. The moon is often blood red, strangely distorted and flickering, like a distant fire on the horizon. And Venus too – a green sprite, or an icy jewel. It is a fantastical place, Falcon.'

'I can hardly see the moon at all,' said Falcon.

Cherry studied his face. 'Heavens, boy. You don't need good eyesight to see the night sky. Come on, let's see if the snow's stopped.'

Suddenly he was on his feet: 'I can't hear it, can you? I know one can't hear it, not in the real world, but I always think there's a kind of whisper to falling snow, so perhaps our luck is in.'

4

The snow had stopped, and for evermore Falcon believed Mr Cherry could hear when it fell.

Behind the curtains Cherry showed him boots and scarves, and then threw open the French windows. The garden ran away from the house – now a perfect snowfield worthy of Antarctica.

To the right was the walled garden, and what they called the 'Tudor Gate', which Barton said had been salvaged from the original house. To the left lay 'The Dell', a mysterious circular dip that wound down to a summerhouse, where they held a garden party every year for the staff. It was a ruin, but what Mrs Potts called 'picturesque'. There was also an ice-house, which was locked by order of the master and never used because he'd bought what they called a refrigerator, which had been installed in the engine house, although Fletcher had passed on another story, that back between the wars Mr Cherry had started 'night walking', and that they'd had to send out the dogs to find him, and he'd been there all the time, in the ice-house, writing his book by candlelight and drinking whisky.

'Follow me,' said Cherry, leading the way down the cork-screw path into the Dell. The master seemed transformed; his stiff limbs supple, his movements almost joyful. The small adventure seemed to have broken some kind of deadening spell.

'Wait here,' he said, when they reached the ice-house. 'We need light, and a lunar map.'

Cherry fumbled with the keys, then slipped inside.

Falcon looked up at the sky. The moonlight was harsh, catching each crystal of ice, and making it blink, so that the Dell's grassy slopes appeared to be signalling to the stars, which lay in a depthless black sky.

Cherry was back, locking the door behind him. 'All's well,' he said, holding high a lantern already lit, a leather-bound book under his arm. Falcon noticed that he checked twice that the door was locked.

Back up on the lawn they could see the house was still in darkness, although the dining-room windows glowed with candlelight, and the silhouette of Barton was behind the glass, still and watchful.

Cherry walked on towards a small hill that marked the high point of the plateau on which Lamer stood. They began to pass the great trees, which were centuries old: Cherry identified each – holm oak, sweet chestnut, mulberry, hornbeam. The very top of the hill was marked by a stone block, with a strange hieroglyph on the side depicting an arrow and a line.

'The surveyors who made maps left this here,' said Cherry. 'It's two hundred and ten feet above sea-level.'

Cherry put on his spectacles; they were wire with circular lenses and he had to find each ear before engaging the arm. He opened the book on the surveyor's stone to reveal a map of the moon. 'You see. It's very mysterious,' said Cherry. 'Great craters, and seas – *mares* – and there's even the Oceanus Procellarum – the Ocean of Storms. But no water – apparently – which is a bit awkward.'

He stared at the moon, and Falcon thought he was letting the light flood into his eyes, as if it was energy, or even life.

'Science is a wonderful gift, Falcon.'

Then Mr Cherry did an extraordinary thing. He knelt down in the snow, slipped a hand inside his coat and produced a small copper telescope, which he smoothly extended and held to his left eye – having pushed his spectacles into his hair – turning the bevelled edge to adjust the focus.

'Here, stand behind me, and use my shoulder to rest on – that's the key, boy, everyone's obsessed with the magnification powers of the instrument, but the absolute necessity is a solid platform. I've adjusted the focus but you'll have to fine tune. Come on.'

Falcon's hands were cold and he nearly dropped the precious telescope.

'Snap-snap,' said Cherry, kindly. 'The dreaded party looms, Falcon.'

As if on cue they heard a motor-car crunching up the long drive, hidden from sight by the wall, and a line of poplars, like saw-teeth.

'It sounds odd,' said Cherry, in a smooth conversational way, which seemed comical to Falcon, given the lord of Lamer was on his knees in the moonlight. 'But because you focus on the image produced on the lens, you don't need glasses at all. In fact the view is better without – as long as you don't have what they call astigmatism. I think you'll be fine. It's even easier with a reflecting telescope, because then you can just focus on the mirror image. Tell me what you can see, but be quick about it. I sense Barton approaching to starboard.'

Falcon blinked the image of the moon into view. 'It's not a full moon,' he said.

There was a cheer and a thin veneer of yellow electricity spilt across the snow from the house. South, in the black folded hills, a few lights showed in cottage windows.

'Well done, Falcon,' said Cherry. 'Not quite full. It's what we call a gibbous moon. Do you see? It's shaped like a beer belly, like the one Roberts the butcher hauls around. That's what "gibbous" means in French. If you can, look to the 'terminator' – that's the line between the lit surface and the shadow. It's where day and night end. Then tell me what you can see.'

Another car was moving slowly but invisibly towards the *porte cochère* of the house.

Falcon was transfixed: in the narrow corridor between the dark and the light he could see mountains and valleys, craters and strange cracks, all in intricate detail because the light was at a low angle and created a landscape of shadows.

'It's like a real world,' he said.

'Mr Cherry, sir.' It was Barton at last, carrying a smart overcoat and a scarf. 'Lady Angela wondered if you would join the rest for dinner.'

'I shall be the life and soul of the party, Barton,' said the master, still on his knees.

This was clearly a shock to Barton. 'I'll tell Cook,' he said, half turning away.

'I'll be one minute,' said Cherry. He stood, one hand on Falcon's shoulder. 'I don't think exploring is much fun any more,' he said. 'There's nowhere left. I'm not much use on a mountain. I miss it – the South. The space. The endless emptiness. That's the key – it's an absence of things, do you see? All that really matters is who we are.'

Falcon looked at the moon and tried not to think of rockets.

'I think the moon might be a wonderful place to go,' said Cherry. 'Don't you? Empty, and with the stars above all day. And great mountains they say – one of them is half the height of Everest. What a sight on such a miniature world.'

He turned to look at the house, the lights blazing, then back at the moon. 'We'll get there one day. What do you think, Falcon? A hundred years, or even less. Maybe you'll go, Falcon. You can tell me what it's like.' He took one more wistful look at the sky. 'I always look for the moon – it's often there in the day, drifting between the clouds. Always look for the moon, Falcon. Always look for the moon.'

5

Three months later

The night the burglars broke into Lamer even Barton had slept deeply: it was as if a spell had been cast over the house. The first Falcon knew of the outrage was when a police constable was shown into the servants' hall just after breakfast by Mr Cherry (a unique appearance below stairs). The master was brisk and business-like, although Falcon thought the whites of his eyes were pink, and his cheeks looked damp. A window in the dining room had been forced, and footprints had been found in the flowerbeds, leading back to a gate on the Ayot path, which hung from a mangled hinge. An inventory of the house was immediately undertaken and revealed a series of thefts: a watercolour from the hall (John Sell Cotman, 1826), two Delft figurines from the dining room (a wedding present), a silver platter engraved with an image of the *Terra Nova* leaving Cardiff for the Antarctic in 1910 (presented on the city's quayside by the captain of the *Deutschland*, Wilhelm Filchner, leader of the rival German expedition to the South Pole) and finally the framed picture that had hung over the fire in the library, which had hidden the safe on the wall. The real blow was only revealed by Cook: the master had risen early to walk the dogs and found them in the kitchen passage. The vet, called from Wheathampstead, said their food had been laced with rat poison.

Two weeks later Falcon was in the kitchen eating what was left of a gala pie for tea when Barton told him Mr Cherry was in the library and wanted to speak to him. The

silence among the rest of the staff as he slipped down off the
stool – socks again – was mildly shocking. Since that day in
New Cross, when the V2 rocket had changed his life, he'd
been content to let each hour pass unconsidered, perhaps
hoping on some unconscious level that he would simply be
reunited with his family – an event as likely, surely, as them
being blotted out randomly by a falling rocket. He lived a
life sustained by counterbalancing anxieties, a fear of what
lay before and what behind. He was now six and a half years
old. His future was unknown and had never been discussed
in his hearing. Asking questions seemed reckless.

Cherry's recovery had taken everyone by surprise. The
Harley Street doctors had worked wonders, according to
Barton. The master's bed had been packed away and he had
returned to the rooms on the upper floor. Even the burglary
had failed to dampen his improving spirits.

It was getting dark, and the French windows of the library
were open, but this time there was no moon. It had been in
the sky all day, shyly describing an arc over the Hertfordshire hills. Falcon had, as instructed, established a lifetime's
habit of always looking for it when the sky was clear, or
between the clouds.

The master was standing in front of the unlit fire.

A man Falcon had never seen before sat awkwardly in one
of the wing-back chairs but jumped up now to be introduced.

'This is Mr Parkis, Falcon. He's a lawyer – a clerk to
chambers. It's a firm that deals with my affairs. I wanted you
to meet because he's going to play a big part in your future
– if you want him to, of course.'

Mr Parkis extended a long arm and a set of bony fingers.
He was very young, perhaps just twenty, and very tall, possibly six foot. His limbs were stick-like and he seemed, to
Falcon, to be a collection of joints, like a puppet. A wide
smile did not waver.

'Hello, Falcon. I've heard a lot about you.'

They shook hands. Falcon wasn't offered a seat. Mr Parkis sat down with his hands clasped around one knee, watching intently, rocking slightly back and forth.

There was an awkward silence, which did nothing to modify Parkis's smile.

'Lamer is up for sale, Falcon,' said Cherry. 'In fact it's sold, lock, stock and barrel. Perhaps you can keep that to yourself until Barton has told the staff. You're good at keeping secrets, aren't you?'

Falcon nodded. He made a supreme effort not to look at the spot above the fire where a pale mark showed the outline of the stolen photograph. He'd seen the safe as soon as he'd entered the room; the metal door half open.

'Lady Angela and I will live in our flat in Bloomsbury – it's a mansion flat, so the servants come and go by a special lift, and there's a view over London from a balcony. We're on the sixth floor. The . . .' Cherry searched for the word '. . . the recent intrusion has upset my wife. It's time for us to go. Which brings us to you. Mr Potts is going to work at Bride Hall – they've got a carriage, and they ride. But he's going to go on living at Stable Cottage here – by arrangement with the new owner. I asked him if he would continue to take you in, which would be helpful. There are documents to file. The Pottses would become your legal guardians. If that's what you want, we'll go ahead.' He stepped forward and put a hand on Falcon's head. 'I'll miss you, Falcon. But remember – I'm keeping tabs. You might not see me, but I'm there. Mr Parkis is my eyes and ears. If you ever need anything, you'll have his number and there's a phone you can use at Bride Hall.'

Cherry lit a cigarette, and then there was a little ceremony of throwing the match into the fireplace, once, twice, and only letting go at the third time.

'Do you remember that night we first talked here in the library? I have to ask, Falcon, did you tell anyone about the red notebook?'

'No, sir.'

'Good. It's even more important now to keep our secret. We'll talk of this again when it's safe. For the moment the less you know the better.'

Mr Parkis nodded gravely.

'Did the thieves take the notebook, sir?' asked Falcon.

'Good God, no,' said Cherry. 'It was safe. I hid it in the ice-house that night we looked at the moon.' A childish smile lit up his face. 'They'd tried before, you see. You made me real-ise how important it was to keep it safe, so I can pass it on.'

Mr Parkis nodded at this, patting a leather satchel on his lap.

'We need to think about your education, Falcon,' said Cherry. 'The school sends good reports.'

The school was ghastly, but Falcon had a head for num-bers and a careful, meticulous intelligence, as well as a won-derful memory. Not being able to see the blackboard had been an unexpected bonus.

'Perhaps we should find a more challenging institution – a boarding-school? And then university. What's your favourite subject?' asked Cherry.

'History, sir.'

'Why?'

'It's about the past.'

'Indeed it is,' said Cherry. 'Work hard. Mr Parkis will keep me up to speed. I've told Mr Potts' to stay in touch. I'll watch your progress with interest. I'm sure the doctors will always claim that they got me back on my feet – but in some ways it was you.'

Cherry shook his hand awkwardly. 'So, thank you very much, Falcon.'

It was a kindly way to dismiss him, but Falcon couldn't move. Cherry had to go and get Cook, and once they managed to stop the tears, he was taken back to the kitchen and given sweet tea, but he couldn't hold the cup.

Mr Parkis arrived and suggested they allowed Falcon some privacy. He sat with him in the old dairy, a whitewashed stone room with large windows that seemed saturated in light.

Falcon's skin was dotted with globes of sweat, and his eyes were closed, but the violent shaking had stopped. Parkis sat beside him with an arm around his shoulders. Cherry had told him that if the boy was poorly he'd ring for the family doctor. Parkis checked Falcon's pulse, which was racing but strong, and decided that the best thing to do was wait.

In the meantime, he decided to talk. 'Mr Cherry looked after me too, Falcon. I was fifteen. I left school and started work as a clerk at Bootham's – that's what they call the firm, off Chancery Lane. Every time he came to the office he'd ask how I liked it – how the partners were treating me. He asked what I did when I wasn't at work and I said I ran. I've always run you see – four hundred yards, eight hundred. It's my gift – that's what Mr Cherry says.

'One Christmas he left some money with the senior partner to pay for kit – shoes, and fees at a club, at Barnes. I won a medal – at seventeen. I showed it to him when he called. He said physical endeavour was important. He said a whole generation had been lost in the Great War and it was up to me – my generation – to fill the gap. When I was nineteen I was selected to run for England, Falcon, to run in Paris, and Mr Cherry paid again, for the trip, and a hostel, and food. My father was a railwayman – we didn't have cash at all, not after food and rent. I came third and I brought the bronze medal to work, and Mr Cherry told the senior partner to make a little speech to everyone, and he got me to stand on a desk. Everyone had to clap.

'I still run, but that was the best day, that run in Paris. Best day of my life – except for family things, of course.'

Falcon's eyes were open, and his breathing had settled, but he struggled to be still, to stop his feet rearranging themselves.

Parkis wondered if he shouldn't have mentioned family.

'Mr Cherry insists, you see, that I do all the leg-work on the Lamer account. I deliver the documents and take his messages and go up in the car now every month. The partners don't like it but they can't upset Mr Cherry. He's going to look after you, too. That's good news, isn't it?'

Falcon looked exhausted. His skin was like lard, and his eyes distant.

'What's wrong, Falcon?' asked Parkis.

'I can't stop them.'

'The memories?' guessed Parkis. Cherry had told him the boy's history: about the V2, his family, and sanctuary at Lamer.

Falcon nodded.

'Why now, today, in the library?' asked Parkis.

'Mr Cherry was kind. It reminded me of home. And then I can't stop it – I'm walking up the street to the house after the rocket fell. It's like I'm there – but I know what I'll find. I try to hide it when it happens, but I couldn't today.'

He shook his head, and Parkis guessed he was searching for words. 'It's that I always think they'll wake up this time,' said the boy at last. 'I know they won't. I went to the funeral at Woolwich.'

Mr Parkis had two children, a boy and a girl, so he went to his car and got a bottle of pop – R. White's – from a crate he'd bought as a surprise.

Falcon was sitting up and Cook came in with a straw.

For several days, if not weeks, he was prone to sudden collapse, and he really didn't know if he cried because he was lonely or some other, darker, emotion that seemed just out of reach. And it was beyond argument that he often felt better after the tears, and his mind felt less cluttered, less restrained by the scenes he was constantly fighting to suppress. His dreams were full of splintered images: the flame playing in Edie's pram, Barton sleeping soundly with the gun under his pillow, and Mr Cherry double-checking the locked door of the ice-house.

6

Ten years later: 1957

It was the end of Trinity term, Falcon's first year at Christ Church, Oxford, when he decided to trace the V2 rocket back to the secret factory that had given it birth: a complex of underground tunnels called the Mittelwerk in the foothills of the Harz mountains of Germany. This reversal of its trajectory seemed to offer some form of redemption, as if he could rewrite the past. It might help make the future less daunting. He was still a victim to collapse, although even more skilled at hiding his episodes of terror and loss from those around him.

Getting into the East was a bureaucratic nightmare. Moscow's coup in launching Sputnik – the world's first man-made satellite – had added a further dimension to the simmering Cold War. The spaceship's plaintive 'beep' had taken America by surprise. The Space Race was under way. But Oxford offered nothing if not strings to pull. The university branch of the Labour Party helped him secure a trip with the World Confederation of Labour to promote post-war reconstruction. For his part all he had to do was write a short article, for an obscure journal, on the role of trade unions in East Germany. He was shoehorned onto an RAF flight into Berlin, otherwise packed tight with soldiers heading for Brooke Barracks, opposite Spandau Prison. A Russian flag-car picked him up from Brooke, and his papers were stamped at the crossing on Friedrichstrasse.

At the checkpoint he was interviewed by a Red Army captain, an officious bureaucrat in a tawdry uniform, who no doubt saw the young man before him as a degenerate, an imperial imitation of a beatnik. A growth spurt had left Falcon at a gangly six foot. His face was still pale, the shadow of a beard and a wispy moustache just visible, and a lot of brown hair left to curl. Grey eyes – of course – that seemed to collect information without broadcasting anything in return, shielded by a pair of circular NHS glasses. For the captain he set out details of meetings planned with trade-union leaders in Nordhausen, an industrial centre in Thuringia, 150 miles south-west of the city. After a silence, in which his proposed journey seemed to hang in the balance, he was told he had three days in East Germany; his passport would be held while he was out of Berlin. He was issued with return tickets to Thuringia.

He'd been told not to take photographs, but the old city, when he finally arrived, was no great temptation. Once a medieval jewel, Nordhausen had become a centre for military-arms engineering during the war and had been destroyed by the RAF. Trams ran through a half-built grid of new wide streets. Stagnant bright green water lay in bomb craters. Vast new factories belched smoke into the sky above the suburbs. He got a room above a bar and went for a walk in a park with no grass. In the distance he saw two giant silos in the shape of *Korn* bottles – it was a kind of grain brandy and, his Baedeker guide said, a local industry. He found a bar and ordered a beer with a *Korn* chaser. It was like vodka, but grainy – a slightly bleak taste he really liked. He ordered another. The bar was called Die Aussicht, the View, and stood at the top of a spiral path that ran through a patchy botanic garden.

Looking south (no compass required, but glasses essential), he saw the Kohnstein, a blue whaleback hill, with flashes of exposed chalk, a thousand feet high. Once, they'd sent men down to mine gypsum, and the whole edifice was – according to Baedeker – riddled with tunnels and caves. (An identical guidebook had been used by the pilots who'd destroyed the old city.) Cherry's telescope, a present sent on his tenth birthday, brought the Kohnstein into sharper focus: he could see two tunnel entrances, engineered as for a railway. The scale was grand, the darkness within absolute.

He ordered a bottle of *Korn*, some potatoes and sausages, and another beer. The sky was a sickly pink once the sunset had gone. It was a colour that suited Germany, making him think of icing on cakes, sugared biscuits, and decadence. He drank the spirit and the beer, his mind drifting, calm.

Postcards of Nordhausen showed old pictures of its pre-war glory. He'd chosen one for Mr Cherry: a line of horse-drawn carriages – one of the coachmen was a ringer for Mr Potts. A wall of his room at Christ Church was decorated with cards from the Cherry-Garrard cruise-ship travels mainly: Nice, Naples, Alexandria. Pictures from a life of leisure, stately and civilised. The scrawled note on the back was invariably a record of the food on board. There was never a mention of Scott's notebook.

His postcards – sent to Bloomsbury – were little better, and he pushed the latest aside untouched, setting down his pen.

Instead, he closed his eyes and began to run the pictures of his life in reverse, as he had many times before.

He'd start in Tapton's sweet shop asking for a Milky Way. He'd feel the visceral churning shock-wave of the V2, then hear the explosion, and the sound of it rising up into the clouds. Woolworth's would remake itself from the ground up, like a Hollywood silent movie, and the dray horse would settle back on its hoofs.

He poured himself a fresh shot of *Korn*.

His backward life continued: the V2 rejoined the parabolic curve that would inscribe its path back over the North Sea, over the Frisian Islands, to a forest on the coast, and a lonely sandy road, where the launcher was parked, jacked up on four metallic feet. Then the rocket would perform a balletic turn, until the nose cone pointed up, and the burning engines would lower it nicely into its cradle, which folded down, the feet retracting, so that the driver and crew could set off for the railway station, where it would join others in a line, ready for the night journey south.

Through war-torn Germany it would trundle past villages and towns where no light showed, until at dawn it reached the old station at Nordhausen, then set out across the dull plain, to the Kohnstein. Then the V2 – *his V2* – would be unloaded and slipped back into the shadowy tunnel entrance to join the production line that had brought it into the world.

Falcon wished to follow, to walk down that tunnel into the mountain.

The next morning he asked the hotel doorkeeper how to get to the mountain and was directed to the museum in the Rathaus. They recommended a man called Georg, who worked as a school caretaker. They found him in the basement of the town's *Académie* beside a cot bed and a pile of blankets. He had some English, and textbook German, which Falcon could follow. He was Hungarian, a Jew – a one-time slave 'in the mountain', who'd lost all the teeth on the right side of his jaw, so that he looked crushed, distorted. He had a dog called Pest, which ran at his heels.

They walked a dusty track, marked by roadside shrines, for three miles, then struck off into the foothills of the Kohnstein. The labour camp, Mittelbau-Dora, which had provided the slaves for the factory, had been razed to the ground, although the rigid geometry of huts and perimeter was still visible. There was no birdsong and Georg knelt down and showed Falcon the soil, which had been mixed with a white powder.

'Lime from the mountain, to kill the stench,' said Georg. 'Nothing grows. Nothing lives.'

It was a barren valley – even the stream had gone, seeping down into the chalk.

'In winter a flood,' said Georg, with his half-made smile. He walked among paths and rotting wood, until he found a spot. 'I die here,' he said, 'but the Americans come in time. Now I live here.'

Falcon knew that the US Army had liberated the camp, getting to the factory before the British, but Thuringia fell into the Soviet sector, and in the end they'd had to give up the mountain to the Russians.

A path led up, offering them views of a railway line sunk into a deep chalk cutting.

They crested a bank and the tunnel entrances were there, fifty yards away, gapping, toothless.

Georg was on hand with facts. Labour for the V2 factory had been marched to the site each day. Sixty thousand men had been brought here, many of them desperate survivors of the death camps in the east. More than twenty thousand had died, many of them living skeletons even the Americans couldn't save. The factory was two mile-long production lines dug into the mountain, with connecting passages. Barbed-wire fences had been strung across the entrances, but there was a metal gate, and Georg had a key. Falcon stood in the shadows, where the weak sunlight gave up to the darkness, the stale air moving past him. They left Pest, whimpering, in the dust, and walked inside Tunnel A. (The signage was still visible. The tunnel was S-shaped, so they could not see if daylight lay ahead.)

Georg had brought spotlights, and they walked carefully between the rails.

Out of the gloom the nose cone of a rocket appeared.

Falcon climbed on to a gantry and touched the apex, feeling that he'd somehow closed a circle. It was odd, but he sensed nothing of the void, the fears of that day in New

Cross. Fleetingly, he hoped that this marked an end to his episodes, and a new beginning.

The air was cold, foetid, but he saw that Georg was sweating.

'We work like animals. Every hour. Each day hundreds die, beaten. They burn the bodies. We have no beds, no food, no doctors. In the winter the bodies are piled up, stiff with the ice.'

He looked around him and Falcon knew that he could see them. His mouth hung open, the lips wet, his old back bent, to make it easier to breathe.

'Your friends?' asked Falcon.

'My brothers. They leave them on the floor.'

They walked on, past workbenches and tool shops, lathes and drills, huts and empty fuel drums.

The Nazis who ran the Mittelwerk had been desperate, Falcon knew. He'd read the original paperwork seized by the Americans – half-burnt pages from gutted filing cabinets. Berlin demanded rockets, better rockets. Hitler wanted a 'miracle weapon' to turn the tide of war. But the V2's guidance system was inadequate, poorly designed, and produced failure after failure: explosions on the launch pad, in mid-air, the rocket's trajectory often erratic.

Sabotage was the excuse. The workers were blamed, beaten, murdered.

Georg said he would go back to the sunlight, and Falcon was tempted to follow, but in the darkness ahead there was a reflection from paintwork. He could see the shape of a machine: a capital L upside down, like a gibbet. It was a crane, and he'd seen its picture before. To stem the 'sabotage' they'd hanged thirty of the slave workers at a time using the long metal arm: an image captured by the liberators of the Mittelwerk. They'd been left hanging for days as a warning to others. As he touched the cold steel the image slid from the page into his heart. Until that moment Falcon had never thought of the V2 as evil. But the slaves had been worked to death to produce the rocket that flew from the coast, arced over Kent, and fell on the New Cross road. It had sprung from evil.

He went back to the gate and found Georg sitting in the shade with Pest, eating lunch. His guide had brought a dish in his satchel, and he'd filled it with water for the dog.

'The tap still works,' he said, leading Falcon to the second tunnel entrance, where he'd already opened the gate. Water dripped from a standpipe into a stone horse trough. The entrance there was crowded with offices, set to either side, with glass partitions, smashed, wrecked.

On one door the name had survived: Marcus von Braun.

Georg spat on a cloth and cleaned away the grime. 'The rockets do not find the targets – the remote control is faulty. Hitler tells *Wernher* von Braun this must be fixed. Von Braun, yes? The great man. This job he entrusts to his brother, this Marcus. Not a good man,' he added, and something gave way in his face, and tears fell.

He held up his hands, ashamed, then led the way to the next office. 'And Mr Rudolph sat here . . .' said Georg. 'Factory manager.'

The furniture was in ruins, the filing cabinets empty, twisted.

'The Americans took them away, and a V2 rocket, before the Russians could offer more money, or the British. Look here . . .'

Out in the tunnel a board held newspaper clippings and photographs, pages torn from books.

'One day a museum,' said Georg.

'I hope so,' said Falcon.

'Now these men are all Americans, the past is forgotten,' said Georg. 'Mr Rudolph design Saturn V rocket. Yes. Space Race begin here, in Mittelwerk. There will be an American on the moon.'

'And Marcus?' asked Falcon.

'He work for Chrysler – he make cars.'

And that was the image Falcon took away – the clean, dashing, arrogant lines of a Plymouth de Luxe perhaps: the American Dream on four wheels, emerging from the tunnels of a catacomb.

7

The last time he'd seen Cherry he'd met him in the bar of the Randolph Hotel in Oxford, opposite the Ashmolean Museum. It was sad that this *was* the last time because it wasn't the best time. In a peculiar way he resented the intrusion, the peremptory note in his pigeonhole. Life at Christ Church was superficially idyllic, in that he was left alone with his books and a view of Lady Bridge from his room, often shrouded in mist rising from the Isis. He was at the end of his second year and his studies embedded him in the past, not his own personal story, but great sweeps of adventure and glory, which led to Cherry, of course, whose old room was across Tom Quad. At dusk, or after formal hall, when he was returning to his room, he'd look up at the green glazed window and try to catch the shy face, pulling away.

The trip to the Mittelwerk had opened his eyes to a wider world. As research for his article, he'd gone on to visit several factories in the outer suburbs, riddled with poverty, choked with fumes. On his return he found his college painfully rarefied. His school, a private boarding establishment north of St Albans, had delivered a classical education, paid for by Cherry, but he was still the orphaned son of a south London brewery worker, an impostor in that gilded world, a visitor entitled to nothing for which he didn't work. He was a member of the poetry society and drank red wine with other 'progressives'. He'd joined the Labour Party, like his father, and spent dreary evenings in damp rooms discussing the imposition of a super-tax, which made him a hypocrite given the identity of his benefactor in Bloomsbury, who, if he wasn't on a cruise in the Caribbean or the Aegean, would undoubtedly qualify to pay it in full.

He'd made one concession to the Randolph, dragging a comb through his hair, but otherwise he was his imperfect self.

Cherry arranged to meet him in the bar, because he'd dined earlier with his wife, as they were bound for Keble to see a special screening of *Scott of the Antarctic*, ten years old now, but the university film club had invited Cherry to a special showing, along with its star, John Mills. Falcon suspected that such provincial trips were rare, as Cherry avoided publicity, and that therefore the outing might have been contrived solely so that they could meet. It was more than a decade since he'd stood before the cold fireplace in the library at Lamer. The mystery of the red notebook remained obscure. He was beginning to suspect the whole thing had been a figment of Cherry's fevered imagination, best left unmentioned.

The master looked older, puffy and formless, as if he was no longer defined by his bones. He wore an immaculate slate-grey suit, a Winchester College tie, and said the cocktails were first-rate, but Falcon insisted on a pint of Morrell's bitter in a straight glass – specifically not the dimpled tankards beloved of the saloon-bar crowd. The conversation was painfully awkward, which was odd, in that they had never had trouble speaking before. But then Falcon wasn't a child any more. Cherry, who had a second cocktail, was complaining about the government and taxation and saying what a relief it had been that day he'd driven away from Lamer for the last time, and that the flat was ideal because they could get to the West End easily to see theatre or hear music at Wigmore Hall. And he could always go to lectures at the Royal Geographical Society.

Finally, when this line of conversation petered out, he leant forward, looking into Falcon's transparent grey eyes. 'I'm still pursued by the Black Dog, Falcon. I'm struggling to enjoy life. The doctors won't leave me alone. We're off to Bermuda on Tuesday, from Southampton. Angela says the sun will do the trick. The food's good – it's the *France,* which is stylish I know, but not a patch on the *Normandie.*'

It seemed to Falcon a life lived in reverse, with all the adventure and drama at the start, and then a long, slow tail of comfort and domesticity. The sense of playfulness seemed to have deserted him completely.

'I hear reports. It's going well I know . . .' he said. 'Parkis is full of praise.'

The legal clerk had visited Oxford twice, to check Falcon's allowance and that all was well in college. They'd taken tea, in the covered market, and gone on for a pint of beer at the Turf Tavern.

'I'm enjoying it, sir.'

Again, the conversation faltered, so they turned to the news, still dominated by Sputnik. Cherry said it was uplifting to feel again the excitement of exploration – even from a deckchair on a cruise ship. He wondered if he might live to see a man on the moon after all.

They moved on to the debacle of Suez, the fall of Sir Anthony Eden and the humiliation of the withdrawal from Egypt.

'It's the end of Empire,' said Cherry, summoning the waiter with a raised finger.

'It was over already,' said Falcon, taking off his glasses and sliding them onto the polished table. 'War's ruinous. We've fought two. We can't afford our pretensions any more.'

Cherry looked at his watch. 'What will you do when you go down?'

Falcon worked a finger between collar and neck, brushing back his hair when he'd done. The waiter arrived with a fresh pint of Morrell's, which he lifted to his lips, sipping. He owed Cherry everything, but that didn't mean he had to like being spied on, or the idea that he had a duty to deliver a commentary on his life.

He ignored the question. 'I see Mrs Potts every month – she's alone now.'

'She's not in need?'

'No. The women at Bride Hall set aside a cottage – down by the ford. She has a garden, a small income. I suspect that's your work again, sir. We're all in your debt.'

'I don't mean to pry,' said Cherry, a hand passing over his eyes.

'There's a possibility of doing a doctorate – at Cambridge,' said Falcon, relenting to scrutiny at last.

'College?'

'Caius – Wilson's *alma mater*, of course. There's interest, and I can take supervisions, pay my way.'

Cherry's eyes focused on the mid-distance and Falcon guessed he could see Wilson – Scott's mentor – lying in the tent on the day they found the dead.

'The subject?' asked Cherry.

Falcon smiled: 'The Scott Polar's doing work on mapping, sir.'

'Will you go south?'

Falcon shook his head. His episodes, the blackouts and flashbacks, had got worse. Tracing the V2 into the tunnels of the Mittelwerk had brought only temporary catharsis. He still needed control of his surroundings: the triggers must be avoided as best as he could. The idea of being confined: a ship, an aircraft, a hut, a tent, made the blood rush to his heart. And there was a darker reason: both Poles had a reputation for inciting madness. There was something about the sudden invisible swirl of magnetic forces at the ends of the earth, the spinning vortex of longitude, which seemed to break the minds of men. It had unseated Cherry's, after all.

'No. I doubt it. I'm a backroom boy. But who knows? I've got the degree to finish first. My dissertation is on the archaeology of Antarctica.'

'Good God. Are we that old already? Am I of interest to Howard Carter – or do I actually have to be dead?'

'It was the Golden Age, sir. It's remarkable what *has* survived. Amundsen, Scott, Mawson, Byrd, Ross – they all left a mark. Bleached wooden huts, ice-covered encampments, cairns and man-made "landmarks". I shouldn't lecture you, sir. You know, it's a featureless world so in an odd way the landscape is made up almost entirely by the stories told. The place where the dogs were shot, or the ponies, or where men died. There are the skeletons of ships, crushed in the ice, or beached in coves. I'm just making an inventory, if you like, of what is there to find.'

'Goodness. That was a speech, Falcon Grey. I doubt you've said as much in all the years I've known you. And then Cambridge?'

'Well, I hope so. The idea is to start looking under the surface. A lot of artefacts are in the ice. There's some new kit – the Scott Polar is leading the way. It's called RES.'

'Didn't we use that in the last lot?' asked Cherry, knocking out a fresh cigarette.

'That's it. Radio Echo Sounding. A pilot can bounce a signal off the ground to work out the height of an aircraft. Useless on ice – the radio waves go right through. The Scott Polar is using it to map the underlying geology. My idea's slightly different.'

He'd edged forward, thrilled to see Cherry's face animated again, the blue eyes catching the light. 'One of the scientists at Christ Church is helping develop the kit,' said Falcon, his voice now lighter, betraying excitement. 'We got talking about Antarctica one night over a drink. Thing is, sir, these radio waves don't pass through the ice unhindered. There are layers, strata, which show up on the read-out. Deciphering it all is the trick of it. With skill you can see things in the ice. I can see them. But it takes practice to decipher the signals.'

'Could you find them – Scott and the rest?' asked Cherry, his drink forgotten.

'No, sir. You see, we need aircraft to fly "search patterns" to produce the data. We can't afford that – neither the institute, nor the university nor the country for that matter. The only option is to piggy-back off US naval flights, which restricts the areas we can investigate. For now RES goes where the Americans fly – but one day maybe.'

Cherry checked his watch, his shoulders slumping. 'I shall be in the doghouse, Falcon. Angela will be waiting. But it's good to know you're still following footprints in the snow. If you have the time, write – I'd like to know how it's going.'

'Yes, sir. The plan is to try out the kit in about three years' time, which is ideal for me. The Americans are planning a new base and they're flying in the hardware from Chile so they'll go over the Weddell Sea. We're going to try to find *Endurance* – Shackleton's ship.'

'But she was crushed by the ice.'

'Possibly – or she's on the seabed, or embedded in the ice, in which case she's drifted north towards the Antarctic Peninsula. It has to be worth the shot – and the Americans are happy to recalibrate their flight paths for each trip, so we get the coverage. My job's to do the historical background, and help interpret the RES printouts . . .' For the first time Falcon saw a conflict of emotions on Cherry's face, a kind of anguish and a flickering joy.

'As I said, write, Falcon. Keep in touch. My life may be coming to its end. Who knows? I'm not a god . . .'

Lady Angela appeared at Cherry's shoulder, slipping on long gloves. 'My word – is it really Falcon?' She laughed. 'Every inch the student, I see. Thank you for visiting

Emily Potts. It means a lot to her. They never had children but you were a son to them. I know it didn't feel like
that. Still waters . . .'

Cherry struggled to his feet.

'Oh dear. I've come at the wrong moment, haven't I?' she
said. 'I'll be on the steps, Apsley – we've got ten minutes.
There's a student here to take us to Keble – as if we don't
know the way. Still, it's a kindness. Goodbye, Falcon.' She
left, light on her feet.

Cherry got his stick in hand. 'Come to the bar with me.
A parting cup.'

There were stools but they stood at the far end, which was
deserted.

Cherry ordered two whiskies with a splash of water.

'Howard Carter,' said Cherry. 'He's buried at Putney
Vale – Angela's sister lives close by. There's a line on his
gravestone: "May your spirit live, may you spend millions
of years, you who love Thebes, sitting with your face to the
north wind, your eyes beholding happiness." Wonderful –
it's from one of the ceremonial cups he found in the tomb.
I'd take the south wind, but otherwise . . .'

Cherry took a step closer. Falcon could see the broken
blood vessels in his eyes and he thought, even then, that this
might be the last time they'd speak.

Cherry lit a cigarette. 'Scott's notebook,' he said, his eyes
flitting about the bar. 'There are still forces at work, Falcon.
Official forces – let's call them the authorities. And others.
Outside forces. As you know the burglary at Lamer was not
the first. I am not entirely free, as you know, to make public
the truth, which is a situation with which I have struggled
for many years.'

Falcon went to speak. *Could he not share the truth?*

But Cherry held up a hand. 'It's best for now. You could
be placed in danger, my boy. What did Macbeth say? "Be

innocent of the knowledge, dearest chuck." One day the time will be right. The notebook will come to you. It does not tell the whole story – that will fall to you to find, I'm afraid. That night in the library at Lamer I thought you might be the right person. I was right. I'm proud of you.

'Remember – it is the *original*. Scott planned it so. Without it the truth can be denied.'

Falcon drank his whisky in one draught. What possible story could Scott's notebook hold? The Last Expedition was history, almost legend. The secret thoughts of its leader might amount to no more than grudges, gossip and recrimination.

Cherry ordered two more drinks.

They touched glasses.

'If you can, Falcon, pursue that doctorate at Cambridge, stay with the Scott Polar. The quest – your journey – may begin very soon. I'm sorry if it leads you away from the life you want to live. I wish you luck, and courage. And then peace.'

He put a pound note on the bar and a hand on Falcon's shoulder. 'Remember the last line of my book: "If you march your Winter Journeys you will have your reward . . ."'

'". . . so long as all you want is a penguin's egg,"' finished Falcon.

As Cherry walked out he tipped his hat and Falcon noted that several guests watched him leave, a man nudging his wife and telling her, no doubt, in a whisper, to catch a glimpse of the hero before he was gone.

8

Cambridge: 18 May 1969

It was ten years to the day, and Falcon had been up since dawn. Cherry had died in a hotel room, near Piccadilly Circus, after breaking his arm in a fall and suffering heart failure. Falcon thought the irony was almost tangible, in that a man who had sought the open horizons of Antarctica should leave the world so close to a symbol of crowds, and lights, and bustle – a place so magnetic as to be christened the Third Pole. A few days earlier Cherry had walked among the daffodils at Kenwood with Lady Angela. He didn't die alone, and he didn't die in pain – another irony, thought Falcon, because he'd lived his life in pain. He cried when he got the news, and it was worse at the memorial service, where he stood at the back, feeling again the self-pity of the left-behind. The will was read at the solicitors' offices – Falcon was not invited – but a letter informed him he'd been left three hundred guineas.

There was no mention of Scott's notebook. In those first weeks and months after Cherry's death he'd waited for the way forward to reveal itself, but that moment never came, and he decided that the master had taken his secrets to his grave, which lay in the churchyard of St Helen's in Wheathampstead, beside a tall Celtic cross, the shadow of which moved like the hour hand of a clock, as Falcon watched, which he did on Cherry's birthday – the day after the New Year – when he'd go back to Bride Hall to see Mrs Potts, in her cottage by the ford.

When he thought of the notebook he imagined Cherry burning it in the library fireplace, deciding at the last that Falcon should live his life unburdened. But he didn't forget Cherry, or his secret. The anniversary of the master's death provided the opportunity for a small ceremony of remembrance. Falcon took the copper telescope from its allotted drawer below his bunk and stepped out through the open sliding door of his VW camper van (NOD 59G) to climb the metal ladder to the roof. He spent a lot of time on the roof of the VW, which had been adapted to fulfil its role as an observation deck: the view dominated by the lazy Cam, heading north to the sea, through broad water meadows. There was a guide rail, and a slatted wooden platform on which he could sit, but the key addition was a custom-built tripod for the telescope, which slipped into three brackets fitted to the steel roof panel.

Sofya appeared with the coffee pot. They'd been together for six months and she'd been initiated into the many small rituals, incantations and habits that to Falcon seemed to give time a pattern. The night before, around the fire, he'd checked the calculations: the moon would rise at 10.09 a.m. He would track the thin crescent with the telescope, remembering that evening long ago at Lamer, a memory he'd shared with Sofya many times.

She passed him up a coffee. 'A good day to follow the moon,' she said.

Later, at about six that evening, Apollo 10 would take off from Cape Kennedy – the dress rehearsal for landing a man on the moon. It would fly half a million miles and enter orbit, allowing the lunar module to detach from the command module, descend, and fly-by a few miles above the surface, before climbing back to dock with the mother ship. If all went well, Apollo 11 would take off that summer, and put two astronauts on the moon. The world was watching every moment of the drama unfold.

It was the moon, and its story, that had brought them together.

'Will you come to the party? I give invitation, yes?' she asked, settling on a camp stool with her cup.

Sofya worked at the university. A party had been arranged to watch the launch of Apollo 10 on TV. Sofya was keen for Falcon to meet the scientists she worked alongside.

'You will be on the best behaviour.'

Sofya's English, especially its inflections, was still awkward, and freighted with the syntax of her native Russian, so this sounded like a command.

He'd met Dr Sofya Sarkisova (she'd hidden her doctorate for several weeks until he noticed it on a letter) at a pop concert on Coldham's Common, held in a marquee on the lawns going down to Jesus Ditch. Waiting for the Strawbs he'd slipped out during the support act's set to have an illicit smoke and look at the moon: 25 September – a rare penumbral lunar eclipse. He had the telescope in his inside pocket, and found a stone wall on which to lean, and was watching the shadows move over the mountains a quarter of a million miles away when he heard a match strike, and then her voice – for the first time – the accent sticky and nasal, but sinuous too, as if the words hung from a graceful washing line.

'The shadow of the heavens, yes?' she'd said, standing about twenty feet away, on top of the wall he was leaning on. She was slim, and sinuous, like her voice, but not petite – even then, in the half-light, he could see the wide cheekbones, the angular face.

He held out Cherry's telescope but she shook her head. 'My eyes – twenty-twenty plus. I can see Gassendi A.'

Falcon doubted this because it was a delicate feature, a tiny crater on the edge of Gassendi itself, which he needed a telescope to see. But then eyesight wasn't his strong card, so he kept his silence.

He walked along the wall, tall enough to rest his arms on the top, looking up.

She did have remarkable eyes, black, wide.

Falcon thought of Yeats's cat, which lifted to the changing moon its changing eyes.

She'd produced a hip flask and, with a flourish, he produced his own. They swapped: Talisker in his – a nod to Cherry – and vodka in hers, but not the root-vegetable variety. This contained the strange uplifting scent of new-mown grass.

'It's passing,' he said, pointing up at the moon, where the trailing edge was beginning to catch the full force of the white light of the unseen sun.

He thought she might be drunk – or at least tipsy – because she bowed from the waist and held out her hand. This was the silhouette he would take away: a small body, the jagged inflections of elbows and knees oddly smoothed away, the feet and hands simply defining the end of a series of curves.

'Sofya Sarkisova,' she said.

'Falcon Grey.'

Inside the marquee there was uproar for the next group – the Newcomers – and the first ragged drumbeats of the set.

'You like the moon?' he asked, taking off his circular John Lennon-style glasses, and pushing long unruly hair out of his eyes

'It's my job. And this is boring – it is not *the* moon.'

'Looks like the moon to me,' said Falcon, scratching his fingers through the stubble on his chin.

She wagged a long finger. '*A* moon. The earth's moon, yes. But not *the* moon. There are nearly two hundred in the solar system. They all have names. She is no different.'

'It's a woman?'

'Yes. Of course. And she is called Luna. Selene in Greek – this is my favourite.'

She drank more vodka. 'The stars are different at home,' she said.

'Where's home?' he asked.

Her head went to one side: 'For work, Kurdistan, home Moscow. For now University College. I work from here.' Her hand, the fingers as pliable as the wrist, fluttered to the south, very precisely, becoming a pointing finger. 'The university's great telescope?'

'The Mullard? Do you have to go every day?'

'I have to do everything. Comrade Brezhnev is watching.'

'I thought there was a Cold War. But we're working with the Russians?'

'This is academic world. We cooperate always – even in my field of study. And it is not Russia. It is Soviet Union.'

He could see the smile, breaking slowly, but not evenly. She spun round on her toes, and Falcon guessed she'd been unable to suppress the urge to check that they were really alone.

He offered her a Ducados, which she examined carefully. He'd worked for a term at the university in Vitoria and become addicted to the acrid hit of Spanish tobacco. The smoke leaked out of her nostrils, and he saw her eyes water, but she manufactured a smile.

'You examine my face,' she said.

'Sorry.'

'One dance, only,' she said, as if he'd asked.

She stood closer and quite formally they drifted on the grass to the music from within. He thought her short velvet jacket might be handmade, and the mini-skirt was daring. Her tights were black too, and her shoes polished. He thought she was nervous, highly charged, and he wondered if he'd interrupted some crisis, a moment of decision.

'How will you get home?' he asked.

'This is a question of the existential, I think,' she said. 'Tonight, I walk home or take a taxi. To Moscow I must return.

I will be taken there. I am not free to do otherwise. I dance, I look at the moon, but I am not free.'

She pressed a finger into his chest. 'How will *you* get home?'

'I live in a camper van out on the Fen by the river. I'll walk.'

'You go north, I go south. We may never meet again.'

But they did: they saw *Planet of the Apes* at the Regal, and *Gerry and the Pacemakers* at the Union, and they joined a protest march against Vietnam – although Sofya produced dark glasses and a headscarf for the occasion. She said she wanted to live as ordinary people might. Sometimes it was as if she liked to try out aspects of everyday life, as if she was a tourist, with a list of places she had to visit before going home. It unnerved Falcon because it suggested he might be one of the items ticked off the list.

Cambridge was clearly a surprise to Sofya: it was in the vanguard of what everyone was now calling the 'sixties' – music was in every pub and club, protests on the streets were common, fashions usually restricted to the King's Road were a common sight on King's Parade. Drugs, from alcohol to LSD, were freely available, at a standard street price. Sex was less furtive, and undergraduates could be seen entwined on the grass by the river, or in shady doorways.

Falcon told her she was lucky – the sixties weren't happening everywhere.

Her life he assembled as an incomplete jigsaw: the daughter of a Soviet engineer, she'd studied at the Moscow State Technical School, her degree in electrical engineering. Her mother had been an English translator in Moscow, so they'd been bilingual at home because her father was always away. She was part of a delegation invited to Cambridge to track and analyse signals from Soviet probes – to Venus, Mars, but specifically the moon. The Luna robotic probes were unmanned and had first flown past the moon a decade earlier. Later versions had reached the surface or achieved orbit. Now, with

Luna 15, Moscow planned a soft landing – although its launch had been delayed, then postponed, due to undisclosed technical problems. Sofya described her role in the team as menial, explaining that she had largely been included in the group to act as an informal translator, although she admitted that her doctorate had involved interpretation of radio signals in astronomy. She was reluctant to bore Falcon with the details.

One evening, after a drink in the college bar (self-service with an honesty book), they'd gone to her room. Once inside Sofya placed her index finger across his lips, sat on the counterpane, and turned the bedside lamp upside down. The bug was innocuous, but she explained later that in Moscow everyone checked appliances regularly, and there was no doubt. She'd packed her bag while Radio Luxembourg played, and they'd slipped out across the lawns to walk to Fen Ditton – an hour by moonlight. She said she wasn't surprised by the discovery: the KGB had interviewed her before she'd flown to the West. A 'press attaché' had travelled with the party and was undoubtedly an agent.

Later, in the narrow bunk of the VW, Falcon had opened the clam-shell roof so they could see the stars. He felt obliged to be curious: 'Why did the KGB interview you before you left Moscow?' he asked.

But she'd fallen asleep.

9

Sofya left by bicycle so Falcon sat alone, cross-legged, on the roof of the VW, which he'd bought from a man in Ventnor on the Isle of Wight, who'd taken it over the Solent to see Bob Dylan and Fairport Convention and never gone home. (He'd never seen Dylan either – unless you could count a glimpse from a mile distant of a small figure on the stage.) The owner had been very proud of what he called the 'paint job', which was light blue with white clouds. It made the van look like a scrap of sky on four wheels. It was indoors, but outdoors, and Falcon rarely slept anywhere else. He had rooms at Caius, while he continued his post-doctoral research at the Scott Polar. He saw history students for tutorials or supervisions, but he used the bedroom for storage, and told the bedders not to bother, handing over a crisp five-pound note at the start of term. The location of the VW was a moving feast. Its current spot at Fen Ditton, two miles north of King's College Chapel, was rented from the publican of the Ancient Shepherds a mile down the track. It had become a regular pitch in spring, sheltered in its copse of Scots Pine, but with a wide view of the river, and the Fens stretching to an unbroken horizon.

He sipped his coffee and waited for the moon. It was a Sunday, so the towpath was quiet, but he noted a single scull on the river, a cyclist on the far bank with a pannier in which was set a French loaf, a man walking downriver with a dog, which trotted ahead, its lead in its jaws, and on his side two grazing horses in the rough grass of Stourbridge Common, a foal just visible, lying in the sunshine.

His heart missed a beat because he recognised a symptom – hypervigilance – which might herald one of his fits. When he saw the world like this, in tiny details, he had to brace himself for the worst. The triggers were legion: a smell perhaps – often most potent. Brick dust, hot pavements, gas. Or a sound. The birdlike fluttering of his eardrum, a voice asking if he was all right, a siren. Touch – the subtlest of all. Linen, a doorknob, the slippery skid of blood on skin. Sights less so: a sweet shop, a pram, an empty sky. Often the symptoms would flare, then fade away, as they did now. But if the memory, fully realised, returned, it always crushed him. At night it left him sweating, wide-eyed, in the bunk. During the day it drove him to lonely places, the bank side, or the middle of Parker's Piece, where he could lie down and let the past wash over him.

Inevitably, Sofya had witnessed an episode, a towpath walk interrupted by the sudden roar of a fighter jet over-head. He'd passed out, shivering, and she'd been holding him when he came round. He'd told her then all about the day he'd lost his family, right up to the point when he'd said, 'I'm sorry I'm late.'

'It's not your fault,' she'd said. 'If they're lost to you then this is Fate – you cannot go back. Live for now, Falcon. I learn to do this too.'

They'd sat for an hour watching the river flow. He admitted that it wasn't just the episodes. As the years passed he felt increasingly numb – physically at first, as if he sensed the world from the wrong side of a pane of glass, and then emotionally, as if everyone close to him was getting further and further away. 'It's like being in a play at school but not having any lines,' he told her.

'I am happy with silence,' she said. 'It is a noisy world.'

He heard the city's bells now, marking ten o'clock. He extracted a cigarette paper, rolling the tobacco expertly, before adding a few threads of dope. The first time he'd smoked, in the small yard of a city pub, he'd come back to his pint and sat happily, waiting for the high. He'd thought about the void in his life, and how it seemed to leave his chest empty. And then there it was: a flame of almost pure joy, a sense that he was lying on that bed in the flat but they were alive – all of them – and there was a life behind him that led, in a straight line, to the life ahead of him. That first smoke blew him away for two hours. It had to end, but it meant there was a place he could go to escape.

Now, lying flat on the wooden platform, his eye to the telescope, his mood gently soared as he looked north, the flat fens dominated by sky; nine-tenths of everything was blue, the rest billowing thunderclouds, including one the size of a housing estate sliding to the west. Oxford was a city that obscured the horizon; Cambridge seemed to reach out to it. Overhead, thunder rumbled, but the sun still shone.

The telescope found the cooling towers at King's Lynn, and – unexpectedly – in the mid-distance Ely Cathedral, one side of its octagon tower catching the sun, flashing, as if relaying a signal from God.

He was a human compass so he knew – to within a few degrees – where on the horizon the moon would appear. And then, at 10.09 a.m. precisely, there it was, occurring to the sky, a tip of the crescent; laidback, stylish.

He fished quickly in his back pocket for his hip flask. 'To footsteps in snow,' he said, toasting the past, the malt whisky burning his throat.

The thunderclouds had massed with astonishing speed. There was a flurry of large drops, like marbles, splashing on the VW's sky blue and white paintwork. Within a minute the deluge struck, and Falcon had to swing himself down and inside the van. The noise was a cacophony, as if he sat inside a kettle drum. Outside the world faded to grey, with the riverside poplars just visible as darker shadows.

As the storm cloud passed he took a seat outside and sat under the dripping awning, so he was looking towards the unseen river when a figure emerged, walking towards him, pencil thin, with a hat and carrying a briefcase. He stopped twenty yards short and, looking up, took off the hat.

'Dr Grey,' he said.

'Mr Parkis? Good God. You look like a drowned rat.'

They shook hands. He'd seen Parkis often in his university days, but not in person now for two years. Questions would have to wait. Falcon could see water running out of the lawyer's lightweight suit and over his black polished shoes.

'Let's get you dry – I'll make tea,' he said, sliding back the door of the VW and sorting out fresh clothes. He left Parkis two towels, grabbing a kettle and gas burner, cups and teapot, and leaving him some privacy.

Emerging, Parkis looked comical in Falcon's old clothes. The jeans were a good fit, the multi-coloured socks playful, while the T-shirt still carried the faded letters of BAN THE BOMB.

Falcon put two mugs on the grass by the camp chairs. 'It's the day Cherry died – the anniversary. May the eighteenth.'

'Yes, sir. Ten years to the day. That's why I'm here.'

Parkis had a satchel, which he picked up, shuffling through papers. 'Lady Angela visits at Lincoln's Inn. Two weeks ago she had lunch with the partners and they revealed Mr Cherry's instructions. She came and found me afterwards and suggested a cup of tea at High Holborn. She wanted me to make this visit.

'She told me a story,' he said, cradling his mug. 'When they met – on a cruise in Norway – they went for a walk along the shore of what she called a fjord – it's like a lough, isn't it? He gave her a piece of quartz he'd picked up on the beach. Not a word of explanation. She's only recently found out it's a sort of mating ritual of the penguin.' Parkis met his eye for the first time. 'Are you well, sir?'

Falcon smiled. 'Not too bad. I've met someone. She's called Sofya. I think I feel better.'

Parkis beamed, then checked his watch. 'To business,' he said. 'The original will left Lady Angela the flat in London and a gilt-edged annuity.'

Rowers swept past noisily on the river, but still unseen in the mist, to the military command to *stroke, stroke, stroke.*

A sudden fear gripped Falcon. *Please, God – don't let there be any money.* The debt he already felt to Cherry was overwhelming. A gilt-edged annuity could be the death of him.

'But he left instructions for a further bequest on this day. He left you this,' said Parkis, handing over a small worn leather document pouch. 'This was Mr Cherry's in the First World War when he served briefly on the Western Front, until his various illnesses brought him home.'

It was light and, for a terrible moment, Falcon wondered if it might be empty. Or did he hope it was?

'There are documents inside,' said Parkis, as if he could read minds. 'I haven't read anything, you understand – nobody has. But I suspect you'll know what it is. That's all I can say officially, other than good luck. I'd rather you didn't read it in my sight. I should leave.'

'What can you say unofficially?' asked Falcon.

Parkis looked around, as if about to reveal an indiscretion. Falcon had the very firm sense that this was all part of his instructions, that some distant series of obligations and promises were about to be finessed.

'Mr Cherry asked for advice from the firm in 1912 – on his return from Antarctica – about various aspects of the Official Secrets Act 1911 – a revamp of the original legislation of 1898,' said Parkis. 'There had always been secrets of course, state secrets. Elizabeth 1st kept the diaries of Francis Drake a secret on pain of death.'

Parkis had produced a wad of papers. 'The Act in question,' he said, putting on a pair of wire-rimmed spectacles: 'makes it an offence if any person for any purpose prejudicial to the safety or interest of the State'

(a) approaches [inspects, passes over] or is in the neighbourhood of, or enters any prohibited place within the meaning of this Act: or

(b) makes any sketch, plan, model, or note which is calculated to be or might be or is intended to be directly or indirectly useful to an enemy; or

(c) obtains, collects, records, publishes or communicates to any other person any secret official code word, or password, or any sketch, plan, model, article, or note, or other document or information which is calculated to be or might be or is intended to be directly or indirectly useful to an enemy . . .;

'they shall be guilty of a felony.' Parkis quickly removed the glasses. 'The penalty back then was penal servitude.'

'Why did he feel the need to find out such legal details?' asked Falcon.

'I think he was being careful. He'd signed the Act, he said, with respect to some documents deposited with the Foreign Office. We can presume this was Scott's notebook and that something in it constitutes a state secret. Cherry said he kept the original, as per Scott's instructions. The government has a copy. He wanted to know to what extent he was bound to keep such secrets and, specifically, the extent to which he would be bound in the future.'

Parkis leant forward in his camping chair, grasping his knees. 'I think that's the key to it, sir. He wanted to publish these documents – in the legal sense, of distributing them to more than one person. At the time he was restrained, ultimately by the foreign secretary, Sir Edward Whyte, overseeing what was then the Secret Service Bureau. Scott may well have feared the notebook would remain shrouded in secrecy. Perhaps that is why he wanted Mr Cherry to keep the original. It's proof of itself, evidence if you like. Now Mr Cherry has left it to you.'

'I see. And what is my position?'

'I'm not a lawyer. I'm a lawyer's clerk. You'd have to take advice. But to do that you'd have to know what information it contains. It's unlikely the threat perceived to the nation's security in 1912 is still real – but who knows?'

The mist had finally cleared off the Cam, and a line of barges carrying sugar beet, drawn by a horse, slid across the landscape.

'But I haven't signed the Official Secrets Act,' said Falcon, reaching into a bag hanging from the VW's passenger-side door handle and retrieving his Ducados.

'Ah. I'm afraid the whole "signing the Official Secrets Act" is misleading – a term of art dreamt up by the film industry. It's true Mr Cherry would have been asked to sign something – that's common practice within the Security Service. It simply reminds someone of their responsibilities under the law. But the law covers everyone anyway. You don't have to sign up. That would be like saying you can happily steal something if you haven't signed up to the Theft Act of 1968.'

'So I may have to keep this secret *secret*?'

'Yes. And you might have to give back the original – even though it may be technically your property.'

Something about Parkis's cheerful face made him feel uncertain. 'The Security Services have never made enquiries at the firm? Never asked if Mr Cherry deposited documents?'

'Given client confidentiality, we would demand an instruction from a judge before answering that question.'

Just for a moment Falcon considered that answer, concealed by the fuss of lighting his cigarette. Something told him to let the matter rest – at least for now.

'So, I'm safe for a while – and possibly for ever. It was nearly sixty years ago,' he said, affecting a cheerful tone.

'Yes, although several members of the expedition are still alive,' said Parkis. 'Skeletons in cupboards are always tricky. When is there a good time to tell the truth? And if it's a state secret – which it technically is – it may have repercussions for our allies and our enemies. We are in the middle of a Cold War.'

The blind terror of the Cuban Missile Crisis was still a vivid memory. He'd been at Oxford and there'd been marches, and vigils, as Kennedy dared Khrushchev to start a nuclear war. During the crucial hours he'd walked down to the river and along to Iffley. It was uniquely unsettling for Falcon: the idea that rockets would rain down again as they had done before.

'What if I declined the bequest?' said Falcon, unhappily.

'You can't say no in any meaningful way. You are the owner. You could give it away, or throw it away, or burn it, or hide it. Or just leave it here, I suppose, and drive off in the VW. But it's a historical document of great worth – possibly. And you're a historian. It all really depends on the contents of the notebook. As I said, I can't give advice. But I'd read it, sir. Quickly. Then you can decide.'

They shook hands.

It had been an odd meeting, because he felt they'd started out as friends and ended up as client and lawyer.

'When will you run next?' Falcon asked, trying to reclaim a sense of warmth.

'Tonight. The house is at Teddington, so I can use the towpath.'

Falcon thought that legal clerks – even chief clerks – must be well paid to live in leafy Teddington, where the boats rode the tide up to Richmond Hill.

'I should go,' said Parkis.

Falcon gave him a bag for his wet clothes. Parkis promised to post back the socks, jeans and T-shirt. He put his hat, still damp, on his head and shook Falcon's hand a second time.

For a moment they looked each other in the eye, and then Parkis marched into the distance. Falcon felt there had been something unsaid between them, almost a farewell, which made him feel unsettled. Parkis looked lighter walking away, unburdened. Falcon picked up the satchel, sniffed the leather and, flipping back the flap with its copper buckle, saw inside a wax document pouch – and, rising from it, what might have been the smell of history itself.

10

Falcon chose his favourite bench, under a lime tree, close to the river, in deep shade. He'd put Cherry's satchel in his knapsack, with a Thermos of tea, a sandwich and the master's telescope – largely because it was a talisman, but also in case he wanted to track the moon again. He didn't need glasses to read but he retrieved them now to survey the scene, assailed by the conviction that he was being watched. A white river-cruiser went past, and the water came alive, Canaletto waves catching the light. He glanced back – a reflex only – towards the VW, parked among its shield of Scots Pine and silver birch. There was a figure standing under the awning by the van, which Falcon had left up, and which had buckled under the weight of rainwater, springing several leaks.

The telescope brought the intruder into sharp focus: he was knocking on the van doors, peering in at the windows. He wore a checked shirt and jeans, with a knapsack. Falcon's only visitors were friends; his post went to Caius, his 'address' as such was Nagg's Lane, Ditton Meadows, but his passport, and all official documents, gave his college as his place of residence. And when he thought of friends who knew where he was, he counted six – two of them former girlfriends. Besides, he often moved with the seasons, so the idea that somebody had found him was startling.

He watched his unknown caller. From the knapsack the man produced a small camera with which he took pictures through the windows of the VW. With a series of deft movements he tried the window latches, and the door handles. He circled the vehicle, and took a note of the registration in a book, possibly adding some data after peering in at the dashboard – mileage, perhaps, or a few letters left in view: a tax form, a college notice. Finally, he produced what might have been a stick of chalk and marked each one of the tyres at twelve o'clock. Rising, he straightened his back, so Falcon saw his face. He was older than a student, fair hair, a wispy beard, a psychedelic T-shirt. The sunlight, which had broken through again, dappled the van, and it caught something in his hand, a cigarette case, blindingly metallic. It was another detail that didn't fit.

His caller stood smoking, looking towards the river, where crowds were now emerging from the trees to sit in the sun again. Falcon felt safe in the dappled shadows, but it was pretty clear a return to the VW was out of the question. If this was MI6, or Scotland Yard, it prompted three questions: how did they know about Cherry's bequest, how had they found him so quickly, and did they have the authority to demand custody of the documents? He had to find somewhere to read the notebook, which, given the crabbed handwriting, might take hours, or days. If possible he needed to make a copy, then hide the original.

His visitor set off on foot north towards Fen Ditton, so Falcon went south, on the towpath into Barnwell, on the edge of the city. The telephone box stank of urine, so he wedged his foot in the door and punched in the number for the Mullard Observatory. Instinctively, he trusted Sofya, but the ringing tone, plaintive and weak, like a distant signal from outer space, seemed to inspire doubts. In truth, he had nowhere else to turn.

Then it was too late: a voice, smooth and slightly bored, cut through the static: 'Mullard Observatory. West Gate.'

'Dr Sarkisova, please. Is she in?'

'I'll try. There's an event at the station later – I think everyone is there.'

Falcon recognised the voice; a chatty young woman at the Observatory 'checkpoint'.

'It's going to be quite a party. There's visitors, too, from NASA. And children – everyone's brought their children, so you can imagine. It may be best to ring later, if you can?'

'Can you try her line?' He hoped he didn't sound desperate, but the idea that he was being hunted had taken hold.

Sofya picked up on the first ring. 'Sarkisova,' she said, business-like, abrupt.

'Sof, it's me. I need help.'

He heard her put her reading glasses on the lab bench.

'You never ask for help.'

Their relationship was defined by self-sufficiency and independence. They were close, closer with each passing day, but always separate. To be in need seemed to break an unspoken code.

'Well. Here I am. I need to lie low. I can make the party – that's safe. It's six o'clock, right? Can you get us a room at The Railway?'

The Railway Inn stood opposite the gates to the Mullard.

'I'll explain everything later.'

'You are not in trouble, Falcon?'

'Depends how you define trouble. Speak later.'

'Later.'

Falcon walked to Parker's Piece – the city's great green urban square – and sat down to read. Lazy traffic ran along three sides. Several makeshift football matches were taking place, with bags and jackets for goalposts. The Scott Polar Institute stood at the south-eastern corner. Falcon's office was on the second floor, at the back, with a view over the Victorian terraced streets of New Town. On Sundays there was a precise routine at the Scott Polar. Only one porter was on duty, and there would be a changing of the guard at just after two o'clock, using the side door. If Falcon kept to the shadows he'd be able to slip in unseen. The front doors were out of the question: if they were after him, and the notebook, he'd be in full view of Parker's Piece – and they were bound to know where he worked. Once he was inside he could make a copy – possibly two. Then he'd slip away to the Mullard.

He had an hour before the shifts changed.

He sat on the grass, opened the waxed pouch and found the old red notebook, slightly stiff, which creaked when he turned back the cover. It was marked RFS – Robert Falcon Scott – and dated November 1912.

The first page held a message:

For Cherry
There's no time for sentimentality . . .

Falcon read on hungrily, devouring the words, despite Scott's scrawled hand. A few hundred yards away Kathleen Scott's bust of her husband on the façade of the Scott Polar looked out with blank eyes. Falcon read the brutal accusation in the note again, then again: that Scott had been murdered, they'd all been murdered, hunted down, that the truth – and the identity of the killers – if divulged, could bring war. They'd died in the tent dreaming of vengeance. That burden, to seek out the killers, had passed to Cherry.

For God's sake find the truth,
RFS

'And now it comes to me,' whispered Falcon, alone amid the crowd.

He looked up into the blue sky and saw a chalk-white seagull hovering, as if impatient for him to begin the task. Perhaps Cherry's soul had taken wing.

He turned to the first page of the journal.

II

Attention: Sir Edward Whyte, Foreign Secretary

21 Jan 1912
First Depot after Pole

Sir

I undertook to keep a separate record if required.
The diary tells of our humiliation at the Pole. It needs no
elaboration here.
At present only Wilson knows of our discussions concerning
sabotage – and then only in summary. I told him there was
intelligence that an attempt would be made to sabotage our
expedition. All evidence pointed to agents of the Kaiser. I made
it clear the information is sketchy and we should not presume
the Germans are the only suspects. I further divulged that by
your order we have a government agent within our crew –
Cecil Meares. He turned back towards Cape Evans with the
dogs at the foot of the Beardmore and should, by now, be back
at the hut. We agreed that if he spotted any evidence of sabo-
tage en route he would leave a message at a depot.

Falcon looked up from the diary. An ice-cream van was on
the edge of the grass playing its idiotic tune. So, the British government had suspected sabotage *before* Scott sailed
south. What was more they'd put a spy inside the expedition to help Scott keep watch. Had the vital 'intelligence'
mirrored the truth? Were they really being hunted down?
He read on.

There are five of us still. Myself, Wilson, Bowers, Oates and Taffy Evans.

We are forty-eight miles from the Pole, more than seven hundred miles from the ship.

Privacy – never mind secrecy – is incredibly difficult to achieve. These notes will be brief. We haul for eight hours and then huddle in the tent. My decision to bring Bowers and swell our ranks has had repercussions: five men in such a cramped space is wearing on the nerves, although we benefit from the body heat. But cooking, reading, writing are acts requiring communal action, a ballet of domestic perfection. To keep this secret we have had to be swift – every time Bowers fixes our position with the sextant Wilson and I walk out with him, stand aside, and snatch a brief interlude, heads together.

The wind is not as helpful as we supposed. Our sail gives little advantage. Morale is low, spirits outwardly high – a debilitating combination. The days are shortening, the dusk creeps earlier, I feel we are on the edge of night.

My official diary tells a more buoyant tale.

I am using the spirit lamp by which to write this note.

The problem – which has provoked this report – is Taffy Evans. My diary relates his decline since his fall on the glacier. His injuries won't heal. But Wilson detects other symptoms. There is evidence that what we took as a minor head wound suffered in the fall has led to internal bleeding. Wilson fears an injury to the brain. Taffy has become morose, silent and, to some extent, pitiable. We are agreed he's done for – which is a calamity. We can't leave him behind, and he's beginning to slow us up. He drags his feet, unable to muster the will to lift his boots.

But it is what he said that has prompted this report.

Wilson was examining his injuries in the tent. They were otherwise alone. He cannot have it word perfect but he has tried his best – and was happy with this version of the conversation, if we can call it such. His signature is in the margin as a warrant of its authenticity.

Falcon looked up. The gears of a distant bus grated on
Regent Street. A kite in the shape of a diamond cast a jittering shadow on the grass. A child with a toy rocket ran wildly
in circles. He examined the scrawl in the margin. He could
check it later with his files but it looked authentic, although
there were signs of stress and a cramped, cold hand. Sunlight played across the page . . .

Once alone the Welshman broke the silence.

'I know the others are keeping quiet,' said Taffy.

The doctor was applying a cream to his frostbitten fingers.

'About what, Taffy? Quiet about what?'

*'I saw him at Half Degree Depot – off to the east, always
to the east. I think Soldier sees him too but he won't say. He'll
think it madness but it isn't. The snow was blowing and he
must have got too close to our camp. Then the wind dropped
and he was there, sir. It's God's truth.'*

*'You're saying you saw a man – not one of us five – but one
of our crewmates?'*

*Taffy covered his mouth with the back of his hand. Then:
'He's always there, sir. But out of sight.'*

*At this point he began to shake his head mechanically, as if
refusing to answer questions, which Wilson did not put. The
doctor simply went on tending the poor man's hand.*

By this point the Welshman was weeping.

*Then, Wilson said, it was as if he emerged from a dream,
looking about the tent in wonder, and then dread. 'Thank you
very much, sir,' he said, standing, thrusting the injured hand
back into the mitten and then the gauntlet. 'I don't expect
they'll be any more trouble. They were nipped by the frost.'*

*Outside Wilson joined in the work but kept an eye on Taffy.
He worked diligently, as of old, for twenty minutes, but when
I called a break so that we could gather our strength to haul
he slumped down, sitting on an empty food box, staring at his
boots. Oates offered him a smoke but he just shook his head, not
looking up.*

Later, when we found the last cairn of the day, Wilson reported on their conversation. It is extraordinary that the ravings of a beaten man should conjure up fears. But for nature this is a benign world. There are no bears, or wolves, or wandering tribes. When I look out into the frost smoke I have never feared a looming silhouette. Now all is changed – and for what? This madness. The man has broken down.

What else can we conclude but an injury to the brain? Taffy's drivel – if given credence – implies either a plot among my own men, or the attentions of a foreign enemy. As for our own expedition there can be no one but us five on the plateau. The last returning party left us twenty-seven days ago. They will be within sight of the hut by now, God willing. As for an outside enemy – who? Amundsen beat us to the Pole by six weeks. He will be within sight of the Bay of Whales by now. He returns home a hero – why delay to snuff out the lives of the vanquished? The Germans were set for the Weddell Sea – on the far side of the continent. Who could want to hunt down the losers in the great race?

I talked to Bowers and Oates, and both reported that Taffy had not spoken to them of his visions. Bowers let himself down by suggesting the Welshman may have told the truth but that the apparition is supernatural. He insisted on retelling old sailors' yarns about guardian angels – spirits that accompany men in times of great trial.

In other words: ghosts. Pathetically, he failed even to be straight about the myth: it is not at times of great trial, it is at times of approaching death. I told him if he couldn't spit it out he should keep his peace.

I brought the discussion to an end. It seems to me that God has forsaken our venture. All that he can control – the vast movements of the heavens, the compass of the winds, the lie of this desperate land – has been turned against us. Against me. I doubt he would afford us the comfort of angels.

I undertook, sir, to report back on any signs of sabotage. Our considered position is that Taffy Evans, petty officer, is deranged, perhaps intermittently. The idea that a foreign agent

*could be shadowing our progress on the Antarctic plateau is
fanciful and safely beyond belief. But you have this record. I
promised to report anything sinister.*

*I told Oates and Bowers to omit any mention of Taffy's
visions from their own journals. This will be the only record.*

RFS

Falcon blinked to clear his eyes. A game of football had
started in the shadow of the University Arms. Was this to
be the heart of the matter? The crazed visions of a dying
man? The most alarming aspect of the entry was Scott's
own mood: embattled, bitter. That line, 'God has forsaken
our venture', was pitiful. Hoping for better, he read on.

*Upper Glacier Depot
7 February 1912*

Sir

*This is our third depot homeward bound, but the first to
show a severe shortage of oil. The cans hold an imperial gallon,
and we estimate the deficit as a quart. Wilson decanted what
was left and made accurate measurements. He did this in plain
view of the party, so everyone is now aware that oil shortage
is a threat. It has always been a hindrance, but this is of a
different order. Our lives depend on fuel. We cannot survive
on frozen rations, not to mention the morale-boosting heat and
light. What rankles is that the usual notes left for us by the
returning parties do not mention any shortages. But, of course,
for them there is enough. We are last and must suffer if others
take too much.*

*The shortages could be down to shoddy work by the last two
returning parties or evaporation through the caps – although I
ordered leather washers, which should have resolved the matter.
(Oates says that when contact was made with Amundsen at*

the Bay of Whales he had ordered his cans welded shut. They break them open when needed. This seems a hammer to crack a nutshell.) The oil cans leak – we knew this on Discovery *and* Shackleton *reported similar, although his notes on the issue are poorly kept and of little use. It may be the practice of piling the cans high – to build the cairn and facilitate navigation – is part of the problem. They sit in the sun during the day and the frost at night. This must accelerate losses. Wilson has also detected pin holes in the cans caused by metal fatigue.*

Most irksome is the possibility that we are short because the last two returning parties took more than their fair share – although I cannot believe this was deliberate. My decision to take five men to the Pole (instead of the allotted four, depleting the last returning party to three) means that they had to divide depot supplies on a ratio of three to five. This presents a challenge to those who went before us – though hardly an insurmountable one.

But Lieutenant Evans, who led the last party, is not a first-class officer. I have studiously avoided criticism of my second-in-command in the official diary – to the extent that this has been possible. This is a private note. The man is despised. It is not the job of any officer to be popular, and those who are – and here Shackleton springs to mind – are often flawed by the need to be liked. Lieutenant Evans is cheerful enough, hail-fellow-well-met, but when he is not being watched he is idle and slipshod. Wilson notes that he looked weak and thin when he set off for home. His dislike of seal meat is well-known. He has instead set aside extra rations of the meaty pemmican – to the detriment of others. Wilson fears he may have been showing the early signs of scurvy as a result. I had to say that when I told him he was not going to the Pole he was crestfallen, dignified, but I thought I detected bitter disappointment. If he has fallen ill as well it bodes badly for his men. Crean and Gwynne are Titans, and would be the last to flag, but if Lieutenant Evans was stricken perhaps they needed extra oil for warmth and food. Or he may be slowing them down, in which case they need more oil between depots. If he has allocated to himself the task of dividing rations on the basis of three eighths then it is quite

*possible the shortfalls are a mistake – a charitable option. As for
deliberate sabotage – by a slighted man – this is, as I say, unthink-
able. He is an officer and must be considered a gentleman.*

　　*Wilson and I had a further private conversation out on the
ice. I said, with regard to oil, that sabotage was out of the question – because we are not the victors in the race for the Pole.
Why would anyone wish to snuff us out? Wilson – always per-
ceptive in terms of human nature – voiced a subtlety that had
escaped me. Our enemies, if they exist on this virgin continent,
might not know the outcome of the race, if they sabotaged the
depots after we passed through going south. It is also possible
that the oil cans could have been tampered with on the voyage,
or when we re-stowed the ship at Christchurch at Lyttelton.*

　　*Taffy continues to confide to Wilson. He has seen our shadow
again – last night just after dusk. The Welshman walked away
from the tent and stood alone for twenty minutes in the biting
cold. Oates said he could hear him talking, quite plainly, but
that the sense of it was lost on the wind. Later Taffy told Wilson it was the same figure, a man, hooded, in heavy gear, with
goggles, standing about a hundred yards away.*

　　*Lack of oil will not kill us unless we slow down. But Taffy is
slowing us down. The expedition is in peril.*

　　RFS

Falcon set aside the diary. The tone of recrimination had
deepened. A mood of dark suspicion permeated Scott's
view of his comrades. He wondered what Cherry had made
of this – would he really have wanted the world to read
it? Or did it in some way provide Scott, and even Cherry,
with others to blame? He'd thought better of the master.
He turned the page . . .

　　Sir
　　8 March
　　Middle Glacier Depot

Sabotage certainly. The game is up.

I must set the scene. We arrived here yesterday, although we came perilously close to not finding the depot at all. The food was welcome, the sheer relief of not being lost in a maze of ice made us all giddy. But the fuel was short, one can by more than half a gallon, one entirely empty. Today I let them rest and we collected geological samples nearby. As I write this I'm perched on a rock at the edge of the vast chasm of crystal that flows away from my feet. It is difficult to get any sense of scale: the human mind is dwarfed by grandeur. Below the surface of the glacier lie ballrooms of ice. Traversing this translucent world is like trying to walk over the glass roof of a vast railway station. Darkness is gathering. The feeling of falling, of tipping into the void, is hypnotic. We are silent, allowing the view ahead to fill our minds, so that we can perhaps forget our desperate plight.

It was Oates who made the discovery on our return with the samples. He was the last into camp – he is limping badly. He knelt down beside the empty oil can – which Wilson had set back on the spot where we discovered it. The Soldier's head slumped forward – I thought for a moment he had fallen asleep. He is exhausted, poor chap. But then the sleepwalker stirred and taking off one of his mittens began to feel the snow beneath his right knee, digging down with bare fingers. He produced a small iron tool – a centre punch, the type used to put a dint in metal before using a drill.

Oates held it up for all to see.

Wilson's brain works quicker now than my own. He picked up the empty can and stood it on its end. And there was the punched hole, clean through the tin, a perfect square.

I saw it then, the saboteur at work. A moment of panic, surely. He must have driven the centre punch home with a blunt instrument of some kind, and the blow sent the tool spinning away, but he had no time to search for it. This means he works against the clock – which suggests he has companions who do not share his designs. Or that he is wary of our arrival? Is he that close? Are Taffy's ravings a cruel distortion of some truth?

'Look – it's inscribed,' said Wilson, holding the punch to his eye and spelling out the letters. 'MV BJÖRN – there's a diacritic over the O. I think that suggests Norwegian, or possibly German.'

'A ship then?' offered Bowers and I agreed. Our tools were all marked MV TERRA NOVA, the initials for motor vessel.

'Filchner's ship is the Deutschland,' said Wilson.

'A second ship?' said Oates.

Motor vessels can be hired by any nation. So the field is open. This led to another debate in the tent. Bowers said he heard at Lyttelton, before we set sail in the Terra Nova, that an expedition was about to leave Tokyo for the south led by Nobu Shirase – a veteran of the north, the noted explorer of the Kuril Islands and Shakalin. Intelligence, which was sketchy, indicated he was bound for the Barrier and that most of the crew were expert skiers. There was much talk of a lightning 'dash' across the ice. Are they the enemy?

I said the Japanese were our staunch allies and should be beyond suspicion but Bowers, who has served in the east, said Shirase was an army officer dedicated to the glory of the Emperor. Perhaps he hoped to take back the ultimate prize – the Pole – and make sure we were not competitors, or at least prevent us from reaching civilisation with the news of our triumph, or that of the Norwegians – for Bowers pointed out that Amundsen may also be a victim of sabotage. Is he being hunted too?

Bowers sees enemies everywhere. Mention of Amundsen prompted him to ask if the Norwegians might not be the saboteurs. But this is ludicrous: they were six weeks ahead of us by the time they reached the Pole. Their base is four hundred miles west of Cape Evans. They were almost certainly descending to the Barrier along their own route before we began the climb. Amundsen's conduct has been less than chivalrous – but I know he seeks only honour for his country.

I pocketed the punch. If we die out here on the ice it should be found with my body.

I decided that the time had come to face our situation openly and together. I let them know of our conversations about potential sabotage. While Germany was the chief suspect, I made it clear that the Foreign Office had also cited foreign revolutionaries, and anti-imperialists. Oates chimed in, pointing the finger at our own Russians. Were they spies? The man's mind is failing, as is his strength.

I had to stop such wild talk. I made it clear that no mention of such matters should appear in any journal but the one notebook destined to be taken back in secret to London. The news agency requires a diary for publication, and the contract is binding. Our families will benefit. The agency must publish immediately. And if we fail, and our bodies are found, the diaries will be a comfort to our people. And there must be a story for the public. So it was agreed.

We all sat in silence then, haunted by the same fear. We may talk of foreign powers and wild revolutionaries but we all know that the prime suspects must be our own men of the returning parties, who passed through these depots long before us. But I won't hear it discussed. I chose the men; I stand by them. But in my heart I know any one of them could have punched the hole in the oil can because it was at the bottom of the pile and the damage would not have been discovered until now. Who might the traitor be? Atkinson led the penultimate party of Wright, Keegan and Cherry-Garrard, while Lieutenant Evans led the last, of Gwynne and Crean. Not knowing adds dreadfully to our torment.

Taffy is failing fast, Oates ailing. We must hope for milder temperatures, no more storms, and luck. Fate owes us a benefaction. Otherwise, we march into oblivion.

RFS

Falcon laid down the diary carefully, making sure it was safely within its leather pouch. He had to make a copy – quickly. The story had moved from ambiguous anxiety to outright fear of death in just three entries. And finally there was evidence: the centre punch. Did it lie with Scott's body? He was nearly certain it did not appear on the list of artefacts held by the Scott Polar. Items from the tent were highly prized, and meticulously documented.

The great clock on the Church of the English Martyrs stood at a quarter to two: there were just fifteen minutes until the porters changed over. Opposite the institute a shop sold TVs, and a small crowd had gathered to watch the BBC's broadcast from Cape Kennedy. Several identical black-and-white pictures flickered in the window, showing the Saturn V on the launch pad, leaking fumes and steam. The crowd – young and old – was excited, rapt. One man had a small boy on his shoulders. A path was cleared to let an old man through to the front.

Falcon stood in the back row, using the crowd as a screen. He felt his heartbeat tick up at the sight of the Saturn V, a slight coolness in his hands as his blood withdrew from the extremities. He was a child of the Space Race so he'd become inured to this trigger, able to stem the progression to panic and fear. Perhaps it was because he'd never *seen* the V2, only heard it, smelt it, felt it. He'd seen film, and there was something snake-like, predatory, about the V2's flight. By contrast the Saturn V looked like a force of nature, upright, noble, its flight aimed at the stars.

He made his shoulders relax, his lungs take a little more of the warm summer air.

Sofya would be watching now – out at the Mullard. He knew what she was thinking, feeling. She hated the Space Race because of what it had done to her. But one night, after they'd been together for a month, she'd finally told him what it had done to her father: a story that explained so much – including the watchful eye of the KGB – and had begun in the Kremlin three years earlier, although he sensed she had not told him the whole truth.

12

Three years earlier: Moscow

Once upon a time there was a church in the middle of a forest. Sofya's mother, Nina, had told her this story many times as a child. And now, aged twenty-five, she stood beside her, looking down on the modest dome of St Saviour-in-the-Forest from the windows of the Kremlin. The trees had all gone, many centuries ago, and now the church stood in the middle of the Great Palace, in a courtyard, which in its turn was at the heart of Moscow. In a room nearby, which they could not see, her father lay on an operating table, his chest opened by the surgeons of the Politburo so that they might save his heart, which had been failing for years.

A man in a worker's jacket appeared carrying three wooden stools, and told them to follow, pushing open two vast silver doors, which moved with an almost liquid ease despite their undoubted weight. 'The Hall of St Andrew,' he said, setting down the chairs and lighting a cigarette. 'They'll come for you at the right time,' he added, flicking ash in the direction of the Imperial Throne. 'Nicholas 1st sat there – his great-grandson took a Bolshevik bullet in the head. It's a lesson in history.'

Her mother, breathless, taking in the scene, whispered to herself: 'There are seven hundred rooms.'

Sofya's brother Maxim sneered at the gaudy magnificence of the hall. The parquet flooring was made of many kinds of wood and lay beneath fluid-like wax and polish, so that it was as if he stood on water.

Light flooded in from the south, through two flights of windows (from the outside the palace had three floors, but they saw now that the top two simply lit the state rooms with a double line of sparkling glass). On the north side there were identical windows, but the glass here was silvered mirrors. The room was thirty metres long, pillars on either side of a ceremonial nave. There were several violet jasper fireplaces, great bronze chandeliers and, over the throne, a glittering starburst of gold, with at the centre what her mother said was the 'all powerful eye'.

'How do you know this?' asked Sofya.

'I worked here when I met your father,' she said. This was happening now, little glimpses of a past life offered up casually. They would have meant so much more when Sofya and Maxim were children.

They'd read about her father in *Izvestia* and *Pravda*, but he was never accorded his name. The world called him 'The Great Designer', the mastermind behind the race to beat the Americans to the moon. She had asked her father once, in his office at Baikonur, why they could not call him Sergei Pavlovich Korolev and he'd explained that the CIA, who had agents everywhere, planned to kill him. He must remain shadowy, insubstantial. In this he had succeeded, even to his children.

She sat in the splendid mirrored hall and wondered if this was one of the reasons he was fading away: that he'd been denied his own identity.

At the far end, opposite the throne, a pair of copper doors opened a foot, and a man's head appeared, then retreated. Beyond him, in a hall of marble, Sofya glimpsed men in white coats and a single blinding light.

'Is he going to die?' she asked her mother.

'No. No. This is the Kremlin and your father is in the hands of the professors. If it goes well I am told we may be able to talk – an hour, maybe less.'

They heard the bells of the citadel's four cathedrals, and two churches, mark the hour. In the hall the sound lingered long after the bells had fallen silent.

Her father had another family, and at least one former wife, but he loved Nina and Sofya, although Maxim was a disappointment: he wasted his talents in mathematics on small acts of petty rebellion – editing an underground newspaper, refusing to train with the militia, organising protests against nuclear weapons and the rockets that would fly them to their targets.

Her father was forgiven many things because of what had happened before the Great Patriotic War. He had been arrested with many others, and there had been a trial lasting an hour in which he was accused of passing secrets to the French. This was the charge they all faced. A generation. Stalin suspected everyone. Her father was sent to the Kolyma gulag. For two years, he told Sofya, every waking moment was dominated by hunger, until the minute after the evening meal of potato soup when the cold made his teeth ache. One night, many years later, when he came to the flat for dinner and to put her to bed, he gave her his most precious treasure, a tin mug he'd used in the gulag, inscribed with his name, etched with a nail.

The Kremlin relented, and he came back to Moscow and worked in a government laboratory on Radio Street designing rockets. Then came the Patriotic War. He fought in the Red Army in Hungary, at Buda, in the final days. He was given a medal he never wore. German scientists, enticed east, worked there too, while their luckier colleagues went west with Wernher von Braun to Texas, and the desert.

The stain – the gulag – never faded, but her father's genius could not be set aside. He worked at Baikonur, the new Space City in the deserts of Kazakhstan. He came back to Moscow when Khrushchev summoned him, demanding yet another *coup de théâtre* – the first man in space, the first woman, the first docking, the first probe to the moon. He was given a *dacha* at Oboldino in the countryside outside Moscow and they went often to stay. Each time he looked a little older, irritable – but never with her. Sofya studied, revealing she had inherited her father's mind. Maxim rebelled, because he needed his father and he was hardly ever at home.

Then, one day, she too flew south to Space City. She had her degree from the Moscow State Technical School, and now a doctorate in aeronautics. She was there by right. They shared a prefabricated house on the edge of the new city, although her work was in one of the laboratories and his in a bunker close to Pad 1/5 – Gagarin's Start. In the winter, ice was a veneer on all the windows, their breath frozen inside. In the summer evenings the heat was too much so they would sit outside in the long shadows, while on the horizon rockets shimmered in the heat, rippling like corn.

She drank vodka; he drank tea.

'What's he like?' she'd asked.

'Khrushchev?' It was the face of her father she'd always remember, caught in the red light of a sunset, looking towards the distant cosmodrome. 'Belligerent. Vicious. Jovial. When he shouts I get spit on my glasses.'

'Why must it be a race?' she asked, sipping the vodka, which was warm, even though it had been iced a minute earlier.

'One day,' he said, setting his glass of tea in the red dust, 'bombs will fall from space.'

He turned stiffly in his chair and pointed to the moon, which had risen unseen behind them.

'In the meantime we must claim a new world for the children of Lenin,' he said, pulling a doubtful face.

Which was when Sofya realised they sat outside each evening in the dust for a reason: that the house was bugged.

That first summer her mother and Maxim visited and there was a family outing because they had fuel for the car. They drove along the dry course of the Syr Darya to the coast – but there was no water there, the boats beached on sand, a saltpan, among the heads of dead fish. This was the Aral Sea – lifeless, no sign of water beyond a mirage, and no way out to the wider oceans. Her father bought them all ice-creams at a hotel where minor party apparatchiks lay beside a murky pool.

As she kissed Maxim at the aerodrome, he whispered in his sister's ear: 'His heart is weak. Mother says this at the sink, every day. His heart is weak.'

This is her family, and this is their prize: that the Kremlin will fix his heart.

For the first time they heard feet running. Because the room was only half lit by the windows there were hundreds of electric lights, and they dimmed now, faltering, then recovered.

Sofya thought of her father's heart, the heart she loved.

There was silence in the seven hundred rooms of the Great Palace. Sofya had never felt this before. It was as if the world pressed down on her, suffocating, echoless. Finally, they heard a child crying – it was not the sound of grief, but perhaps of confusion.

They sat for an hour. Sofya watched the rectangles of sunlight edge across the wooden floor. Maxim paced the nave, complaining that he'd run out of cigarettes.

Then the copper doors opened again and she saw it all. In the next hall the windows had been covered with sheets. They had seen no furniture in any of the halls but here she could see, at the far end, perhaps twenty metres away, a hospital bed, the surgical lights above now lost in a grey shadow. A sheet covered a body on the bed.

A man appeared in the doorway. Her mother stood and Sofya heard the breath leave her body. Maxim hung back in the shadows beneath one of the old chandeliers.

'Comrade Secretary,' said her mother, and Sofya looked at his face. She recognised only a man from the Politburo, seen on the balcony in Red Square, anonymous and familiar, the perfect Party man. The face was without a wrinkle, the taut skin shiny and very pale. Sofya thought that when he died the embalmers would preserve him but he would look no different to his family and friends.

It seemed unlikely but one cheek was wet with tears. The rest of him was stiff, mummified, and Sofya wondered if he wore a corset.

'Irina Borysivna,' he said, with a slight bow. 'The worst news. Please take a seat. His heart was too weak. It has failed at last. He is a hero of the Soviet Union. We will lay him to rest in the necropolis.'

Sofya would always remember his hands. They were a peasant's, but the left shook now as he straightened his tie. Her own heart missed a few beats, and then began again, reluctantly.

Her mother swayed back, as if struck by an invisible blow. 'Now I have nothing,' she said, slumping into the seat.

'Would you wish to see him?' said the comrade secretary, standing slightly to one side, shuffling heavy shoes. Sofya smelt him then, an aftershave perhaps, but to her the oils of the embalmer.

Her mother shook her head but Sofya took her arm, hoisting her to her feet, and they went through the copper doors, and Maxim took his mother's other hand, as she began to cry.

The comrade secretary walked ahead.

Her mother whispered: 'It is Andropov. From the Central Committee.' She took Maxim's arm, so that her lips were close to his ear. 'Say nothing, Maxim. Nothing.'

Sofya counted 135 steps to the hospital bed. It took long enough for her to accept that she'd lost a future in which her father would have loved her, even from afar. She felt empty, untethered, as if she might float away.

A nurse appeared, nodded to her mother, and pulled aside the sheet so that they could see his face.

'A good death,' said her mother, because they could see his soul had departed.

Sofya thought there was something stern about him, the soft line of his lips now straight and angry. She knew then that he hadn't fallen unconscious from the world but had slipped away knowing what he had lost. And then she received a wonderful gift. She knew with absolute certainty that the last thing he had thought of was his daughter Sofya.

'A great man,' said Andropov. 'I was an engineer too. Water transport – at the highest level. We could talk about this.'

'If he'd had a name they'd have given him the Nobel,' said Sofya, and she felt her mother squeeze her hand savagely.

'That honour was for the nation, no single man,' said Andropov.

'Where are his other loved ones?' asked her mother.

Andropov looked to a set of doors painted in white and gold. 'They have paid their respects.'

'I see,' said her mother, already bitter, already understanding that she would be excluded from the official ceremonies, the lying-in-state, the procession.

Maxim edged closer to the bed and took up his father's hand.

'I will leave you alone,' said Andropov.

But he paused beside Sofya. 'You must continue with the work. Your father was proud of you.'

There was a silence and Maxim let go of his father's hand.

'The Luna programme – sending probes to the moon – would benefit from assistance from the British, at Jodrell Bank,' said Andropov. 'I have recommended that you, Sofya Irena, should travel with Professor Valentinov. You went to

Houston, I think, in 'sixty-three, with Cantor? These are great honours. There will be other duties. You will hear from Comrade Semichastny's secretariat.'

They stood still as his footsteps receded. Maxim moved to the foot of the bed and Sofya thought he looked oddly elated, as if he could see some bright, bitter future. Their mother always carried prayer beads, although the Party frowned on dogma and ritual. They stood apart, listening to the clack of the wooden rosary.

Somewhere in a corridor, finally, they heard the advance of a mop and pail. They retraced their steps to the Hall of St Andrew where the old man was waiting to show them out. He took off his cap.

'Where is Comrade Semichastny's office?' asked Sofya. 'Do you know?'

His eyes slipped from her face to the far end of the hall where the sunlight had caught the gold starburst around the 'all-seeing eye'.

'Not here. Lubyanka Square. You must go there.'

13

The great clock began to chime the hour, so Falcon left the crowd in front of the TV screens, flickering with images from the two o'clock news – a riot in Northern Ireland, petrol bombs being thrown, a Cabinet reshuffle in London, then a return to the waiting Saturn V. Crossing the road he slipped into the shadow of the plane trees next to the Scott Polar. To one side an iron harpoon gun stood on a plinth. He could see Scott's carved face in profile, the stone chin weak, the brow noble. His death gave the building a peculiar resonance, as if the museum and laboratories were simply additions to a shrine. Visitors often whispered as they crossed the threshold. Through one of the playful arched windows he could see into the museum rooms, cases of artefacts, sledges on the wall, a stuffed penguin in a case.

Shackleton, the resident cat, sprang to a window ledge and tried to stare him down.

He stood with his back to the building and got out his cigarettes. Through a cloud of bitter fumes he looked down Lensfield Road. The sensation of being followed, watched, was again almost palpable. One detail would not leave him – why had his visitor chalked a mark on the tyres of the VW? He studied the cars parked opposite, thinking it through. If the chalk was set for noon, it meant its position was important – and then he had it: if Falcon slipped back, and moved the VW, but returned it to its usual spot, the chalk mark would no longer be in precisely the same position. It implied they were prepared to wait, happy for him to show his hand. It gave him confidence.

And then Brookfield, the night porter, was marching up the road towards him.

'Dr Grey,' he said, touching his bowler hat. Brookfield was undoubtedly a creature of the night – pale, with sunken eyes. There was something slightly grimy about his white shirts, and the shiny university tie.

'The very man,' said Falcon. 'Can you let me in, Brookfield? Some midnight oil needs burning. I wanted to use the Electrofax and get into the files while the place is quiet.'

The outgoing porter appeared, tipped his hat, and wordlessly fled.

Brookfield held open the door. 'It'll be a graveyard, sir. Tea?'

'I'm fine. I've got a pile of work – if anybody calls, can you fob them off for me? I don't want to be disturbed. I'm not here.'

The porter retreated, whistling as he turned the corner, '*Yellow Submarine*' gradually fading as he disappeared into the bowels of the museum.

Falcon's office was on the first floor, but as he shared it with three other researchers, he'd quickly found an alternative place to work in the artefact store in the basement. It also housed the latest American copying machine. He tripped down the concrete stairs, the chill gathering, and as soon as he opened the door he caught that dead smell of old things. The basement was arranged like a library, with metal drawers, and movable stacks operated by fly-wheels. Three Antarctic sledges were set one on top of another, the metal runners gleaming. A whole wall held tackle: man-hauling harnesses, as well as those for dogs. He thought of Cherry, a Stakhanovite in man-hauling, with an unbeatable record on the ice. This image had always worried Falcon, because he imagined him trapped in the team, unable to see ahead, relying totally on the man in front – a lifetime spent *following* footsteps, not making his own.

Beyond the artefacts was a service lift for large objects, and then a concrete cubicle with a fine cedar table, a cubbyhole he'd made his own. The table was covered with his maps, while the walls held the photographic versions of the radio echo soundings (RES) sent from Washington – the communication hub for the US Navy planes. After the unsuccessful hunt for Shackleton's ship they'd transferred their search for artefacts to Wilkes Land in the hope of finding traces of an Australian expedition, which had been on the ice in 1912 – half a continent away from Scott and his men. They'd already scored one triumph, locating the Vickers monoplane the explorers had taken with them, still in its crate close to base camp, hidden under the ice. He had a large newspaper picture of it reassembled at the museum in Christchurch, New Zealand. It looked brand new: the arid, freezing winters had left it untouched.

He opened his flask, poured tea and took the diary out of its wax pouch. He was surrounded by the playthings of the dead, as lifeless as the fossils in the Sedgwick Museum down the road, crammed with the once teeming life of the Cretaceous. He'd always thought of Scott and his men as fossils too – for ever trapped in the solid strata of the past, sinking through layers of ice.

But here was Scott, speaking to him, on a summer's afternoon in Cambridge.

He took off his glasses and blinked the words into focus.

23 February
Lower Glacier Depot

Sir

The death of Taffy Evans is reported fully in my diary. We have left his body behind, under a thin shroud of snow. To be candid, morale has lifted, as the prospect of having to shepherd the man home has been removed. He broke down in mind and body.

This entry is to record a note from your agent Cecil Meares, left in the message cylinder at the depot. I agreed with him a code in case of sabotage, or danger of such. Each returning party will read the notes – so content is severely restricted.

Meares's message:

Depot shipshape in all respects. In good spirits. Dimitri entertains with tales of bygone feasts. Dogs hungry – but pony meat worked wonders. We shall do our best to make the hut before winter strikes hard. We dream of a celebration drink when we make landfall. Whisky for me, vodka for the proud Russian. Dimitri says out in the stables the idle talk – led by his countryman Anton – was of navy rum in a bar in Lyttelton. God speed. CM.

The reference to landfall in New Zealand is contrived to allow for 'navy rum' – our code for sabotage. So he reports that – according to Dimitri Girev – the men, or some of them, gossiped about sabotage in the winter at Cape Evans. And the leader of the discussion was Anton Omelchenko, the Russian groom. This is grist to Oates's mill – do we have an anarchist in our midst or, worse, a revolutionary? Has he found fellow travellers among the crew? And then there are Taffy's ravings. Are they founded on overheard gossip?

Was there a plot? Is there a plot? The reference is infuriatingly vague.

Meares's note was not the only one. The parties that came after him, including those led by Atkinson and Lieutenant Evans, mention no shortages in biscuits, pemmican, pony meat or oil, but then they were simply drawing from the well. Atkinson is flying, and Keegan is better. Lieutenant Evans, last through, sounds down – I hope he does not broadcast a defeatist attitude to his companions. Wilson notes that his hand seems unsteady.

*I shared Meares's coded message with all. The news that
we had a government spy among us was greeted with knowing looks. It appears Meares's reputation as a wanderer on the
edges of the Empire went before him.*

*Bowers tried to dismiss any fears of mutinous talk. He said
the stables at Cape Evans were often full of gossip. All sorts of
insubordination were aired, but it was just talk. Girev – presumably with Meares acting as an agent provocateur – had
simply revealed the usual state of humour below decks: that of
bitter resentment of authority. Oates, who made of the stables a
private fiefdom, given his role as chief groom, stayed silent. He
is often mistaken for a crewman – at Lyttelton he was ordered
about by the subalterns on the dock. Kathleen thought his
casual, tattered demeanour was a scandal. He is a gentleman,
of course, and paid the full thousand pounds to join the crew.
But he aspires to be Everyman. One wonders to what extent he
took part in this malicious talk.*

*Having tried to scupper talk of mutiny Bowers turned to Lt
Evans and his party – did they deliberately take more than their
fair share? I said I wouldn't stand for my second-in-command
being accused – although privately my suspicions are harden-
ing. Wilson suggested that Lieutenant Evans might have fallen
ill and remains unaware of the actions of Crean and Gwynne.
Crean, left out of the final party, was bitterly disappointed his
place was taken by Taffy. Is this revenge? Bowers – a kind soul
at heart – suggested that they all might be struggling badly in
the cold, and with their allotted rations, and have convinced
themselves that they can take more than their share, given the
slim chance we will ever follow in their footsteps.*

*We must press on: if we'd had Shackleton's luck with the
weather we'd be faster between depots and wouldn't need to
make our meagre oil stretch so far. We deserve better. Leaving
land behind. It is the Barrier now.*

RFS

Falcon set aside the notebook. He was desperate to read on, but the priority was to copy it quickly, then hide the original. Fifteen minutes at the Electrofax and he had finished; the neon fluttered, then died, and he left the artefacts to their own polar night, having slipped the original journal into a box of seal's teeth collected by Shackleton from Elephant Island in 1917. One further task: by the door, a bound inventory of artefacts hung on a chain. He found the entry for the tent: no mention of a punch or any other tool.

Closing the door, he listened to the silence. To avoid the noise of the cables running in the lift he took the stairs.

The library was open so he put one copy on the shelf between two volumes of the *Polar Review* for 1901.

Retracing his steps to the museum he could hear Brookfield talking to someone at the main door.

'. . . but not always,' said the porter.

'It's nothing too urgent, it's just we've got a mutual friend, and he's in town, and it would be great to meet.'

It was a woman's voice, light and young.

If Falcon stood behind a glass cabinet of polar relics he could see the front desk. His visitor had on a tie-dye shirt, her hair up in a multi-coloured scarf, revealing wisps of red curls. A broad face was defined by wide cheekbones and a pale forehead. He'd never seen her before. Her eyes scanned the museum, even as she talked to Brookfield.

'I'll leave a message, madam. A name?'

'It's OK. It'll be too late. There's no chance he's here?'

'None. I'd try him at home,' said Brookfield. 'Or his college, or possibly the university library.'

'Thanks.' She didn't look grateful. She turned on her heels.

'Can I say who called?' asked Brookfield, taking on the butler role with relish.

She turned back, nodding. 'Tell him Oriana was asking for him.'

14

It was a message, of course: Oriana was Edward Wilson's widow, the wife of Scott's mentor and friend. There could be no coincidence with such a name. Again, like the man investigating his VW, the threat was tangential, but insidious. They didn't mind if he knew they were after him because they thought there was no escape. For a moment he stayed in the shadows, a few feet from the glass cabinet that contained Oates's sleeping-bag. Someone had once described The Soldier brilliantly as a hero without heroics, a quality Falcon desperately needed to emulate. He had to finish the diary. Sofya expected him at the Mullard for the Apollo launch. He had time to spare – enough to decode another few pages of Scott's idiosyncratic scrawl.

Brookfield let him out by the side door and he slipped into the rear vehicle yard. Several of the senior staff kept cars there – a dusty Hillman, a newly waxed Rover, and two Minis, one with a soft top. In the far corner he'd negotiated his own space for his motorbike and sidecar, which he'd bought second-hand with part of the money from Cherry's will. The sidecar, which Sofya had christened 'Primrose', was decorated with hand-painted flowers, and had a roll-back roof. Its presence at the institute was a matter of controversy: it leaked oil onto the hard-standing, so it stood on various tin trays sticky with a gum-like lubricant. He put the document pouch and his ruck-sack in the sidecar, kick-started the engine at the third attempt, then slipped on his white helmet, and adjusted his goggles.

Rolling forward he paused at the gates. Opposite, sitting on the iron railings of Parker's Piece, Oriana was licking an ice cream, her eyes fixed on the façade of the Scott Polar. Beside her sat the young man who'd examined the VW, an unlit cigarette between his lips.

The city flew past in a blur, the Fitzwilliam Museum a streak of white marble, the river green and soupy. He headed for Grantchester and the Orchard tearooms, where he endured a long queue at the wooden café to get his pot of Earl Grey, then headed out past the apple trees, and through a gap he knew in the hedge to the water meadow beyond. A few deckchairs were dotted about, and in the distance a punter propelled himself upriver. Given the Sunday-afternoon crowds, it was an ideal place to hide. A slight breeze helped keep the wasps at bay, circling abandoned plates smeared with jam. The general air of genteel society couldn't have altered much since Rupert Brooke had met his friends there before the Great War – Woolf, Wittgenstein, Forster and the rest. The 1960s had made no impression whatsoever. No wonder the church clock still stood at ten to three.

The sun came out, lighting the page.

24 February
Southern Barrier Depot

Sir

Bowers found an entire wooden box of pemmican missing from the depot. The meat store was also short of pony. Wilson measured out the oil: I told him we needed all the facts collated. We were a fluid ounce short of a half-gallon down. While the men broke camp, Wilson and I walked away to smoke. He made a pertinent point: if someone was trying to kill us they would take all the oil. We'd be dead in days with no hot food to eat. But perhaps they wish to kill us by degrees, leaving the alternative theory a possibility – that evaporation, and poor management of the depots, has killed us, literally by degrees. Which makes the discovery of the centre punch and the vandalised oil can of the utmost importance.

*Then Bowers came over to report the discovery of tracks: a
single line of prints leading directly west. It is the singularity
that has chilled the company. The snow often tells lies but it is
still rare to find a set of lone tracks, and it surely means only
one thing: one man, on his own. This is not possible – unless
others held back. Taffy's ghostly apparition was suddenly made
real. We followed the trail westwards – a mystery in itself. If the
apparition was following we should have gone south, if ahead,
then north. West took us out into the heartland of the Barrier.*

*Away from our gear and the depot the immensity of this cold
desert freezes the heart. We trudged three hundred yards, and I
was about to order a retreat when Wilson's botanist's eye spotted
a depression beside the track where there were several footprints.
He dug in his gloves and we saw that the snow was 'fill' – piled
into a hole. The surface condition of the snow rules our lives and
we have become as adept as any Eskimo in divining changes
in density and consistency. This was loose snow. Digging down
for a few minutes we found the provision box. Wilson took a
jemmy to the lid – and there was the pemmican, which cheered
us, but not once the implications were clear. This was sabotage,
undertaken by a man who had no need of the food. What man
is this? Clearly Lieutenant Evans's party – or any of the other
support parties – would have taken the food with them if they
were prepared to steal it. So who is our shadow? The tracks
ran out just beyond the stash. We marked the spot with a ski
pole and each of us walked away by a hundred yards. Then we
walked towards each other, completing a circumnavigation of the
spot, but there was no sign of our visitor.*

*We discussed events in the tent. As I spoke my breath turned
to snow, a moment of wonder, which might have cheered us in
happier times. We discussed the implications – although Oates
now stays silent: his old war wound is opening up. I suspect he
is in great pain: he resists the simplest of conversations.*

*The returning parties who went before us have left notes,
none of which mention any shortage of supplies. It is possible
they were satisfied with what they found and did not notice the*

*missing box – but unlikely. Which means our shadow raided
the depot after they passed through. Logic appears to rule out
the returning parties, for they must be desperate for food. Faced
with hauling on such a surface, even Girev's imagined cabal of
revolutionary plotters could not resist pemmican.*

*Which forced us yet again to consider a well-provisioned for-
eign enemy. We must consider the possibility that the Germans
altered their plans and have landed on the edge of the Barrier,
rather than the Weddell Sea. Or that the Japanese have struck
– a lone skier, perhaps, or a small group. Why do they wish us
dead? Do they think we are the victors?*

Fear makes us weak, but we must not yield.
RFS

Falcon closed the notebook, slipped on his glasses and looked
up through the branches of a pear tree. His eyes ached, for
Scott's scrawl was deteriorating rapidly. And with each page
the story grew darker. The evidence of sabotage was mount-
ing at a sickening rate. He felt a sudden empathy for these
men, exposed upon a featureless white plain. He at least had
a city to hide in, and a folded landscape of fields and streams.
Beyond the hedge the gentle sound of teacups and saucers, the
barking of a dog conjured up the scene: Sunday afternoon on
Grantchester Meadows.

If he could have finished the diary there and then he would
have done. But at the current rate it would take hours. He had
time to decipher one more entry – and flicking ahead he saw
it was short.

3 March
Northern Barrier Depot

*Fire at last – the polar curse. There is no defence against the
flame: all the water is frozen, and everything flammable is as
dry as bone. At least we did not have to suffer the sight of it or*

*bask guiltily in the fleeting heat. It was Wilson who saw it first
– the smoke rising – and shouted, 'Fire!' The night before we
had let our imaginations stray to the possibility that a rescue
party might have reached this far and replenished the depot.
If the orders I gave Lieutenant Evans had been followed this
should have been a priority. We should have heard the dogs by
now. We dared to hope. But now this . . .*

*But there were no flames, just a thin string of smoke, which
rose directly for about a hundred feet, then, meeting an inver-
sion, spread out in all directions, so that a ghostly cloud hovered
over the scene. As we drew close it was clear a pyre had been
built. But it wasn't smoke rising: it was fine ash, being drawn
up by a current of air. The oil cans, upturned, were on the top –
no doubt their precious fuel had powered the flames below. The
store boxes were cinders, the meat reduced to blackened bone,
the pemmican burnt. The evidence of intent could not have been
more brutal: whoever had done this (man or devil, we no longer
care) must have known – or hoped – that we would experience
this exquisite torture. The memory of the promised heat and food
and shelter hangs in the air, like the shroud of ash.*

*How close are our hunters? A month, a week, a day, an
hour? The ashes were cold – small comfort. Later, in the tent, we
returned to a consideration of evil. What would send a man to
this dreadful place with such a dark soul? We are all prepared to
die for our country, and if war comes, to kill for our country. But
this stands outside the circle inhabited by civilised man: a renegade
then, acting alone or with like-minded desperate men? Oates, sullen now, finally spoke. It was clear that the actions taken against
us were escalating – from petty theft concealed as slipshod work to
arson. Why? The obvious answer was that the perpetrators knew
their earlier attempts had failed. They wanted us dead but could
see that we were alive. Perhaps they fear a rescue party is close.
After this contribution he spoke no more. His spirit is broken.*

*The fire brings the end close. Only a small amount of food
was salvaged – although they did miss a box of pony meat buried under the oil cans. We are desperate for oil to provide light*

and heat for cooking. We must reach the next depot quickly –
but Oates is a dreadful burden.

We march on tomorrow and we are agreed: no one will look
back at this dreadful sight.

RFS

It was an image that would never fade in Falcon's memory:
the charcoal black pyre of the depot, the men struck silent
by the knowledge that an enemy they couldn't see wanted
them dead, and that the hunters were – almost certainly –
close at hand.

The church clock tolled the hour. Time had run ahead of
him. With a kick-start the motorbike came alive and he left
Grantchester in a cloud of blue exhaust.

The sleepy villages went by, shaken slightly by the Triumph's labouring engine. The road unfurled before him to
match the map inside his head, leaving his brain to process
again that last entry. The fire marked the crossing of the
Rubicon: a clear act of lethal vandalism. And yet . . . one
suspicion lingered, and Falcon was disturbed to find that it
was beginning to dominate his thoughts. There was something melodramatic about the fire: the black-on-white stark
image. The neat device, by which only Scott's diary would
tell the full truth, meant no corroboration was possible – as
long as none of them got back alive. Cherry believed Scott
– but then his judgement was impaired by guilt. Meares
appeared to offer corroboration – but of what? Gossip
below decks. No doubt Sir Edward Whyte had left independent testimony – but only of the *threat* of sabotage.
No, until further proof emerged, Scott's story stood alone.
Was it the truth or the creation of a broken man, desperate
to excuse his own shortcomings? The vital clues – if they
existed – lay still within the ice.

15

At the main gatehouse to the Mullard Observatory, at Lord's Bridge – a now abandoned railway station on the old Varsity line to Oxford – the barrier stayed down and he was forced to dismount and sign the book. Clearly security had been tightened due to the visitors from NASA. The young woman on duty, who'd taken his call earlier, was smoking a cigarette.

'The party has begun, I take it,' he said, carefully filling in the 'address' of the VW van.

'It's in full swing, sir. They'll be dancing on the tables by now. And brown ale – crates of it. The astronauts brought their own box of Pepsi-Cola. They're handsome,' she added.

The barrier bounced up and he found Primrose a spot beside an open-top lemon-yellow Cadillac, which looked out of place in the dour surroundings of the old station. Commandeered by the Observatory, it had never shaken off the down-at-heel atmosphere of a lonely country halt.

As Falcon approached the buildings, he could see along the old rail line – arrow straight – now used to allow the Mullard's telescopes to trundle across the open chalklands. The five dishes – bowls turned skywards on pedestals of steel – were in the distance, two still under construction, so that they looked like leaves, partly stripped by greenfly or slugs. That was the trick of the Mullard: not for it the huge bowl of Jodrell Bank, the world's largest telescope, but a lot of smaller dishes each collecting a piece of the celestial jigsaw. Then they moved the telescopes in a synchronised dance, by radio control, to fill in the gaps or let the rotation of the earth do the job for them. Collectively the dishes could see stars millions of light years away, which thrilled Falcon because, of course, it meant they were looking into the past.

Falcon checked his watch: it was 5.35 p.m. Lift-off for Apollo 10 was less than half an hour away. The old platform ahead was crowded, mostly with men in white laboratory coats. As he got closer he saw women too, in party print skirts, and children in Sunday-best shorts or dresses, hair combed, or held back with clips. An ice-cream van, the sliding window catching the light, stood at the end of the platform, besieged.

Sofya appeared from the crowd and smiled, two bottles of beer held expertly in one hand. She was the only woman in a lab coat. She introduced him to a few of her colleagues as Dr Falcon Grey, of the Scott Polar. The group separated to allow a small man with a barrel chest and white hair to offer his hand: 'Dr Grey. Professor Yuri Valentinov. Your institute does great work, sir. In the south we too cooperate – at Vostok.'

Valentinov – an expert in solar radiation whom Sofya described privately as the group's only eminent scientist – tried to tell an anecdote about Bellinghausen, the great Russian polar explorer, but everyone's attention was taken by the sounds of the TV drifting out through the open doors and windows of the Old Station.

'T-minus twenty-five minutes.'

In the end the Russian shrugged. 'We must endure the triumph of capitalism,' he said, laughing. 'But we still have a few cards to play. Soon a robot to wander the lunar surface, a probe to the dark side, and a space station above the earth – these are our goals. We must keep the Americans guessing – yes?'

Everyone else began to drift indoors.

Falcon noticed that Valentinov's eyes settled constantly on Sofya, then moved on rapidly, only to return. Falcon was adept at this kind of observation: his inability to express emotion had led to the development of other skills – reading body language, tone of voice, gait, or the subtle clues of the spoken word.

'Our American friends are here,' said Sofya. 'The children want to know which one will be the first man on the moon.'

They were difficult to miss, with crew cuts, slacks, sneakers and NASA name tags. They looked tanned, well-fed, bored. Sofya had explained that the British were happy to allow visiting scientists to use facilities at the Mullard and even Jodrell Bank. Inevitably, Russians and Americans might work side by side but relations were formal, cool, wary. After all, Britain was hardly neutral ground.

'There are more Americans down at the Cavendish,' said Valentinov. 'They cannot be important – otherwise they would be at the launch. Tomorrow the senior men fly in. There is a meeting, then they go to Jodrell Bank. They need Lovell's help to track their spacecraft – and in case of problems.'

Falcon produced a cigarette and strolled away, taking Sofya with him by the arm. 'I think our professor is in love,' he said.

'He enjoys the game,' she said. 'I keep one step ahead . . . I have booked the room,' she said, now they were finally alone.

'Thank you. I have to keep my head down for a day, maybe two. Some people are looking for me. They tried to get into the VW.'

'You must tell me everything. It is only fair. As I have told you.'

'Is there somewhere I can go now – while the party's on?'

'Yes. Even here I have a *dacha* of sorts.'

He patted the satchel over his shoulder. 'Documents – historical, historic. Priceless. I need to read them, quickly, privately. It'll take hours.'

'You steal this – it is the police you are hiding from?' asked Sofya.

'No. Well, we're not talking bobbies on bicycles two by two. My guess is Scotland Yard – MI6 perhaps. The Secret Service.

I've seen some – a man and a woman. Young, thirty perhaps, pretending to be younger. And they're not stolen – at least, not by me. The legal position may be complicated. They've tracked me down to the VW, and the Scott Polar. I've nowhere else to go.'

'I can't show you now the way to the *dacha*. It will be noticed. I must see Apollo fly, then I'll take you. And you must tell me more.'

It was at moments like this that she reminded him she came from a different world, where a knock on the door at midnight could change your life, a set of headlamps on a dark road, a summons to a bleak car park. It made him realise that not everyone lived life inside their own head.

'They did not get *inside* VW?' she asked. It was an odd question, and she looked quickly away, as if checking they were still alone.

He shook his head. The progress of their relationship was marked by the things she left behind at Fen Ditton: a new toothbrush, a drawer for tights and pants, a notebook, a black-and-white snapshot of them both in front of Scott's bust at the institute. They'd taken the van to the beach at Brancaster, so there were pebbles, and a piece of driftwood, and later she'd given him a framed picture of the lake at Oboldino, near the *dacha* outside Moscow, with her teenage face just above water, her father alongside, his features lost in a sudden movement. And she left books in English by the bed: *The Gambler, Lucky Jim, The End of the Affair*.

'They – he – looked in the windows,' said Falcon. 'They might get a warrant – but it takes time. I need to talk to a lawyer. I need to know my rights.'

The station had a brass bell, and someone rang it, while one of Sofya's colleagues beckoned stragglers to come inside. The old waiting room had become the staff room as such, and a new 19-inch TV set had been placed in front of three neat rows of chairs. A trestle table was laid out with teacups and saucers and a large mahogany-brown teapot. Biscuits were arranged on plates, and there was a pile of sandwiches, which Falcon judged to be fish paste and cucumber. It was remarkable the degree to which the wartime aesthetic, tight-belted and functional, had survived. The sixties wasn't so much a time as a place: if you left the clubs, or the city-centre pubs, or the boutiques on Petty Cury, you were back in the fifties.

Beyond the doors to the old ticket office a computer emitted random noises, communicating in its binary dialect with a printer, which chugged out data describing a point of light that had probably begun its journey to earth before Christ was born. Falcon thought the juxtaposition of technology and cheerful austerity was very British.

He was desperate to get back to Scott's diary. But he felt he was safe, and soon he'd be able to read at leisure. He took a seat in the back row – the first two were full – while the children had decided to sit on the floor at the front in a circle around the TV, which was on BBC1, the broadcast in black-and-white.

The scene was the familiar one: the studio was murky but dominated by a large model of the full moon. A newsreader he could not name was the 'anchor' – while the studio experts, whom he could name, were the popular astronomer Patrick Moore and the science journalist James Burke. Various aspects of the action about to unfold were being explained in an excited way. The picture was in fact grey, or certainly shades of it, and a pale band of interference crossed it from left to right every few seconds. The only variation was an occasional dislocation of the picture, which would slip upwards, allowing a black band to intrude until, with a seeming effort, it would halt its journey and return to the base of the screen, although occasionally it lost the fight, and the whole picture would roll over, like a tombola.

Burke had a model of the lunar module, attached to the cone-like command module, and he was manipulating the two, illustrating how they could separate, then dock in a new formation. It occurred to Falcon for the first time that the cone was almost exactly the same shape as one of Scott's polar tents, and that both carried explorers, separating them from the elements that could kill them: a vacuum in the case of the astronauts, the searing cold in the case of Scott. And he saw how Scott's route – the long straight line, the rebound from the goal – mimicked the unperturbed orbits and flights of Apollo.

The studio shot cut out, to be replaced by a grainy long-distance view of the rocket, seen across marshland, the motif CBS NEWS at the top right corner. The audio coverage had shifted to the BBC's man at Cape Kennedy, who was outlining the schedule for Apollo 10: the long journey to the moon, the orbit to the dark side, the lunar module's fly-past over the surface, tantalisingly close to a historic landing. Everything was a vital dress rehearsal for Apollo 11.

Sofya produced a hip-flask and added petrol-blue liquid to a glass of lemonade. She drank it quickly, then mixed another. He knew what she was thinking, what she felt. They shared many secrets, and this was one she must hide today. Falcon could tell she found deeply unsettling the presence of both sides – NASA and Valentinov, the Kremlin's man – in the same room. Falcon had thought, initially, this was because of her father's death. But the heart of the truth lay further back, in a suburban park where the sun had baked the grass brown and lit a scene the world would never forget, however hard it tried.

16

Six years earlier

It was a holiday weekend so Sofya had three days of freedom. The rest of the delegation was back at the Lone Star Motel off Route 45, not far from the building site at Clear Lakes, which would be NASA's Mission Control. Most of the wives had been by the pool, lapping up what they called the 'Hollywood light', while the men had elected to hire golf clubs and go to Memorial Park. It was officially playtime, because the meetings, held in the hotel casino in the striped shadows behind blinds, had gone well. Memos had gone back to Moscow and Langley. History was being made.

Sofya bought a ticket and climbed onto the Greyhound bus. It was steamy and smelt of tobacco and sugar. At the back men and women, all black, some holding children, sat crowded in the last five rows; three men and a woman with two children stood in the aisle. The front of the bus was half empty, so Sofya took a window seat behind the driver, and enjoyed the thrill of knowing that soon the engine would cough into life and they'd inch forward off the bay to hit the open road north. Sliding past the front of the bus station she saw a banner, strung up between futuristic towers: Welcome to Space City. NASA was changing the world. The year before, Kennedy had said they'd put a man on the moon by the end of the decade. Johnson, his vice-president, secured his hometown the glittering prize of Mission Control. To the west Sofya could see the new Astrodome, its dinosaur bones rising on the horizon.

Soon the city bled away into the yellow desert, although one side of the road was a darker brown, because to the horizon a herd of cattle stretched, kicking up a dust storm, which hissed at the glass and turned the sunlight to sepia.

Sofya ate pretzels. She was an expert on freedom, because she often had little. The special quality of freedom here was the freedom not to have to explain yourself. It was intoxicating, but she'd also bought two bottles of beer – Schlitz – and opened one now, drinking from the neck, which seemed to scandalise an elderly woman across the aisle, because she looked doggedly away east, towards the Gulf coast, just visible as a livid blue haze beyond the green bayou.

Sofya had been included in the 'trade mission' to Houston, thanks to her father's influence. There were eight senior scientific staff from Baikonur. Sofya was – officially – the translator and technical assistant. There were two KGB men, nominally drivers. The real purpose of the visit was secret. Kennedy may have declared the goal of reaching the moon, but the White House had had second thoughts. The price tag, at $20 billion, was eye-watering. The Cuban Missile Crisis deepened the gloom. But the world had moved on from Armageddon. A hot-line was installed between Washington and the Grand Palace in the Kremlin. Treaties were signed to limit nuclear weapons. Then, just three weeks earlier, the young president had made a speech to the UN suggesting that Moscow and Washington might join forces to reach the moon *together*. Officially the Kremlin ignored the offer. Behind the scenes her father was told to organise a delegation to Houston to see if a joint project was viable.

The Greyhound sped north. They stopped at a gas station and she bought a popsicle, then stood in the shade of a cactus watching families eat in the diner, the Technicolour food laced with tomato ketchup. She thought of the family meal at Oboldino, only a month before, the dining table taken out into the garden where her father grew vegetables. The food was earthy: *pelmeni*, the dumplings drenched in a pungent soup. Her father drank vodka. Her mother sat watching him, studying his face, glimpsing joy as he talked to Sofya about the trip to Houston. If the Space Race was over, her father's heart might beat longer, stronger.

But it was not the only thing at stake. The memorandum agreed at the Lone Star Motel suggested the formation of two teams: a Russian unit in Houston, an American one in Baikonur. Sofya had been told she would be stationed in Texas for the duration of the project.

She looked out of the window to the far horizon where oil derricks dipped. The idea of a decade of freedom made her dizzy with joy. She thought of all the things she could do: buy a newspaper every day, hitch a ride west to the coast, try out her new swimsuit, visit Berkeley and listen to Einstein, sit in the sun all year, telephone her father in his office, talk through the science.

They reached Lancaster – City of Trees – before they slowed down to edge through an angry demonstration. Sofya read the placards: RACE MIXING IS COMMUNISM. PUT A WHITE MAN IN THE WHITE HOUSE. A row of clapboard houses, no more than wooden shacks, flew what she had come to recognise as Confederate flags. She saw a sign with a swastika on it, but looked away, absurdly shocked. It was the first time she regretted the day trip, but not the last. The bus slowed to walking pace to squeeze through a police cordon, the crowd pelting the back windows with rotten fruit.

On board no one said a word.

They flashed through the affluent Dallas suburbs, two police outriders ahead, until they met more crowds – but these carried the Stars and Stripes, and there were families, and hot dog stands, and children riding on shoulders. The driver had switched to KLIF Radio, Dallas, and *The Ken Knox Show* was interrupted to announce that a police department spokesman had said a quarter of a million people were on the city's streets. A reporter spoke to a woman from Waco, sixty miles south, who said it was set to be the best day of her life. 'I can't believe I'm going to see him,' she said.

Sofya had bought a new camera and she unpacked it from her handbag, trailing the strap around her neck, as the Greyhound pulled into a bus station identical to the one they'd left four hours earlier. She had a simple belief in the geography of the American Dream so she headed for Main Street and found the crowd was three deep on the sidewalks.

A marching band with cheerleaders went past, and in the sudden silence she heard a voice, frail but confident: '*Ya uvizhu yego otsyuda?*' A Muscovite, hoping for a clear view. It was an old man in a wheelchair and she helped his family edge him forward through the ranks to the front. She squeezed his hand and asked where he was from in Moscow and he said the name of a village just five miles east of Oboldino, so she chatted about snow in the woods, wolves, and the sound of trees cracking at night.

'We can't go back now,' said a man called Frank, who was his grandson.

Frank had an American accent. 'He wants to be buried in the village but this is what the Cold War means – he can't be with Grandma.' He shrugged. 'But we are Americans now.' He embraced two toddlers who must have been the old man's great-grandchildren, then introduced his wife Lowella, who clutched a portrait of the president. They could hear shouting now, from up the street, and the swelling chorus of a crowd cheering.

Frank had three cameras around his neck. 'I know a better place, where we had the picnic last summer. You OK here, honey?'

Lowella nodded, one hand on the back of Granddad's chair. 'Go for it, Frank.'

'You wanna come?' asked Frank, seeing that Sofya was struggling to see over the heads in front. 'He's heading for the trade mart. So I know where to catch him – we'll get a great view.'

Frank started walking quickly away from uptown into a maze of city back-streets and alleys. Outside a bar, where they could see a baseball game on a TV, a teenager in a Dallas Rangers baseball shirt was standing on the corner. 'Where's you running on a hot day?'

'Dealey Plaza,' said Frank, and the kid tagged along.

Later, in the years that followed, when Sofya told this story, it was from this moment that every detail seemed to come alive: every lamppost, every flag, every voice. There was, finally, an alleyway full of trash cans, and then they were out onto a wide area of parkland. The grass was brown, but several families had spread picnic blankets on the field. They could see from the people gathered along one side that the motorcade was due to turn left by a big warehouse, down a hill, towards an underpass with three arches, and out of town.

Frank was jogging ahead, looking back over his shoulder, and then he shouted: 'He's here. It's the Lincoln.'

Sofya looked over her right shoulder and saw the first car, a white 'hardtop', then a black shiny car with dark glass, and then an open limousine – the Lincoln she presumed – with the back seat raised. Even then, from a hundred yards, she could see Jackie's pink dress and hat, with a navy trim. Finally, there was another black limousine, with men in suits on the running boards.

Frank didn't run towards the motorcade, but away from it, towards the hill that led down to the triple underpass. The president's car was moving slowly along the side of the park, so they were at the roadside by the time it took the corner and picked up a little speed. Sofya had a perfect view, watching the cars approach, and thrilled, she took Frank's hand. The teenager who'd tagged along stood on her other side, his hands in his pockets, grinning broadly, and bouncing slightly on his feet.

President Kennedy was looking from side to side, and Sofya thought how beautiful he was, and she would always remember that the word 'golden' had come to her just then, and it didn't just describe his hair. There were four other people in the Lincoln, two in front of the Kennedys, then the driver and what she guessed was an FBI man in the passenger seat.

There was a helicopter above, and motorcycle outriders, but the sound of the crowds was fading so they could hear the limousine's engine, and the shout of a woman on a grassy hill in front of a billboard: 'Jackie, we love you.'

Sofya is disappointed now that he's waving at people on the far side of the road on the grassy bank, but then he drops his arm, as if tired, and turns towards her, and she thinks he'll look at her, but she hears a sharp sound like a firecracker and he stops and brings his elbows and hands up and holds his throat. Jackie puts an arm around him, and the man in front of Kennedy turns round.

In the dusty park near their flat in Moscow the boys from the militia practise at nights with their guns and tin cans, so Sofya knows what a bullet sounds like, although this percussion is higher, almost inaudible, but still hurts her eardrums. It's as if someone has punched a hole in the air. She feels the breath leave her body.

The man in front of the president shouts: 'My God, they're going to kill us all.' The car slows, and Sofya thinks it will stop for her, as a man from the shiny black car behind jumps down from the running board and runs forward to the president's car. There is another shot, and the man in the front of the president slumps into his wife's lap. A few seconds, two or three, tick past.

The car is opposite them. Frank says, 'My God.' Sofya hears the third shot, and there is a cloud of blood, a sudden scarlet halo around the beautiful man, and there is a terrible movement – the spine, the neck, jerks the head backwards.

There is a lot of shouting, and the car accelerates, and Sofya sees Jackie climb onto the back of the car where she helps the secret-service man onto the boot. The car diminishes, she hears sirens, and then screams for the first time. There may be another shot, but she is never sure. For some reason Frank is kneeling down. The teenager is still standing with his hands in his pockets but is shaking violently. People point: towards the underpass, at the grassy hill beyond a picket fence, up the hill towards the old warehouse building.

Sofya looks down at her summer dress, which is pale yellow, and sees that it is spotless still, but the dream of an end to the Space Race is dust.

17

The telescopes of the Mullard Observatory trundled unwatched, for everyone was in the Old Station, all eyes on the flickering TV images from Mission Control at Houston. Then the picture switched to the launch control room at the Cape, the languid NASA technicians, smoking, unwrapping cigars, delivering the laconic commentary, in that distinctive Southern drawl: 'T-minus three minutes.'

Sofya was watching the rocket leak liquid fuel from the deserted back row of seats, but she turned to whisper in Falcon's ear: 'I have lost patience. Tell me now, what is it you must read?'

Falcon had told her many times about Cherry, and his childhood at Lamer. He'd often talked about the final expedition, shown her the maps, Ponting's photographs, the diaries, even the moving film. It was a story that defined him, and she'd absorbed it by touch until it was a backdrop to their life together.

They were still alone in the back row, the children creating havoc in front of the TV, the NASA men edging closer too, sipping from Coke cans.

'Cherry left me something in his will,' said Falcon. 'A short diary kept by Scott and found with his body. Not *the* diary – this is something else. Its contents have never been made public. I have it. It alleges that Scott and his men were murdered, possibly on the Kaiser's orders, or by anti-Imperialists – Russian revolutionaries and the like. Or skiing Japanese explorers under orders from their own emperor. It is also possible – even likely – that the culprit was one of his own men, embittered at being denied the glory of reaching the Pole, or working for an enemy power.'

He took a deep breath. 'It's technically possible that it's all a fiction, created by Scott to obscure his own shortcomings.'

Sofya nodded, and he could see her analysing the information, assessing risk and truth.

'Scott promised evidence, but so far I've found precious little we can verify. But I need a day, maybe less, to finish. It's in Scott's hand, which is deteriorating as his body begins to fail. I have to finish it. Then it won't matter if they demand it goes back into a safe.'

'But you believe Scott?' she said.

She'd cut to the heart of the matter. 'I have to. Unless I can prove the opposite.'

'T-minus two minutes.'

The BBC coverage had cut to Jodrell Bank. The camera panned around a small room with a wide panoramic window, finally resting on an elderly man: thin, imperious, studying computer printouts. A caption read 'Sir Bernard Lovell'. Around him stood acolytes in white lab coats, several smoking pipes.

The Americans, suddenly animated, lit up Lucky Strikes.

'T-minus sixty seconds.'

The TV broadcast switched to a long-range telescopic image of the Saturn V, which shimmered in the heat. For the men from NASA this was the key moment: a successful launch, a faultless dress rehearsal, and the way was clear to put a man on the moon. The next minute was probably the most important sixty seconds in the decade of the Space Race.

The countdown ticked by with the numbers on the screen. Falcon closed his eyes and thought of the *Terra Nova* leaving Cardiff Bay, the King ashore, the crowds cheering. He thought that the moment when a voyage began held glory and peril in equal measures.

'Ten, nine, lift-off sequence begins, eight, seven, six, five, internal systems on, four, three, two . . .'

The buffeting cacophony wiped out the voice. Falcon imagined the TV picture. The flames beneath the rocket, the belching gases, and then the vast machine rising, passing a stationary camera, the picture flecked with white cladding falling away, and then the slow majesty of the vast rocket passing the lens, the huge letters USA sliding by. He felt a distant echo of fear, memories stirring, so he opened his eyes and looked at Sofya, not the TV.

There was a round of applause. The NASA men were transfixed, several kneeling, most clapping. There was a single whoop, with a clenched fist.

The party began after the rocket disappeared from view, jettisoning its stages, slimming down for the ascent into orbit. Someone had brought a record player and there was a light-hearted debate over the merits of the Rolling Stones versus the Beatles. 'Honky Tonk Women' was greeted with cheers.

A crate of champagne and glasses appeared. Corks were popped.

Sofya was not impressed. '*Sovietskoye shampanskoye,*' she said. 'Cheap and nasty. We threw out the Frenchmen who made Russian champagne – the very best, *Novyi Svet, Abrau Dyurso*. Now it has plastic corks. But still better than this.'

She smiled broadly and raised her glass when the toast was proposed. 'Apollo!'

Then one of the British scientists was on his feet, trying to get silence, turning up the volume on the TV. The children were shushed.

James Burke was holding a piece of paper, which he'd just been handed live on air. 'So, yes. To repeat,' said Burke, unhurried and authoritative.

He nodded for emphasis, his heavy-rimmed glasses magnifying mildly startled eyes.

'The Kremlin has just issued a press notice. The delayed launch of Luna 15 – a probe to the moon – has been scheduled for June the eighteenth. The unmanned spacecraft will fly to the moon, enter orbit, then jettison a probe, which will descend to the moon's surface, to the Sea of Crises – that's here . . .'

He got up and went across the studio to the giant map of the visible moon.

'Once on the moon it will receive radio signals to activate a robotic arm, which will collect samples of dust and rock. It will then re-launch, rising up to rendezvous with its mother ship, and return to earth.'

Burke rearranged his glasses. 'A coup, certainly. But no great surprise – they've been sending probes into space for years. But look at the dates. Luna 15 will land at the precise moment the crew of Apollo 11 are due to take their second walk on the surface of the moon – as long as Apollo 10's mission is a success.

'The two spacecraft – American and Soviet – will be less than a hundred and fifty miles apart on the surface of the moon.'

Again, the trademark shuffle of the glasses. 'One detail. At present we have no timings on Luna 15's return to earth – but it is possible it will get back before Apollo with that precious moon rock. That would be a coup.'

The NASA men were in a huddle.

18

Sir

Morning: 4 March

*A note on leaving the scene of the fire. One tantalising clue.
We were packing up the tent when Oates made another discovery. He is unable to lend an able-bodied hand so is often left
standing, mute and alone. He called us over.*
    'This was on the wind,' he said.
    *It was a scrap of newspaper, mostly blackened by fire. Our
own packing cases are often lined with scrap paper, usually old
copies of papers collected at the docks in Cardiff – the* Western
Mail, *or the* Cardiff Times. *It is possible this scrap was used
to light the fire. It was delicate, and eventually disintegrated
in Oates's hand, but we all saw a little of the typeface before it
was gone. Japanese characters – or possibly Chinese. Perhaps
we have been victims of the Dash Patrol, after all.*

Falcon lit a cigarette and closed his eyes. He was sitting in a
deckchair outside Sofya's secret *dacha* – in reality no more
than two small huts, each with a window, set beside what
appeared to be an overgrown orchard or possibly allotment:
it was difficult to tell. If Sofya hadn't shown him the wooden
frames supporting wires, lost in the weeds, he'd never have
known this was the fabled Interstellar Scintillating Array, the
radio telescope with which the Mullard had found that first
pulsar, a star that really twinkled, a discovery that would
almost certainly win a Nobel. The huts, which still held
the computers and monitors with which the scientists had

looked into the past, revealed some homely touches: a bunk bed, an old armchair, a sink – and, fifty yards away, in the pine trees, an ash closet. Close by, unseen, the telescopes trundled along designated paths. On such a calm summer's evening the only noise was the occasional *brrr* of the motors slowly turning the great wheels below each dish. Only one was visible through the treetops – the eastern dish of the One Mile Telescope, tipped back in search of distant worlds.

Sofya appeared with two bottles of beer and some sandwiches. She held out a key on a wooden fob: 'To the room at the Railway Inn,' she said. 'He gave me one of your old-fashioned looks.'

She got out a second deckchair. 'I must go soon. Valentinov wants to see us at the lab. The embassy phoned – we must go to Moscow for debrief, then back to Jodrell Bank for the Luna launch. This must be a success.'

'You didn't know?' asked Falcon, drinking his beer.

'We know only what we need to know. Even Valentinov – although he pretends to be the best informed. A friend of the comrade chairman.'

'And then – after Luna 15?'

'Back to Moscow. It may be I come back – Luna 16, and then Lunokhod – this is a robot that wanders the surface. Another first. We will see each other. It is the best there can be.'

'Is it?' he said. It was a conversation long postponed.

'Yes, Falcon. Yes. You said yourself: everyone you love must leave.'

'Why do you have to go back? I thought you said they all gossip about defecting, your scientists. That it's easy – the Americans want the skills, we want your skills, the inside knowledge. Or is there someone else?'

She looked serene, her face tilted to a crescent moon that had just parted company with the treetops, but she let out a small gasp – as of a swimmer coming up for air. She looked suddenly stricken, the façade of brisk efficiency gone in a single breath. 'Maxim,' she said.

Falcon knew he should go to her, touch her, but he couldn't move his limbs. 'Your brother? You said he's studying – in Moscow? A mathematician.'

'He was a student, yes. A rebel – I said this too. He was arrested for running a printing press. They find books they shouldn't – Solzhenitsyn, others. My father made this go away. But now we have Brezhnev. Maxim is determined. He thinks the Kremlin took away our father. Now he will take revenge and sweep away the state. Three times he is arrested – and then he disappears.

'My mother says not to ask. A moment I cannot forgive. She is adrift in the suburbs, holding on to her flat, which the state gives her, and a small pension. We must not ask.

'But I did. Six months later we are informed we can visit. The gulags are gone but there are new gulags. Maxim is diagnosed with "sluggish schizophrenia". This is the perfect illness. There are no outward clinical signs. The patient exhibits anti-social behaviour. This is enough. He is a patient in the District Twelve psychiatric hospital in Moscow. Periodically they send me a permit to see him. He is given drugs, so we can never know if he is really ill.

'This is not the worst that can happen. There are other hospitals – Perm, even Aramas. I am told I should never want to see these hospitals. At District Twelve Maxim has a room – he has solitude, he is a human being. Not the person he was, but he is alive. The nurses are kind, there are no bruises. He lives in a make-believe world in his head. Do you know what is in his head, Falcon?'

She drank her beer and looked at the trees, and the distant church tower at Harlton. Falcon had learnt to wait for answers.

'Our old *dacha* at Oboldino. This is where he goes to escape reality. He would walk with Father in the woods, talking about science and the stars. And when the cosmonauts came, there was a dining table, and a feast, a fire in the pit. And vodka. Maxim loved this. He could climb trees, and listen to wise words, and become lost, but only just out of sight of the smoke from the fire. He was frightened of the city, frightened of its complications. The *dacha* was a simple place. I go there too, in my dreams. Perhaps I will meet him one night.'

Falcon felt a moment of fracture, a crossing-place. This story was now his story and he had a right to interrogate, to know the truth in three dimensions.

'You could leave him there – in his imagination.'

'Yes. I have thought of this many times. I would. But as I say there is a worse place than District Twelve hospital. They would take this from him, this half-life. In the sanatoria in the east he would be treated as an animal, and he would die. They all die. From disease, malnutrition, the cold. Pneumonia in winter. I would get the death certificate, but all it would say is pneumonia. His friends have died like this and are buried under snow that never thaws.

'This has been made clear to me. I must do my duty for my country and remain loyal. This is why I must go back. I cannot desert him – even for you.'

19

Sir

9 March

Mount Hooper

If they'd torched Mount Hooper we were dead men.

A low blizzard, just a foot above the ground, had blown for three days. We had to keep hauling because we don't have the food and fuel to stop. We saw it ahead from two miles – the largest depot on the traverse.

'No sign of fire!' shouted Bowers, leading. Closer, I could see the wooden food boxes, the oil cans, the loose gear – pony harnesses, the leashes for the dogs, a broken sledge.

Out of his harness Wilson marched ahead the final yards with my blessing.

As we stowed the sledge and pulled out the tent we watched him approach the 'mountain'.

He lifted an oil can and pulled the wooden slats from a food box. 'She's not been touched!'

Four desperate men with smiles on their faces at last.

Wilson pulled out the message cylinder and quickly rifled through the notes.

'Lieutenant Evans came through five weeks ago – he's ill. Scurvy. They're in a desperate fix. They plan to pull him all the way.'

I could see them then, two of them hauling, straining, Lieutenant Evans lying uselessly on the sledge. It will kill them all. We may find their bodies. If they had the strength they could relay two sledges – one for the food and gear, one for Evans. But they'd need twice the rations.

'Atkinson says his party was hale enough to make it to One Ton,' called Wilson.

We fell upon the stores, like carrion. Not only was our share of pemmican and biscuits adequate, the oil was down by just a fluid ounce – due solely, I suspect, to the tins being stacked in the sunlight.

There is now a chance we can make One Ton – if only Oates was not stricken.

While the men put up the tent I walked a half-mile north towards home. I can hear the dogs. I hear nothing else. The huskies have a raucous choral howl. I hear them all the time. But only I. Am I haunted by them? We had to slaughter so many of the beasts. It is barbaric, and surely not a sign of civilised people. We shouldn't have given them names. I don't think Cherry, for one, will ever get over it. It is their ghosts I hear, baying, waiting perhaps for their turn to feed on the dead.

In the tent there was only one question: why is Mount Hooper untouched? Do they think we are already dead? Wilson put forward the theory that as we have now crossed the 82 Parallel a rescue party could appear at any time – do they fear detection? Do they know a rescue party is at hand? This idea lifted spirits – although Oates's weak smile would break any heart. And that was the unspoken thought – that they can see Oates, crippled, limping dreadfully, a shell only, head down, alone in his private hell. Perhaps they see our civilised dilemma. We should leave him, with promises that we will send back help when we can. But how? There is only one tent. Do we walk away from the man, leaving him exposed to this dreadful place, waving, and, God forbid, that last brave smile? No – we will stick together. They know that. We may well all die together.

RFS

There was a neon strip outside the *dacha* and it had begun to attract moths, which made the light flicker, and reading difficult. Falcon set aside the diary. An image began to form in his imagination of Oates limping into the white distance, but then he heard brisk footsteps, light but confident, and Sofya returned, carrying a bottle of champagne and food from a buffet prepared by wives and girlfriends: Coronation chicken vol-au-vents and sausages on sticks. They sat for a moment, eating, and then she opened the champagne. This had become one of those small ceremonies that can define a relationship, the sitting in silence, the avoidance of an immediate opening gambit.

'Valentinov make a speech,' said Sofya, eventually, gesticulating with her glass. 'He said the Kremlin announcement was a triumph of propaganda, given Luna 15 actually blew up on the launch pad six weeks ago. In the Soviet Union we do not name our mistakes. If the rocket fails we simply avoid publicity, and mark it up as a test flight. So there is now great pressure on us to steal the show when Apollo lands. A new Luna 15 will rise from the ashes. There is little hope of this, but Valentinov's career is in the balance.'

'So you are back in the race?' said Falcon, unkindly.

'We are back in *a* race,' she said. 'The race to the moon is lost. But if we can get rocks back to earth first it will tarnish the Americans' glory. Ever since Gagarin we play this game. We give the Kremlin what it wants: we make headlines when they are needed to undermine the Americans, to divert the attention of our own people from the squalor they live in, work in, die in. First man in space, first woman – sorry, I forget, first dog. First earthlings to the moon . . .'

'They were turtles,' protested Falcon.

'Turtlenauts,' said Sofya, in mock triumph. 'And now first moon rocks returned to earth by Luna 15. A day *ahead* of Apollo.'

She had a slim, stylish briefcase he'd bought her in Cambridge – orange with black circles. Out of it she produced a black-and-white picture with a flourish.

'The embassy will release this to the press. Behold *Luna 15*.'

The probe was a strange bulbous object with wheels and mechanical arms. Falcon was always amazed that Soviet technology seemed to echo Russian imperial culture – it looked like pieces of the Kremlin had been welded together, complete with onion domes and baroque flourishes. It was about the size of a small bath.

'How did the NASA men take the news?' he asked.

'They leave early – with their cans of Pepsi-Cola.'

'Is it safe? The moon's been deserted for a million years. It'll be like Piccadilly Circus up there.'

They looked up. The moon was high above. Falcon thought of Yeats again and Sofya's changing eyes.

'Valentinov ends with this: there is no need for alarm. Baikonur will liaise with Houston. There is no danger. This is a lie, of course, because we do not have complete control over Luna 15 in moon's orbit. We failed to control it on the ground. But there will be no collision. The numbers are almost infinite.'

Falcon cradled his champagne. 'You enjoy the race as much as they do?'

'I despise the race,' she said, 'but it's a race I can't leave.'

There was a long silence in which they could hear the distant *wrrrr* of the trundling telescopes, and a dog barking on a farm, chickens fussing.

'What does Scott say in his new diary?' she asked finally. 'Is it murder?'

'At the moment the killer would have to stand in the dock alongside the usual suspects – the cold was mutilating, the food too short anyway, and the work, Sof, the sheer animal effort of hauling sledges for hundreds of miles. It would have killed me. I'm not at the end yet. Sabotage certainly – *if* we believe Scott. Someone spiked their fuel, hid their food, set fire to a vital depot. It's murderous, that's for sure.'

20

Sir

15 March

Our fifty-seventh camp since leaving the Pole homewards. When I look into the eyes of the others I see their people – wives, children, mothers, fathers. We're living with them now as they slip away, as we slip away. I think of Kathleen, only Kathleen. The cold is crippling, the surface cloying. We move too slowly, using up food and fuel when we should be at the next depot. We now have two days' meagre rations to make the eight days to One Ton Depot. It is possible, but I think we all know the truth. Even our nemesis has given up the cause. He knows he has done enough.

My thoughts have turned to death. This is a destination we will reach.

Oates left us this morning. My official diary records his last words: 'I'm just going out, I may be some time.' The truth is it wasn't all he said. I can't produce a verbatim record but this is close. He didn't even try to get his boots on. His right foot is bad, but his left foot is grotesque. I was not the only one to look away.

He had his head down but I think he spoke to me alone.

'I wish I'd had a gun. There's some honour in that. We should have set out the path months ago. None of us will survive if you wait for me. We're done for anyway – but I can't live any more with your pity or your hatred. You'll die together and there's some comfort in that. I wish you that final gift – from where I stand it's a bright light in the gloom.'

At this point he got down on his knees to get ready to crawl out through the vent, and I think he faltered then, but his voice was much stronger the next time he spoke.

*'I don't believe any more in German ships and Japanese skiers
– or even Russian spies. Neither did Taffy. When I was alone
with him the day he died – at the foot of the glacier – he told me
many truths, weeping all the while. I said I'd keep them secret. I
won't break my word. But you should look for the culprit within
– that's all I'll say. Meares is right – we're not the happy ship
we're told. It's not just whispers and gossip. There's a plot.'*

He began to unthread the stays on the tunnel.

*Birdie tried to get him to stay – he found the right words but
we all knew they were just that, words. We didn't want him to
stay. If he'd been a sick animal we'd have put him down, but
now this passive self-destruction is all that's allowed. The cold
will kill him. Wilson had given him morphine, but not a lethal
dose. When I think of the dogs and the ponies we despatched
with the gun. Man is a strange creation. We give to the brutes
what we withhold from those we love.*

*At the last he turned round and looked me square in the face.
What I saw in his eyes stopped my heart. 'It's you they want,' he
said, 'and what you represent. Empire. The Old World. Above
Decks. It's a bad plan, because they'll make you all heroes. Even
I may be a hero. Taffy knew the names but didn't tell for fear.
They have a secret sign – but that's no good to you now.'*

*And then he was gone, and Wilson sadly tied the stays. He
said Oates's last minutes reminded him of a story from Greek
mythology – Philoctetes, the hero of the Trojan War, stranded
on an island alone for ten years by his shipmates because a
snake bite on his foot had festered so horribly. The stink of it
was too much to bear. In the end he was rescued and went on
to glory. 'But there's no ship coming for Soldier,' he said.*

*We tried to find the body later but there was no sign. We
marked the spot where we'd pitched the tent and said a prayer.
Taffy's last words we put down to delirium – although it was a
worm in the apple, and I for one could not think of our crewmates without the question: was a traitor really among them?*

*Our appetite for gossip has gone. Each of us lives alone in
the casket of his own head. Our outside world is governed by*

small measures of cocoa powder, pemmican and biscuit, and fluid ounces of oil and paraffin. This is no Greek myth. Our world has imploded: from the white continent of legend to a store box rattling with biscuits.

RFS

Sir

23 March
The tent: ten miles from One Ton

There was no great eight-day storm, of course, forcing us to wait for death. That was a tale for the official diary.

This slim notebook tells the truth. A short storm blew itself out and now there is total calm – the inside of the tent is an ice box. Snowflakes form in front of our eyes, our breath in tangible, beautiful, crystalline form, lighter than the green air. I told them, finally, that I would write of a storm, and this gave us all leave to prepare for death in our own ways.

We are dying, each one treading a different path. We are ourselves each, not a body of men. We did not have the will to move, and so we will die where we have come to rest. I realised today that the diary the world will read, this year, probably next, if ever, tells many half-truths. It must. It should tell a story to inspire, not bring despair. This will be our victory over the men who have hunted us down. We did not yield to man, but to Nature.

If there is a war coming, then let that be the battle cry.

I have taken up the pencil for the last time.

This paragraph tells the true story of these last few moments of life.

I feel diminished. The legend seeks immortality, but I do not want to die. I want to see Kathleen again, and the hills of England. The longer my life plays out the less heroic it seems – so I will hasten the end. I will open my jacket, take

down the hood, and let the cold air have my last breath. I
am bitter. My friends are dead. In the very pit of the silence
I could hear the air between their lips. But no longer. I can't
recall their last words. I think Bowers said he would sleep,
and then wake Wilson, and see if they might not walk out
as they had planned. 'To die in the traces,' he said. An hour
later Wilson whispered the Lord's Prayer. 'Bless you, Robert,'
he said, not looking at me, and shook himself down into his
sleeping-bag.

I have forsaken God. I do not feel His presence here, only
His absence. I feel the cold logic of Nature. I leave this world
willingly. This is a bitter peace, but it is the bitter peace I wish
to make. There are no mysteries, just questions yet unanswered.
Enough.

RFS

21

Behind the medieval walls of Magdalene College stood the Master's Lodge, a slightly sinister 1930s confection of metal-framed windows and blind walls. The college itself – a chaotic range of fourteenth-century brick and stone – stood in silhouette behind a garden of trees, a thicket, which provided a suitable *cordon sanitaire* between students, fellows, and their master. The college walls kept the town at bay. Falcon walked through the open gate, up the gravel drive, aware as he so often was of the peculiar hush behind academic stone: the sounds of the city were muted; he could hear a bus not twenty yards away beginning the ascent of Castle Hill, and bicycle bells rang on the Great Bridge, while the strains of a jukebox leaked from the closing door of the Pickerel Inn. He could hear all of this – the life of a city in 1969. He could even see the upper deck of the bus on the hill, as if angled for take-off, poised at the lights. A chilly spring evening, so the upstairs – lit from within – was obscured by condensation, although a few hands had inscribed portholes to look out on the passing world.

But none of this disturbed the essential calm of the master's garden.

The door was an art-deco creation, with a glass panel, showing a light within. Overhead a steel lantern hung, the light brutal, revealing the geometric carvings in the wood of the door. There was a bell-pull, and an inset panel for a microphone. That was what he found most disturbing – the juxtaposition of twentieth-century technology and neo-Gothic baronial. There was something Fascist about the combination, telephones in castles, coats of arms and TV sets. He thought it was what the world would have looked like if Hitler had won the war – with Halifax's Britain standing at his side. The past would have had a new lease of life. The old world would have gone on summoning its servants, but by electric button.

He shot the cuffs on his dinner jacket and pressed the bell.

The invitation to dinner had arrived at the Railway Inn the morning after he'd finished Scott's secret diary. There was a handwritten note on the back: *Drinks at 7 at the Master's Lodge. George Benet.*

Again, the playful but insidious reference: George Benet were Cherry's second and third Christian names. It was as if he was being led into a trap, step by intriguing step.

They knew where he was – this was the next step. He could have ignored it and gone back to the Scott Polar to work. Instead, he'd put the invitation on the mantelpiece and imagined – even relished – a confrontation with his pursuers. He'd used the rest of the day to reread and make a note on the diary, while they buried another spare copy in a biscuit tin (left over from the party), among the tangled raspberry bushes of the Interstellar Scintillating Array.

A tall man, slightly bent, answered the door.

'Do come in,' he said, mumbling a name with the elaborate deference of the rich.

A woman stood behind him in a striking amber dress. She must have been in her sixties but had clearly, and expertly, embraced the fashions of the current decade. Her hair was short, boyish, revealing large geometrical earrings. The dress was knee-length, the flat shoes red patent leather.

The man turned out to be Sir Henry Strood, the master, democratically welcoming guests at the front door.

'Dr Falcon Grey, Scott Polar,' he said.

'Great you could come,' said the woman in amber, as the master studied his polished shoes. 'I'm Margaret,' she added. 'You're very welcome to our house.'

There was a long corridor, the length of the building, leading to what looked like a stairwell in which a modern crystal chandelier hung: dazzlers all cubes, cut to perfection.

On the left a door stood open revealing a study.

'That isn't the original, I suppose?' said Falcon.

The woman in the amber dress – presumably Lady Strood – politely followed his line of sight, as if he were a child who'd spotted a signpost he couldn't read.

Sir Henry had walked on, oblivious, so she'd taken charge.

'The Dollman?' she asked, leading Falcon into the room and up to the work, which he could see now was in pencil, not the famous painting, but clearly a precursor.

'*A Very Gallant Gentleman*?' asked Falcon.

'Yes – preparatory sketch. It's been languishing in the archives at the Fitzwilliam. We're trying to get works of art circulating more – do you see? Get them out of the dark and into the light. Original's in the Cavalry Club – Oates's regiment paid for it. I think this is better than the oils.'

Her face was remarkably animated. She was one of those rare people who appear to devote their entire attention to others.

She craned her head back to take a second look at the sketch. 'They've both put Oates on the right of the canvas, struggling to move on into the blizzard. You'd expect him on the left, but then he'd have to cross the canvas before he's lost from sight. With this composition he's just about to disappear. We're about to lose him. It's effective.'

Falcon was now sure he was in the right place. The interest in Scott was too neat a coincidence not to be designed. He didn't know what MI6 agents looked like but he had faces to go on: Burgess and Maclean, for example, both Cambridge students, were fleshy, slightly gone to seed, anonymous. Lady Strood was hidden in plain sight.

The door was open and other guests were being welcomed.

'They say – the art historians – that Dollman's early work influenced Van Gogh,' said Lady Strood. 'I'm not so sure. Most of it's a bit sickly – Victorian story-telling. He liked legends.'

Falcon smiled. 'I guess Oates was a legend too. Do you paint?'

She looked less eager to talk about herself. 'No, no. History's my thing. Henry is a historian too – but he's classical, I'm modern. So we've got lots to talk about but our own hinterlands, which works well.'

A guest arrived and spotted her from the doorway.

'We must talk later,' she said, a hand on his arm for just a second too long to be polite.

A reception room held about twenty people. They were offered champagne and canapés by waiters.

Someone somewhere sounded a gong gently, and Sir Henry began to corral his guests. Falcon had eaten at Magdalene before: the food was excellent, the cellar sensational, but he appeared to be heading for the high table, which didn't bode well. It was pretty much Russian roulette: conversation across the silver was impossible, which limited the potential to one's immediate neighbours.

The French windows had been opened and the guests were ushered out directly into the garden. Falcon suspected this was a theatrical flourish, an ancient college custom invented in the 1920s when the house was built. There was an atmosphere of almost childish excitement. Sir Henry led the way with a lantern, following a snaking path under trees, which, in spring leaf, completely blotted out lights from the town. Lady Strood's stylish flat shoes were now explained. He could see the college ahead, the range punctuated by ancient slit windows, lit within. As they emerged from the trees they saw one of the windows had been thrown open, allowing steam to escape from the kitchens, as if the inside of the building was boiling over. They could hear the clatter of pans and ladles.

The dining hall was without electric power – a peculiarity of which the college was clearly proud because it was so often cited. A few candles showed through stained glass. A woman's scarf caught on a branch and there was a brief chaotic interlude while she was freed.

They reached a blue door studded with ironwork locks, which Sir Henry negotiated with practised ease. A light came on to reveal a small, exquisite room, in Georgian eggshell blue and gold, so perhaps the whole rigmarole really was from a bygone age. It might have been a first-class cabin on a sailing ship to Calais, marking the start of the Grand Tour. Academic gowns hung from pegs. There were two mirrors, in which bow-ties were straightened and powder applied. Falcon was silently handed a gown by a servant who'd followed them into the room. He noted that they'd done their homework: a Cambridge gown, with doctoral lace. Then they all sat on the bench that ran round on three sides.

There was a small escape door – half-size – in one wall, and on the other side they could hear students filing into the hall to eat. There was a hubbub, and the grating sound of wooden chairs on a wooden floor. Sir Henry lit a candle and turned off the light (presumably permitted as the secret room was *outside* the hall). They heard a stern voice calling for order. Silence blossomed, first slowly, then like a trap shutting.

'Ready,' said Sir Henry, and knocked lightly on the small door, which was immediately thrown open to reveal the high table, the end gable of the hall with its portraits, and several guttering candlesticks, dazzling the glassware and cutlery. Everyone stood to file out but a hand touched Falcon's arm and he turned to see Lady Strood, the amber dress now hidden within a splendid gown.

'I can do without the smoked eel. Would you keep me company?'

Falcon nodded, noting that while the voice of his hostess was still modulated and polite, there was no way he could decline the offer to stay behind.

A servant closed the escape door and they were alone.

Falcon wondered how often this little stratagem had been used. There was clearly going to be no independent record of the meeting, so he felt the sudden need to concentrate, despite the champagne.

Lady Strood got up and opened the door into the garden, producing a packet of cigarettes – Embassy. Falcon reminded himself of Napoleon's epithet – that if you want to understand someone you need to understand the world when they were twenty years old. It was 1969 – but Lady Strood was probably sixty: she'd come of age in the years after the Great War. She might have been one of those rare women admiited to a university. She might have been a suffragette. In the last war he could imagine her breaking codes or utilising near perfect French as a spy.

He thought the gamine face had hardened slightly, and she picked a piece of tobacco off her lip.

They listened to grace through the strange half-door.

'Henry's Latin is third rate,' she said. It was the first unkind thing she'd said. 'People can be so cruel. That's why academics are so cutting, of course – there's so little at stake.'

He wondered if Henry had been a disappointment over the long years of academic and married life, and whether the Secret Service was in some ways a distraction.

'I graduated in history here in Cambridge in 1936,' she said. 'My first language is German – I was born in Berlin. My father was a dealer in art, and we wanted to stay when Hitler came to power – he felt he had a right to live in his own home, in his own village, beside the Rhine. But we were Jews, pursued, betrayed. The future was bleak. So we escaped to London. We made our home there. I was grateful. So I do what I can. I'm repaying a debt.'

She paused, then ploughed on: 'I was approached after graduation by what I think we are now supposed to call MI6. Then it was the Secret Intelligence Service, which sounds magical, doesn't it? I was told it was a matter of national security. I was given a brief outline of the contents of a leather document pouch retrieved from the tent in which Captain Scott and his comrades were found in 1912. A notebook within contained the allegation that he was murdered – possibly by Germany on the orders of the Kaiser, possibly by the Japanese or even foreign nationals among the men – Russians, even a Norwegian.

'We dispensed with the German allegation pretty quickly. There was ample evidence that Filchner's expedition had landed on the coast of the Weddell Sea, which put him out of the picture.'

'What about the centre punch used to sabotage the oil cans. MV *Björn*?' asked Falcon. 'German, surely. And Filchner was secretive about the voyage. There was never any mention of the famed motor sledges.'

Falcon felt that demonstrating he'd read the diary closely was a clear signal that there was no point in trying to get it back, even if it did in some way put his own person at risk. His brain was a state asset. His head a casket for secrets.

'A Chilean expedition found the sledges last year – three miles inland of the Weddell Sea,' said Lady Strood. 'No wonder Filchner tried to keep that a secret – even Scott got ten miles with his. Filchner fell out with his captain – Vahsel. A drunk who died of syphilis on the way home. The whole thing was a disaster.

'The centre punch is a detail. But, yes, a worrying one. Filchner's ship, the *Deutschland*, was originally a coaler called the *Björn*. But our view is that it was a deliberate effort to lay a false trail. Quite a sophisticated one.'

Falcon felt it was a detail that needed to be considered even further, but he decided to move on, because there was no way the Germans could have reached Scott from the far side of a frozen continent. 'So you concluded it was an inside job,' he said. 'One of Scott's own men was the killer.'

In the hall they could hear plates being set out, the buzz of conversation growing louder as the wine glasses were refilled.

She nodded. 'We must also consider one other possibility. What if Scott made the whole thing up? It's a cunning agreement, isn't it? Only his secret diary will tell the truth. The others all agree to censor their own writings.'

'He met the foreign secretary, Sir Edward Whyte, at his country estate in the Borders at Etterick shortly before the expedition sailed. There was intelligence that sabotage was planned – specifically by Germany. That's on the record. But that's not the point. Is it? The fact is there is no independent corroboration of any of Scott's claims. It could all be a work of fiction.'

'Or he was delusional,' said Falcon. 'Such hardship would break stronger minds.'

Lady Strood's story had come to a natural pause, and she offered a second cigarette.

'Look, we have no intention of stopping publication,' she said. 'I'm sure you've made copies. It would be a simple thing to post a set to, what? The *New York Times*? The *Irish Times*?'

'The diary deserves to be published as a historic document. The problem is that it carries an accusation which is open-ended. Who killed Captain Scott? We want you to investigate and provide a definitive commentary on the diary to be published at the same time. If we're never going to know the truth, we need that to be plain. A handful of expedition members are still alive,' she added. 'We've lost so many these last years – one this very month, in fact. So speed is of the essence. Others were interviewed after the Great War – I can let you have the files.'

Falcon felt he was already being given orders.

She hadn't finished. 'You have our permission to communicate a verbal summary of the diary to those you interview – but they must be reminded that until we give permission the contents fall within the ambit of the Official Secrets Act, which covers foreign nationals within our jurisdiction. It might be best to describe sabotage as a theory – and not refer directly to the diary. But we'll leave that to your good offices.

'There is also one other source. The diaries of Lawrence Oates have never been published – a few chosen paragraphs, but large parts are apparently lost. Oates's mother, Caroline, felt they should remain private.'

Falcon drew sharply on his cigarette: 'There's always been gossip – that he fathered a child, that the mother was no more than a child herself. Maybe he regretted not providing for the child – maybe he says as much in black-and-white.'

'Yes,' said Lady Strood. 'It's also possible Oates ignored Scott's orders and wrote about the sabotage. Any reference to the issue would be invaluable, of course, as it would lift any suspicion that Scott was manipulating the legend – if I can put it like that.'

'Didn't Oates's sister burn the diary?'

'She was told to. But copies may have been made. If so, it would be a priceless document. The Cabinet Office has made representations. In fact, the foreign secretary has spoken to a senior member of the family. They may – *may* – be willing to help. You can see the implication: if they can consider our request then the diary exists in some form.'

The buzz of conversation in the hall had reached a crescendo.

'It's a sensational opportunity, Dr Grey – you reveal to the world Scott's secret diary, possibly uncover the culprit's identity. All we ask is a level of cooperation in terms of the date of publication.'

Falcon stood and went to the open door, breathing the sweet scent of honeysuckle. 'So, when?'

'Now would be problematic,' she said. 'The culprit – if they exist – may well have been one of Scott's men, either a British subject or possibly Russian, or Norwegian, or working for the Germans. But the point is we *suspected* the Germans – and the Japanese, for that matter. It would be seriously embarrassing if this came to light at this time.

'Two issues spring to mind: the United Kingdom is currently engaged in preparations to reapply for membership of the Common Market. We need the goodwill of Germany. There is a Cold War – our relations with the Soviet Union are tricky. Japan is being courted as a long-term trade partner – and a possible substitute for the European markets we may be denied if the French say, "*Non!*" again.

'Then there is the Antarctic Treaty. It is a fragile accord. It preserves an entire continent from conflict, and the vandalism of mineral extraction, fishing and so much else. It is a nuclear-free zone. It has been a sensational – and unexpected – success. Any one of the signatories may be implicated by your investigation – notably the Soviet Union. The Germans are preparing to join. Their feats of exploration in the region are second to none. In five years everything will be different.'

'And I have to keep quiet until the time is ripe?' said Falcon.

'You're a quiet man. Even we found it difficult to track you down. It gives you five years to research a book that will make your name. And you're a patriot – I assume – and would not wish to harm national interests.'

Falcon could see her as a fly fisherman, casting bait. He wondered if she had several personalities, and that he was simply seeing one. He tried to imagine her as a child, fleeing Germany, the dark shadow of the camps. Perhaps she'd learnt quickly the arts of semblance.

'How *did* you find me at the Mullard?'

'We didn't. We were keeping an eye on Miss Sarkisova. In fact, we're keeping an eye on all of them – the whole Soviet delegation. And their KGB minders. You appear in Sarkisova's file – it's not particularly thick, even though she is the daughter of the Great Designer.'

'Indeed,' said Falcon.

She stubbed out her cigarette in a small clam-shaped ashtray fixed to the wall.

'If you decline our offer we would request a stay – a month perhaps – so that diplomatic contacts can be advised. We are not going to stop you, Dr Grey – in all probability we can't. Unless we bundle you into a car and throw your weighted body into the Cam. But that's never been our style.'

He smiled. 'I'll do it. I have one request of my own. Do you know what RES stands for?'

'Your file contains a brief extract on your work.'

'Good. I'd like a request taken to the government – the Foreign Office, I suspect – to fund a short series of RES flights over the Barrier. I think we should try to find the tent – after all, if Scott's telling the truth it's a crime scene, and there's evidence to collect. The party that found the dead may have missed obvious clues. But most of all there's the bodies. A trained pathologist could answer the key question: how did they die? Perhaps they were being tracked by a vindictive killer, but maybe they would have died anyway – of the cold, or lack of food, or tainted food. These factors need to be weighed against each other. We need the facts.'

'I can make enquiries,' she said, 'but the costs would be prohibitive. And could we really find them? This isn't a needle in a haystack. It's much more difficult than that. It's a five-foot-wide tent in an area the size of France. And the tent is drifting – each year it moves a few hundred yards closer to the edge of the Barrier. If you found the original spot it wouldn't be there. Tricky?'

Falcon buttoned his jacket, pulling off the bow-tie. 'There's a way of narrowing the search. All I need is the aircraft and the diplomatic clearance to go ahead. We don't need to tell anyone why we're looking – it's a perfectly rational venture as it stands. It's not a needle in a haystack, you see. It's a line eight hundred miles long. A necklace if you like. There's the depots, the cairns, the waymarks, the one-off landmarks – like Mount Hooper, fifteen feet high. Every single one of those points is drifting with the sea ice, each one at a slightly different speed. All we'd need would be a few contacts from more than a hundred sites. Think of it as a string of lobster pots drifting in a current – that's better than the necklace. Locate two or three of those pots and you can find the rest. And the depot at Mid-Barrier was burnt out, according to Scott, so there might be evidence of that. It's not difficult to find, carbonised wood in ice.'

The clatter of plates indicated the approach of the main course.

'We should take our places,' said Lady Strood, standing.

'Forgive me,' he said. 'My appetite has fled. I'll slip away. But I want to be clear. The tent should be found, then tagged, electronically, so that it's never lost again. Scott wanted the bodies left in the ice, and we should undertake to return them to the ice, but first they have to tell their story.'

She nodded, not meeting his eye. 'I must eat,' she said.

'One final request,' said Falcon. 'I'd like to go home, to Fen Ditton. What is my position? Am I to be carted off for interrogation, or left alone unless I publish? I don't like being hunted down.'

'Why on earth can't you go home?' For the first time that evening she looked genuinely surprised, which seemed to make her profoundly uncomfortable, because she was not in total control of the situation.

'Within an hour of the diary being delivered – by Cherry's law firm – I had a visit. A man with knapsack and camera. I watched from a safe distance. He was dressed like a student but he had a silver cigarette case. Then, later, a woman came to the Scott Polar saying she was an old friend and wanted to look me up – the porter palmed her off, but I saw her face. I'd never seen her before. She left her name, Oriana, which I take as a sour joke.'

It was only now, remembering, that he realised the woman had had an accent – hidden, but just discernible. American possibly, from the south, soft and pliant.

'I have no idea who these people were. Not us, Dr Grey – you have my word.'

For the first time Lady Strood looked her age. 'Parkis was told to deliver, offer some astute advice, then disappear for ever. I was to take over from there.'

'Parkis? Parkis is an *agent*?' The word seemed foolish, even stagey.

'Yes. It was felt necessary in the interests of national security. Cherry-Garrard kept the original diary, following Scott's instructions. We asked him to hand it over but he refused.

'We were always concerned with its safe-keeping. After all, what use are copies if we cannot prove their authenticity? Without the original we could hardly accuse someone of murder without evidence that would stand up in court – so to speak. I'm afraid a rather botched attempt was made to take the diary by force, as it were . . .'

In an instant Falcon was back in the kitchen at Lamer, listening to a police constable questioning the servants. 'The burglary?' he said.

'Yes. A mistake. He certainly never trusted us after that. Three attempts were made in all. Then he asked Parkis for help. He arranged a deposit box at Coutts and, following instructions, the release of the documents this year. So that was that. But we had to keep an eye on developments. One of the partners is sympathetic to the needs of the Secret Intelligence Service. Parkis was brought on board. He alerted us to the details of Cherry's will. He has undertaken other duties for MI6. If "agent" sounds melodramatic we tend to use "operative". He's a very effective operative.'

She tightened the silk scarf at her neck. 'But, as I say, it is not us this time. I have no idea who has been your shadow. We'll make enquiries. After all, if we knew who they were we might have a better idea of who killed Captain Scott. If you see them again, Dr Grey, get in touch here – you can always leave a message. Get in touch quickly.'

22

Six weeks later

Cambridge was awash, a summer shower, which made the pavements glow with sunlight when the clouds moved on, leaving the Fitzwilliam Museum a glistening marble iceberg run aground on Trumpington Street. Two great carved lions guarded the entrance, steaming gently, as if recovering from a hunt. Once through the copper doors Falcon could look up at the dome, where a bird flitted in the sparkling air.

He felt light, as buoyant as the great painted ceiling above, transfixed by an idea: other than Cherry, he had never met anyone who had been there, had walked with Scott, had spent that long, lightless winter in the hut at Cape Evans, had seen his heroes trudging off into the white mist. Now the day had arrived.

He took the great stairs one by one, each flight encrusted with the fossils of the granite age, and moved swiftly through half a dozen rooms overloaded with Renaissance altarpieces until directed, by a solitary handwritten sign, towards a special exhibition of contemporary portraits by Scandinavian artists.

The room was the size of a tennis court. A skylight above swam with bouncing raindrops as another black cloud swept overhead, giving the gallery an odd, shifting atmosphere. The soundtrack seemed to help compress the room, concentrating the colours, thickening the polished air. Most of the portraits were masterworks of the past but the far wall had been reserved for the exhibition – a dozen contemporary figures in cool Arctic colours.

He sat on a leather sofa and looked at the disembodied faces around him. He heard a noise – considering the moment later he concluded it was the creaking of one of the polished floorboards – and looked to the door. Beyond, in the next gallery, a woman's face regarded him from a gilded frame. There was something familiar about her, the red hair, the pale forehead catching the limpid light. Then she moved, deserting the frame, revealed as a mirror. He ran to the door, but she was gone. He stood, listening to the carpeted silence, then heard distant footsteps descending unseen stairs, and knew Oriana had eluded him.

He'd seen her twice before after that first day at the Scott Polar. Once on a passing bus on Castle Hill – had she just jumped aboard to avoid detection? And then again from a window of the university library, carrying books, walking through the small area reserved for motorbikes, no doubt on the trail of Primrose. He'd left a message for Lady Strood in the pigeonholes at Magdalene.

Her return – to Caius – was brevity itself:

Enquiries continue. We feel sure you are not in personal danger. There are three personnel. They are not armed. Century House has tapped phone in rented house off Jesus Lane. English speaking – possibly not first language. M.

Falcon returned to the leather sofa and tried to put aside the feeling that he was still being watched. Oriana's surveillance had coincided with a sudden spate of episodes – fits, memories crushingly vivid. One, in the bunk at Fen Ditton, had left him sweating in Sofya's arms. Another had been in broad daylight on Trinity Street: stepping off and onto the kerb had seemed the trigger. He'd had to stagger down Garret Hostel Lane to the river, and lie on the grass bank, despite a steady drizzle.

In six weeks his hideaway at the Scott Polar had become his own secret Mission Control. Lady Strood had arranged for the files on the Scott case to be delivered, and the Scott Polar had been briefed on his work in outline. His timetable had been cleared of teaching to allow for a 'special project'. Meanwhile, the Foreign Office had formally turned down his request to fund RES flights over the Barrier. The box files on what had been dubbed Project FALCON numbered eight, Lady Strood's original investigation taking up two. The rest spanned interviews and reports on the Japanese expedition led by Nobu Shirase, the so-called Dash Patrol; and eight cursory debrief sessions with survivors of the expedition, taken between 1923 and 1932. All had been asked about below-decks disaffection and had been circumspect. None had heard specific talk of sabotage or seen evidence at the depots.

Cecil Meares – confirmed as a government agent – had made a brief official report on his return to London in 1913. The only evidence of possible sabotage he'd listed was the shortfall in oil at several depots, all of which could have been consistent with evaporation. He was able to expand on Girev's reports of gossip back at Cape Evans the winter before Scott set out. The Russian had named four principal malcontents: his countryman Omelchenko, the cook Mills, Butt, a junior member of the scientific staff, and Taffy Evans. Girev's grievances had amounted to little more than bitter disappointment at the poor rations while hauling, and he'd listed only two actual acts of sabotage mooted, both in what he called 'jest' – the 'spiking' of the engines on the three motor sledges, and the idea that the dry fodder for the ponies might be set alight. Mills and Butt denied any sabotage, or insubordination of any kind; Omelchenko was beyond reach, back in his native Ukraine.

Meares was clear: there had been no signs of overt sabotage at any depots on the way back to Cape Evans. This narrowed down the suspects within the expedition, for they had to have come through the depots *after* Meares and Girev, but *before* Scott. This limited their number to seven: the last returning party, of Lieutenant Evans, Crean and Gwynne, and the penultimate, of Atkinson, Cherry, Keegan and Wright. Lieutenant Evans's party were now all dead – but, nevertheless, the prime suspects. All three had been bitterly disappointed by Scott's decision not to select them for the final glorious push to the Pole.

Lieutenant 'Teddy' Evans was the prime suspect of the prime suspects. Falcon had pinned photographic portraits to the noticeboard. Lieutenant Evans looked effete, the eyes the weakest feature, above a strong jaw disfigured by a ready smile. In every picture he'd seen of Scott's second-in-command he'd thought the man self-regarding, yet unsure. There was a strong echo of Scott himself. Crean was the Celtic giant, a face clustered with big, honest features, the inevitable pipe hanging jauntily, and finally Gwynne, the West Country stoker: there was something private in the hidden eyes, but also a look of belligerent honesty.

He'd tracked all three men through the rest of their lives after sailing home on the *Terra Nova*: the rise and rise of Admiral Evans, the hero Crean at Shackleton's side during the epic tale of survival after the loss of *Endeavour* in the ice in 1916, and his retirement to run a pub in Kerry, and finally Gwynne, working his own fishing boat between wars. All had been remarkably circumspect in talking about Scott at all – Gwynne had never spoken to the press, Crean only once, and Lieutenant Evans's genuine heroism and success in later years had allowed him to set aside the past with ease. There were no clues here of a hidden secret. But he was not done with Lieutenant Evans yet. He had to hope that interviews with the living would reveal the truth.

From his comfortable sofa he could see Tryggve Gran's face at the far end of the gallery in a simple wooden frame:

Scott's ski expert, recruited in Norway on the recommenda-
tion of Fridtjof Nansen, the Arctic explorer, was an old man
now, but the painter had brought him intensely alive, with
almost colourless blue eyes, the skin taut and weathered.
Gran had been with Scott, a witness to history.

Falcon got up and took a closer look at the brushwork.

'Good, isn't it?'

He turned to find the subject in real life – leaning on an
elegant stick.

'Dr Grey?'

They shook hands, and Falcon felt it then, the athletic
grip, dry as paper. This man had been there the day they
found the dead in the tent and had to endure the congratu-
lations of the men when, on reading Scott's diary, they'd discovered that the Norwegian flag flew at the end of the earth.

As the rain fell on the skylights small-talk covered their
choice of a leather banquette, and cursory introductions.
Falcon had rung various museums in Oslo, and the university, where he was told Gran was in England for the opening of the exhibition at the Fitzwilliam. He was standing in
for his wife, the artist, who was unwell. 'I hope your wife's
recovering,' said Falcon.

The Norwegian nodded, brushing away the question with
a movement of the hand. Falcon sensed that talk of weakness or failure was always unwelcome.

'How can I help, Dr Grey? My office mentioned new
information on the expedition. *New?*'

Falcon was prepared for this: 'There is new information.
It comes – in part – from Her Majesty's Government. It is
in the interests of national security to keep it private. You've
been a friend of Britain in the past. Are you able to give me
your word it will remain private until such time as it can be
published – which may be several years from now?'

Gran looked at his own portrait. 'Of course,' he said.

An attendant had come in and sat on a seat peeling an orange.

The sound of the falling rain filled the room.

'Captain Scott kept a secret journal,' said Falcon, 'although not secret from the four men with whom he died. He became convinced attempts were being made to murder them all by sabotaging the depots on the return journey. The principal suspect was Imperial Germany – and he divulged that before leaving Cardiff on the *Terra Nova* he had been warned of such an eventuality by the foreign secretary, Sir Edward Whyte.'

Falcon thought Gran's eyes were slightly more distant, even wary. The Norwegian was a patriot, but in some ways he could be seen as a mercenary too: in the Great War he'd been a pilot for the British with the Royal Flying Corps; in the Second World War he'd been the poster boy for Quisling's pro-Nazi government, standing trial for treason when peace arrived.

'The Germans? That's all bunk,' he said. 'Filchner's expedition was a fiasco and he was half a continent away.'

'Indeed. But Scott didn't know that. He also considered the Japanese, but never the Norwegians.'

'Small mercies,' said Gran. 'Is that it? What was the evidence of deliberate sabotage? It sounds fanciful to me.'

Despite the tone of incredulity Falcon could see that he had the old man's attention, so he ignored the question.

'In the tent they discussed world geopolitics. The more obvious possibility, that they had been betrayed by one of their comrades in the returning parties, was initially set aside, but eventually confronted. Taffy Evans, whose decline was swift, said he'd seen a man shadowing them as they crawled home north. But this vision was his alone.'

'So, just short rations and fuel?' asked Gran, and Falcon could see his fist clenching and unclenching. 'It's hardly surprising, is it? The men were exhausted, desperate really, struggling to put up the tent at the end of the day, to see the flame of the stove, to smell hot food. Your clothes freeze so there's a slow thaw. You turn to meltwater. The pain is excruciating – in the joints, the feet, the frostbitten fingers. It's not conducive to carefully decanting oil or unpacking and repacking parcels of seal meat or pemmican.

'Then Scott split the last two parties unevenly – that must have created chaos. How do you take three-eighths of a case of frozen pony meat? Tell me that.'

He stood up suddenly, as if to relieve pain, perhaps, in old bones.

'Maybe they're all guilty,' he said. 'Meares admitted taking more than his fair share – you know that? He left a note to say he'd done it. He had no choice. Scott made him drive the dogs south to the Beardmore Glacier and they hadn't taken that into account laying the supplies. Scott himself said it was a "dreadful jumble".' Gran threw up his hands as if the mystery was explained.

'The sabotage escalated,' said Falcon. 'The North Barrier Depot was burnt out. Food crates were taken away and buried – intact, with their food. At least one oil can was punctured with a centre punch. This was all clearly deliberate.'

Gran shrugged. 'If we believe Scott.' The speed with which he'd moved to this possibility was shocking.

Falcon felt this was Gran's birthright. The wealthy golden son who'd met a Kaiser, garnered medals and honours, could simply brush aside impediments to his version of history.

They were twenty feet apart, their voices raised, but the attendant had left to complete a round of the galleries.

'If we believe Scott, suspicion must fall on the last returning party,' said Falcon. 'Lieutenant Evans, Crean and Gwynne.'

'Teddy was roundly despised,' admitted Gran. 'In private his appointment was a matter of regular discussion. Out in the stables, with Oates and Meares, it was the leitmotif of gossip. Everyone knew he'd been taken on solely – solely – to

avoid the embarrassment of two rival expeditions with the
Union Flag heading for the same point on the map. He was
determined to lead his own but was behind Scott and the
RGS in terms of raising the funds. The King's not going to
countenance rival British efforts, so they bought him off with
the number-two slot with Scott. Then Scott named our base
Cape Evans in his honour. The British have an expression –
"tongue in cheek".

'There were other problems. There's a line, Lady Macbeth
I think, when she wants the lords to do her bidding: "Stand
not upon the order of your going." There was work to do – it
was no place to worry about rank and status. Teddy Evans,
on the other hand, never forgot it. In the hut, the officers
lived on one side of a partition made of crates, the men on
the other. But once we were out on the ice the world was a
different place: there were no uniforms, everyone mucked
in, and a tent hasn't got room for an officer's mess.

'Teddy didn't deserve his rank, so he clung to it. Which
in a way cost Scott his life. Originally, they were going to
take Reggie Skelton with them – he was the man for the
motor sledges. Best in the world. A mechanical genius. But
he outranked Teddy – so Teddy said no. Scott's decision,
I know – but I bet you strings were pulled back in London.
So we got Day, who tried his best. But look at the results.
One thousand-pound motor sledge in McMurdo Sound, the
other two clapped out after thirty miles.'

Gran straightened his spine. 'Arrogant too. He was told
seal meat helped reduce the incidence of scurvy. Atch gave a
bloody lecture on it. But he didn't like the taste. So he refused
to eat it. A few times he secured extra supplies for himself of
pemmican to avoid the seal – that didn't go down well. Silas
Wright said he wanted to throw him down a crevasse. Cherry
said he'd help. Cherry, for God's sake – the world's most
forgiving man. If Crean hadn't walked thirty-five miles on his

own in a blizzard to get help he would have died out there
on the ice. They had to carry him, you know, on the sledge.
Oates walked until he couldn't walk. Only Teddy got a ride.

'And he expected to go to the Pole. He thought it was his
right. That's what's really at the root of this, that he was disappointed, angry, slighted, so maybe he did take revenge. It's
an awkward truth but Scott probably should have taken him –
not Bowers or Oates. He took Wilson, of course, but then they
were in cahoots. Too close, I think – it certainly undermined
Evans's authority. But that's no excuse for dereliction of duty.'

It was quite a speech, the embers of a sixty-year-old bit-
terness flaring into life in the middle of an English rainstorm.

'After you got back, to Europe, the issue was discussed?'

It was the key that opened the lock.

'Yes. There was a conspiracy – it's the right word, I think.
The view was taken – in the end – that there should be no
inquiry. So the questions went unanswered. Had Teddy Evans
had more than his share because he was ill? Was it revenge
for being left out of the final party? The trouble was that the
men in power feared these questions would lead to others: had
Scott botched the whole thing? Why did five men die when
back at base there were food, ponies and dogs. Why were
most of the good men out on "side shows" and not focused
on the main party? It is one of the primary duties of a leader,
of course, to pick others to lead if he is absent. Scott knew he'd
be gone. He left instructions, but that's not the same thing. In
the end Atch led us – a good man, but not a dynamic leader.'

Gran was transformed: he looked ten years younger, revi-
talised by indignation.

'The trouble was the diaries, Scott's, Bowers's, Wilson's
and Oates's, when we eventually saw a few extracts. It was
a noble story unsullied by disaffection. But even the diaries
had been tampered with.'

The words were premeditated, explosive: 'tampered with'.

'By whom?'

'The widows and the mothers were *advised* – and the result was considerable editing and revision. Criticism of Lieutenant Evans was cut, Scott's role sanitised.'

'Who was behind this?'

'Clement Markham – president of the Royal Geographical Society, Lord Curzon – the patron – and a man called Lewis Beaumont, an admiral, again, at the heart of the Royal Geographical. They worked on Kathleen Scott and Oriana Wilson, Bowers's mother and Caroline Oates. There were visits, genteel cups of tea, and solicitous letters. Ironically, the biggest issue was Oates's mother, who wouldn't publish at all, but then worked tirelessly behind the scenes to try to get Scott into the dock. I never did understand that. But Kathleen Scott played ball.

'So the truth never came out.'

'No. But I know Teddy Evans was hiding something.'

'How?'

'He changed his story. And I think he made Gwynne change his too. Crean never told one in the first place. When Teddy Evans got back to London he said he'd gone down with scurvy three hundred miles from the hut near Mount Hooper. Six months later it was five hundred miles from the hut at the foot of the Beardmore, which meant he could claim he'd taken the extra rations because he was ill – or even taken them by mistake. Gwynne sent Cherry bits of his own pretty sketchy diary for *The Worst Journey*, which backed up the five hundred miles – and even claimed they'd left "extra" rations behind for Scott.

'There's guilt there, Dr Grey. What did they feel guilty about?'

'But there was no inquiry?'

'No. Evans's wife died suddenly in London, and I think it was felt he'd suffered enough.'

'So we'll never know,' said Falcon. 'And, anyway, what about the fire, the deliberate sabotage? Are we saying Lieutenant Evans could have done that unseen by the others? Or is it a conspiracy? Impossible, surely?'

'It's possible he acted alone,' conceded Gran.

'Pitching camp in such conditions, and taking it down, then setting off with the sledge packed are all coordinated operations. Each task is allocated. The men work separately. In this case there were three men, not the usual four. He could most certainly have sabotaged the fuel can, and even hidden a case of food. The fire's the problem, I'll grant you. Did he set a timed fuse? If he was the last man to leave camp it is possible – especially in mist, or a blizzard. They carried powder, you see, for blasting in case they got caught on the glacier with no way out of the ice.

'And you can't dismiss the possibility the fire was an accident: it's the Antarctic curse. It's a desert – the driest on earth.

'What if they decided to burn the old wooden cases for heat and it got out of hand? Was that the secret Teddy was trying to keep? Or did they douse a fire, but it flared up after they left?'

A picture of Richard III hung on the far wall, the deep-set dark eyes reaching out into the aqueous gloom of the gallery.

'Perhaps he paid for the silence of the others,' added Gran. 'Crean went home to that pub in Ireland. I think Gwynne got his own boat. He always talked about that – his father was just crew, so the family ambition was always clear. I remember he even had a name ready – the *Josephine*. It's what we all talked about, you see – our dreams. Perhaps Teddy bought them off.'

Falcon shook his head. 'Lieutenant Evans *was* a hero in later years. An admiral. A knight of the realm. Can you really believe this of him?'

'Yes. He failed to put the interests of others ahead of his own. He failed again when he got back to Cape Evans.'

The attendant was back with a Thermos flask.

They moved to a picture of Sir Edmund Hillary, the pin-
nacle of Everest behind him, a wild sky above.

'How did he fail again?' asked Falcon.

'It was clear – certainly to me – that Scott wanted a relief party
to go out and meet him halfway to the Beardmore, not One Ton,
further south. Teddy knew Scott had to be in trouble – it was
obvious. They had to haul hundreds of miles further than he had
and he only just got back alive. I think Scott gave explicit orders
for a relief party when Teddy left him on the polar plateau, but
they were never passed on officially to Atch back at Cape Evans.

'Then he packed himself off on the boat to New Zealand,
leaving the expedition behind in limbo. Not very heroic, is
it? Meares went with him, but he'd got word via the ship of
a crisis at home, a death in the family, an estate to sort out.
But Teddy just fled.

'And he wasn't that ill. I went aboard the *Terra Nova* to
plead with him to send out a rescue party. He wouldn't have
it – he said Scott's *written* orders were clear. Men and dogs
should meet him at One Ton to help speed the good news
back to Europe. If he wasn't there they should leave supplies.'

For the first time Gran held his gaze. 'But Scott must have
given that second order, Dr Grey. Just read the diaries. He is
constantly on the watch for the dogs in those final days. He
expected to meet a relief party. He expected to meet it at Mount
Hooper. It was the one hope that kept them alive. By that point
Teddy was on his comfortable way home aboard ship.

'Heroes and villains, Dr Grey.' He was looking round at
the portraits. 'When I see his face, especially later in life, as
an admiral, of course, and a great winner of medals, I see
him for what he was: a man of no real substance.'

Gran examined his watch. 'I wish you well, Dr Grey. But
you'll not prove anything now. The truth was covered up, buried now for half a century. It's a bitter pill to swallow, but I'd
let sleeping dogs lie.'

23

Falcon let the motorbike idle as he came to the village green, trundling onto a verge in front of the church, the two-stroke engine continuing its guttural coughing long after he'd switched off the ignition. Sofya, who'd rolled back the cover on the sidecar for the journey, extricated herself through the single latched door, hauling out a wicker picnic basket she'd bought on Cambridge market – the essential ornament, apparently, to a traditional English picnic. The civilised symmetry of a cricket match completed the scene. Her return flight to Moscow left the following morning so these few days of English summer had been a checklist of cultural clichés – punting from the Mill Pond up the Granta, fish and chips at Wells on the north Norfolk coast, a trip to Oxford across country to walk up The High, then to Blenheim. The arrival of her return air tickets had heralded a truce: she flew back to London for the Luna 15 mission by military flight in early June. So this wasn't *The End of the Affair* (she'd decided that was her favourite Greene novel), but Falcon knew it might be the beginning of the end, because she'd have to go back when the time came: a week after Luna returned with its precious rocks, or earlier if disaster struck.

Falcon heaved the bike up on its stand and, taking off his helmet and gauntlets, surveyed Old Hall – a Georgian manor with a red-brick façade, which stood behind a high wall, a garden of cedars and oaks beyond, crowding round a pond, with an ornamental island. But the landscape was cramped, and a pale imitation of the splendours of Lamer. Unfolding his cloth map, he saw that the 'park' lay beyond the house, a few hundred acres sweeping down to the Belchamp Brook, over which, according to a note in *White's Almanac,* young Lawrence Oates had jumped his horse in pursuit of the fox.

Sofya found a warm sunlit bank of grass and spread out her blanket, exhibiting her cat-like ability to luxuriate in her surroundings.

The village of Gestingthorpe was locked in time. The Pheasant, at the south end, had been open, a few locals on a bench outside against a whitewashed wall. The high street had incorporated two farms; a herd of cows dripping manure in one yard, a horse tethered to a cart in the other, its head lost in a nosebag. The church, understated but perfectly proportioned, stood firmly in its corner of the green. Everything was in its place. One discordant note: someone had painted a CND sign in the bus shelter.

Oates's father had bought the estate, and a place in rural society, quitting a townhouse in Putney. His mother had thrown a lavish party for her son on his return from the Boer War. They'd all played their part that day – Falcon had found a newspaper cutting from the *Sudbury Times* in the file. There'd been a picnic meal served in front of the house for 281 people: beef, mutton, plum pudding, nut brown ale.

Oates was a hero of the Empire. He'd been ambushed with his men in South Africa and when offered safe passage in return for a white flag had sent back the message: 'We came here to fight, not surrender.' Eventually the Boers gave up and left him to die – he'd been shot in the thigh bone. The *Times* correspondent dubbed him 'No Surrender Oates' – and there was speculation he'd have got a Victoria Cross if there hadn't been fears that the fuss would have revealed the botched planning which had left him and his men exposed to danger in the first place. Back home he'd been called upon to make a speech at the party, saying all his men were proud to be British soldiers. He limped badly.

Falcon checked his watch. He had an hour before his appointment. Unless Oates's diary provided vital corroboration of Scott's allegations, his quest for the truth was on its knees. He had a prime suspect – Lieutenant Evans – but no evidence, and he still struggled to see how Scott's second-in-command could have torched the Northern Barrier depot, unless Crean and Gwynne were traitors too. Tryggve Gran was right: the passage of time hid the real killer from sight. Oates's diary was probably his last chance.

For an hour he'd forget his burden and enjoy the picnic.

But, of course, he'd underestimated Sofya.

As soon as he sat down and opened a Tupperware box (another of her recent purchases) he sensed the tension, noted the way she sat, knees up and embraced by her arms. He had a brief moment of peace in which to appreciate the skill with which she'd set the trap: the plea to come with him on a rural ride, the picnic basket, the carefully chosen summer dress – black-and-white sixties squares – the request to arrive in good time.

'You could come to Moscow too, one day, if we had the right papers,' she said. 'We'd have to get married. That church would be nice,' she added, and they both studied St Mary the Virgin as if some subtle aesthetic flaw might rule it out. Falcon had the presence of mind to realise he'd just received a proposal of marriage.

'I'm just saying we've given up without a fight,' said Sofya. 'Sometimes I think the episodes – the flashbacks – are an excuse not to connect to another human being for fear of being left behind again. You've failed to let go of the child you were. I think you should be braver. I'm sorry. I practise this, but it is still not right. You have to leave the dead where they fall. I have done this.'

He nodded, unable to eat the ham sandwich in his hand, the cricket playing out a thousand miles away. He felt his heartbeat picking up, put the sandwich down, took a paper cup and a bottle of beer, but set them aside.

To speak he had to take in a lungful of air. 'What about you? Isn't Maxim your excuse? You have to go back to Russia, you have to take part in the great race, even though it killed your father, and you feel guilty because in a way it's put Maxim where he is – in that hospital. If he wasn't your brother he wouldn't be part of the game, in play.'

'That's different. I can't desert the living.'

'I can't desert the dead,' he said.

'I think that's another excuse.'

'I think it's a key. That if I can find out what happened – clear Cherry's name and Scott's, then somehow I won't feel my own guilt any more for being late. For letting them all down. It's Cherry's gift, because he understood guilt, that it can be assuaged, atoned. It's my only hope. The episodes – the fits – are getting worse, Sof.'

'You were a child. There's nothing to put right.'

His hands were shaking so he put down a wine glass he was going to fill. He'd bought a bottle of Blue Nun, planning to ask her if – when she came back to Jodrell Bank – they could have a holiday, walking in the Peak District, because it was one of his favourite places, open and barren, windblown. But now he was back in New Cross, on a busy Saturday afternoon.

He could feel his heartbeat in his blood, his limbs going cold, the dizziness whirling. He was aware that she was holding him, and saying she was sorry, but she thought Jodrell Bank would be the end, that they'd station her at Baikonur, or in Moscow if she was lucky, because with Kennedy's death the dream of a joint mission to the moon was over.

He fell, unconscious, into the past, emerging slowly to the distant sound of the cricket match.

When he was able to stand she led him to the church, into the shade, and away from the heat. It was a shelter, and serene, even if it was a symbol of what they seemed unable to achieve. Falcon still felt light-headed, but the anxiety had gone out like a tide, leaving the usual sense of emptiness and loss.

They sat in the back pew. She'd told Falcon she loved English churches, for their cool, spiritual calm, the absence of votive lights, glittering gold and the women in black, diminished by prayer. 'I'll enjoy the silence,' she said, throwing her head back, a signal perhaps that for now the discussion of their future was over.

A woman appeared, from a small side door, loaded with flowers, and showed him the brass plaque to The Soldier – paid for by Oates's regiment, the Inniskilling Dragoons. Then she pointed Falcon across the church to a set of new windows, modern, arts and crafts, in milky colours of green, and yellow, and blue. One showed a Biblical scene – possibly Moses and the burning bush – but the other was striking: a rocky ledge, a great waterfall, a creeping jungle arching over a brave explorer. The dedication was to the memory of Oates's uncle Frank, who'd died, apparently, in Matabeleland at a young age, big-game hunting and collecting specimens for the London museums. The plaque said he was only the fifth white man to witness the majesty of the Victoria Falls. Falcon wondered what Oates had thought when he sat in the family pew on a Sunday and saw the light shine through this image of Empire. Of what glories had he dreamt?

The woman fled, perhaps sensing the tension.

'I make a confession,' said Sofya, standing, her voice dangerously hard. 'This place is fitting,' she said. 'In Moscow there would be boxes here – in which to tell sins. I have a sin. You must listen. Everything – the *dacha,* my brother's life, my work, my *status,* my position, all this – depends on the state. I must work for all parts of the state, Falcon. The Lubyanka too.'

Falcon stood in a pool of sunlight by a clear window. 'I know.' At some level he'd always known.

'I am not a spy or an agent. I am a slave. I observe my colleagues, closely. I report back: what they eat, what they say, who they meet. I pass this all to my handler. He is called Shelepin, and he can break my life with a phone call. I have been given a specific task – I cannot say more. It does not concern you. After it is done I must go back to Moscow. I am sorry, Falcon.'

Falcon picked up a small, printed sheet entitled *Historical Notes* and stood pretending to read, willing himself to ask the one question that really mattered.

'This is our situation,' said Sofya.

She was at the door already, hauling open the oak, letting the sunlight fall like a deadweight on the stone floor.

'Did you tell them about me, about the diary?'

The door closed. He thought the sound, of the door finding the worn embrace of the frame, the latch lifting to fall neatly, was how he would always remember the moment of betrayal.

He sat in the first pew and gave himself up to the loss until the tears came.

24

The clock chimed three. Out on the cricket field the dead air of a Sunday afternoon pressed down, a fleeting mirage making the figures at the wicket buckle and weave as they ran. Primrose stood in the shade of a chestnut, Sofya, sitting on a blanket, appearing to watch the game. Falcon turned his back, crossed the dusty road, and walked through the open gates of Old Hall, marching up the short gravel drive.

The door opened before he could knock. 'Dr Grey? John Walton – family solicitor. Thank you for being prompt.'

There was a hint of a smile, but no more. He wore a three-piece country tweed suit, but his face revealed the kind of tan reserved for holidays on yachts between Greek islands. Falcon had been expecting a country journeyman, but this felt more like the Inns of Court.

'I thought we could talk in the drawing room – it's where they used to hold dances and parties, very grand,' said Walton, as if speaking to a child. The family was trying to sell the house – according to Walton – although nothing as crude as a For Sale sign had been visible to the village.

Most of the furniture lurked under dust sheets, but the drawing room had been cleared. The ceiling plaster depicted a hunt in full cry. Falcon put on his glasses, wondering if young Oates was one of the riders. Walton had two chairs ready by an open set of French windows, so they were looking out to the woods, the land tilting down to the unseen brook.

'We thought it best to meet here rather than in chambers,' he said.

'Who's we?' Falcon thought the interview was a little too patronising. He wanted the family's help but felt he'd been relegated to 'below stairs' – a supplicant seeking a low rent, or permission to take duck eggs from the pond. Walton's manner was irritating, and he kept thinking of Sofya, sitting on the grass, pretending to watch cricket, making plans without him.

'Er . . . Well, the family. All of Laurie's siblings are dead, of course. So we're into the next generation, and the next. They're keen to preserve certain principles – protecting privacy where they can but serving history when they can.'

This sounded like a practised line, so Falcon didn't react.

'Laurie?'

'Yes. He was always Laurie. The family don't wish to encourage the nick-names: The Soldier, Titus. He's still Laurie to them.' Walton crossed his legs and straightened the crease on his trousers. 'Just so we're on the same page,' he said. 'A résumé.

'Laurie left instructions on the flyleaf of his diary. He left it to Edward Wilson to deliver to his mother – Caroline. There was a verbal message too, according to the diary, but sadly that died on Wilson's lips in the tent. When they were found – the dead – so, too, was the diary. It came here, to Old Hall. Caroline guarded its contents fiercely. She felt it was a private document. She understood that her son had played a public role – for other soldiers, schoolchildren, he was a model of sacrifice. She didn't want that sullied. She didn't think people had the right to know his intimate thoughts.

'But there was another reason. At the time – 1913 – Caroline was approached by the government of the day who wished to check that all the diaries had kept to an agreement to allow Scott alone to record certain "suspicions". They wished to read Oates's diary, to verify this stricture had been followed.

'She declined to release it. She said simply that she had
no plans at all to publish, which satisfied the requirements
of the Foreign Office.'

Walton drew stylishly on a cigarette.

'You've read the diary?' asked Falcon.

Walton ignored the question. 'As you will know, Caroline found evidence in the diary of what she took as Scott's
incompetence. She consulted the other next of kin – Mrs
Bowers, Oriana Wilson, Lois Evans, even Kathleen Scott,
although she was less inclined to listen as you might expect.
They agitated for an inquiry. When the King gave out the
posthumous medals she alone did not attend. She kept her
peace. The diary itself remained private.

'When she died in 1938 she instructed Violet, her daughter, who'd remained here to care for her, to burn it. It seems
this was part of her agreement with the government in 1912.
Violet was of an independent mind. She decided to copy relevant passages of interest. These have been passed to a historian who plans a biography. The rest she said she burnt.'

'Did she?'

Walton held up a hand. 'The family was approached by
the Foreign Office – and indeed the Cabinet Office – two
weeks ago. A personal request has been passed on from the
prime minister. A decision was taken to allow you, Dr Grey,
to read the whole diary. It's felt that this would be in keeping with the wishes of the two most important women in the
story . . . Caroline and Violet. Shall we meet them?'

They went through into the dining room, which still had
its table, covered with painter's sheets. Over the fire was a
'swagger' portrait of a woman standing by the hearth.

'Here she is. Caroline, and here is Violet.'

Caroline was the matriarch, stolid, formidable. Violet,
captured in a modest frame in a shadowy corner, looked less
substantial, but Falcon thought he could detect a smile; the

artist had caught light reflected in her eyes. But despite her haughty dignity it was Caroline who looked bereft.

'The whole diary,' said Walton, finally answering the question, 'is on that table. Other than the family you'll be the first person to read it from cover to cover. A few stipulations: you can report on what you read but not quote the diary directly. We'd like a note to be attached to any articles making it clear the family released information in the national interest.'

Walton was still looking at Caroline. 'Laurie died at thirty-two. Most of his siblings remained hale and hearty into old age. Caroline could never forgive Scott for what she felt he'd taken away.'

Falcon walked over to the table.

'You can hold the diary,' said Walton.

'There are complete and accurate copies?'

'Yes. There's one on the seat by the window. You can take that with you. Laurie had a good hand, and they're not voluminous. He left a lot of the daily data to the others. I'm told they're the most personal of the diaries. In many ways they form more of a memoir. An insight.'

Falcon picked up the original notebook. The cover was brown and carried a date, with Oates's signature. He raised it to his nose and thought he caught the echo of ice, paraffin and pemmican. He felt as if he was holding a holy relic.

'It's extraordinary, isn't it?' Falcon said. 'I can't think of any adventure in history which is so defined by the written word. Sometimes I have to remind myself that they died, the five men. That it isn't just a story.' He saw the landscape then for what it was: an icy blank page, over which men could write stories.

They went out into the entrance hall and stood on a chessboard of black-and-white tiles.

'What will happen next?' asked Walton, finally giving up control of the interview.

Falcon slipped the copy of the diary into his leather satchel. 'How much do you know?'

Walton stiffened. 'Only that certain new documents have come to light. That Laurie's diary may provide corroboration.'

'I see,' said Falcon. The Oates family really did know how to keep a secret. 'It depends on what the diary reveals,' he added. 'I must read.'

They heard a shotgun and the sound of birds clattering in the woods.

'The villagers say that every week Caroline made her way to the church to polish the plaque to Laurie's memory. It would be a shame to see it tarnished.'

'So he mentions the child?' said Falcon.

Walton looked disappointed, as if let down by a little boy who had failed to calculate a simple sum. 'What do you know?' he said, his voice flat.

'There's been gossip for years, ever since I started studying the expedition,' said Falcon. 'That Oates – sorry, Laurie – fathered an illegitimate child, a girl, in 1900. The mother was twelve at the time, eleven when the child was conceived. Even then that was an offence. A very serious one. The mother turned up here at Gestingthorpe after the Great War but I understand the family gave her short shrift. She never came back.'

Walton looked Falcon in the eye. 'The Cabinet Office – when they got in touch – made it clear they wanted the whole diary handed over or at least its contents. The family assures me there is not a single reference to the child or the mother. Given these are Laurie's most intimate thoughts we hope that puts an end to the gossip. He was an honourable man. If he'd made such an error of judgement I think it would have played on his mind. And Caroline was absolutely sure he would have sought to see the child was cared for – *if* he'd been the father.'

Falcon judged that if Oates had faced a court for his crime, even at the close of the nineteenth century, the phrase 'error of judgement' would not have saved him from a prison sentence.

Walton hadn't finished. 'I think it is fair to say that any young woman who found herself with a child and no father in those years after the Great War might well have wished she'd met a very gallant gentleman. He was a hero. An idol. Rich, handsome, and gone – lost for ever. He was ideal for the role. The family thought the mother was a gold-digger.

'Laurie loved Caroline, his sisters, his country. We trust that any material made public will be treated with sensitivity. It is a harrowing tale and Laurie was dying – perhaps he reveals too much of his own frailties and fears.'

Falcon nodded: 'Did she have a name, the child?'

Walton pretended not to know, but Falcon saw now that as a lawyer he was mildly handicapped by fleeting honesty, 'Kit, I think,' he said finally, opening the front door and standing aside. No hand was offered.

'Kit' was short for Kathleen, of course, a strange echo of Scott's widow. It struck Falcon how different their lives must have been. Walking away from the house he thought of Dollman's painting, Oates stooped, abandoned, exiting right. He wondered what secret regrets, if any, he'd taken with him that day.

25

That last night, when they returned from Gestingthorpe, they lit a fire in the iron pit and drank malt whisky until the early hours by the VW's lights. It was a soft gentle evening, coloured by regrets. They talked about many things, but not the KGB or the machinations of the Lubyanka. Falcon had to accept that all she had done she had done under extreme duress. So they did not think or talk about the past or the future. He thought this might be the gift they shared – a necessity to live in the moment. He was a light sleeper, so he had no idea how she'd slipped away at dawn without waking him.

He swam before the sun had left the horizon, the green river emerging from the shadows, the water cool and silent. Armed with a flask of black coffee he put out a folding chair and opened Oates's diary. Walton was right – The Soldier seemed less interested in the minutiae of sledging totals and the state of the ice than the observation of character. Entries were limited and often covered several days.

He skipped back and forth until he found the entry for

Middle Glacier Depot

Scott can't raise our spirits. He just tells us what we've done wrong, what to do right. He says the dogs will reach us out on the Barrier, but even he doesn't believe they'll meet us at the foot of the glacier. I reckon One Ton's the limit, and that's three hundred miles away. I heard plenty of officers rally the troops in the Cape. There's a trick to it all right – you must give people hope but you can't make it sound like wishful thinking. You've got to be straight. Scott's crooked.

The oil was short again. This time there's no doubt we're done for. We won't be able to melt our food, let alone cook it.

It was a rest day but we were sent out to collect geological samples. Madness: we'll have to drag them home. For a while we lost sight of the depot and I thought we were back in the glass maze, which had nearly killed us the day before. Finally, we found it by sheer luck. I knelt down by the packing cases – I was done for. The old wound has opened up and my feet are rotting. If those dogs don't come my body's never going to lie in the old church. So I knelt down, exhausted, and felt something sharp pressing into my knee, so I rooted around and found a discarded centre punch, inscribed with letters. Wilson quickly found the corresponding hole in the fuel tin. Someone wants us dead all right. The inscription on the punch was MV BJÖRN. Scott and Wilson slid off for one of their little private conferences – do they really think we can't see them? It's puerile – like schoolboys keeping secrets. This time they came back and said we all needed to talk, once we'd had some hot food.

Turning the page, Falcon used a bookmark so that he could come back to the entry: the first independent corroboration that Scott's version of events was not a total fabrication. It might prove the most important page of any diary written on the continent. Scott had been murdered: there was no room for doubt.

Taffy and I went to collect some rocks for ballast on the groundsheet and he confided, again, that he'd seen our 'shadow' – a man, to the stern, just in sight. I'd heard the Welshman's voice the night before – at dusk, out in the darkness, talking to his apparition. Until now I'd put it all down to Welsh nonsense and the fact that since the Pole he's been transformed: gone the cheery workhorse, now he's morose, slow, idiotic. But this latest discovery has cast a chill over us all. Maybe he isn't deluded.

We made a sorry bunch in the tent. I think everyone's trying to forget what it means. It's torture being so close together but

*so far apart in our thoughts. I get by thinking of Gestingthorpe
– riding down along the brook with the hunt, or nights out
in Dublin from the Curragh. There were plenty of taverns at
Temple Bar and the girls were pretty. But most of all I think of
the* Saunterer. *I never did take her out to the Arrans. She's a
fine boat, and sailing's my kind of life because it's one thing after
another. There's always a job to do, and you can learn with your
hands. It doesn't require introspection. That's a mug's game.*

*I haven't shown Wilson my feet. He doesn't ask, which is
surely a dereliction of his duty as a doctor. If we'd all been
examined on the way up I doubt half of us would have made
the final party, not me, not Taffy. My toenails have gone, and
there's a frostbite line on the left leg – the one that took the bullet in the Eastern Cape during the war. The old wound is raw.
I'd swap those headlines, 'No Surrender Oates', and the b----y
Military Medal for a swift amputation and a ticket home.*

*We all waited for The Owner to speak but the routines –
now sacred – were observed. We each know our duties – and
with five of us in a four-man tent the boundaries are never
crossed. I set up the trivet for the food and stir the pemmican, and add some of the pony meat, which is grey and
glistens and never browns. Scott tends the spirit lamp for a
little light and heat, which we now use to save fuel. Wilson
takes up his notebook to record the log.*

*At the current rate we'll not make it back by a long reach.
It's the surface – Scott says it'll change but he doesn't know.
It's the temperature, way down on predictions. Either Shackleton can't read a thermometer or it's a freak winter. Just our
luck. The snow was like porridge to the edge of the glacier, lines
of sastrugi at right angles to our route, each one an icy foot tall,
each one a mountain. (Birdie fell foul of them – as we crossed
a ridge he lost it entirely and thought the far side was a hun-
dred-foot drop. He clung to the sledge for his life.)*

*The food takes less than a minute to eat. It is the only time I
think of anything else but the pain. I keep my mouth shut. I'm
not a whiner.*

*Once we'd eaten, Scott called us to order. (It's a tent not the
House of b----y Commons) We had to accept the possibility that
the shortages of oil and food are a deliberate attempt to sabotage
the expedition. I thought this a statement of the obvious, and
I caught Birdie's eye. Scott told us that before leaving Cardiff
he was briefed on intelligence reports that German agents were
planning to derail the enterprise, possibly at sea. Uncle Bill –
no doubt primed to chime in at the given moment – gave us
chapter and verse on the Kaiser's imperial ambitions and the
coming threat of war. Birdie was first to pull the rug: if the*
Deutschland *had made landfall on the Weddell Sea, and if the
Germans' much vaunted motor sledges can cover fifty miles a
day, then to get to our stores he'd have to pass the Pole en route!*
  But they'd thought of that.
  *Wilson said we had to consider the possibility that – like
Amundsen – they'd switched to the Ross Sea and made a late
camp mid-season on the Barrier edge. If that were true and the
motor sledges were efficient, anything was possible.*
  *It's the kind of solution Scott loves. Blame someone else.
Blame the Germans. I couldn't help thinking of the* Saunterer
again. The first time I took her out – across to Larne – I took
The Riddle of the Sands *to read at the helm. Half of England
had read it first, and reports of a German invasion were two
a penny. Childers was right, of course – we were wide open to
invasion along the creeks and marshes of the east coast. But the
hysteria was universal. For a while spotting German spies in
Clacton or Malden was all the rage. Scott's happy to feed the
same old paranoia. Then Birdie said he'd been told in Lyttelton
that the Japanese were sailing late, but hoped for the Pole too.
So that's added spice to all the talk of foreign enemies.*
  *I took my moment. Scott's authoritarian style bridles at
back-talk, but I'd had enough. During our long winter at Cape
Evans I'd spent most of my time outside with the ponies in
our makeshift stables – with Meares, whom Scott sent to the
Far East to buy the beasts. He happily agreed he knew nothing about ponies and that it was a classic example of Scott's*

inept judgement. Meares is a dark horse: he's spent a lifetime travelling in the back of beyond, apparently without the need of papers or visas. My money's on him being a government man.

Anyway, I told them what he'd said about Russia: that the country was in chaos, that there were revolutionaries every-where. He said that even out in the Far East, where he'd picked up the dogs and ponies, the wild tribes were ready to rise up. Moscow sends all its convicts out there too – to an island called Shakalin. And they don't just hate the Tsar. Japan won this last war against Russia so they had to give up half this frozen island to the Emperor. They'd love to strike a blow against Kyoto – and their new allies the British. They're desperate to get their island back, even if it is just ice and rock.

That made Wilson pipe up: 'But the Russians have no plans for an expedition,' he said. 'You can't really believe we're being hunted down by the wild men of Siberia.'

I could see the fear in Scott's eyes.

'No,' I said, savouring the moment. 'But we have Russians of our own – and one at least is from the Far East. Girev's father was a prisoner on Shakalin. How do you think he knows how to run dogs? He's learnt from the Amur – that's the tribe. And Anton's no lover of the Tsar – after a few drinks he's more than happy to talk revolution.'

Scott held up a hand. 'I won't hear it. I chose the men. They are above suspicion.'

This is one of Scott's half-truths. He didn't choose the Russians, Meares did. Scott chose Meares – although there was a rumour back in Cardiff that he was foisted on us by the powers-that-be.

We moved on quickly to consider what action to take in future. We can hardly post guards – the damage is done before we arrive. Wilson suggested that on arrival he and Scott would inspect the site for footprints, any sign of dogs, or sledges. Meanwhile Birdie and I will circle the spot at a distance of a hundred yards, if conditions allow, in the hope of spotting motor-sledge tracks, ski tracks, or other signs of our malevolent shadow.

But the truth hung over our heads like a noose.

Yes – someone's trying to kill us. But they're one of our own. Out at the Curragh we liked a bet on the horses. My money's on the Russians, but the last returning party is coming up on the outside. Teddy Evans is transparent – like Scott. They think they're invisible behind the rank they hold. He was certain he'd make the final party. He wasn't upset when Scott gave it to him straight, he was distraught – and we didn't see him until ten minutes after he was given the news. Gwynne, the Cornishman, is an enigma. He's a listener, keeps his own counsel, unless he's invited to tell us about the Josephine *– the boat he's going to buy with his pay when he gets back. When the talk turned on Scott he'd listen, but rarely speak. But he had no love of the Navy – he told me after all the wine at the midwinter feast he'd have cheerfully sunk a boat hook into the back of every captain he'd served under.*

Crean, the great Irishman, always kept cool, but there was a bitter edge to it when he realised Taffy was going to the Pole and him already looking done in. Crean's a giant, and showed no signs of failing, but they took Taffy – why? Nothing's been said but my money's on Scott having orders to try to keep the Irish out of the picture: Bowers is a Scot, Wilson, Scott and I Englishmen, Taffy Welsh. There's enough plain prejudice against the poor people of Ireland – if he'd been a nice Proddie from the Pale, preferably Trinity College, they'd have taken him in a flash, especially if he'd been an officer. It didn't help he was always kissing some paper tag he wore on a necklace – that'll be Catholic mumbo-jumbo. You could see Scott's lip curl. So it was Taffy, not Crean, and me, instead of Lieutenant Evans. Why me? The Army – that's why. Petty politics again. And the fact was Scott couldn't look his second-in-command in the eye. Lieutenant Evans will have walked away with a black heart. If the motive's vengeance – the personal variety – he's our man.

Falcon put the diary on the grass and stood to stretch, then lit a cigarette. The sun fell dappled through the trees, but the Soldier's world was a shadowy one: he seemed to see the worst in everyone, or was he just a sharp observer of human nature? They all stood exposed: Wilson, Bowers, Crean, Gwynne and, above all, Teddy Evans. But most suspicion fell on the Russians – and he'd known them well. Oates was the pony man, the stables his kingdom. Several of Ponting's photographs showed him huddled by the blubber stove, head-to-head with Dimitri Girev, the groom.

Taking up the diary, he shuffled his chair into the sunlight, an antidote perhaps to the brutal story unfolding on the page.

17 February
Lower Glacier Depot

Taffy finally collapsed short of Shambles Camp, but he'd been on his last legs for days. I said I'd stick with him while the others went ahead to get the sledge. We were alone for an hour. I knelt down on the snow with his head on my lap, so that he was looking north, towards home. I thought I could write something for his widow so tried to remember everything we could see. He died a few hours later in the tent but this was the final scene. I kept thinking of Nelson, lying in the lamplight below decks. I can't do it justice. I'm a soldier, not a painter like Uncle Bill. I'm a practical man. I enjoy tasks not thinking games – just ask all those tutors Mother brought to Gestingthorpe. But I thought if I get home people – Taffy's people – will want to know what it was like.

So I took it all in. I looked back at the glacier, the scale of it all beyond me: a hundred miles to the top – the air so clear there was no sense of distance. It was awesome – I think the word's sublime. It was overpowering. A staircase? You could put London on one of the steps, Paris the next. To each side the mountains, pyramids of carved stone with not a tree in sight, towering, unearthly really – like peaks on another world. As a deathbed it would have suited Nelson – it would have suited a pagan god. Thor, perhaps. There wasn't a single sign of humankind: our

*own footsteps perhaps, but they'd be gone by nightfall. Not a trail
of smoke into the sky, or a lonely cabin, or castle tower.*

*North, over the Barrier, nothing. A slight haze. My heart
sank – it was the way home, but not for Taffy. I talked about a
bowl of hoosh, and a warm tent, and then the ship, and Lyttelton, and a pub in the town for a smoke and whisky.*

'We'll sink a few,' I said, gripping his shoulder.

*I prattled on, but I felt a fraud. I was worried about myself,
not Taffy. The right foot's nearly gone. I won't make it – I
know I won't. It'll be a bitter end. I won't take Wilson's
cocaine pills even if they are dished out. I can't brook self-destruction. If the ice takes me, fair enough. Or even a pistol shot
– at least that's a soldier's way. We should have got all this
straight once and for all before we left the hut. Are we going to
stop here – for days, even a week – until Taffy finally breathes
his last? Why not leave him? Let the ice have him.*

*At first he was rational. We talked some more about what
we always talk about: food. I said there was a bar in Dublin
that served white pudding as well as black, and venison sausages, and duck eggs, and kidneys around the plate. And the
stout was black as tar and just as thick. Taffy said he was
going to buy a pub in Wales and eat Bakers' Oven twice a
week – whatever that was. He was happy then and I thought
he was giving up, his body relaxed, not tensed against the cold.*

*Then I saw a snow snake – the first at least since the Pole.
There must have been the first hint of a wind, slipping down
the glacier. It picks up the frozen snow on the surface and rolls
it into a ridge, and then it begins to tumble, like a long snow-
ball, and to twist and meander, like a desert river. Of course
the hiss is the wind – but if you're not prepared you'd reach for
a stick or a gun. It got me proper the first time because of the
war. We shot snakes for target practice. It's b----y tricky.*

*Once there's one snow snake there'll be more. They sort of start
each other off. A few minutes and the place was alive with them,
moving together, like sand on a windy beach. I don't know what
Taffy saw, but it terrified him, and then it made him angry.*

'It's Hell,' he said. Now, writing this, I think he meant it. He knew he was dying and he thought this was the place where he'd spend eternity. I started looking out for the others then, bringing the sledge, because he'd spooked me. I'm no hero like that.

'Will you kill me, Soldier?' he said, back with the living. I couldn't tell if it was what he wanted, or what he feared.

'Uncle Bill says we should stick together,' I said.

We'd tried to broach the subject on the way up to the Pole. In better days, when it was hypothetical, we chewed it over. If a man broke a leg on the glacier you were done for: either he died there, or you all died there. That was the choice. Wilson said you waited for a relief party. But that's crackpot. What he was saying is that we all die for the sake of one. He's not afraid, of course, because he's going to Heaven. He's got a note.

'I won't swallow the pills,' said Taffy, taking a juddering breath that shook his chest. 'I shouldn't have come. I don't know why the Owner chose me. Tom was in better shape. He'd never let you down.'

'You haven't let anyone down,' I said. 'We're all crocks now – just like the poor ponies.'

Taffy was unlucky. Scott likes him – owes him somehow for the past. He's turned a blind eye to the booze and the women. He fell off the dock at Lyttelton and they let him back on the crew. But he's the biggest, and we're all starving, so it's hit him hardest. I reckon that's it. And he's the only blue-jacket – we're all gentlemen, but he's below decks. So he's no friends at all, not really. He's not been right for six weeks.

I don't think Taffy cared about the Pole. It was a job. That's how I see it. I never thought I'd be picked for the final party: I didn't dream of it or strive for it. I kept the ponies alive. Taffy hauled a sledge.

'If he'd asked about the Pole I'd have said no,' I said to Taffy. 'It's not a military expedition – I don't have to take orders.'

'Oh, well,' said Taffy, and tears were falling then.

'Look. They're on their way back,' I said, pointing.

I think he thought this was his last chance.

He took my hand, and laid it on his chest. 'Tell her I'm
sorry. She should tell the girls too, and Ralph. I do love them.
I'd have put it all right. But I've lost myself – I can't put a foot
in front of the other.'
'Tell who, Taffy?'
'Lois. My wife.'
He broke down then, and the snakes hissed because the wind
had started blowing harder. When the snakes got near he kicked
out his legs and grabbed the collar of my jacket. 'Don't tell
The Owner. I should have said. I could have saved us. I heard
them talking on the Barrier, and at Shambles. I kept an ear
out. They'll kill us, Soldier. I'm done anyway. They'll kill The
Owner. That's the idea.'
'Who are they?' I said.
It was dreadful to see. He wanted to speak but he was too
scared – a man that close to death, afraid of life.
'I'd to keep my peace or he said they'd find my lovely ones
and cut their throats. I said too much over the whisky at Mid-
winter. But they riled me up. They said I'd a kiddie in every
port but I said I only loved my three.
'I said Ralph was a fine boy, and the girls were angels,
and one new-born. I only come south again to make sure the
pension would set us all up. I was boasting. They know where
to go, Soldier. Everyone knows cos I never stop the talking.
'They said they'd put Ralph in the ground alive if I spoke a
word of it.'
His breathing was erratic, his eyes full of terror.
He started then, and pointed, away to the west.
'What can you see, Taffy?'
But he wouldn't speak. I think he saw the man who'd been
following us. A man who didn't exist but for him. There was
no one. I felt sorry for him then, because he must have been
haunted for weeks, and that must have made living unbearable.
'There's nothing to fear, Taffy,' I said.
'Keep a watch, Soldier. I can't save Scott, but maybe you
can. Watch out for the sign. I know their sign.'

His eyes rolled back and I thought he'd gone. He slumped,
and as I had a moment, I got out my diary to make sure I
remembered what to say to his widow.

But he rallied, his eyes swimming, and then he tried to take
the pencil.

On the page he drew three lines: one curved, one straight,
one sinuous, three sides of a void. It meant nothing.

'It's the sign. Keep it safe – The Owner will read your diary.
When we're dead – they'll read them then. They can't see the
sign, or they'll kill my loves.'

With a shaking hand he tore the page from the notebook and
gave the slip to me. I tucked it inside the lining of my boot. I
won't tell his wife about the ravings. It's shameful losing your
mind, breaking down.

'Keep it secret, Soldier – for the children. Don't tell. But if
you see the sign you'll know them.'

As I say, he died later in the tent, but he didn't utter another
word after they all got back with the sledge. Did he tell the truth?
I don't doubt he told it as he saw it. But was his mind unhinged?

This diary is for you, Mother. No one else. But you have
to keep the secret too. I promised. Even a vow to a madman is
sacred.

Falcon set down the notebook and put on his glasses. Sea-
gulls bobbed mid-stream in the wake of a college boat heading north. The river was the peculiar deep blue reserved
for the reflection of a clear summer sky. The dislocation
between the savage brutality of Oates's memoir and the soft-
ness of the scene made Taffy Evans's death throes all the
more shocking. The notebook had so far exceeded Falcon's
expectations: not only did it provide corroboration of Scott's
claims of sabotage, it identified a piece of vital evidence – the
mysterious 'sign' scrawled by Taffy Evans.

Scott had said Oates walked to his death in his socks,
unable to face the pain of squeezing his swollen, frost-bitten

feet into his boots. So where were the boots? Had they been brought back to London? He'd have to return to the Scott Polar to check the inventory. Were they in the tent with the lost explorers?

Desperate to read on he made himself fill the percolator, smoking a Ducados, which conjured up an image of Oates tending the pemmican in its hot pan, the flame thin and guttering. Would he mention the lost daughter? Could he bring himself to confess to his crime? Entries now were sporadic and often incoherent. The Soldier was failing fast. The next significant entry was the last. The handwriting had deteriorated horribly to a jagged scrawl.

15 March

The pain now is like the Barrier itself: featureless, searing, without end. I can't haul, and when we rest I sit on the sledge. I'm baggage now. At the Southern Barrier depot we discovered our killers are without mercy – they dragged a full box of food away from the camp and buried it in the snow. If Birdie hadn't spotted the tracks and the pit we'd be dead by now. All of us. A glimmer of hope kept us plodding on. Would our hunters leave us now – sure that they'd wiped us from the face of the earth? Our hopes rose beyond Mount Hooper – untouched – but approaching the Northern Barrier Depot, Birdie saw what looked like smoke ahead.

For a moment hope was alive. Smoke: fire, heat, warmth, food, friends, rescue, home, all within reach.

A bolt of joy masked the pain for a heartbeat. My eyesight's blurred – I'm as blind as dear old Cherry – so I couldn't make it out until I was ten feet away, but I knew it was bad because of the silence. Our tormentor is done with subterfuge: the cairn had been opened and the oil cans lit. The meat had charred in its tins. Uncle Bill knelt down and said a prayer to himself. I'm not sure The Owner believes in God, but they're both in thrall

*to Fate. It's as if we've all succumbed to a lack of free will.
The lifeblood's gone. When we lost Robinson on the ice at Cape
Evans that first summer Uncle Bill said it was a blessing for
the lad to have gone to his Maker at such an early opportunity.
He was twenty-four. I think we should have been led by men
who keep their god to themselves.*

*I must have been bad – my arms shake now, and one knee.
Birdie appeared with a roll-up and lit it for me. He even
placed it between my lips. We're all overwrought, of course,
but the kindness was almost too much. My eyes flooded and
he turned away. When the tears had fallen I was looking
down into the pyre. One of the oil cans was on its beam end,
standing up. It was black with the smoke, but in the top
corner the sticky soot was disturbed by three thin confident
strokes. I hadn't thought of Taffy for weeks. It was the sign:
the three lines – one curved, one straight, one sinuous. The
scrap of paper was still in my shattered boot. The sign could
have been mistaken for a random blemish – there were others,
amid the curved insanely beautiful patterns of smoke. But
for Taffy's deathbed confession it would have meant nothing
to any of us: why had it been left? A last act of bravado?
A moment of completion perhaps: we were all dead now. In
truth we all died at around five o'clock on the afternoon of 4
January when Amundsen's black flags came into view. But
we walked on, dead men. Taffy left first. Now it's my turn.*

*As the light bled away I made one more discovery – it's
because my eyes are down and I've got no duties to distract me
from the world we're all going to leave. It was a scrap of paper
– burnt, newsprint, with Chinese or Japanese type. I nearly
crushed it underfoot. Why give Scott more grist for the mill? But
I think Birdie spotted me looking at it in my hand. He's a good
soul. He knows I'm done for and he keeps an eye open. No doubt
tonight the Japanese will step forward again as our shadowy foe.
The truth is we used plenty of newsprint for insulation – it was
gash, from a warehouse, and a lot was from overseas. I remember*

pages of German because one of the scientists – Silas Wright, I think – can speak the lingo. But for Scott the plot will thicken.

It's because in some ways he's the killer. I think we all know. We're all the victims of incompetence. The saboteur's a side-show. Meares had it right one night in the stables: the motor sledges – one of which we dropped in the sea off Cape Evans – cost a thousand pounds each. The ponies – which Meares cheer-fully agreed were 'crocks' – cost five pounds each. I was hired as the horse man and should have gone to Russia to choose the beasts. I kept them alive, they did as well as they could – but it was terrible work, and they suffered. The dogs cost thirty bob apiece – and you can feed them to the others when they break down. They were the answer all along.

No more mention has been made of Taffy. Scott refers to his 'breakdown' and the pity we must feel for his inability to rise to the standards set by the rest of us. If he could hear himself as I hear him. It's bilge, of course. I may follow in those foot-steps soon. He's looking for scapegoats. I wonder how I will fare in the official report? Will Taffy suffice to provide the excuse required? Scott regularly reminds us that he held us back sev-eral days. Or am I another sacrificial lamb?

Last night I asked Uncle Bill for help with the pain. In that ditch outside Aberdeen, when I'd taken the Boer bullet, I lay twelve days in agony. I passed out once, when my own heartbeat seemed to overwhelm me. But that pain was specific. It had a root, and with an effort of will I could separate it from my own body, let it drift away. But my rotten feet have won a victory: the blackened toes are dead flesh; the gangrene in the left leg has reached to just below the knee. My left hand has gone too – frostbite, and now an infection. I can do no work. When I walk all the tortures of life are compressed into each step. The pain intrudes on sleep. I am the pain. There is nowhere to go to find relief.

I hope, each time I close my eyes, I will not wake. But the nightmare continues, bathed in white light.

Wilson gave me morphine while the others pitched camp and checked our perimeter. 'This will help, Soldier,' he said. 'But no more.'

What had I hoped for? A lethal dose, perhaps, so that I could close my eyes, after a last meal, a last smoke, The Owner's rum. But the good doctor won't do it – it's against the moral code. And I won't take the cocaine tablets. Scott was lucky with Taffy – he had the good grace to die the day he fell. I can't die, however hard I try. I'm holding them back, dodging the work, eating the food. It's the pain I long to leave behind. And this diary. I've asked Uncle Bill to give it to my mother if they get through – if not, leave a note to that effect. The diary must stay private. I promised Taffy.

I'll go tomorrow morning. I know they want me to. I'll walk out and lie down and it'll be over. Scott will write my story. If I could talk about going – about giving up – it would be so much easier to face, but no one looks me in the eye.

I'll sleep now. I've been given a little more morphine and the effects last about three hours. Now I've decided I can feel how sleep calls. When I wake up the pain will be back – but I'll leave it behind for ever soon enough. In the life that is left me it is all I desire.

Mother – Dr Wilson has my last words for you. Seek him out. Honour my wishes.

Your son,

L. O. R. Oates

26

The Mond Building, the latest addition to the Cavendish Laboratory, was modern and brutal, a round tower next to a cubical extension, the outside curiously decorated with an incised outline of a crocodile. His guide, Charles Wright (Falcon had been briefed not to call him *Sir* Charles, and certainly not Silas), explained, 'It's by Eric Gill. It's good, isn't it? They really are living fossils,' which made Falcon recall a line from one of the diaries, that Wright had picked up a stone imprinted with the outline of a primeval sponge-like organism on his way up the Beardmore Glacier – the first sign ever found by man of ancient life on the continent.

Wright – one of Scott's scientists, who'd been in the party that found the tent – was almost as famous as the men he'd watched trudge off south to death and glory. He ranked along-side the men who'd made the modern electronic world in this oddly dilapidated set of buildings hidden in the heart of medi-eval Cambridge. These dull red-brick walls had seen the dis-covery of the electron – that strange spherical particle with its own 'poles', a miniature model of the earth. Much more had followed: the revelation of the structure of DNA, the unveil-ing of the neutron, and finally the artificial controlled splitting of the atom. All here, off Free School Lane, a back-alley half blinded by the walls of Corpus Christi, the entrance over-looked by the Eagle public house.

'The story is,' said Wright, still considering the crocodile. 'That you could hear the great man coming because of a booming, gruff voice – it reminded Gill of the crocodile in *Peter Pan*, which had swallowed the ticking alarm clock.'

Wright, clearly a scientific sceptic in all things, shook his head. 'Who knows? But that's the story.' Falcon wondered if he'd met Rutherford, the 'great man', a fellow Canadian, a Nobel laureate, a legend already by the time Wright came to Cambridge to study cosmic rays in 1910.

'Let's keep going to the laboratories. We'll find a quiet spot there. The place is full of stuffed shirts, Dr Grey – a visit from NASA no less, the top brass this time. They're bound for Jodrell Bank. But they'll want to see Rutherford's lab first. Then there's some kind of ceremony – speeches and the like. Odd to think there'll be a man on the moon before Christmas. I wonder what the great man would have made of that.'

Falcon followed his guide across a courtyard and up some stairs to the second floor of the L-shaped block. He considered his tactics. He'd called Wright at St John's, where he had a room, asking for the interview, explaining that he was hoping to use RES to locate Scott's last tent. What he really wanted to do was track down Oates's lost boots. There was no record at the Scott Polar. The Oates family were adamant that nothing had been brought back to them except the notebook, and Laurie's sleeping-bag. Museums in Christchurch, New Zealand, and elsewhere had drawn a blank. And what to make of the curious instruction to his mother to seek out Wilson and 'honour my wishes'?

Rutherford's lab was an extraordinary sight – not unlike Ponting's pictures of the interior of Scott's hut at Cape Evans: lab tables, walls partly obscured by books and packing cases, a rough-hewn floor and ceiling. Scattered about were various experiments: Bunsen burners, electrical circuits linked up in bewildering sequences, fume cabinets, and a strange elongated metal tube, possibly a particle accelerator. There were about fifty scientists in the main gallery, none in white coats, most talking, a few smoking. Notebooks lay around, inscribed with numbers and geometric designs, and careful spidery notes. In one side-room, where a group of hulking computers had been housed, spewing out tape, two students sat playing chess. At the far end a middle-aged man was bouncing a tennis ball against the wall while smoking a pipe.

The Cavendish – the world's first purpose-built laboratory – was on the move to new premises on the edge of the city: a plate-glass temple to physics, quantum theory and cosmology. Wright found them a 'cubbyhole' among packing cases and went to get tea. Young Charles had been here when he applied to join Scott's expedition. He was turned down – just like Cherry. He walked the sixty-five miles to London to ask Scott to reconsider in person, which did the trick. It was pure luck that both had survived. Cherry was certainly on Scott's list for the final party – and so was Wright, who'd called Scott a 'fool' for selecting others for the final push, sending him back just a few hundred miles short of glory. At the time, trudging back, he'd been too angry even to write in his diary.

Since then he'd lived a life of glittering scientific success. Officially retired, he was back in Cambridge a final time, perhaps, to receive a medal at the Senate House. In the university library Falcon had scoured the newspapers for mentions of him over the last few decades. He'd been back to Antarctica twice – once to mark the fiftieth anniversary of Scott's death. He'd stubbornly avoided discussing the expedition, despite being guest of honour at Scott Base. The *Manchester Guardian* had recorded something of the event. As Wright climbed aboard his plane on the iceway for home, a reporter had tried one last question: how have you found the return to the south? The paper had coyly reported his reply: 'Personally, I've always hated the f------ place.' But he'd been back four years later, and this was another polar trope: if they survive they can't help being drawn back to the icy flame.

'The NASA men are on the move,' said Wright, returning. 'I don't know what they expect to see here. The controlled splitting of an atom is a private affair.'

Now he was sitting down, Falcon studied the man: white hair, close cut, busy, upbeat and sharp – what Falcon would have called 'bushy-tailed'. Technically, Wright was still on Falcon's list of suspects. He reminded himself to be alert for misdirection.

'How can I help?' asked Wright. 'You mentioned RES.' He was composed, both hands clasped round one knee, raised so that a foot could rest on his captain's chair. Falcon could see him then, bursting cheerfully out of his tent, quickly tackling the reindeer hide finnesko boots before getting into the harness to haul the sledge.

'Yes. If we can get funding I think we can find the tent.'

Wright didn't blink. 'Good luck, money's tight.'

'I know. Whitehall turned us down. And the Pentagon. We need the US Navy to fly the kit – NASA relies on their pilots, the very best. Armstrong and Aldrin, who look set to fly the lunar module on Apollo 11, are both naval aviators. It's been suggested we might get them, or one of the other astronauts, to plead for a favour – half a dozen flights over the Barrier. It's worth a try, modern explorers making a gift to their predecessors. It's the main reason I'm here.' Falcon took out a notebook. 'I'm meeting someone called Mattingley – he's down for a future Apollo mission, and he's ex-Navy too. I'm hoping he's a fan of polar explorers. After all, they have so much in common, risking everything to reach a desolate new world. I'm told he's got friends on the Hill, as they say. The Senate is our best bet. Apparently, he's going to find me in the Old Laboratory at noon.'

'Then you're in the right place. And we have half an hour. So how can *I* help?' asked Wright.

Falcon wanted to get him talking, before mentioning sabotage.

'If we're going to find the tent I need detail. We might be able to get within half a mile – but then we need to know the lie of the land, so to speak. Could you tell me about the day you found them, and then the next day, walking south looking for Oates – until you turned back? There might be something . . . The diaries are fine, but spare. I guess everyone was in shock?'

For a moment Wright considered the question. 'I saw the tent first,' he said at last, and there was a hint of emotion in the eyes, the past occurring with a slight visceral shock. For all the academic distance the past still cast a spell over Silas Wright. Falcon liked him a little bit more.

'I said: "It's the tent." I'm not prone to nightmares, Dr Grey, but when they come that's what I'm trying to say – but I can't get the last word out.' It was an insight, and for a moment he looked sorry he'd let it slip.

He seemed to notice Falcon for the first time: 'Sorry. Yes – you want detail. It was about three hundred yards off the direct bearing south, SSW. Atch – Edward Atkinson, leader by default – said, "How do you know?" and I thought, Well, what *else* could it be? I think at that point there were probably less than fifty people on the continent. I could see it was something man-made, so there wasn't really an alternative. But, as I say, it was just off the line – a point you should note. Did I say three hundred yards? Maybe less. Even with the cairns and the depots, keeping to the line was always a difficult task. One of the reasons poor old Cherry didn't plug on from One Ton was he felt – quite rationally – he might miss Scott going the other way. If the weather closes in you can't see your boots.'

He studied his mug of tea, which was decorated with a red Canadian maple leaf.

'Atch and Cherry went in first. Then we made camp and Atch summarised the story he'd gleaned from Scott's diary. Then we all went in, two at a time. I went with Dimitri Girev.'

He paused, struggling to carry on. The finding of the dead seemed to hold a spell over all the men involved, as if some great taboo had been challenged, and they were for ever cursed: it was a tomb after all.

'It's the ice, of course, that fools you. If we'd found them in a tent in the jungle, or the foothills of Tibet, it would have been different. Freeze then thaw. They'd have rotted, which is natural. Faded away in the end – even the bones. But because they were there . . .' he made a claw of his hand '. . . fossilised. You think they'll always be there. Or even that one day they'll thaw – and then they'll be alive again. Not rational. But it wasn't that sort of day.'

'And you pitched tent. How far away?'

'Yes. Good question – about fifty yards. It didn't seem right to get too close. But there'll be no trace. We took all our gear back – at least, everything metallic.'

'Then, the next day, you set off to find Oates?'

'Yes. Scott's log was pretty accurate. We had about twenty miles to cover. We trudged along and finally spotted Oates's sleeping-bag – about five miles short of their last camp.

'Scott must have stopped there a while – trying to lighten the sledge. By that point the bags were iced up – they were heavy, cumbersome. They certainly didn't need it. I suspect they hung on to it for a few miles in case they found Oates on the path. After a while it must have been obvious he'd gone in any direction *but* north. He didn't want to be found, which I think shows how brave he was. There was a boot too,' he added, sipping his tea.

Falcon tried not to react, making a careful note. 'That's not in the diaries, is it?'

Wright smiled. 'It was in mine. But then nobody reads mine. A hundred yards further – maybe less. One boot – finnesko. The three in the tent were still in their boots – so it had to be Soldier's. Again, weight, I guess.'

Falcon cursed himself: he'd read *all* the published expedition diaries, but many years ago, and had forgotten the lone boot. 'Why just one do you think?'

'It was to hand – or they discarded both and the other was there but we couldn't see it. It only takes the wind to move the snow and you've no hope.'

'What happened to the boot?' persisted Falcon.

'We took the sleeping-bag back with us on the ship. Not sure about the boot – why's it so important?'

'A loose end.'

'It might be in Scott's tent. When we got back – having marked the spot close to where Oates died with a cross – we decided to leave pretty much everything there, except for the diaries and some personal effects for families back home, a few mementos, perhaps. I doubt anyone bothered with a spare boot. "Tigger" Gran took Scott's skis and left his own, set as a cross to mark the burial cairn. He thought that something of Scott's should make the whole journey, as it were, there and back again. They have metal bindings by the way – so possibly helpful.'

The sound of Falcon's pencil scratching on paper filled the cubby-hole.

'I saw Tigger only yesterday, in fact, for lunch at the University Arms,' said Wright. 'He said you'd met. Sworn to secrecy, I know, but he felt he could trust me. He can. So can you. A new diary then – and sabotage?'

'Yes,' said Falcon, oddly surprised that old comrades should still be so close. He felt blind-sided nonetheless. The interview was now out of his control. The time for direct questions had arrived.

'Do *you* think Lieutenant Evans had anything to hide?'

'No, no. Tigger mentioned arson, and theft of the food? That's not Teddy. Frankly, I don't think he had the courage for outright evil.'

'Oates suspected the Russians,' said Falcon. 'I've read his diary. He says that on his deathbed Taffy said there was a plot back at Cape Evans – below decks – to "get The Owner", his words.'

'*Two* new diaries? How extraordinary.' Wright set aside the mug of tea, clasping his hands: 'The Russians, you say? I liked them – we all did. The only man *I* couldn't figure out was Cecil Meares, He recruited them, of course, out on the banks of the Amur. Meares was an adventurer – that's the word put about. Irish – Kilkenny, I think – then the Army. The Irish don't like empires, especially the British variety.'

Falcon noted how deftly Wright had put Meares in the list of suspects. 'Meares was Secret Service – sent out to keep an eye open for saboteurs – personally appointed by the foreign secretary.'

'Good God. Maybe he changed sides,' suggested Wright. 'That's the thing with those chaps. All that cloak and dagger, and they forget who's paying the bill.

'But you mentioned the Russians. That might be closer to the mark.'

For the first time Wright looked excited.

'You see there's something I'd forgotten. I went to see Cherry after the Great War – 1925, maybe, a little later – at his house up in the country, and he told me something that's not in his book, in any book. We talked about Dmitri Girev because news had just come through that he'd died, a heart attack out east. You'll recall that in *The Worst Journey* Cherry says that when they went out to One Ton to meet Scott the Russian suffered from a mysterious illness, one of the reasons they couldn't press on further south. He begged Cherry to head back to Cape Evans. Cherry insisted they wait.

'It's what happened next that's been kept secret. After a few days Dimitri recovered and struck a deal. He offered to do a quick recce, see if Scott was within striking distance, as long as they set off for Cape Evans as soon as he got back. He took a light sledge, rations and all the dogs, and set off into that storm. The plan was to be gone a day, but he didn't come back for three. He said he'd found nothing, that he'd only got five miles, when the storm forced him to hunker down. But one man, a light sledge and dogs – he could have reached the Northern Barrier depot. Tigger said it was torched? He could have lit that fire. Why was he so desperate to head home? Perhaps he was afraid he *would* see Scott. Did he offer to go out one last time to make sure nobody ever saw Scott alive again?'

Falcon felt cheated. Why had Cherry not told the whole truth?

Wright read his mind: 'Cherry said they agreed to leave it out of the record because Scott's written orders were not to risk the dogs. Dimitri pleaded with him not to tell any-one because he thought he might not get his back-pay if everyone knew they'd defied orders – and the dogs were his personal responsibility. He certainly didn't want any more questions about the mysterious illness, which sounds a lot like a loss of nerve.

'And I think Cherry was deeply ashamed that he couldn't run the dogs himself, that they hadn't taken the risk together. So it suited them both. And Cherry believed Dimitri. Maybe he shouldn't have.'

There was a sudden silence outside, a stilling of the hub-bub in the lab, as everyone left for the ceremony in the Mond Building.

'What are we saying?' said Falcon, half whispering. 'That Girev – possibly with Meares's help – sabotaged the depots on his way back to Cape Evans? Then when he was sent back out with Cherry to meet Scott he made absolutely sure they would never reach One Ton by torching the last food and fuel?'

'I'm not saying it – you are. I liked Dimitri – and so did Cherry, which is why, as I say, he never told the truth about the recce.' Wright was struggling to get into a jacket with patched elbows. 'Have you tried to find out what happened to the Russians – to Anton and Dimitri?'

'MI6 are trying. But there's no progress, not even through the usual back-channels.'

'Tigger and I – and Atch – kept tabs as best we could on both of them once we got back to London,' said Wright. 'We all felt they'd done a fine job but had been written out of the story, so to speak. We wrote – even sent some money when the newspaper and wire contracts paid up. When we heard about Dimitri's death we thought we'd find out more for an obituary and get some extra money to his family. We roped in Teddy Evans, because he had the contacts. A rising star after the Great War. So, Dimitri originally went back to New Zealand and married a local girl, then got homesick and took her back to his village in the Amur. He turned his hand to gold mining and dredging on the river.

'Teddy found out all of this after Dimitri's death. Anyway, the revolution came and went, and then the purges began, and the camps returned. One day in 1930, I think it was, agents from the NKVD turned up in his village – it was called Chlia. This was Stalin's secret police – the men who would become the KGB. They took him away to Vladivostok for questioning.

'They held him for eighteen months, then let him go, without charge. The line Teddy got from the intelligence people was that they thought he might be a capitalist lackey, the Russian who'd helped get Scott to the Pole, that kind of thing. Was he really a loyal son of the revolution? Perhaps he'd been boasting about his heroic past in the local inn. He liked a drink.

'It was winter when he was released. The law was – and this goes back to the tsars apparently – that when the prisoner is freed it is up to them to get home. Tough country. Dimitri was six hundred miles from home. He befriended two fur traders travelling by sledge and hitched a ride. The sledge journey took six weeks. When he came in sight of his village he must have felt he was home at last. But he was denied that: a heart attack was the story. He died out in the snow, a few miles short of his own front door. He was forty-five or -six. Nothing, really.'

He shook Falcon's hand. 'I'll leave you to lobby your NASA man.' Wright paused with his palm on the door handle. 'I wonder now if we got the whole truth about Dimitri. We tried to pass the news of his death to his compatriot Anton – this was 1932, so not easy. He'd gone home to Ukraine – a Party man apparently, running a cooperative farm. But we were too late. Weird coincidence, really: he'd died the same year as Dimitri, hit by a bolt of lightning on a lonely country track. Again, that's the story.'

27

The walls of the lab were furnished with blackboards, most embroidered with equations and geometric diagrams. Falcon had the components of Taffy Evans's mysterious sign in his head: the curve, the vertical line, the sinuous wave. For the thousandth time he drew a random symbol comprising the three lines.

Wright's recollection of finding the boot offered up the hypnotic possibility that the symbol – after half a century – might still be tucked within the boot, stowed away in the tent. Which made inveigling the Americans into flying over the Barrier critical. The chalk squealed and he stood back, lighting a cigarette, letting the nicotine blur his vision for a moment. He tried several iterations of the symbol. Not for the first time he felt the timid stirring of recognition, just out of reach.

The ceremony in the Mond had begun and the soft sound of applause was like a distant waterfall. Falcon put the chalk down.

'A puzzle – yes?' said a voice he didn't know.

He turned. A tall man in a fine suit stood by the door smoking a cigarette. He had very large features, conventionally handsome, with fair hair. Later, Falcon told Sofya that he knew then, on some subliminal level, but even he felt he was using hindsight, that he didn't know, couldn't have known, but he certainly felt it, a sudden encounter with the edge of the void.

The newcomer sat on the corner of a desk, one leg swinging slightly from the knee, smoking elegantly.

'Ken Mattingley?' asked Falcon.

'A lowly substitute, I'm afraid. Ken's the only Apollo astronaut in the group. He's very much in demand. But I have been briefed, and I've said my piece to the crowd. I've bored everyone.'

He took a short sharp breath and removed the cigarette from his lips. 'I'm intrigued by your plan, Dr Grey, to use RES to find Scott and his men – it just might work. I'm sorry to intrude,' he added, nodding at the hieroglyphs. 'Is this part of the plan?' He walked forward.

The light, almost colourless blue eyes made a direct connection with his own: fleeting, but daring. The man was mesmeric, a kind of human lighthouse – signalling, directing, flashing.

'Just doodles,' said Falcon, picking up the duster and obliterating the chalk symbols.

Then he had it: the face he'd seen so many times, in newspapers, magazines, or glimpsed on TV in the white-shirted cauldron of Mission Control.

So he picked up the chalk again and drew a circle encompassing three matchstick bodies. He wanted to draw this man in, because he recognised that this brief encounter was rich with possibilities, not all of them unwelcome.

'The tomb?' asked the visitor, walking towards the board. 'The tent – yes?' He pressed a beautifully manicured index finger to the chalky surface of the blackboard. 'You must find them in the vast wastes of ice and granite.'

Falcon shook his hand, touched dry skin. 'Falcon Grey,' he said.

'Wernher von Braun.'

And there it was: the void, opening. This man had conceived the rocket that had obliterated his family in an instant. Three bodies shrouded in a white sheet.

Falcon pulled out one of the strange tall metallic stools and perched on the curved seat. 'Yes. Scott and his two comrades in the tent. I want to find them. I need your help.'

For a few minutes he talked about RES, and the technicalities of interpreting the readouts, the problems of persuading the US Navy to fly over the necessary terrain, the vast featureless Barrier. They wanted to find Scott, the final tent, so that the men were not lost for ever. He didn't mention why he really wanted to find the tent: that it was a crime scene, and there might be vital evidence to gather at last. He drew a ragged map of Antarctica and plotted the approximate position of the tent, its likely path of drift northwards, and westwards, to the open sea.

'Why now?' asked von Braun.

'Because we can. This is the moment when technology becomes the solution. By the end of the year there will be a man on the moon. Can we not find three men on our own planet?'

They laughed together, recognising something in each other.

'And if we take the long view we're running out of time,' said Falcon. 'They're drifting, edging away from the spot where they died. The further they wander the less chance we have to find them. In a century, maybe two, they'll reach the edge of the Barrier. An iceberg will calve, and they'll float out into the Southern Ocean, the ice will melt and they'll be free – but lost for ever, unless some bones find a distant shore, where no one will know it's them.'

He ran the chalk around the circle of the tent. 'The time has come to find them. With modern science we can discover precisely why they died. Scurvy, perhaps, or lead poison from tins, or the cold, or lack of food. And we can tag the site so it's never lost, and then we can map their long journey. It's fitting.'

Von Braun lit another cigarette. 'But first you need your aircraft?'

'Yes. Which we don't have. Which is where you, sir, come in. Otherwise, it's a pipe dream. The UK government might help in five years or ten. But we don't have our own long-range aircraft so we'd need your help eventually.'

Von Braun let cigarette smoke drift out of the corner of his mouth. 'What did Scott say at the Pole?' he asked. '"God – this is an awful place." In a month's time, God willing, Neil Armstrong will stand on the moon. I wonder what he will say.' He shrugged. 'Something uplifting I am sure. But Aldrin next – he may be tempted to be truthful.'

'Is it worth it?' asked Falcon. 'To plant a flag?'

Von Braun smiled. 'Yes. The Stars and Stripes. I am an American now. So I will be proud.'

Falcon could suppress the image no longer: the V2 falling towards New Cross.

'No. Was it worth it? The Mittelwerk. Twenty thousand innocent lives.'

A wave of applause came to them – louder, even joyful.

For a moment von Braun broke eye contact, examining the glowing tip of his Lucky Strike. 'A very different rocket,' he said. 'A different age.'

'I went there as an undergraduate,' said Falcon, brushing aside the apologia.

'I was given a tour – if that is not the wrong word. A man from Nordhausen, a survivor of the camp, will show you round for a few East German marks. Tunnel A, and then across to B. We saw the crane where the mass hangings took place. It's somehow fitting that it's all underground. A hellish place.'

'I did not know,' said von Braun, and Falcon could see him fighting the urge to turn on his heels. 'I did not know *everything*.'

It was a concession, so Falcon thought he would be truthful too. 'I lied. It's more than an academic interest. My family died in a rocket attack – New Cross, close to the Thames, in 'forty-four. My parents, my sister. I found the bodies. They were killed by the shock-wave. I still ask myself, why them, why not me? I feel guilty. I always have.'

Von Braun let his eyes leave the blackboard and settle on Falcon. 'It was nothing personal, Mr Grey.'

'It's Doctor Grey – but it doesn't matter.'

Von Braun executed a small bow, a distant echo of a Prussian childhood. Falcon recognised that this was how the man had survived – thrived. He rose above accusation, not recognising perhaps that he stood accused. What a contrast to Cherry's life of regret.

Von Braun's eyes shone now with the glorious memory of the past. 'In 'forty-three we had problems with the targeting – it was very poor. We needed to observe at close range the impact of the rockets. The test range was a village in Poland called Sarnaki. My friend Arthur Rudolf and I went to Sarnaki and stood in the middle of the bullseye – as it were. Right on the target. The guidance system was so poor it was the safest place to be.'

Again, the dismissive flap of the sinuous wrist, and a brief smile.

'Do you know how we measure the accuracy of rockets? There is a number – the diameter of a circle within which fifty per cent of the rockets will land. The smaller this number the better. Our ambition was four point five kilometres. In reality, perhaps twelve. So, you see, we aim at the docks, I think. But the impact is in Kent, or Essex, or the Thames. Later a radio beam was developed so things improved.

'I am sorry, Dr Grey. This was a weapon of terror. Its indiscriminate violence is a key component of its effectiveness.'

Falcon wondered if the German's inability to empathise was arrogance or some emotional flaw.

Von Braun took up a piece of chalk and drew the trajectory of a V2 rocket: the rise, the swivel, the arc, the fall. 'I went twice to the factory in 'forty-four – before the end, before the killings,' he said. 'We had to make V2 rockets there because the original factory at Pennemünde on the coast had been bombed. There was a camp – Mittelbau-Dora – which provided the labour. We had our orders directly from the Führer's office – the V2 had to be improved, it had to be manufactured, it had to fly to London, and Paris, and Antwerp. It had to kill thousands, terrify millions. Otherwise, Germany was lost. There was sabotage in the tunnels. The rockets malfunctioned. Examples had to be made. It was that simple.'

Falcon had found a series of articles von Braun had written in America about the future of space for a magazine called *Colliers*, which had made him a star on radio and TV. He'd envisaged spacecraft – initially carrying monkeys to see the effects of weightlessness on life. Readers complained this was cruel, that when the spacecraft re-entered the atmosphere they would die a horrible death. Von Braun later wrote that he'd solved this problem: he would install small capsules that could be triggered from earth to release a lethal gas before re-entry, killing the monkeys before they were consumed by the fireball. By that time details of the camps in the east were better known. Von Braun's solution for monkeys seemed crass, cruel, even provocative. Could this really just be arrogance, a lack of empathy?

'Was it sabotage – or did your rockets just fail?' asked Falcon.

'That is a question for Arthur Rudolf, the factory manager. He's in the other room, listening to the speeches. He may not wish to engage in such a debate today. He is a citizen of the USA, as am I. I am sorry. We have left the past behind.'

It occurred to Falcon then that there might be two kinds of human being: a species separated by the ability to leave the past behind.

'How is your brother?' Falcon asked.

'I have several brothers,' he said, the playful note instantly gone.

'The youngest. Magnus,' said Falcon. 'There was a particular problem with the rockets, of course, the vane servometers, I think, which gave you remote control of the flight. As I say, perhaps sabotage was an excuse. The engineers were sent into the Mittelwerk – below ground – to fix the problem. I was told Magnus faced being sent to the frontline so you got him a job as a manager of this project. So *he* knew. Did he witness the hangings? I was told they were a required spectacle.'

'Dr Grey. A miracle weapon was required. Do you know Berlin spent twice the entire cost of the Manhattan project on V2 rockets? I was not asked to do this. I was told. There were plans for submarine launches, too, off the American coast. But there was no time. A year, two, Germany would have won – or at least been able to settle for an honourable peace. What of the Allied scientists and their weapons? Is Barnes Wallis pursued by such questions, or Whittle? No.'

Falcon thought von Braun would walk out, walk away, and forget this conversation for ever. But for now he went up to the board and examined the circle and three matchstick bodies Falcon had drawn.

'Is it a flag, blowing in the breeze?' he asked. He adjusted his jacket into line. 'I must go back to the proceedings.'

They shook hands, a small ceremony over before Falcon was aware it had begun.

'Magnus works for Chrysler in Milwaukee,' he said, letting his dry hand fall away. 'Many of us went west – some to the east. The Russian space programme owes them much. Even the British – they, you, used what they found in the Mittelwerk.'

He fixed Falcon with the falling-water eyes. 'It is not about means and ends. The V2 was not the end – it was the beginning. Now Apollo 11, then perhaps Mars, and the stars beyond. The Pole is an end – the end of the earth, a fixed point. You cannot go further without going away. It defines itself. Was *that* worth it?'

'For everyone who wasn't there,' said Falcon.

And that was partly the truth of it: that it built a legend, and countries, nations, empires thrive on stories, but the crowd has little time for the lives it cost.

'Yes, for everyone who wasn't there,' said von Braun. 'Wisdom at last.'

28

Moscow

It was a grey city, bereft of neon, populated by shuffling women in black, moving from stall to stall, trying to find fresh fish, or suet, or a ball of wool. Sofya knew what *she* looked like: a rare tourist on a bench, smoking, pretending to look at Dzerzhinsky's statue, but secretly examining the three ornate floors of the Lubyanka. It wasn't the cigarette brand that marked her out – Belomorkanal was a Moscovite favourite, the strongest in the Soviet bloc, with its little cardboard filter. (She would buy 200 for Falcon, because the filter was a perfect roach for dope.) No, it was that she was a woman smoking in public. On the metro all the men had sucked the life out of their cigarettes, eyeing her beret and leather handbag. One had got too close, and there were always pickpockets about, so she'd stamped on his foot. *'Day mne dyshat', tovarishch!'* Give me room, comrade! Wide-eyed, he'd backed off, grinding his own smoke into the ribbed wooden floor. The city was a man's world: you couldn't buy a hairpin, however deep your purse, and tampons were only available on the black market. Pillows were curiously absent too, reserved for hotels and the *dachas* in the suburbs.

She studied the façade of the Lubyanka: the third floor had a clock set in the centre, amid the ornate cornices and painted stone. She had half an hour until her interview: no doubt Shelepin wanted to know the latest about her colleagues – one in particular – before the delegation moved from the Mullard in Cambridge to Jodrell Bank for the launch of Luna 15, and its epic journey to the Sea of Crises. Half an hour, so she'd have time for Detsky Mir, the Children's World, Russia's premier toy shop, which took up one corner of the square. This was in her blood, the juxtaposition of sickly fables and real-life horror: in the vast arched windows of the store, mechanical dolls dipped and jerked their dead arms, while opposite stood the headquarters of the secret police: they said it was the tallest building in Moscow, even with its modest three floors, because you could see Siberia from the basement cells.

Sofya knew the truth: they kept locals in the basement for misdemeanours. The real interrogations were conducted on a hidden fourth floor in the roof, and those cells had no windows. She lit a second cigarette and examined the packet, with its stylised map of the great canal – Stalin's waterway. No one mentioned that now. It had linked the White Sea in the north with the Baltic and the West: a triumph of Soviet engineering and endeavour, but dug by the hands of the prisoners from the gulags. Men like her father. Russia was a stone best left unturned.

She checked her watch: time had flown, so she'd brave the clunky lifts of Detsky Mir after the interview – she wanted to take care in choosing presents, so it might take hours, because the heating was always on and she'd get disoriented in the cavernous halls, jostled by mothers distraught at the prices, surrounded by train sets and toy soldiers, spacecraft and *nevalyashka*, the self-righting dolls that tipped and swayed with a manic intensity. Her nephew Viktor, Maxim's son, was three, and his mother had hinted in a letter he wanted a kaleidoscope that showed the stars and Gagarin's capsule. His sister Galina was eighteen months old. She wanted a puppy but their block leader said it was not allowed – although it was, but only for Party members. She wanted to be generous because her brother could not bring presents: his struggle with 'sluggish schizophrenia' was endless, decreed by the state.

Briefly, that morning, she'd visited him at the *psihushka* in the suburbs. The commissar at Baikonur insisted that she accept the gift of such visits whenever possible: all fares were covered, and the paperwork complete. They reserved a room for her in the Hotel Moskva and she could run a tab in the cocktail bar on the fifth floor, which served champagne at breakfast. None of this amounted to a gift. It was a warning – you could lose all this, it said, with one typed sentence on an internal memo, activated by a single scrawled signature. And Maxim would be lost too. She wouldn't be told until the funeral was over: there'd be a grave in frozen ground, unmarked, and a package by post of his possessions: a notebook, pencil, wedding ring.

The hospital maintained an antiseptic façade. A cheerful painter was whitewashing the perimeter wall when she arrived, and she had been booked in by a nurse at the front desk in a smart blue uniform and fob watch. But beyond the first locked doors the acoustic was brittle – as if a group of wayward children had been let loose in a dilapidated swimming baths: shouts echoed, the top notes left for chains and bolts, the bass for an electric floor polisher operated by a man in grubby overalls. White tiles, reinforced glass, steel doors. Everything had an echo.

Then she'd been told to sit and wait in a soundproof booth, which left her twenty minutes to wonder what noises they wished to hide. Maxim appeared and sat on the far side of a Perspex screen without looking up. She'd asked if the straitjacket was necessary, and was told by the male nurse that he'd tried to attack the woman who changed the bucket in his cell. The nurse was called Evgeny and Sofya's sister-in-law had said he was kind, and that when she visited he whispered to her helpful things: 'He eats well. He has started sleeping again. He listens to the radio.'

Sofya asked Evgeny how her brother had been, and he said he'd been unwell – his eyes would not focus, but that this was a side-effect the doctor knew well. Maxim was distracted: during this discussion about himself, he was studying the view outside the barred window, where a tree stood in the yard. When she thought of her brother she tried to imagine what was inside his head: after their father's death he'd refused to continue with mathematics, or physics or aerodynamics and had joined a cooperative underground printing works. But the notebook he was allowed to keep was always full of equations, and when he showed Sofya he'd trace their logical progress with a shaking finger. So perhaps he took refuge in the silent world of numbers.

She'd talked at her brother for fifteen minutes while a guard made notes. She told him about the Mullard, and Luna 15, and how proud Viktor was, and that he wanted to be a cosmonaut. Maxim's face did not change. His eyes seemed to struggle to stay aligned within their sockets, one persistently falling below the lower lid, like the moon setting. She said that once the Luna 15 mission was over – and the samples of rock returned to earth – she would return to Baikonur, and then, eventually, there would be another visit. She said she would kiss the children. Maxim's good eye filled with tears. She had a bag of fruit she'd bought in the Central Market from an Uzbek farmer with no teeth: the prices were exorbitant, but there were no queues. The stall was beside one selling goat, the heads hanging, dripping blood. She examined Maxim's face then looked away, remembering the eyeballs in the butcher's stall, lined up in tin trays.

She made herself say it at the last moment, splaying a hand on the plastic glass: 'We all love you, Maxim. We think of you always when we are together.'

The only desperate moment came as she left the building. Every night she'd slept in Falcon's VW she'd wished that death would release Maxim of its own accord, a gift that would release her as well. But outside, on the street, there was flat sunshine, and the traffic went past in a blue fug of exhaust fumes, and a woman walked a small white dog with a jacket, and she knew, with a dreadful certainty, that Maxim would live a long life.

29

The clock on the Lubyanka struck two. She crossed the square, passing briefly through Dzerzhinsky's shadow, before entering the foyer. She had her paperwork ready – including her special blood-red Communist Party card, and was directed to a lift, which took her up to the third floor.

Her 'handler', Fydor Shelepin, was a KGB colonel, who played the role of favourite uncle. If she was ever tempted to believe in this projection as the true basis of their relationship she had only to imagine what was going on above her head. The cells were soundproofed but she'd once heard a single cry. She'd often thought that if you could see emotions – their footprints, even – the air in the building would be thick with fear, a miasma of despair and desperate hope. Every time she entered she lived for the moment when she could walk away.

'Sofya,' he said, sliding a packet of cigarettes across the table. The desk was large, and included an iron ashtray, which was full of mangled butts. She was afraid of Shelepin, terrified of what he would do to Maxim before they killed him if she let them down. But her heartbeat was steady and her skin dry, because she had learnt to be a machine in which the components whirled, but silently.

'Has Valentinov revealed his hand?' he asked, his match flaring in an unpredictable bonfire.

She had an image of the professor then, sitting up in bed drinking his tea in his rooms in Cambridge, the hair on his chest damp from the exertion, like black worms. Valentinov's requirements in bed were easily met, usually once a week in the afternoon. In many ways he was otherwise a kindly father.

It was a truism that an academic intelligence is easily fooled in matters of emotion.

'Yes. He's made contact with Century House.' On a day trip to London Sofya had strolled past the headquarters of MI6, unable to believe Lubyanka gossip about its legendary inadequacy as the nerve centre of the Secret Intelligence Service. But the rumours were true: the twenty-two-storey building was largely made of glass and had a petrol station at ground level.

'How did he make contact?'

'Ernesto Kan,' said Sofya. 'They've kept in touch by post-card. They were students together in Minsk. Kan's defection hardly caused a ripple. He's been quietly working at Porton Down in the germ-warfare labs. I suspect they set up the back-channel before Kan jumped. Valentinov met a British agent in the café at Selfridges last week. Then, this weekend, there is an invitation to a cottage in Dorset.

'He plans to defect after Luna 15 lands on the moon. He will be leaving Jodrell Bank by "embassy" car, provided by the British. The arrangements are in place. He expects the probe to fail – even a soft landing is problematic. The technological challenges are immense.'

'There's no suggestion of sabotage on his part?'

She shrugged. 'No. He's a passive man. He waits for events to fall into place. If the landing was an absolute success, and the probe returned to earth with the samples, I think there would be a loss of nerve. Why decline a victor's return to the Kremlin? I think that in some ways this is what he hopes for most – unexpected success, then a new *dacha*, medals, a Hero of the Soviet Union, perhaps. One day a state funeral.'

'Either way he'll get his state funeral,' said Shelepin. 'It may be sooner than he hoped.' He smiled. 'If he goes with the British, are you included in these delightful plans?'

'Apparently. There's a safe house in a place called the Peak District. He doesn't know the address. He's in their hands. He says the British will let me work as his assistant.'

'He risks so much. Does he hate us?'

'No. He's proud of the past. It's just that they've given him the prospect of a dazzling future. Cambridge, the Rutherford, once the furore is over. Then he can work with the Americans. The far planets – this is his dream. The Lunokhod can be developed for the conditions perhaps – Mars, even Venus. He feels our own efforts have stumbled – the death of my father . . .'

Shelepin held up a hand. 'We all grieved. But he would have wanted us to press on.'

For the first time Sofya wondered if the surgeon responsible for her father's botched operation might be a fellow inmate in Maxim's suburban hospital.

'We cannot let Valentinov go,' said Shelepin. 'When you get to the safe house you must slip away before nightfall and ring Harrington House. Our men will be there with you within the hour. There may be violence. He has a gun?'

'Yes. He is entirely incapable of using it. Why Harrington House?'

'You don't need to know,' said Shelepin, shuffling notes on his desk. Harrington House was the ambassador's residence. The basement contained a KGB suite for use when Kensington Palace Gardens was deemed insecure.

'He will be driven to the nearest east-coast port – Hull or Grimsby. A fishing boat will take him to the Baltic, then Shipyard 189. He will be interrogated on Vasilyevsky Island. You will be driven to the defence attaché's residence in Highgate, then flown out of Gatwick with the first secretary's staff. Your presence on the island will be required – so, a weekend in St Petersburg, Sofya. A fitting reward for good work.'

There was silence in which, above their heads, they heard a voice cry out. Sofya tried not to react, turning her left foot on the ankle, dissipating the stress.

'And the rest of your colleagues: Khariton, Tkatchev, Suslov?'

'No – immovable,' she said. 'Each has ambition, but none has the talent. Valentinov knows this and is happy to leave them behind. They are placemen. Our world is full of such people.'

She'd gone too far. Shelepin coughed, and turned the pages of her last report. 'If Valentinov jumps, your contact at Harrington is Aldonin – he'll organise the operation on the ground.' Shelepin closed the file. 'The Englishman?' he asked. 'Dr Grey.'

'He found the bug,' said Sofya.

'Yes. A shame. But you did the right thing. He thinks he can talk openly now?'

'Absolutely.'

Shelepin licked his lips. The Scott diaries were a minor affair, but Sofya's diligence had given them a ringside seat while Washington, Berlin and Tokyo floundered to catch up.

'He's achieved little since my last report,' said Sofya. 'If he secures a breakthrough I will make contact. You'll know within hours. Girev is in the frame – but we always knew he would be – Omelchenko too, but Girev is more problematic.'

Shelepin steepled his fingers. 'We are in a strong position. If we were hunting wolves we'd be leading the pack.'

'The Americans?' she asked.

'The Americans don't care – although I'm sure they've been briefed by the British.'

Sofya nodded. 'He's asked NASA for help in locating the tent.'

'Yes. This is what they call a "long shot", yes? They will not help. The bill would be prohibitive, and they know nothing but the cost of things. Our principal aim – our only interest – is the same: there must be no suggestion it was Girev, or Omelchenko, and certainly not a Bolshevik-inspired action, or Menshevik-inspired for that matter.'

He opened a lower drawer in his desk and produced a bottle of vodka and two glasses. The liquor held the violet hue of the finest spirit.

'Happily, we are on the side of truth. You can take this file . . . It gives the details on Girev and there's a note on Omelchenko. Read it somewhere private. Memorise what you need, then take it back to old Zamyatin in Research. Sign it back in – don't let him just take it. I realise he's an old comrade of your father's and he dotes on you but he's a menace to good bureaucracy. Pass on the general gist of the report to Dr Grey. Tell him Zamyatin let you see the file. This is plausible. It will free Dr Grey to move on to other suspects.'

The interview was over, but Sofya could tell Shelepin wanted to play: he might suggest a drink at Dom Kino, the cinema club where he was a member, and hint at a meal later, or a visit to Gogol Boulevard, the headquarters of the Russian Chess Federation. There would be more champagne, and caviar, because the KGB was providing security for the world chess championship. Everyone pretended to be neutral but Shelepin quietly hated the Armenian Petrosian, while his superiors loved Spassky, born of Russian parents in St Petersburg. The match would last months and was largely incidental to the opportunity to rub shoulders among the higher echelons of the KGB. And then there would be the inevitable suggestion that she go back to his hotel. On her last visit she'd turned him down, but it would be very difficult to turn him down again. It wasn't her life that hung in the balance.

But Shelepin had another plan. They took the back stairs up to the next floor. Here the original décor was intact, laid down by the All-Russian Insurance Company, which had built the Lubyanka – parquet flooring, pale green walls. A traffic-light system operated, which allowed guards to know when prisoners could be moved – it was of fundamental importance to ensure their guests did not see each other. Shelepin ignored a red light, no doubt a privilege of rank, and led the way down a corridor of cell doors. At number 32 he stopped and slid back the observation slot. A young man lay still on a bunk bed in shorts, one leg in plaster.

'Our deadly assassin,' said Shelepin, swelling with importance.

Viktor Ilyin had joined the Red Army to get access to weapons – finally taking two pistols, then stealing the police uniform of his brother-in-law. He'd gone to the Borovitskaya Gate to the Kremlin and waited in a crowd to see the cosmonauts from Soyuz 4 and 5 drive past in an open car. They were heroes, having just completed the first transfer from one spacecraft to another in orbit – a technical coup that, at least for a few months, removed the lustre from Apollo's triumphs. But they were not his target. That was Leonid Brezhnev. So he shot fourteen bullets into the second (closed) limousine in the motorcade. The general secretary was uninjured, but Ilyin killed the driver, and inadvertently injured (slightly) several cosmonauts from previous Soyuz flights – including Valentina Kureshkova, who had been the first woman in space. A police motorcycle outrider ran him down.

'Comrade Andropov has interviewed him,' said Shelepin.

Andropov: the grieving face of the Kremlin, who'd stood at the foot of her father's corpse on its bed and set her on the path that had led to this dull room in the Lubyanka. Andropov was now the director of the KGB.

Shelepin shut the observation slot. 'He told the director he was going to use his court appearance to advocate a solution to Russia's ills – a tax-free payment to all citizens to cover basic needs, such as food, education and health care. This transfers control to the individual, away from the state, and cuts costs and bureaucracy. It's crazy, of course – but unfortunately a policy advocated by the economists at the World Bank, the Bank of England and the US Federal Reserve. So maybe no day in court, after all. I understand that after a brief appearance in camera he may be heading east – the Kazan State Psychiatric Hospital. I visited it on one of my regional tours, Comrade. A truly dreadful place.'

For the first time that day he looked Sofya in the eye.

'And no visitors.'

30

The picture, black-and-white, showed a man's *pince-nez* being held to a rack of rotting meat, acting as a magnifying glass, to reveal the wriggling bodies of the insect life within the dead flesh.

Sofya translated the subtitle with unconscious ease. 'Maggots!'

A mutiny was brewing on the battleship *Potemkin*; below decks the ratings were starving, but had refused to eat the borscht, served up in tin bowls on the swinging tables rigged up by rope in the galley. The doctor, summoned to adjudicate on the beef, pronounced it edible – all that was required was a wash with brine.

Sofya was waiting for a certain scene, which had chilled her blood when she'd first seen the film – right here, in the 'nosebleed' seats at the Khudozhestvenny, on Arbat Square. That night the house had been packed – a rare showing of Eisenstein's classic, which had not always been in official favour. They'd had to watch it here – her mother had explained – because this was the very screen on which it had first been seen. At the *dacha* there was a picture, showing the façade of the Khudozhestvenny – its classic frieze of centaurs and lapiths obscured by a large model of the battleship.

She could feel her mother's hot breath on her cheek that afternoon. 'Tolstoy came to the first night,' she said, as if it was the first line of a prayer.

Sofya ate potato crisps as the scene moved to the deck. The captain, astride a raised turret, told the sailors that if they did not eat the borscht they would hang from the yardarm: and

there it was, as frightening as it had been that damp afternoon in 1948, when the grey city seemed to seep inside the
cinema and onto the wide screen. The yardarm, stark against
a white sky, was a black silhouette, but – hauntingly – the
merest hint of grey began to reveal the silhouettes of bodies
hanging, coalescing, turning in a light sea breeze.

Enough: she'd come here to work.

She'd thought about taking the files to the *dacha* but it
was a long metro ride, and it would only disappoint, as the
house had been reallocated to a senior technician at the university. She could sit in the allotment, it was a fine day, but
the place was full of memories she had no wish to disturb.
The forest had gone, the suburbs bleeding out. Besides, it
would remind her of Maxim, who'd loved to run wildly in
the cherry lane, in and out of the summer shadows.

The cinema had seen better days – the luminous fountain
had gone from the foyer, the orchestra pit too, and a false
ceiling hid the plasterwork above. Even the palm trees had
been neglected. She'd hoped to be alone and had paid ninety
kopeks extra to secure a seat on the balcony. Below, twenty
Moscovites sat smoking, drinking beer from paper cups. But
the balcony was empty except for Sofya and, six rows forward, a man with white hair, inexplicably reading a book by
torchlight, while to her left by thirty seats a couple sat in the
back row, entwined.

She had a small torch to illuminate the note attached to the
file from Yevgeny Zamyatin, the head of the research office.
She'd known the old man all her life and loved his soft, low
voice: her father had called him 'gravel-guts'. He was Uncle
Zheny to her, and always would be. He had lived, with his late
wife, above Sofya's childhood flat. The story, told by others,
was that he'd been trained as an agent but discovered that he
fainted at the sight of blood or the sound of a gun, and had
won banishment to the library in the Lubyanka's basement.

His prose was direct, and careful.

Note to Col. Shelepin re Agent 5H's request for intelligence on Dimitri Girev.

Sofya smiled in the shadows. Zheny knew she was Agent 5H, and she imagined the delight he must have enjoyed, a sense of superiority over the detested Shelepin.

Dimitri Girev was interviewed by the NKVD in 1930 at a safe house in Vladivostok. This is odd as the NKVD had a building by the dock, so this implies a second level of secrecy. The officer in charge of the interrogation was O. G. Irkutsk. His version of the arrest and interrogation is very different from Agent 5H's hypothesis – that Girev was seen as an Imperialist lackey. The fear, in fact, was that Girev was a revolutionary, not a reactionary, and he'd either acted alone, or conspired with others to sabotage Scott's expedition. Such action was not sanctioned by the Party and would have been a severe embarrassment if made public at that time. Irkutsk had witness statements to the effect that the subject had boasted about his exploits in the taverns and drinking dens of the Amur River in the years after the revolution. Girev claimed to have sabotaged motor sledges, and to have stolen food and supplies. He wished to be seen as a Hero of the Soviet Union. He had been happy to tell anyone who paid for vodka that he had gone south in 1912 to strike a blow against Great Britain, and their new Far East allies, the Japanese, who were sworn enemies of Russia, and indeed of the people of Shakalin, who had suffered a brutal Japanese invasion.

Under interrogation he insisted he was neither a Bolshevik nor a Kulak. He had gone south for the money, and for adventure, and because he trusted the British agent Cecil Meares (see File AM 677). Agent 5H outlines in her note the acts of sabotage inflicted on the polar party. Girev was unable to recount any details of the fire, the hiding of stores, or the puncturing of oil cans. It is quite clear he was not a dedicated saboteur – and neither was Meares.

The NKVD left him in a cell for three months. They thought he was a dangerous nuisance. Then they offered him a way out. Girev was proud of his homeland, the Amur River, and of the native tribe, the Nivkhi, who had taught him to run dogs. After his return from London he had, in part, picked up the life he had left behind. When he could he'd been back to Shakalin, where he was born (see certification attached, and for father). At this time Moscow was considering using military force to take back that part of the island lost to Japan. Girev was supremely equipped to attempt a reconnaissance mission on behalf of the Kremlin. He was released and landed by ship on Shakalin, at Alexandrovsk – the capital – in early 1930. This mission was disguised by his long spell in 'prison'.

He travelled alone, and partly in winter, a considerable achievement. It appears his time with Scott was not wasted. It took him four months to reach the southern tip of the island – a bleak spot, marked by a lighthouse. The Japanese town of Wasalki was nearby, and the strategic port facility. He made maps, observed troop numbers, then set off back to Alexandrovsk, and took a boat to Vladivostok. The intelligence gathered was rated as 'excellent' and despatched by ship to St Petersburg (File TX 8). But there seems to have been a final crisis of nerve at Vladivostok. Could they really trust Girev? Moscow's invasion plans (eventually shelved) relied entirely on the element of surprise. Girev had already shown himself to have a loose tongue.

When Girev was released winter had set in, but he secured a sledge in a caravan heading for Nikolaevsk, the main port on the Amur. The two fur traders in charge were NKVD agents. He was killed on the final leg of the journey, and his body delivered to the village. The story about the heart attack was agreed beforehand (Report – Agent Y785). There is no doubt he was innocent of trying to kill Scott or involved in any plot to do so.

I also attach police file 67/8870 – Kiev CP. I asked them to look at Omelchenko's death. There was a storm; he was running for cover with two fellow farmers. He was the last through a metal set of cattle gates when the lightning struck. There is a picture from the state morgue, also attached. The blackening of arm, left leg, indicates lethal shock. So, coincidence after all.

YZ

She left the crew of the *Potemkin* up in arms, and walked out into the blinding sunshine. She loved her country, but it was typically a Russian doll: layer inside layer inside layer. The metro had reeked of onions so she decided to walk back to the Lubyanka via the Alexander Gardens, stopping to buy a greasy parcel of *chebureki,* expertly allowing the fat to spurt harmlessly onto the grass from the triangular pastry as she took the first bite. She found a canteen for tea and vodka, and thought of Falcon sitting outside the VW, watching a college eight, smoking a cigarette, woven with dope, in pursuit of oblivion.

The Kremlin had nineteen towers in its walls, a fact instilled by her father, and learnt from lists – a feat of memory she bequeathed to Maxim. As children they'd walk here, along the bank of the river, past the south-facing towers, heading for Zaryadye and the funfair. They'd always been fascinated by two towers: the 'unnamed tower' and the 'second unnamed tower'. Maxim said that if he'd been the Tsar his first proclamation would have dealt with this deficiency. So this was their game – he must name the first unnamed tower, she the second. Each time they offered up new names. But Maxim's favourite for the first unnamed tower was the Fibonacci. Only that morning Sofya had seen the numbers of the mathematical sequence written on her brother's arm in blotchy ink: 0, 1, 1, 2, 3, 5, 8, 13, 21, 34. In his head Maxim dreamt of following the numbers to infinity. Her tower she called many things, but after her father's death within the walls she knew it only as the Korolev.

Threading her way through Kitay Gorod – with a brief rest at St Barbara's to say a prayer beneath the icing-pink dome – she found herself back in Dzerzhinsky Square at dusk.

The sun caught the roof of the Lubyanka, but the door she wanted was at the foot of a shadowy set of steps and marked 'Issledovatel'skiy otdel'. Most of the work here in the record office – trawling through files – was done for agents abroad, and communication was via the relevant embassy. But there was a front counter for internal enquiries and Zamyatin was at the desk, reading a single sheet of typed paper. He had one set of glasses on his nose, the other aloft, held in place by the folds of skin on his bald head.

'Sofi,' he said, taking her hands in his. 'The world lights up when you're here.' His soft rumbling voice seemed to embrace her.

'You look tired, Zhenya,' she said.

'Always truthful,' said Zamyatin. 'Maria will want to know your news. Is there still romance in England?'

Talking to Zhenya always reminded her of her lost father. 'There was,' she said, and burst into tears.

He came round to collect her and led her down a corridor to a set of doors that led into a small garden. At the designated break times the secretaries came here to smoke and gossip. Now it was empty, although the brown earth was scattered with filters and matches. They sat on a bench together and smoked. Zamyatin had read Sofya's diligent reports on Falcon Grey, the Englishman's attempt to decipher the mystery of Scott's death, and those of his companions. The character that emerged, of a man driven by the mistakes of the past – both in his past and that of others

– made him a poor candidate for the husband of his beloved Sofya. He tried not to rejoice at the tears.

'I miss your father too,' he said, hoping to suggest that her sadness stemmed from a wider sense of loss. He had been at the university with Sergei, and he had been her father's principal witness at his wedding. In the front room at the *dacha*, on the mantelpiece, there had been a framed photograph of Yevgeny, arm linked with her father's.

'You have emotions to spare,' she said. 'Can I take some away with me to England?'

'Cold people,' he said, holding her hand. 'When you come home finally all will be well. Until then write to me at Tretyakov Street – the old flat. You can be frank: the censor still thinks I'm at the old party compound in Okhotny. But I've moved back in with Maria. She's a dutiful daughter but a sad widow and I'm ready for retirement. I'll be honest – the food is better.'

Sofya held on to his hand. 'I was walking in the sunshine but Moscow is all past, no future.'

'Live today, child.'

'I have to sign the book,' she said, handing back the file on Girev.

'I'll do it later,' he said, waving away the red tape.

She cuffed his shoulder. 'No, Zhenya – no. Shelepin said you would be lazy – which means he's watching. Don't let them find an excuse to move you on – or out. It's cold in winter on the street. You won't see the spring.'

He struggled to his feet. 'They won't get rid of me. Comrade Andropov knows the files are useless. There is no system. Only here is the key, in an old man's head.'

He came back with the book and she signed the file back into the archive.

'Andropov sees Brezhnev,' he said, whispering. 'They drink together at seven in the morning – before sunrise in winter.

They say the old man's had a stroke and that Andropov makes the decisions. That he'll take his place.'

He couldn't resist probing further on the issue of romance. 'And Dr Grey?' He gave her a sideways look and she flamed into a blush. 'Do you think he will find the icy saboteurs?'

'I must trust so, Zhenya. It is the only hope for us.'

31

20 July 1969

Falcon had bought the Sony TV-8-301 second-hand from a lab technician at the Scott Polar for twelve pounds and a set of Beatles LPs he didn't listen to any more. He'd connected it to the double car battery array he'd rigged up under the VW. The result was a picture, nine inches by seven, that pulsated, revolved, and was periodically riven by what looked like electronic fits – zigzag lines, buzzing. He'd set it up on the rim of the camper van's open sliding door, facing out, positioning the aerial on the wooden rack of the roof. When interference was very bad he got on the roof and transferred it to a branch of the overhanging Scots Pine. So he could sit outside, and later, if the cloud cover broke, he'd be able to watch a man walking on the moon, see the actual moon, and the Sea of Tranquillity.

The Sea of Crises – designated landing site for Luna 15 – would also be visible, but the Soviet probe was still orbiting the moon, awaiting its own moment in history the following day. Sofya had flown into Manchester a week earlier and gone straight to Jodrell Bank with the Russian delegation. A postcard promised a telephone call at precisely six p.m. tomorrow, an hour after the Luna landing, from their designated telephone box: they'd used it before when Sofya had had to spend a week in Oxford for a conference with Valentinov. It stood opposite the Green Dragon at Chesterton, out on the riverbank where an old iron bridge spanned the Cam.

He had no idea what the future held, but she'd sent two further postcards, reiterating the time and place for the call.

So he knew something secret was being hidden. Perhaps the Kremlin planned another coup to steal NASA's limelight.

Falcon carefully threaded some dope into his roll-up. It had been a bad week: Oates's boots were not to be found, there was no trace of the centre punch, and he suspected that von Braun might not prove the enthusiastic advocate he had hoped at NASA.

He filled his lungs and felt better: the fate of Apollo 11 – even now poised in orbit above the moon's surface – would engage his mind for ten priceless hours, a diversion from archives and artefacts. And there had been one good piece of news: Lady Strood reported that Oriana and her associates had left the house off Jesus Lane, under cover of darkness, despite the rent being paid a month in advance. They'd taken the train to London and disappeared in three directions into the crowds on the Tube.

Falcon dozed off but woke to the sound of the city's bells marking six o'clock. On the TV James Burke was holding a model of the command module in one hand, the lunar module in the other, slowly moving them apart.

'At this moment Collins, in Columbus, is two hundred miles above the lunar surface looking out at Eagle as she pirouettes – that's actually the technical term – so that he can check the landing gear is down, and everything is shipshape. And it is a ship, further from port than any other in the history of man.'

Falcon reheated some Vesta curry over the camping stove and was scraping the plate, the sunset overhead spiralling through the branches of the pines, when a car trundled down the track. It was a Chevrolet, electric blue, and it stopped when the pot-holes were bad. A man got out, straightening a smart suit, which reminded him of poor Parkis, delivering Cherry's bequest in a thunderstorm.

It was bad timing. The TV was reporting that Eagle's long descent to the surface of the moon had begun.

A brisk military stride – very unlike Parkis's long-limbed ease – brought the stranger to Falcon's pitch. He had fair hair, and a face that didn't tell Falcon much – like the Action Man toy that kids loved. Bland, generic, honed.

'Dr Grey – sorry to track you down, sir. Eugene Schmidt, lieutenant colonel, sir. Pentagon.'

They shook hands and Falcon fussed, opening up a camping chair.

The Sony crackled, a voice from Houston announcing Eagle's progress.

Schmidt took in the TV, and the crate of beer, then checked his watch. 'I'm just a messenger, sir. A lot of which is tedious. It won't sound any different in an hour's time – you happy to wait?'

'Call me Falcon,' he said, raising his beer bottle. 'You're welcome to stay.'

'Gene.'

He'd started smoking so Falcon offered him a beer, which he downed smartly. 'Help yourself to more,' said Falcon. 'After all, it's really your big night.'

'I guess,' said Schmidt.

They listened to the audio feed as Eagle flew lower. Falcon felt that the measured tones of the astronauts increased the tension, as if they were hiding some lethal reality. Schmidt didn't help, now pacing up and down.

Finally, there was just the sound of Aldrin reading out numbers in a rhythmic series. One of the anchors announced that the estimated TV audience listening was 600 million. It struck Falcon that Cherry would have been amazed to find the final act of an expedition of discovery was a public event.

'That's speed and height – Buzz is just looking at the instruments,' said Schmidt, kneeling on the grass in his suit. 'The computer's flying the Eagle – but Neil's in charge, he's the pilot, looking out the window.'

'You're a pilot?' asked Falcon, eyes on the Sony's scintillating picture.

'Was. Aircraft carriers. Vietnam. Now I've got a desk. My job's liaison with Houston – the crews. I'm over to brief at the Mullard and Jodrell Bank but they gave me an extra detail.' He shrugged. 'Can't complain. Best seat in the house, right?'

He had a watch – metallic, complex, and he couldn't stop checking it, shaking his wrist as if that would give him the numbers he wanted to read.

Aldrin's voice was like a metronome now: '160 feet . . . 120 feet . . . 100 feet . . .'

'There!' said Falcon, pointing east where he knew it would be – the moon rising, dusk gathering, caught between the black cloud cover and the silhouette of the city, its spires and towers.

The open line to the moon was full of static, and Aldrin had stopped reading the numbers.

Schmidt was holding the beer bottle an inch from his lips, mouth open, lips moving. Falcon felt suddenly sick, as if in freefall, because he'd realised that the American was praying.

'Contact light!' said Aldrin.

Schmidt was on his feet, looking at the watch. 'It isn't over yet – contact light means one of the probes hanging from a footpad has touched down – they're still flying. I'm no flight controller but I reckon they've got less than a minute of fuel left. They must have jumped a rock field, or a crater. Neil must have cut in over the computer.'

Falcon thought of the millions listening, trying to interpret the silence, which stretched out to breaking point.

'Houston.' It was Armstrong. 'Tranquillity Base here. Eagle has landed.'

Schmidt's head tipped forward, and Falcon felt tears on his face. There was something embedded in this moment that would change the world – but he had no idea what it was, only that he wished Cherry had been alive to see it.

Aldrin's voice next: 'Okay, engine stop. ACA – out of detent.'

Armstrong acknowledged: 'Out of detent. Auto.'

Aldrin continued: 'Mode control – both auto. Descent engine command override off. Engine arm – off. 413 is in.'

'That's all good,' said Schmidt.

Falcon had a stand-by crate of beer under the bunk so they toasted the crew.

'You've got a bunch of guys about to turn blue,' said Mission Control. 'We're breathing again. Thanks a lot.'

Across the river in Chesterton a firework rose a hundred feet and exploded over the rooftops. Briefly they heard car horns sounding.

For half an hour they talked about the space programme – the plans for Apollos 12, 13, 14, and onwards to 20. Walkabouts, and drive-abouts, and landings near the mountains, and in the deep craters.

The moonwalk and the historic first step were scheduled for the early hours of the morning.

Schmidt took off his tie, and Falcon thought his eyes looked glassy. 'I guess I should deliver my message,' he said.

'I've got good news, Dr Grey. The Pentagon's minded to fund eight flights over the Barrier in October, for the polar spring. Looks like you've got friends in the Senate, sir. The money goes to the Navy. We're happy to run your RES kit in-flight and provide you with the read-outs.'

Sofya had left behind a bottle of Russian champagne, so Falcon tied a length of string round the neck and went down to the river, settling it in the reeds at the water's edge. As he stood there in the dusk, watching the Cam slip by, he thought about Cherry's soul taking wing and, looking up, saw the sky darken with birds flocking north to the open water of the Fens.

When he got back Schmidt gave him the details on the US offer. The New Zealand government had agreed the flight paths, which criss-crossed their zone, and there were contingency plans to send in people on the ground if the RES came up with a fix. The aircraft available would depend on operations, but were likely to include Dakotas, Skymasters, and Hercules.

'The cost to us is nominal – maybe a hundred thousand dollars. We would expect to be informed of any data patterns via the British Antarctic Survey or the Foreign Office, whichever gets us in the frame fastest. And we'd like any updates on the kit – developments, improvements, operational notes. And we'd have to insist on a press blackout unless – or until – we have findings to publish. There'll be more meetings, paperwork.'

They listened to more from Houston – preparations for the moon walk, reaction from round the world.

'You gonna go, Doc?' said Schmidt.

'South? No. I'm a backroom boy,' he said, but Schmidt didn't look convinced, and Falcon thought how disappointed Cherry would have been if he'd heard the words.

Schmidt slept in his chair. He had a room at the University Arms, but he'd said he had jet-lag so he didn't really care, as long as Falcon woke him up in time for the main event. He might even sober up.

At two o'clock Falcon fetched the champagne and spent a moment staring at the blurry moon. Luna 15 was already in orbit, waiting to descend to the Sea of Crises.

A man walked past with a dog on the towpath. 'Amazing,' he said, looking up.

'Amazing,' said Falcon.

By the time Armstrong could be heard, breath labouring, opening the hatch, trying to get out of the Eagle at the top of the ladder, Falcon and Schmidt were standing up. The champagne was ready but they'd found a bottle of malt whisky in the interim.

They'd reached the stage of drunkenness in which sudden intimacies are shared.

'D'you ever give up on ambitions?' said Schmidt, swaying. 'I did – I was twenty-two and I missed out on switching into the NASA flight programme. So I knew it wouldn't happen. I wouldn't do what he's doing now . . . I was with my girl, my wife now. I cried. It sort of takes the light out of life for a bit. Then you find something else. I thought I'd win the Masters too – hell, that ain't gonna happen either. How about you? What do you want?'

It was a question about how he felt so he simply shook his head, laughing.

Schmidt was back on his knees: the broadcast was sound only, voices coming and going, static and echo, until suddenly Armstrong's voice crackled, then cleared, and then the picture from a fixed camera filled the tiny screen, a violently binary image of shadow and light, which meant nothing, then flipped on its side, and upside down.

Armstrong descended the ladder, and CBS added the caption: MAN ON THE MOON.

'There he is – a thirty-eight-year-old American standing on the moon,' said Walter Cronkite, the anchor.

'Nearly right,' said Schmidt. 'He's on the footpad. Now all he's got to do is take a step and say something – anything.'

Falcon wondered how Armstrong would have reacted if he'd seen someone else's flag flying at the spot – or if Luna 15 was within sight, its strange Kremlin-like bulbous shape casting a moving shadow, as its mechanical arm scooped up the precious dust. But he had what Scott had been denied: priority.

'This is one small step for man, one giant leap for mankind.'

'Wrong,' said Schmidt, laughing. 'Christ. Ask a scientist to deliver a line and that's what you get. It's *a* man Neil – *a* man. Let's hope Buzz does better.'

Falcon popped the cork and they sipped their champagne.

As Aldrin struggled down the ladder, Armstrong executed two-footed bunny jumps, using the zero gravity to hop about, positioning the camera on a tripod and preparing the flagpole.

Aldrin, finally standing on the footpad, appeared as a flimsy figure, cut out of a net curtain, the light streaming through.

'You can't broadcast the images direct – they're not compatible,' explained Schmidt. 'So they have to film the monitor and broadcast that. That's why they're all ghosts in the machine.'

Aldrin took his first step. There was a silence, and they could see him standing in the shadow of the Eagle, looking out at the moonscape.

'Magnificent desolation,' he said, and took the next step. It was like an echo coming down the years. Falcon held his breath expecting to hear Scott's voice as an echo.

By the time the astronauts took a call from the White House, Falcon had got the record player working. He missed Sofya, because this was a night to share for a lifetime, and now he was sharing it with a stranger.

There was a cutaway live picture of President Nixon at his desk, a white phone in his hand.

'Hello, Neil and Buzz. I'm talking to you by telephone from the Oval Room at the White House. And this certainly has to be the most historic telephone call ever made from the White House.'

'There was another speech you'll never hear,' said Schmidt. 'We had sight of it at Houston. It was ready in case they crashed or ran out of fuel and were stranded. One of the team had pulled a poem – a guy called Brooke? Cambridge, right?'

'Grantchester,' said Falcon. 'Back upriver three or four miles. There's a church. Brooke lived there a while before the Great War. He died in Greece – blood-poisoning, I think. He's buried out there.'

'Right, right,' said Schmidt, looking up at the moon, eyes closed. '"*For every human being who looks up at the moon in the nights to come will know that there is some corner of another world that is forever mankind.*" That's what he would have said. Thank God he didn't. I need my bed,' he added. 'I guess we shared that piece of history. I enjoyed it.'

He lit a fresh cigarette and pointed east, over the water meadows. 'Look – it's the dawn of a new age.' A flock of swans crossed a pink blush of dark sky.

Falcon thought he, too, would sleep for a few hours.

'Give me ten days and I'll sort out some dates,' said Schmidt, standing. 'We need to get you talking to the Sea-Bees – they're kind of . . .'

'I know. Construction Battalions – they do the heavy carrying for the US Navy.'

'Yup. And the building, and keeping the beakers alive.'

'Beakers?'

'Scientists. You'll need to meet the key people, work through the programme. We reckon the first flight will be October fifteenth – but it's all down to the meteorology people. They rule the roost.

'For now there's this.' He handed over an envelope. Falcon thought it was fitting that Scott's story was embalmed in diaries and letters, and that this new chapter brought its own paper trail.

'It's private – so I guess we'd like you to keep it that way. I'm kinda lost. I don't know what it says. But I came five thousand miles to hand it over, so there you go.' He gave a half-hearted salute and walked away.

By the fire-pit's flicker Falcon read the front of the envelope: Dr Falcon Grey.

The VW had a spotlight, so he took the camp chair and sat in the full glare.

It was a brief letter, handwritten in a crisp copperplate. The signature was a flourish: *Wernher von Braun.*

Dr Grey,

Gene will have told you the news. I wanted to say something else. You can take this note as a confession of sorts. I didn't want you to think that I'd pulled strings here to get your RES airborne as some kind of quid pro quo. It's not a gesture of redemption, Dr Grey. Far from it. You lost your family in the rocket attack – 24 November – launched from Hoodervard. I looked it up in my notebooks. I wasn't there – we'd been called to Berlin. I know you feel guilty about what happened in London, that somehow it was your fault. I don't feel guilty about that rocket attack – and this note is to say I'm sorry about that, that I don't feel the guilt. Perhaps I should. But I don't. I don't feel guilty about anything. This has served me well in life but I suspect it is a gift with diminishing returns. I sense the past is tracking me down. One day it will catch up. Then people will demand I feel guilt. But until then . . . I just wanted you to know that I pulled strings because the truth is important. I hope you find what you're searching for. They were brave men – but it was a prize unworthy of them. A dead-end. What did Scott say? 'God, this is an awful place.' It was the end of a journey, whereas we are witnessing the beginning of a greater one. The greatest journey. It began in the Mittelwerk, so I can't be sorry about that either. I wish I could, but I don't believe in innocence.

Best fortunes to you,

WvB

32

21 July 1969

Sofya sat at a picnic table outside the canteen, a wartime Nissen hut that reeked of cabbage and stewed tea. She felt, briefly, the relief of being excluded from the great drama playing out in the sky, above the clouds, on the surface of the moon. The TV screens in the old dormitory, converted to a press room, had shown the pictures all day, shadowy, box-like figures, executing their strange weightless jumps. In the early hours she'd listened to Armstrong's first step on her radio in her room in the old barrack hut by the gates, one of thirty rooms set aside for technical and admin staff. Valentinov was a guest of the Lovells, whisked away by car to a private house in Manchester. At least his absence spared Sofya the ritual manoeuvres of creeping down hotel corridors.

It was a day that would change everything. Man had stepped on the moon. But the world had changed already for Sofya Sarkisova. In her breast pocket she had the letter that had arrived that morning by courier with other documents from the Mullard. This one was postmarked MOSKVA, and carried Zemyatin's little address sticker, which would have allowed it to pass through the censors' office without being opened. But the letter within was from her sister-in-law, embroidered with doodles in crayon from her niece and nephew: a dragon breathing fire, a sad face, a present wrapped up with a bow. It was astonishing to think of the emotions the letter held: a kind of weightless joy, and an indelible sorrow. It was the combination that had made her cry in the toilet at the canteen, repairing her face in the mottled mirror, beside one of the teenage girls who'd been drafted in to run the typing pool for the press.

'Can I help?' the girl had asked.

'I'm happy,' she'd said, and that was certainly part of the truth.

Alone on the picnic bench she read again the key passage.

In what ways, sister – this you are, and have been to me, so, – sister, in what ways can I soften the blow? Evgeny, the kind nurse, called at the flat. He brought flowers, so I knew. When they went to Maxim's cell on the morning of 8 July he could not be roused for breakfast. This was unusual. A doctor was called. Maxim did not breathe, his body was cold. The medical examiner pronounced him dead at 9.09 a.m. I have the certificate. His heart failed. Evgeny sat with him, wonderful man, for two hours in case his soul left the body. Do not feel guilty. Set these two things on either side of a balance, as I have done. I told the children: Daddy suffers no more, Daddy has gone to Heaven. I rejoice, Sofya, that his life has ended. I miss him. This is all I can say. Evgeny promised they will inform us officially by letter after all the paperwork is done. He thinks the body is to be released to us for the funeral – possibly next week, or the one after. There will be an open casket. Zamyatin wishes to come, and he will write to you separately. I long to hold you, and so do the children.

So perhaps she was safe. Shelepin will think he holds all the cards, she reasoned, and that until the official letter arrives she will remain ignorant of Maxim's death and still be the creature of the KGB. But she is not trapped, she is free, although there is a last scene to play out. The grief she felt she set aside for another day, perhaps for all the other days that lay ahead. Vitoria's letter carried the essential detail: the body was released for burial, and there would be an open coffin. He was not beaten to death: there are no marks upon his skin. A natural death, a good death. An image came to her of Maxim climbing a tree at Oboldino. She pushed it aside, but the tears came again.

She smoked another cigarette, reassembling her face, then set out for Lab 5, a short walk that took her through the creeping shadow of the 'Great Dish', which hummed on its circular rails, inching its centre of focus across the heavens in search of Luna 15's frail electronic voice. While Armstrong and Aldrin enjoyed their last hours on the surface of the Sea of Tranquillity, circling over their heads, slightly lower with each orbit over the Sea of Crises, the probe was preparing its final descent. In the Control Room – off limits to Sofya – Valentinov would already be listening to the messages sent into space from Baikonur, electronic questions and commands, an interrogation demanding details of speed, temperature, height, each prompting whispered responses from the probe.

Sofya climbed the stairs, past the closed doors of the Control Room, to Lab 5 where she took her seat. She took notes by the sound feed, listening especially for the calm, almost sleepy intonation of Lovell, who had begun already a languid countdown to the moment Luna would enter the final stage of her descent. Beside Sofya her tape-recorder turned its reel, her witness to history – or disaster.

Valentinov appeared at the door, cigarette smoke leaking from a cupped hand. 'The signals are strong. Is there any point in assuring the embassy?'

His attempts to disguise his nerves were futile. The chances that the robot probe would successfully collect its moon dust, and return to earth, were calculated at one in five. The plan was set: if – when – disaster struck, the British had a car waiting to whisk him away, ostensibly to the embassy in London, but in reality to the designated safe house. So, failure signalled a new life. Success, on the other hand, presented a choice: to return as a hero, or defect and take his glittering reputation to Cambridge.

'Come and see,' said Valentinov.

They went down the short flight of metal steps. The Control Room doors were open now, a gaggle of technicians on the threshold. It looked like the lair of a mad scientist from the latest James Bond movie. The horseshoe control desk, the wide window, the curved bank of computers spewing out ticker-tape comprised the perfect stage props for a super-villain. Outside, the Great Dish obscured the sky, as if they were under a vast steel roof of curved girders.

Lovell, grey-haired, distracted, sat at the desk talking to two other British scientists while Valentinov, leaving Sofya at the doors, stood at the observation window, head craned up, as if he could see Luna 15, tumbling towards the surface of the moon. The NASA team had briefly decamped to one of Jodrell Bank's smaller telescopes where they were able to listen to Lovell's 'broadcast' at a discreet distance. For them the Great Dish would come into its own as Apollo circled the earth, when it was perfectly placed to pick up signals from overhead.

The PA system crackled, and they heard Lovell's voice: 'Gentlemen – we have contact with Luna.'

They heard a high-pitched whine, oscillating.

Sofya stepped quickly back up the steel steps to her desk.

On the open line from the Control Room she heard Lovell's slightly laboured breath over the PA system: 'The probe has completed fifty-two orbits and has begun final descent.'

'I wonder if Armstrong and Aldrin can see it?' It was Pritchard, the voice brittle and excited. She'd been on site only for two weeks but already she could distinguish the principal players.

Lovell's voice again: 'The retro rocket was fired at fifteen forty-seven UT – on schedule. Professor Valentinov is here with us and is quietly confident. I think I can say that.'

The whining oscillation began to shorten.

'This is very exciting,' said a third voice – it was Fordham, the expert on solar wind. Sofya imagined a pipe being puffed. Thousands of binary radio messages were now bouncing between the Great Dish and the tiny probe nearly a quarter of a million miles away. The pitch rose, and she saw in her mind's eye the spacecraft's shadow, sliding over craters at the foot of the mountains that circled the Sea of Crises – from the summit of which it might be possible to see Tranquillity Base, and its two bunny-jumping inhabitants, out for their last moonwalk.

The signal stopped. Everyone froze, interrogating the silence.

Thinking back, she registered the moment with a three-second imaginary vision: the probe crossing the lunar sky, a streak of silver instantly complete, from its eastern beginning to its western end, where it struck the ramparts of a mountain range, the peaks miles high, razor-toothed, colossal on this miniature world. She even saw the crater made by its impact, smoke hanging vertically above, the pieces of metal debris still in flight, arcing miles to settle in the cloying dust, a few propelled back into orbit – the probe replaced by its own disaggregated self.

The silence was breathless, until Sofya heard the fluid, nervous cough of Valentinov, and the whirring of the computers, hungry for data.

'Transmission has stopped,' said Lovell. 'I'll wait one minute, gentlemen, in case we have a glitch.'

But Sofya knew the science. Silence was disaster. Jodrell Bank could hear Armstrong chatting to Aldrin: it had to hear an accelerating spacecraft emitting radio signals at high velocity.

'Yes. I'm sorry,' said Lovell. He might have been a kindly doctor at the bedside of a child.

'Very dramatic. The probe ceased broadcasting four minutes after de-orbit at a calculated altitude of one point nine miles. Given the terrain, we have to perhaps wonder if it did not crash into a mountainside. I have impact coordinates of 17 degrees north, 60 degrees east, in Mare Crisium. The Sea of Crises indeed.'

He coughed, and Sofya thought he might regret the remark.

'Just to settle the nerves of our American observers, the crash site is 344 miles north-northwest of Tranquillity Base – in a direction, precisely, of 328 degrees.'

Valentinov appeared at the door. He had both hands in the pockets of his white lab coat, and Sofya knew him well enough to guess that they might be shaking. The die was cast: he could return to Moscow and face a series of ritual demotions – possibly even a spell in the camps – or go with the British and face exile.

'Ring the embassy, please, Dr Sarkisova. I will report in person to Moscow from London, after picking up relevant papers from the Mullard. There's no point in delaying our departure. Your data should be radioed to Baikonur when ready. We have learnt much. Ask them to send the car.' He checked his watch. 'We'll leave in an hour.'

This was a speech agreed beforehand with Sofya and made for all those who could overhear. She made the call to the London embassy – correct in all its parts except for the request of a car. The call for the car she made from a payphone in the makeshift press room to a prearranged London number: Tudor 1592. A Century House operative took the call. She delivered a single phrase: 'Comrade Valentinov wishes to leave.'

33

By the time Sofya had taken a summary of the relevant data to the radio room, fetched her (already packed) suitcase from the barrack hut, and offered formal thanks to her British counterparts, Valentinov was outside, putting a suitcase into the boot of the car, Lovell hovering, a hand on the Russian's shoulder by way of commiseration. A gaggle of NASA men stood in a group, smoking, eyes down, eager to get back to the Control Room for Eagle's lift-off, the first critical stage of her journey home. The car was black, slightly dusty, with the usual suited flunkey behind the wheel. Not a Zil, certainly, but exactly the kind of car Kensington Gardens would have sent for a senior scientist.

Sofya had her own small suitcase, which the flunkey took, opening the front door for her, indicating to all those watching that she was a servant too. Valentinov sat in the back, a briefcase already open, studying the computer numbers on a printout. He even manufactured a grim smile for Lovell, with a tilt of the head.

The driver had the radio on the BBC Home Service, so they listened to the news at five o'clock. Apollo still led, with reaction from around the world, then – briefly – the mundane: fighting between Catholics and Protestants on the streets of Belfast, calls from Washington for a ceasefire, then, finally, the crash landing of Luna 15. The Kremlin statement said the mission had explored new ground in placing a probe in orbit around the moon and that Luna 16 was already on its pad for launch at Baikonur. The Soviet Union wished Apollo well, but the next Luna probe would return with moon dust. The one after that would release a robot to wander the surface.

At the gatehouse the barrier bounced up with an almost joyful ease.

Valentinov drank from a hip-flask, and Sofya caught the edge of grain vodka on the stagnant air in the car. The journey took them through industrial suburbs, past dilapidated mills and factories, then up into the high moors – hessian brown, with streams stained peaty black, past an old millstone set by the road, the message chiselled: THE HIGH PEAK. The 'cottage' turned out to be a manor house, slightly gone to seed, set about half a mile from a village. It was in crumbling red brick, with ornate chimney stacks. Moorland rose from the back gardens, up to a treeless horizon. There was no visible security, and one of the iron gates at the foot of the drive hung off its hinges.

The debrief took place in the kitchen. An MI6 operative called 'Charles' said they were at Bosley Manor, the nearby village was Bosley and they would stay for three days while relevant authorities in Russia – and London – were informed of the defections. The address was known only to six people, including Valentinov and Sofya. Two MI6 men would stay with them, one in the house, and one in a cottage they hadn't seen by the gates.

'Charles' had informed the letting agent he was organising a family reunion. He had assured him there would be no parties, and certainly no amplified music. The only noise, in fact, was the wind, which was constant, blowing down from the moors, and the bleating of sheep, unseen, but certainly a flock, which created a wave-like sound that waxed and waned. 'Charles', who had been at the house for three days, said the nights were completely silent except for owls and the alarming barking of deer.

Valentinov's room was upstairs. Sofya was given a self-contained flat in a barn at the rear. Their live-in guard – 'Peter'

– would cook dinner for eight o'clock. Sofya's room had tea and coffee, biscuits and a bottle of vodka, which she thought might be an English joke. Valentinov said he wished to study further the computer printouts. Sofya asked if she might walk – there was still light, and hours till food. 'Charles' said they should all act normally: it was the best way of avoiding gossip. He said the hall was often let to Manchester University for visiting academics so exotic accents were not unusual.

Sofya set out in a raincoat under a dramatic sky of blue and thunderclouds. The village was picture-postcard. Another millstone had been inscribed: BOSLEY. Beyond The Bull there was a small green and a single telephone box. She asked for ale in the pub and was given, to her annoyance, a half-pint. She took it outside and sat at a table chain-smoking. She'd come prepared: she had a packet of the new decimal 10p and 5p coins, and an Ordnance Survey map of the High Peak.

She got herself a fresh drink – stipulating a pint – set it on the table and strolled to the telephone box.

The number was direct to Aldonin's office. She imagined a bleak windowless basement room in the Russian ambassador's mansion.

'The address,' he said, without other preamble.

The village sign – wooden - stood on the green: BOSLEY. There were two more millstones and an artist's rendition of the manor house, in ceramic tiles, with the church in the background.

'Swythamley Hall,' said Sofya, spelling it twice, and adding the six-figure reference from the map. 'It's on the edge of the village of Danebridge. There's a large park around it, which holds the village church. Do you have it?'

'A moment,' said Aldonin, and she heard the tin rattle of his ashtray. 'Yes. The car is ready. They will be there in an hour, possibly two. Where will you wait?'

'There's a pub in the village.' Falcon had taught her to look for the magic three letters: *Inn.* 'I'll be outside. It's a fine evening.'

'Very well. Don't go back to the house.'

Sofya put down the receiver when the line went dead. Change chugged out of the phone, which for some reason made her laugh out loud.

34

At six o'clock precisely Falcon heard the phone ring inside the telephone box opposite The Green Dragon at Chesterton.

He took his pint with him, and wedged open the door with his knapsack, placing the glass on top of the coin box.

'Hi,' he said, knowing it was her. He almost told her then, because he'd been sitting with his pint for an hour, thinking about his life, and how he'd experienced each day at one remove, as if watching time pass behind a glass wall.

'I speak. There is little time,' she said.

But he knew her well enough to decode the voice. 'You're happy,' he said.

'Yes,' she said. 'I have a lot to say. I'm going to talk now, so you must just listen – I have ten pence coins.'

'Go ahead,' said Falcon. 'Then I'll talk. A florin can go a long way.'

'I say, in the Oates church, that I must report to the Luby-anka. The task that Moscow gave me was a simple one,' she said. 'Valentinov wished to defect. I must stop this. So there is a plan. We leave Jodrell Bank together for a safe house where the British wait. I must tell the KGB the address. They will take him back to Moscow, by force.

'I give them the wrong address, Falcon. I have betrayed my country. The British will keep him. I must go back to the house. I, too, must make a life with the British.'

The glass panes in the telephone box were murky and smeared, but he could still see the river, a white boat going past, a dog on the prow on lookout, life carrying on. The sky was brighter, all the riverbank colours vivid.

Then he thought about what she'd said and realised it couldn't be true. 'What about Maxim?'

'Maxim is dead. This is why I am happy, and guilty, and sad – the sadness for ever, the happiness now. His heart failed.'

'But you are free,' he said.

'Yes. Listen, Falcon. To find out what I had to find out I slept in Valentinov's bed. Can you forgive this?'

He didn't think it was fair to ask for an answer to this question so quickly, even though he'd struggled to contain his suspicions given the body-language at the Mullard party. He'd fooled himself that he was wrong.

'If I said yes, I might change my mind. I'll have to wait.'

'If it helps, I had no choice.'

'It helps.'

'Good. There is more. I spy on you too.'

'Yes, but when did you *start* spying on me?'

'Since the beginning. Three months before Cherry's letter.'

'At Jesus – that night. That was the start?'

'I came here to watch Valentinov. Your case is of little interest in Moscow – but I was here, and they wished to be told of any progress made. I followed, and saw you purchase the ticket for the concert, a ticket for one.'

The beeps began and their conversation was halted by the chug of the coin passing through the machine.

Which gave Falcon time to think: 'How did you know the letter existed – before the bequest was executed?'

'The British knew. They have watched and waited. What they know we know because we have people inside MI6 – yes? At Century House.'

Sofya pushed another 10p coin into the slot hoping to avoid the next round of beeps. 'I do not need to share a bed with you to find out what I need to know. I do not need to love you. I do not need to find the bug in the bedroom. This is so they cannot hear the truth, Falcon – the truth which is between us.

'Moscow is not interested in Scott. There is no money for your search for Scott. They know this. There are many suspects, but hardly any clues – and the best is lost, in what you say an "eternity of ice". In Moscow they have looked at the records. Girev is not your man. Nor is Omelchenko.

'Give it up, Falcon. This is what I think you seek: a lost cause. It takes up your life and distracts you from problems for which there are solutions. You cannot undo the past, Falcon.'

'You're right. Whitehall won't fund the search for the tent,' he said. 'But the Americans will. Von Braun pulled strings. We're to start planning the flight schedule in a month. I had it in mind simply to have the RES radiograms sent to the Scott Polar via the Navy's ice cutter – *Endurance*. It's in the Southern Ocean. If I can find something in the data the Kiwis will send out engineers to try to find the tent. That was the plan. I find it on paper, they find it in the ice. But I've changed my mind, Sof. They said I could go. So if they find it, I will. I'll go south. It's not a lost cause any more. I can find them, I know I can. But if I go, Sof, will you wait for me?'

TWO

SOUTH

35

Antarctica: twelve weeks later

The Chapel of the Snows was an old Jamesway – a semi-circular wood-framed hut with a stiff fabric overlay, plus a brick façade added to support a small bell-tower. It had six windows, three on either side of the 'nave', a corridor between collapsible chairs. There was a Virgin Mary in a blue dress, with an ice-white face. A lectern stood to one side with a pile of hymn books on it, the cover of the top one flipping back and forth in the breeze that came through the air-lock doors, which Falcon had wedged open because it was only 4°C outside: this was spring at the bottom of the world. The sunlight that streamed in was pale – maybe white gold was close, maybe ice-cream. Not white – that was almost the first thing he'd learnt: that nothing was white in the Great White. Everything was brilliantly coloured, haunted by rainbows. Even on the ice the spectrum was visible, out of the corner of the eye, as if each molecule of oxygen was a miniature kaleidoscope, wheel-like, and turning. It made the world different, this strange vibrating quality. It was not another place on the surface of the earth, but another place *other* than the earth. The air – everything he couldn't see – was more substantial than everything he could see.

He didn't fear madness any more, or his debilitating fits, because the claustrophobia of the Hercules, the long flight from the Falklands, and his tiny berth here in one of McMurdo's dormitories had given way to this overwhelming sense of space: the blue skies overhead, the frozen sea-ice of the Barrier, the air so clear he could see the curvature of the earth.

And so the fears had lifted, and he felt calm, but on a journey that ultimately led further south. And Cherry was there too, unseen, but thrillingly present. And Sofya: she'd remembered the mating rituals of the penguin, so he carried in his pocket a sea-worn pebble from the beach at Brancaster.

Falcon heard footsteps on ice and a man appeared in the blazing doorway, with a peaked US Navy cap, a quilted jacket, over-trousers, boots – the full McMurdo uniform. The continent's only town could have been anywhere east of the Rockies, west of the Appalachians, just a two-bit run-down collection of sheds and huts. The sign that said WELCOME TO MCMURDO could have said DEAD-WOOD, or LARAMIE. And there was a desert out there too, but it was a cold one, and the driest on earth.

The man's face was lined and weathered, and he looked of an age because his eyes seemed distant, milky, with cataracts. But the luxuriant black hair tufting out under the cap tried to tell another story, although Falcon suspected it was dyed. There was another contradiction in the wide-set cheekbones and the hooded eyes, which hinted of Arctic tribes – Cree or Eskimo. Falcon had the time for this appraisal because the visitor wedged the door further open, knelt at the back row, head up to the altar, with its gaudy Madonna, crossed himself, and stayed immobile for a minute, before hauling himself back upright.

He held out his right hand, two fingers stained yellow with nicotine. 'I'm Frank Maze,' he said, the voice furred up with alcohol and cigarettes. 'Back home I'm county sheriff, White Lake, North Dakota. Here I'm just a US marshal. I don't get no badge to show.' He flipped back the peak on his cap. 'I guess you're Dr Grey?'

'Falcon – please. Thanks for your help. For offering.'

'It's my job,' he said, fishing a mint out of his pocket and crushing it immediately between flexing jaws. 'Well. Let's think about that,' he added, rubbing the stubble on his chin.

'If what they've found out on the Barrier is what we think it is, it's my job. You should know Washington's ordered a news blackout on this – Auckland's on board, and London. All comms are monitored. Until we know what we've got we're not telling the world.'

Falcon nodded. 'Got it.' He'd already had a directive from Century House. Official Secrets yet again.

Maze took a chair. 'If there's evidence that a killing took place, we have a crime scene – even one that's moved fifty miles from its original location, and fifty years from the original date. So we need to administer the law. Question is, whose law? By rights this falls to Auckland. The Kiwis are doing the work out on the ice, so that's fair. But they're happy to stand back in terms of the investigation, if not the crime scene. The Antarctic Treaty's a flexible document. I'm sure we can all rub along. I'm wearing the badge for now, even if I ain't got one.'

They swung their chairs round so their backs were to the altar, looking out down the street through the open door. All the buildings – the berths where everyone slept, the sick bay, the bars, the stores, even the Chapel of the Snows – were just façades, tacked on to metal or brick boxes.

'You feel at home here? It snows, right, in North Dakota?' asked Falcon.

Then Falcon found out why Maze had left the door open. A dog came in, vaguely German Shepherd, but nobler, rangier, with a fawn coat that tended to mahogany at the snout. It walked up to Maze and threw itself down, a mess of legs and paws.

'This is Aput,' said Maze. 'She travels with me.'

'So, snow back home?' prompted Falcon.

'Yeah. You said it. Back home we get minus twenty-five, worse. But when it snows at home it snows – five feet in a day. Here it just blows up off the ground mostly.' He popped another mint. 'I was a sheriff on an Indian reservation – met my wife, settled down. The Native American – he's at home anywhere, because home is where the heart is, right? They wander in the world between the land and the sky – that's what she said. The destination doesn't matter – it's the moving. I'm a half-breed. I know. Well, I know half of nothing.

'Out in the boondocks we're mixed up with the Germans, or Norwegians, or Russians or Irish. I'll be half of one of those. They wander too – but they're looking for something, that's the difference. And then they think they've found it and build a home. I built a home. And the woman stopped wandering – for a while.'

The whole time he'd been talking he'd been looking out at the sky.

Falcon had noticed since his arrival two days earlier that this was the pattern at McMurdo. That mostly people talked about nothing – the weather, the food, the light. But if you hung around for a while they'd suddenly give you a chunk of their lives, a narrative, which almost always hid an explanation to the unasked question: 'Why are you here?'

Maze leant over to a window ledge and took down a small tin ashtray. Falcon knew then that this was one of his places, that he came here and sat by the door, looking out. That was another thing he'd spotted. That everywhere you went people had set up the world around them so they could just sit and look, when they had the time, sit and let the light flood in through the eyes, as if they were charging a battery ready for winter.

The ashtray must have been a comfort because he didn't produce a cigarette.

The silence threatened to become permanent.

Falcon felt he should talk. 'So you've got a police station, a cell. What do they call it? A brig? Anyone in there today?'

He shook his head, taking off his cap, so that the hair spilt out. Falcon knew then that it wasn't dyed, but a gift from a wandering tribe.

'Few years ago one of the Russians at Vostok killed a beaker. Motive? He lost a chess game. We hear Moscow's banned chess. Otherwise, it's a few drunken fights. There's nothing worth stealing and you ain't got a chance of getting it out. So, no. Brig's empty. But it's there. I've never put anyone in it – but a few people have begged to be locked up. That's the winter – it presses against the eyes. Some people can't take it.'

Falcon didn't want to think about winter. His fears of the south had retreated because of the light. Eternal darkness was a place he wouldn't go, although he accepted it would come to him one day.

Maze had dropped his cap on the floor, and he seemed to notice it for the first time. 'See this? This was mine a lifetime ago.'

The cap had a military badge, and an insignia on the peak.

'I was US Navy – a marshal then too. The war. Locking kids up who ran away. Making sure they were back at the dock in time to sail.'

'Sounds like a quiet war,' said Falcon, offering a roll-up, which was turned down.

'Should have been. Dock was Pearl Harbor.'

Maze laughed, but not with his eyes. 'Falcon? That's a name – you could be off the reservation too. *Kiggavik.*'

'It was Scott's middle name, his godfather's surname.' Falcon drew heavily on the roll-up, wishing he could thread some dope through it. 'You get over Pearl Harbor – or is the memory still there?'

'Still there.'

Falcon thought of a few frames of film, a battleship turning turtle, the black dots of the men running across the hull. It always amazed him that people who had survived such horrors could be so still. The dog took her temper from the owner, lying on her side, eyelids fluttering with a soft dream.

Falcon smoked for a few moments in silence, out of which emerged the tinny high notes of a Motown classic played on

the base radio station. Every building had a PA system, save
the chapel, and some of the telegraph poles, which held aloft
a cat's cradle of wires and pipes, carried loudspeakers.

'You're lucky it's spring,' said Maze. 'I over-wintered –
that's great fun for about ten minutes. Then you start looking
at your watch. The Indians think everything's got a life, right?
That chair, that telegraph pole, the Madonna. But only in the
light. Light goes, nothing's got a life. That's true on a level.'

Maze put the unused ashtray back on the window ledge,
and Falcon knew then he'd imagined smoking a cigarette.

'Down to business – right?' Maze took out a notebook, held
shut with an elastic band. 'We've got clearance from Washington to fly you out on the ice. Take a bow, Mr Big Shot.'

Falcon nodded. His line of 'lobster pots' had shown up on
the RES printouts drifting east of the traverse to the Pole.
The clearest image was One Ton. Precisely eleven miles
away there was a blemish – a fingerprint – where the tent
should have been, now about 110 miles north-east of the
Chapel of the Snows.

'The Kiwis sent three weasels – snowcats – out last week,'
said Maze. 'The radio link's intermittent but they've got
down to the target and they report a pyramid tent, with green
vent flaps. That's it, right? I got Scott's story at school – but
I don't remember much about anything. Five fatalities?'

'Three. Scott, Wilson and Bowers. One walked a few days
before the final pitch. He was holding the rest up and they
wouldn't leave him behind. He was called Oates – Lawrence
Oates. They'd lost another way back at the mountains, at the
foot of the glacier. So just three in the final tent.'

'The one who walked – close by, or miles back?'

'Twenty miles.'

Maze patted the dog gently between her triangular ears.
'Hear that? Work to do. I gotta get out there. I gotta get you
there, Dr Grey – sorry, Falcon. This is Antarctica so the

meteorology report rules. There's a window – three or four days tops – before the weather's done. First storm of summer is brewing. So we're going to fly you to the Pole first – they've got three Twin Otters with skis. There's a flight tomorrow, taking up gear. Then we'll hitch a lift down to the site en route for the Bay of Whales. It's a long way round but it takes three days from here on the traverse.'

'What's the traverse?'

'One day it'll be the road to the Pole. Right now it's six hundred miles short of finished so don't hold your breath. It's an ice road – but it's safe, mostly. It's surveyed regularly but you never know when a crevasse might open up under your front wheels.

'We fly tomorrow five a.m. – but, you know, weather changes, it could be a week, a month, next year. It's not worth anyone's life.'

They stood up and stepped outside into the golden light.

A shadow slid across the snow, right in their tracks, and Maze looked up. 'There's luck, Doc. An albatross.'

A flying cross, gliding, the white plumage a reminder again of Cherry's soul taking wing.

'Can I get to Scott's hut?' said Falcon, thinking he might find Cherry there, lying in his bunk, writing a letter home. The idea of meeting him again, the flesh and blood, made him realise what he'd lost.

According to his map the hut at Cape Evans was less than ten miles north.

'You gonna talk to the ghosts? I ain't kiddin',' added Maze, fitting the cap back on over the glossy hair 'Place is full of 'em. Kinda makes the air thicker – you'll see. Can't get there today and we fly first thing. On the way back, Doc. That's a promise.'

36

They set out together along Main Street, McMurdo, heading north, the dog ahead, scouting out the lie of the land. The 'town' spread out on a rough matrix of cinder roads: dorms and labs, the nuclear fuel plant, the post room, the conning tower for Willy Field out on the ice, the main block, the radio shack, a couple of bars. They went past EM, which was for Enlisted Men, and when the door opened they heard the clack of pool balls striking. It seemed like a minor miracle to Falcon that a game based on the nicely poised physics of a circular ball on a flat table could still work here, close to the point where the earth spun on its axis, the magnetic forces raging, criss-crossing, twisting.

They walked on, past the obligatory set of signposts for snapshots: London 10,040 miles; New York 11,800, Moscow 8,800, Christchurch – a hop – at 2,700. It made the place feel sadder, that the only real interest lay in knowing how far it was from home. And overall, Falcon thought, it was a mess – rutted snow, wonky telegraph poles, lines of vehicles parked up ready for the summer. It was mild and there were a few people about, mechanics checking vehicles, SeaBees building a new berth, a posse of beakers setting off to check instruments on the hillside. There was a small area of bare soil marked with a sign that read: McMurdo City Park.

But it was what lay *beyond* downtown McMurdo that took Falcon's eye.

They'd got to the edge of town, the dock to the east. Falcon had sensed it, even glimpsed it between the brutal huts and radio masts, but now, as it opened out before them, the scale of it made his eyes widen, trying to encompass a horizontal world. The clear air brought the distance to the eye – so there was this seeming contradiction of the vast sweep of it all but the sudden intimacy of the detail. It was as if he was in space, orbiting, looking down on the world.

The sun was up, but low, and surrounded by a 'dog' – a halo of gold. Across the water of the great sound lay the Western Mountains – a line of pyramids in blue and acid white, nearly two hundred miles distant, so that their rocky feet lay below the horizon, their tips dipping away towards the north. There was still sea-ice out in the bay, but it was breaking up, and an iceberg wallowed offshore. And in the mid-distance a vast tabular berg, like an aircraft carrier, was surrounded by breaking waves, dotted with penguins, crowds of them skittering, throwing themselves off white cliffs, then breaking the surface in effortless arcs of joy. He recalled Cherry's observation of them, like children, always hurrying to keep up with the rest. What he hadn't expected was the noise: the braying of a thousand donkeys, interlaced with other songs.

'That's Cape Evans,' said Maze, pointing east along the shore towards a low promontory of dark rock, beyond which the gentle slopes began to rise towards the peak of Mount Erebus, smoke drifting from the volcano's summit. Falcon thought it was odd that none of the diaries had ever thought of the cruel irony of Erebus. Even in the long winter when the cold froze the breath in the throat, they'd never considered the fiery depths so close, the simmering magma, and abundant heat.

'That's the Barne Glacier spilling in, right there,' said Maze, pointing out along the cape where a chaos of sugar cubes reached the sea. 'There's timing,' he said, as they saw the white sea splash of an ice block falling. 'That'll be the size of the Staten Island ferry.'

In the mid-distance a red supply ship was effortlessly cutting a black trail through the sea-ice. Closer in, at Willy Field, a Hercules stood on the ice, its cargo door open, attendant weasels trundling out the crates of food and supplies. At the ice dock, close in under the rock, two ships were unloading.

The dog stood perfectly still, nose to the wind.

The far horizon – which led to New Zealand – was razor sharp, broken slightly by a passing rhythmic swell of the Southern Ocean. Above it, embedded in some hazy clouds, there was a strange yellow light. He'd seen it when he'd got off the plane and been told it was 'blink' – a mirror image of the pack ice below reflected up from the sea, and within the light was a dark shadow, the echo of an island out beyond the sight of any human eye – a black fragment of granite reflected in a lemon sky.

'Take a closer look at Cape Evans. Here.'

He offered Falcon binoculars, but Falcon had Cherry's telescope in his pocket, so he took off his own glasses and fine-tuned the focus. It took him a minute to find the hut. He thought about the three years Cherry had spent in this landscape – winter and summer, the night and day of the south. Surrounded by space, but compressed into the hut, and then the tent, and then the ship. All this space felt to Falcon as if it was defined by absence – villages, cities, cars, trains, houses, roads. And not just the absence of material objects, but an absence of the complications of life. For Cherry, it had been family, estates, taxes, boredom, idleness.

Absence was magnificent escape.

Tracking back from the hut with the telescope he found the great cross on the hill above the base, erected to mark the deaths of Scott and his companions.

'Can we get up to the cross?' he asked.

'Ob Hill? Sure.'

Observation Hill was seven hundred feet up, and straight into the wind that blew down from the Pole, eight hundred and fifty miles south. The dog, head down, snaked through the scattered rocks. For the first time the cold made Falcon's lungs ache, and the effort of each footfall seemed to leave him dizzy with fatigue.

At the summit, doubled over, his breath sparked small detonations in the air, the moisture freezing instantly in a personal mist, which hung around his head. His entire skin seemed to breathe – in and out, in and out – coming to the rescue of his shredded lungs. A handful of snow was like crystal dust, dry and gritty, so he rubbed it on his face and felt his bloodstream course, rushing heat to his skin.

The cross – eight foot high – was as sturdy as the day it had been made. Their names were here: Scott, Wilson, Bowers, Oates and Evans, but not their bodies.

Maze, unprompted, read the inscription out loud: '*To strive, to seek, to find, and not to yield.*'

It struck Falcon that it must have been a mournful sight, as Scott's men finally set sail for home in the *Terra Nova*, to see this cross diminish, a symbol of failure, watching the land of their humiliation fade.

The cross seemed to demand a prayer. They stood together in silence for a minute.

'You know what I'm seeking,' said Falcon, finally. 'What about you?'

The wind buffeted, knocking them both back, so that they had to stagger to stay upright. For a moment Falcon thought Maze would decline the invitation, but the voice, when it came, sounded relieved, even lighter.

'Same thing I've always sought. I find bodies in snow,' he said. 'I'm half White Lake – that's a tribe, and a place. I grew up hunting, tracking, wandering in the snow. I know it, it knows me.'

He used the sleeve of his thermal jacket to wipe his broad nose. 'But mostly it's just reading the land, using your eyes. And there's a sense, like sonar, which can see below. The stories that go back say it's a skill, right, like divining. They had to find running water and in the high winter the ice lies over it, over the streams and the rivers, but they flow on, rushing to the sea. We can feel them, below our feet.'

He turned his back to the wind. Falcon thought the people of White Lake had invented their own version of RES.

'I look for the dead in winter. That was my job. Bismarck sometimes, 'cos the city's where people go to die, but mostly out in the boondocks. Some farmer goes out to check his wind turbine and never comes back. I find him in the brush, stiff and blue, off the path, blinded by snow. Then there's murder victims – they die in the city, or the town, and then the killer takes 'em for a ride into the back country. But it's never just a white plain. They always leave the body near a waymark – a water tower, a pylon, a duck shoot, a signpost. Deep down they want to go back – see? Go back and check the victim's still safely hidden.'

The lights had come on in McMurdo below. Falcon half expected a *DINER* sign to flash in neon, red and green.

'I'm here, down south, because I ran out of luck. My wife – she got cancer.'

'I'm sorry,' said Falcon. 'You don't have to tell me.'

Maze shook his head: 'She was at home those last few months, a bad winter, and me working local so I could keep an eye. I told her not to do it because it's a way with her people. But I knew she would. We call it the "long walk". You have to leave while you're alive – but you can't be found. So you need to be lost – alone, so there's no going back. One day I came home and she ain't in the house. The big coat's gone, and her boots, but she's left nothing for me – no note, no letter, just a venison pie in the oven cooking, filling the house up with the smell of it: the fatless meat, the butter in the pastry. That's the note right there: keep living.

'I follow her tracks, with Aput – out along the property, across the Henderson's road, by the old silo. They're crisp, and easy to see, because there's been no snow falling. She knows that o' course – that's another part of the note she didn't leave. You can follow for a while, but then you might as well go back for your dinner.'

Maze shook himself, tightening the fastening at his throat.

They started walking down, and it was only now, looking at his boots, that Falcon realised the light had gone, and his eyes had switched to night vision. The dog was a shadowy presence, only visible when she broke the horizon.

'Never did find her,' said Maze, over his shoulder. 'Tracks went into a copse of birch by the Riccal mine. Never came out. But she wasn't there. False trail somewhere I reckon, walking backwards, and I missed it. Dog lost the scent and then the snow came on – like she'd known it would.

'She got her heart's desire. She out-smarted us and avoided a grave, or the fire. She kinda haunted us after that – me and the dog. So we thought we'd come south for a new life. But it's just like the old one. We get a chance, we'll find your man Oates for you. That's another promise.'

37

South Pole

The trigger must have been the flight to the Pole, which made his ears ring for four hours, as they had done the day he'd stumbled out of Tapton's sweet shop. After landing on the gleaming iceway, he'd fled to his bunk: he couldn't sleep but the darkness came anyway, and he slipped into semi-consciousness. He was back then, climbing the stairs to the flat on Pepys Road, breathless, his heart erratic, desperate to tell them all he'd seen, which would have made it all right – because the images would have been shared, not his alone. The silence, the buried quiet in which he was embedded, was a trigger too. He stood before his parents' bed, and knew they'd left him behind, with their useless pale bodies. When he came to, he felt desolate, because he'd hoped the fits had abated at least, now that he was so close to finding the dead. Instead he sat up, breath ragged, drenched in sweat, pushing aside the idea of madness, the polar curse.

He was in R12, a single berth usually set aside for the AOIC – the assistant officer in charge. Around him 'Old Pole' slept, the entire base now below the snow that had accumulated in the thirteen years since it was opened, swallowed by the landscape it had sought to conquer. The base wasn't supposed to be below 'ground' – but the winds had begun their patient work from the first day. There was a map of Old Pole on the door of his berth: a warren of iced tunnels, sagging broken wooden roofs, and shattered girders. He'd been warned to ignore the sound of gunshots – that was just the metal bolts shearing under the pressure from above. They often found the shrapnel embedded in the ice that formed in the corridors, the crystals clinging together like delicate folds of coral reef.

'New Pole' was on the drawing board, but for now the old station had to function. There were two underground fuel dumps, and an emergency generator, all reached by tunnels. There were dormitories for the science staff and the Navy SeaBees, their mess room appearing on the subterranean signposts as the 'Taj Mahal'. There was a sick-bay, a library, a communications room, a rest room, stores and a galley, all in separate buried huts. In case of collapse, there were several wooden escape ladders leading up to the surface, each exit covered with a protective shed. Falcon had been struck again by the emerging Antarctic contradiction: unlimited space, then imprisonment.

Around him Old Pole shifted in its icy bed, like a ship's timbers, creaking under the pressure. The receding fit left him weak and shivering. He'd flown south in a C-130 Hercules. The belly of the aircraft had held stores, and two rows of fifteen seats crosswise. His only fellow passenger had been Maze – with Aput slumped in the side aisle. He hadn't seen a thing until they landed and dropped the back ramp, revealing a white desert, and a low sun tracking the horizon. The sense of dislocation, of entering an alien world, would have been no greater if he'd landed on Mars. Out by the conning tower he'd seen the Twin Otter, fitted with skis, that would fly them back down on to the Barrier the next day. It looked frail, gnat-like, compared to the vast silver cigar of the Hercules, straddling the iceway.

Desperate for his berth, aware a fit was circling, he'd still caught sight of the Pole – where Scott and his men had posed in weary depression on the day they'd found the Norwegian flags flying. It was oddly comical. It looked like the device beloved of fairgrounds that you were invited to hit with a hammer, sending a counter-balance skywards. It wasn't haunted – after all, no one had died at the spot. It was simply a dreadful place, barren, without note. The last place on earth. Falcon felt no aura at all – history, emotion, nature, nothing seemed to have left a mark.

His watch read 9.28 p.m. The single flashing light in the room must be a signal, but of what?

Then he heard a bell ring and a distant voice in the tunnel shout: 'Chow!'

Out in the corridor he zipped up his thermal jacket, his breath freezing, then turned left, past Fuel No. 1, then left again past the stores. A sign said, 'Club 90°' so he pushed open a chipboard door, walking into the fug of cigarette smoke. A dozen men were in the bar, two playing pool, others playing darts. A card school was crowded round a green baize table.

Maze was at the bar with a beer and a shot of vodka. Aput was at his heel, lost in thought.

'It's the real McCoy,' said Maze, tipping the glass back and forth. 'The Russians are over from Vostok. They always bring a crate of the stuff. It's the workers' paradise so they get the very best, because it doesn't give you a hangover. You can drink yourself numb, forget what a shithole you live in, then go to work the next day. Works in a tractor factory, works at an Antarctic base.'

Falcon didn't like the look of Maze. Alcohol usually works slowly, transforming the mood, the face, the eyes. But for some it's like a light-switch: on or off. Maze was on: he didn't meet Falcon's eyes, and he seemed preoccupied with his own thoughts. He ordered Falcon a beer and his own double round repeated.

'Don't worry,' he said. 'I'm an old soak. It's the Indian disease – anyone'll tell you that. Day the government pay-ments came through to White Lake the men were lying in the dirt by sundown. Middle of winter they had to drag 'em outta the snow – chuck 'em in a truck for town. But I'm half Indian. I'll be fine.'

Out at Willy Field, McMurdo's 'airport', waiting for the meteorology report to be confirmed before take-off, he'd told Falcon Aput's story: the Swedes in Minnesota had brought with them the gift, to teach dogs how to find bodies in the wilderness, under the lakes, under the snow, under the ice. Maze had used placenta from the hospital in Bismarck, and hip bones from the surgical team. On open water the dog could get the scent from half a mile. On snow, less, but not much. It had taken Maze three years, and the dog was still getting better at it, finding minuscule traces of molecules diluted in the chill air that blew from the poles.

Falcon's last question had gone unanswered, thanks to the roar of the engines released for take-off.

'What does Aput mean?'

Maze took a step closer now, the noise in the bar raucous. 'So – the Russians. You'll meet them for food. Don't tell 'em too much about why you're here. Let's just say we're using radar to look for traces of the *Terra Nova* expedition, Discovery, Nimrod. You're here to fly out to the foot of the Beardmore, Shambles Camp, that's our story. And whatever you do don't play chess.'

They sat in tubular metal chairs with orange cushions while the jukebox played Hendrix – 'All Along The Watchtower'. The walls were pine, varnished, and the bar itself looked like it had been picked out of a skip in Soho – curved, with a foot-rest. One wall was lined with a long radiator, pumping out the heat, which Falcon had to remind himself was the only thing between life and death. His life, his death. Above their heads there was ten feet of compacted snow, McMurdo was 850 miles away, civilisation lay another thousand miles beyond. In practical terms he'd be closer to home if he'd been sitting in the command module with the Apollo 12 astronauts, currently in earth orbit before setting out for the moon.

The Russians arrived – three of them – all beakers, so the welcome was polite at least. The music was too loud for any attempt at real conversation, and then they were challenged to a game of pool, which removed the necessity to try.

Dinner, in the galley, was burgers with fries and cold beer. The room was panelled in cheap pine, but the ice had broken through at one end, and in one corner, so that strange crystalline formations caught the neon light, which wavered, tracking the performance of the generator.

The station commander was out on the ice, visiting the base at Beardmore, so Maze took the chair at the head of the table. Folded cardboard signs introduced the guests:

Dr Igor Kapitsa
Dr Pyotr Tamm
Isaak Ginzburg

Soon the conversation turned to 'beaker-speak' so Falcon tuned out. Vostok was close to the South Magnetic Pole so there was an arcane discussion about the shifting mysteries of the electron.

It was Kapitsa, a white-haired geologist, who finally spoke to Falcon. 'Dr Grey, they bring a Britisher to see the fabled South Pole. You are in the footsteps of Scott – yes?'

'Sort of – more Cherry-Garrard. He's my hero.'

'Why?' There was laughter and Falcon felt, even now, the need to defend the short-sighted hero who'd walked away from One Ton.

'Long story. I grew up on his estate – near London. I lost my father in the war. Cherry stood in when he could.'

The Russians raised their glasses, while Maze watched him out of the tail of his eye.

Falcon picked at his French fries, wondering if he'd said too much.

Perhaps Kapitsa sensed the awkward moment: 'This is what they do not tell you: this is not the only Pole!' he said, thumping the table with his hand. 'If you ever come to Vostok we will show you the geomagnetic pole – and the Pole of Inaccessibility. This is the great goal. We plant the hammer and sickle there in 1958. There is still a statue of Lenin. We are very proud.'

Maze handed out more iced beers from a crate. A cook from the galley brought in the standard US dessert in Antarctica – ice cream and popcorn.

They were all laughing, but Falcon thought the atmosphere had cooled.

Tamm, a barrel-chested meteorologist, produced a bottle of vodka and a handful of small glasses from a voluminous quilted jacket. A speaker in one corner leaked tinny music, but in the short gap between tracks they heard an agonised groan, deep-seated, the note pulsing with its own rhythm.

'It's the ice, Doc,' said Maze, kindly. Falcon noted he was drinking Coke.

'There are currents, movements within the great crust,' said Tamm. 'We should enjoy ourselves while we can – one day this will rip the base in two. Vostok as well. We are a plaything, Doctor, of great forces.' His face grew dark, and then suddenly he smiled. 'To the Pole of Inaccessibility!' he shouted, and the Russians thundered their fists on the table.

'How is this calculated – this pole of yours?' asked Falcon.

'Carefully – with Soviet precision,' said Tamm.

'But there are several candidates,' said Maze. 'Depends on where you start – the coast? The edge of the ice sheets? The Antarctic islands? What, exactly, are you inaccessible from?'

Ginzburg, the electron chemist, tried to play peacemaker.

'Everything moves,' he said. 'Our geomagnetic pole wanders too – but not as far as the magnetic pole, which you would need a bicycle to follow, although it may be at sea by now. Even your South Pole here – yes? Or is it all of us who wander?'

Maze picked up his glass. 'To the wanderers.'

But Kapitsa was still staring at Falcon. 'We have a comms man at Vostok. We pick up what you call "the chat". This says your visit here, Dr Grey, is of great note. That out on the ice something has been found – something that was lost.'

'And what is it that I'm looking for?' asked Falcon, taking a fresh beer from Maze.

'I think the question, Dr Grey, is what have you found?'

'Nothing yet. We're trying out some new technology – RES, to search the top layer of the Barrier for artefacts, traces really, from the Golden Age. Scott maybe, but Shackleton too, Amundsen, Shirase, Mawson. I'll publish a report in the *Polar Record*, but it's just what we call small beer,' he added, swinging his bottle of Schlitz from side to side.

Kapitsa looked dubious. 'Then you must work quickly, Dr Grey. The first summer storm is coming – our data says thirty-six to forty-eight hours. A taster tonight, the early hours of tomorrow, but this is nothing to the real thing, which will follow. This will be like nothing you have seen. I am from Perm, Tamm is from Archangel. We have seen snow. But here the blizzards are more snow than air. It blocks the throat, the eyes. It will blow for three days – the sound has sent men mad. This is a lot to risk for small beer.'

Falcon just drank. Maze had zoned out, his eyes focused on a distant point. Falcon wondered if his new friend ever thought about taking the long walk himself, and if it would be snowing.

The PA system crackled and a disc-jockey voice made an announcement: 'It's a niner tonight. It might even get better.

Niner, with a ten on the cards. Use the supply tunnel and the ramp.'

Everyone was on their feet, so Falcon followed. The dog, barking, tried to round them all up.

'It's the aurora,' said Maze. 'These guys are nerds – aficionados. A niner is pretty rare – and once it starts who knows? The Holy Grail is within touching distance. Get your gear. See you up top,' he said, although his own enthusiasm seemed artificial.

Falcon set off through the tunnels to his berth, grabbed his snow suit, a balaclava, long mitts and a spotlight, and headed for the supply tunnel, the ramp leading him up into the night.

At the top the base cook was handing out Thermos flasks.

Falcon stood in line, looking at his boots, delaying the moment.

Armed with his hot drink he walked out, still keeping his eyes down. There was a crowd on the snow, and he heard a few people clapping, the clicking of cameras. He stopped, lit a cigarette, still looking at his footprints in the snow. Some colour was even now reflected in the ice crystals at his feet – an emerald green (not unlike a dragonfly), and a shimmering pink.

Then he brought his chin up, head back. The aurora – a faint glow – was the second most interesting object in the heavens, because across the sky stretched a great sequined belt, which had been twisted with a dark velvet thread, so that it was three-dimensional, not stars and nebulae against a sky, but hanging in the sky, a great circle – only half glimpsed – which divided the heavens like the rings of Saturn. Within the billions of points of light, dark shapes lurked, not voids, but solid clouds wrought in jet, obscuring what lay beyond. That day in New Cross, as the V2 sped towards him, he'd asked for a Milky Way, but he'd never really seen it until now.

He took a step back quickly, thinking he might fall over.

The Milky Way ruled the heavens, but the aurora had deceived him. At present it was merely a baby-pink mist, tinged with green, on the horizon, lighting the scene, lending it a night-club sheen.

Maze was at his shoulder. 'It's a cycle, right. This is just how it begins.'

Around them bristled the topside of the Amundsen – Scott Base, dominated by the balloon launch dome – a strange, Kremlinesque bauble, set beside the telescope in its own protective shell. Radio masts and other instruments broke the snowy plain, hinting at what lay beneath. There were two surface prefabs and several sheds, each signalling an emergency exit/entrance below. They looked like the wheelhouses of trawlers, slightly keeling over. The rest of the snowfield was strangely sculpted, echoing the buildings beneath. Twisted wind tunnels blown by the winter winds ran between ridges, cleared by the tractors that kept the supply tunnel open. The South Pole itself – the metal staff thirty foot high – seemed to shift and weave with the pink light, the encircling flags frozen stiff, hanging down. Beyond the station – about a hundred yards – the polar plateau began again, a blameless white sheet that ran into the night.

There was an audible sigh from the crowd of fifty onlookers as a series of crimson bars appeared in the sky just above the main radio mast. These fidgeted, as if shuffled by the hand of God. The colours – the pink and red – were at a low level in the atmosphere, according to one of the beakers who'd appeared to talk to Maze, at about eighty kilometres.

'They're just the warm-up act,' he said, checking a camera.

The red bars began to pulse with their own electric rhythm. Falcon felt again the giddy sensation that gravity had loosed its hold on his body, as if he was spinning with the planet around the axis, at the centre of all things. It was like the tumbling sensation he felt in bed after beer and a spliff. But instead of trying to stop the roll, he went with it, and somehow stayed on his feet. Aput sat beside him and leant heavily against his left leg, her eyes down, watching reflections come and go.

Then the main show came on, filling a third of the visible sky with a rippling green curtain. This pulsed, every few seconds, expanding to cover the visible world. Then it was a wall, with purple threads, edging across Falcon's line of sight, while above it lime-coloured bolts of light flew parallel with the horizon.

Falcon thought he should hear music, and at that precise moment the PA system kicked in with 'A Whiter Shade Of Pale'. There was darkness as well, shapes within the colours, and for disorienting moments he couldn't tell foreground from background. Opposite the shimmering green curtain a purple tent had appeared, as if the Pole had been covered with a galactic marquee, a silk inner lining hanging as a series of hammocks. Very bright green ghostlike figures flickered. The Milky Way was a shadow now.

Then it was all gone, the stars reasserted themselves, and it began again with the pink mist.

Maze appeared and gave him an icy glass with more vodka. 'The Russians are being friendly. Don't let it loosen your tongue. If they've heard the chat they'll think they know. But from day one we used a code on air. Mawson for Scott. Bay of Whales for Scott's tent. If they've picked it up they'll be none the wiser.'

'They'll know we're using a code,' said Falcon.

'I'm gonna see it from the Pole,' said Maze, setting off for the flags, the dog at his heels. 'Big day tomorrow. Food's hot at six. Get some sleep.'

Falcon set out towards the airstrip, where the Twin Otter stood ready on skis for the flight north. A frozen windsock hung loose from a mast. There was a small nest of buildings, a miniature airport, half immersed, and he had to pick a path along an alley to get out onto the iceway – a river of crystal, hard as glass.

Looking back, the silhouette of the base – masts, telescope, balloon housing, anemometers, fuel ventilators – resembled the superstructure of a ship, emerging from a frozen sea. Over this, limelight played, as if the Beatles, or the Rolling Stones, or Fairport Convention were hidden in the wings, waiting to come on to the roar of the crowd. The first red bars appeared in the sky so he looked up, aware only for a half-second of a movement behind him – the sudden 'thrump' of a footstep in snow.

A blackness came out of the coloured sky, and a slow sickly pain, which seeped across his skull. The feeling was hot, blinding, then ice-cold, as if a switch had been thrown. The white world went black.

38

When he came to he was, for a reason he could never understand, standing up.

He was leaning against one of the corrugated sheds. The aurora had faded away. His watch, the Roman numerals blurred and weaving, revealed he'd lost consciousness for two hours. The snow in the alleyway was pitted with footsteps, and a few dark dots. All colour had gone. It was a black-and-white world, a lunar surface. But he knew the dots were red from the pattern, as if a wounded animal had slunk by in search of its burrow. He took off his woollen hat and felt the back of his head: sticky, and sore, around a brutal bruise.

There was no doubt he'd been coshed with a weapon because the wound had a straight, ridged edge.

The moon had risen, and the surface of the snow, which had been a carapace of ice, was suddenly alive – slithering, flowing, the sound of tiny crystals moving with a gentle whisper. He looked at his boots and saw that both were obscured by the flowing tide of snow. He thought of Taffy Evans, terrified by snow snakes. And then the cold came, and he took a breath, and it froze his throat and he felt his windpipe close so he turned his back to the wind and breathed behind his hand.

What had the Russian said? A storm tonight, near dawn, a presage of winter.

When he looked down, the flowing crystals had reached his shin, and then his knee, and even as he thought, *I must get back*, it was at his waist and around his neck. And then the night was gone, and he was inside this sudden running blizzard. The wind sobbed once, and he heard the metallic whiplash as a radio mast flexed, and the clattering of boards, and the rolling percussion of debris colliding. One of the ceremonial flags – New Zealand – wrapped itself around his leg. Looking up, he could see through a thin film, like surgical gauze, to the Milky Way again, and then it, too, was gone.

A single gust and the storm vaulted to a gale and blew him down; a physical blow, which left his lungs empty.

He rolled over, burying his face in a crooked elbow.

Tiny pellets of snow got into his eyes, so he pressed them shut, but it filled his ears too, and when he went to breathe it clogged his teeth. For comfort he switched on his torch but the light was choked in its throat by the chaos of snowflakes. He thought then – a clear thought, not a shard of panic – that he was being buried alive. Snow had never held this fear for him before, that it could smother him, and that he'd die with an open mouth, trying to suck in air.

He started crawling forward, on hands and knees, although when the wind buffeted it lifted his body, so that his fingers seemed to rise up from the surface of the earth, as if he might be thrown into orbit, thrown off the spinning globe at its axis. The noise now was impenetrable, a wall of sound, like a jet turbine accelerating for take-off.

Every few minutes the storm would abate for just a few tumbling seconds.

Falcon sensed a weakness, so when the next silence came he stopped crawling and listened. The storm caught its breath and he heard in the sudden silence only snow crystals creeping, creating a high-pitched metallic buzz. But there was a bass note too, a *whirr*, the pitch of which was falling, as if a machine was running out of power. And then it was gone, leaving only a rhythmic, but erratic, banging of wood on wood, a universal sound: a door banging in the wind.

The hum began again, an instant acceleration as the wind returned. But he knew now where he was, because the power that drove the whirring machine was the wind. He'd seen a large anemometer on the roof of the meteorological station, each vane of the windmill carrying a brass cup. He felt panic – but hope too, because while the meteorology lab was largely underground he remembered from the map that it had an escape-hatch ladder, leading down from one of the small box-like huts, each with its own door. Here was hope, again, and he felt the sudden energy in his legs and arms.

He crawled on and at the next silence the sound was much nearer – and he could hear the squeak of the anemometer pole as it was blown south/north/east/west by the subsiding gale. The percussion of the door was less angry, desultory as the wind speed fell, but closer.

The storm was abating, but it might be hours until it blew out. At the next silence he got to his knees and, through the white streaming air, saw the hut, the door flapping, before it was lost again. The next fifteen feet took five minutes, but he went carefully because he'd stopped panicking, and the storm still punched, if the blows were uneven.

The idea that he was going to live led, for the first time in his life, to the need to tell someone, to pass on this news, to make a connection. There was a radio shack on the map of Old Pole near the galley. But it could only patch up a link to McMurdo – so he wouldn't be able to reach the Mullard.

But he could imagine the waxing-waning signal, and Sofya's patient, deadpan voice.

'I'm alive,' he'd say, and she'd be happy.

He reached the open door, stood holding its handle, and swung himself into the hut, using a double bolt to lock it. The enclosed silence, the instant warmth were hypnotic and, with exhaustion, he slumped, and a warm sensation of passing consciousness crept across his skull.

'Stay awake,' said a voice, and he remembered a line from *The Worst Journey*: that death would come dressed as sleep and would be welcome.

Below his feet was the escape hatch with its wooden handle, but he guessed the truth before he braced himself to lift it: the snow had blown in, the icy crystals had melted slightly in the rising heat from the shaft below and sealed the narrow join between hatch and shaft: it was frozen solid, shut.

He could have wept. He hadn't been angry very often in his life, but now the emotion was unleashed because he could hear Sofya's voice, but it was fading on the radio waves.

He heaved at the handle until he was dizzy. He thought it was stupid way to die. Locked out.

Then he remembered the Thermos flask in the lining pocket of his fleece. It was coffee laced with whisky, and it was still warm, so he simply poured it round the edge of the hatch and immediately put all his strength into hauling it up: for a second he thought he'd blown his only chance, and then there was a crystalline crack, and up it came, and with it the stale breath of life.

He was looking down a rough shaft, lined with pine planks, encasing a ladder, which led down to an icy tunnel. A thin wedge of lambent electric light fell across the floor below.

He climbed down and, for a minute, on his knees, let his heartbeat slow. Then he set off, still shaking badly but, with the map in his head, he found his berth. The plan was simple: he'd sit by the radiator, let his body heat recover, then report in at Maze's cabin in case his absence had prompted anyone to go aloft. But as soon as he opened the door to his room he could see he was too late: his clothes were scattered on the bunk, his books and papers on the floor in neat, reordered piles. His copy of the secret diary was gone, and a typed version of Oates's memoir.

39

The blow to his head was painful, and the long exposure to the snow and ice had left him with a kind of deep-rooted shudder, an Antarctic shiver, which seemed to go right through his body by working its way up his spine. The radiator was pumping out heat, and he sat with his back to it wrapped in a SeaBee's thermal blanket. He'd told Maze everything and been advised to get some sleep while the US marshal discussed the next move with the station commander – back from the Beardmore. Sleep had been intermittent at best. In a half-dream he was out on the ice again, the snow choking the throat of the torch. Out on the ice he'd thought he'd die here at the end of the world, and the half-life of that fear still made him feel pitifully weak. At the last he'd dreamt of walking the long path to Ayot but there was no sign of the Labradors, or Cherry, just a white gull overhead. The sun was up, but even he didn't have a shadow.

A sharp knock broke the spell, and his legs and arms shot straight, his nervous system still wired. It took him a minute to untangle his limbs, and remember where he was, and why. Maze's head appeared round the door. 'Sorry, an idea – it requires you putting on your kit and following me to the ramp. We may be able to track down our man. It's our best chance: The commander's agreed to lockdown till seven except for meteorology. We got the radio man up too – he's trying to get news through to McMurdo. We'll do a roll call in an hour. There should be sixty-three in the complement. The three Russians left the aurora party and headed straight for their trailer beyond the ice runway. We radioed: all present, and I spoke to each one. They saw nothing.'

Falcon dressed, struggling with the heavy-duty gear, wishing he was cradling a cup of coffee in the milk bar opposite the Scott Polar, watching the cyclists pass by, listening to the discs clattering into place in the jukebox. The comforts of civilisation seemed distant, almost out of reach. A minute later he was in the long corridor of ice that led to Fuel No. 2, following Maze's patient stride, Aput on the lead.

The US marshal paused at the foot of a ladder, resting one hand on a gun in its holster.

'Do we really need the gun?' asked Falcon.

'Depends,' said Maze. 'If our man clubbed you out on the ice to give himself time to search your room, maybe not. But if he put you down after searching the room, then that looks like he didn't want you to live, because of what he found in your room. You're alive – the god of this place doesn't hate you, after all. But that means it might be unfinished business, so I guess we don't take risks.'

They emerged into a diamond world: the sky pure swimming-pool blue, the ice spread underneath a field of mother-of-pearl. There was no movement in the dawn air: sounds occurred to the inner ear as if they were made in the outer. There were no echoes: the snowfall had lagged everything, so that no surface was reflective. The world was vast, but intimate.

The white horizon encircled them, like a collar. The various structures of Old Pole were dimly discernible – only the radio masts and the weather balloon tower punched out through the new snow. Even the Russians' tractor convoy, parked a half-mile out, was swathed in a sinuous drift.

Maze set off towards the distant hamlet that was the airstrip buildings, where Falcon had been attacked. 'Just follow my footsteps,' he said, the sound of his voice right there in Falcon's ear.

He watched Maze's careful strides. They didn't seem as confident any more – in fact, he looked arthritic, awkward and stiff. It occurred to Falcon that Maze had aged in the forty-eight hours he'd known him, as if the magnetic pole had somehow accelerated time.

'Show me where you came round after the attack,' said Maze, when they reached the snow-flecked huts.

Falcon found the place and even the trail of blood spots in the snow.

Maze closed his eyes and seemed to make a great effort to think. Falcon wondered if it was the altitude – they were 11,000 feet up, despite the flat plain, and he'd noticed last night that his own breath came short even before the storm.

'So, this is what we know,' said Maze. 'You were watching the aurora at about ten p.m. The night was clear. But a storm pulse came through at about twelve fifteen a.m. – which was when everyone was called down. You were just coming round at that point. The storm hit. So your assailant left footprints before the storm, which the storm then obliterated.'

Falcon nodded. 'It's bad luck,' he said.

Maze shrugged. 'Maybe. The sun's rising, so the surface of the snow is warming. The snow that fell in the footsteps is newer, less compact, and melts more easily. So the shadow of the print might show – especially if there's a line of them, a bit like your lobster pots. They'll be visible for half an hour – maximum. There's a small differential at this kind of temperature, but it won't last for long. Plus, it's too cold to pick up our man's scent – and, anyway, Aput's taught to ignore the living, which is inconvenient. She's only interested in the dead. And the human nose is a damn poor replacement.'

They both stood aside from the crime scene, allowing their shadows to stretch back to Old Pole. Maze had brought

coffee, so they sipped that, watching the snow, like expect-
ant photographers staring at a darkroom print.

Maze let the dog lean against his knee. 'I guess, as we're
waiting for the sun to do its job, you could tell me the truth.
What's the real story? I know Scott's a victim – but who are
our killers?' He lit a cigarette, waiting, his eyes skipping over
the snow.

The dog sat down, paws out to the front, like a sphinx,
listening.

Falcon told him everything: that at the time Scott thought
it was a German plot, or the Japanese, or the Russians. An
imperial assassination. So – outsiders, tracking them. But
Oates and Taffy Evans thought it was one of the returning parties, an inside job. But the insiders weren't all Brits
– there were Canadians, Norwegians, Russians. The secret
diary said the killers had sabotaged the depots, taking oil,
hiding food, burning gear. There's a clue, a symbol, a sign,
which Taffy Evans drew for Oates, and hid in his boot. A
sign of what? Who knows? Anarchists, Communists, Germans, a plot of some kind. Oates left his boots in the tent
when he walked out to his death. There was no trace of the
boot in any museum. It might be in the tent.

The whole story took ten minutes.

Maze didn't say a word, then knelt in the snow, looking
across the unblemished surface. 'There,' he said, his chin
almost on the ice. 'Footmarks leading away. Then filled in.
Heavy-duty boots – a long stride. See?'

Falcon saw a perfectly level carapace of snow.

'Put your chin in the snow,' said Maze.

Then he did see them, in the low rays of the dawn sun, a
series of grey depressions.

'Let's walk,' said Maze. 'Look, smell, listen,' he said, like
a mantra. 'Give me a fifty-yard start.' He handed over the
dog's lead.

For ten minutes they picked their way with infinite care across the white page of snow. The only sound was the crump of their boots.

Then, without a word, Maze stopped, knelt down, looked up at the sky.

There was something of a prayer about the scene. Falcon stopped too. Then Maze's head dropped, and his body slumped, like dead meat.

Falcon cried: 'Frank?'

Aput leapt, tearing the lead free from his hand.

By the time they reached him he was stretched out in the snow.

Falcon turned him over and saw the green tint to his skin, the blue lips. The dog barked, backing away.

Maze's eyes looked sunken, fading. 'Inside pocket. There's a pill box – blue. I need two. Fast.'

Falcon unzipped the thermal jacket and found the box.

'Water bottle on the other side,' said Maze.

'A minute – less. I'll be good,' he said, swallowing the pills, gulping the water. 'I should keep talking. If I stop, you go back, go to the sick bay, get the doc.'

'Tell me,' said Falcon.

'Heart. It misfires. I don't want surgery. Misjudgement today – I should have taken them, a precaution. I forgot it was morning. I won't miss again. It's the cold – the strain, the blood pumping round. Now you talk.'

He started breathing then, lifting his ribcage, the out-breath shuddering.

'I don't deal well with death, Frank. So I'll take that as a promise – that you'll swallow the pills. When I was six my parents sent me out to post a letter. A German rocket fell and they were dead when I got back. If I hadn't dawdled – wasted time – we'd have all been in the park, and they'd be alive, and I wouldn't be here, at the South Pole, trying to shuffle off the guilt. That's why I'm really here, Frank. How about you?'

The colour had flooded back into his face. 'I'm haunted. I can't face life. Not without Aput.'

The dog sat down at the sound of her name.

'Aput was my wife. It's Inuit for snow. I can't stop looking for her. I thought this was a smart idea, to go south, to the snow and the ice, and leave her spirit behind. That's what I thought. Thinking's overrated. I didn't leave her behind, Falcon. She's here.'

He rolled over and Falcon helped him onto his knees: 'There's no kids so when I take the long walk nobody has to follow. I'm not afraid of dying. I'm afraid of living indoors.'

'Me too.'

Falcon helped him onto his feet, taking his friend's weight, until the old man's limbs loosened.

They picked up the tracks and dogged them to the ice road that ran to the airfield. It was clear of snow, which had been blown from the glazed surface.

Maze, walking carefully, foot by foot, examined the snow on the far side. 'No prints here. He's used the ice as a fox uses the river. He's broken his trail. Maybe he circled back to the base. Otherwise, he's still out here.'

The Vostok convoy was parked a hundred yards out on the plateau, shrouded in its frozen wave of snow.

The dog yanked the lead, so Maze slipped the knot, and she began to zigzag down the ice road.

'There's something wrong,' he said. 'Stay here. I'll do this. Then we go back – I promise.'

He walked along the road, his boot spikes scratching, leaving parallel trails, the dog ahead, nose down, tail down.

Falcon watched, seeing them both diminish with distance. Maze stopped, held up his arm, beckoning, so Falcon jogged through the snow at the side of the road, avoiding the ice.

'Trail turns back,' said Maze. 'See? One of two things. Either he wanted us to think he was heading for the Russians' caravan, then doubled back, or he's lost. Maybe he got caught in the storm like you did.'

Maze walked off towards the base, then stopped, down on his knees again. 'He's crawling here. On all fours – on his belly. There . . . That has to be the blizzard and the wind.'

The dog ran in front keeping her head low, the posture urgent, focused. Falcon could hear Maze's breath, laboured, shuddering.

Ahead, one of the escape huts stood above the snowline, right on the perimeter, covered with glittering frost.

Falcon got the door open, the shock of what lay inside making him stagger back, falling in the snow. The dog went flat on the floor, the bark rhythmic. A man was half sitting, half standing in the narrow space. His head was encased in ice, as if he'd been suffocated with a plastic bag. Opening the door had disturbed the body, and they could hear the tiny glasslike sound of cracking ice on his clothes and skin. Cherry was wrong: death didn't always come disguised as sleep. His mouth was open, one hand was to his throat, as if that was what had killed him: the cold, choking off the air.

Maze carefully unzipped the quilted jacket and, cracking it open, revealed a badge: CE, and the notebooks Falcon recognised as those stolen from his berth. 'CE: construction electrician – he's US Navy, a SeaBee. So that's bad news. If they're the enemy we ain't got a chance.'

40

A few minutes after sunset the Twin Otter banked, tipping them sideways, so that the Barrier swung up into Falcon's view, stretching away towards the Western Mountains, bathed in watercolour pink, mauve and blue. The view encompassed a hundred square miles of pure air. Stars shone where the night rose. The dying sun was blood-red, liquid, molten, not so much sinking as dissolving into the ice. And within this panorama there lay an extraordinary object: a pit, man-made, mathematical, illuminated.

This was SWB, their destination: Scott, Wilson, Bowers. Silas Wright, who had been with those who found the dead, had said that day half a century before, 'It is the tent.' Now it was the grave, and it seemed to exert an extraordinary magnetism, as if drawing the aircraft down from the sky. A new pole perhaps, to add to the magnetic and the geodesic, where lines of emotion collide and can go no further.

The pilot's voice crackled: 'SWB to the starboard side. SWB. Beginning our descent to iceway Kiwi. This is Otter Six, Otter Six to SWB. Please activate landing lights. Activate landing lights.'

Falcon pressed his face to the window and saw the beacons begin to pulse one by one, three on each side of the iceway. A vehicle's blue hazard light blinked at the far end. But in the wide, darkening icescape the safety of the runway looked perilous, fragile, overwhelmed by the gathering night.

If Falcon had flown over the Barrier in the autumn of 1912 he'd have missed them: the last five, a speck that was the sledge, the long traces running forward to the bent figures of the men hauling, a trail behind, and to one side Bowers, perhaps, trying to get a fix from the sun with the sextant, or Scott, calculating, looking ahead, listening in the sudden silence between the winter winds for the sound of rescue. The sheer scale of such a world must have crushed them, as surely as the cold would kill them.

The iceway, rising to meet the Twin Otter, was a half-mile from the pit, which was the real beacon: square, precise, lit brightly within by floodlights. He thought it would be visible from space, an exact geometric feature, a shining symbol of logic and intelligence, a signal of mankind.

He felt the judder of the wing flaps, the sudden decelera-tion, the descent under way. Rigid in his seat Falcon closed his eyes. He wasn't so much scared of flying as scared of landing. It was the expectation, the hurtling face of earth, rising to meet the falling craft. He found a memory – com-forting and safe – an echo of what lay waiting for him out on the ice. He entered that past, and felt the present slipping away, confident for once that this would not lead back to New Cross, but to a joyous fragment of his former life.

The cinema, on Mill Road, Cambridge, was always known as the fleapit but Falcon had struggled to get across to Sofya that this was a term of ironic affection, not a literal descrip-tion. Throughout the short – a travel film about Venice – she'd kept her eyes on the gangway, keen to spot vermin on the move, having already draped her mac over the seat to avoid insect bites. She said she wasn't afraid, just vigilant. It was their third date, and it wasn't going well – especially the ice-cream, which came in a roll covered with paper and was tasteless, frozen solid. It was a matinee, and outside the streets of Cambridge lay compressed under a grey Fen sky, the river pitted with raindrops, the shadows already collecting dusk.

But *2001: A Space Odyssey* lifted the mood. When the screen widened to encompass earth, the orbiting space station, the floating serene spacecraft, Sofya squeezed his hand. This was her dream: benign space travel. And then there was a trip to the moon, to Luna, and the Clavius Base, then a hop to the great crater of Tycho, and a barren landscape – a dreadful place – where a mysterious object had been detected beneath the surface.

This was what he'd seen echoed on the Barrier: an angular man-made pit, a ramp down, lights set – but where the moon hung over the ice, earth had hung over Tycho's illuminated pit. The astronauts approached the lead-black monolith that had been revealed, and touched it, triggering the burst of radio waves, which alerted the galaxy to the ascent of man.

It was a message from the future: what lay here on the Barrier for Falcon was a message from the past.

The Twin Otter's skis touched the ice, the crystals rose, blocking out the view until they'd come to rest. Falcon's nervous system flooded with relief. In a minute he was on the ice, his first time on the Barrier, so he tried to pick up the wave-like flexing of the sea beneath – a world of darkness below his feet, teeming with blind life. Did it move? Every nerve in his body reached out to pick up data, so he felt a sense of light-headedness, which made him set his boots wider apart.

They watched the Twin Otter taxi from the refueling rig, turn and take off, fading with shocking speed. Clouds trailed across the last blemish of the sun, edged in crimson, the rest pulsing between yellow, orange and violet. It seemed that every crystal on the ground mirrored these colours, scintillating, a carpet of kaleidoscopes. Falcon cast the landscape in the role of a distant planet, a place that existed in its own dimension: after time and space, here was colour.

Once the 'fly-buzz' of the plane was gone a silence began to settle, heaving itself up from the hidden depths of the unseen ocean. The mechanical rush, which came and went in Falcon's ears, was his own bloodstream.

The base commander, a New Zealander in Day-Glo with an iced beard, was a forensic scientist from the University of Canterbury, at Christchurch, in the South Island. He had a sinewy handshake, which hardly hid the bones beneath the skin. His name was Dr Jack Finn, but they could call him 'Finn' as everybody else did.

He lit a roll-up and pointed out the camp's distant features.

SWB consisted of three 'long-house' tents – Jamesways – on aluminium frames, and a hundred yards away, a nest of berths, smaller tents for six, with little space other than for the sleeping-bags. There was a separate wooden hut for a generator, and beyond that a radio mast. Everything was spaced out to avoid a fire spreading. The pit lay beyond the long tents, lost to sight, although the strange bloodless glow of arc lamps was visible in the air, which held its own colour – rose now, but deepening by the minute, as the sun finally died, completing a sunset unlike any other Falcon had seen on what he now thought of as 'earth', which lay somewhere to the north.

Finn didn't waste any time with small-talk. 'Comms says Old Pole is locked down. What's up? What do I need to know?' Each word produced a plume of breath, instantly freezing.

Maze readjusted his US marshal's cap: 'You're safe – that's the call. Someone tried to kill Dr Grey, ended up dead himself, out on the ice when the storm struck. SeaBee called Jeff Ward, on his third tour. Home in Boston, wife and five kids, nothing in the file, but we've got everyone on the case back home – CIA, FBI, Boston City. Well, we will have once we've got a message through. The storm stirred the sky up so it's not easy – won't be for another forty-eight hours, maybe longer.

'Nothing from his buddies at Old Pole – liked a drink, ice hockey, dirty mags. My guess he's a loner. If he had a partner on base he wouldn't have been stranded outside the station. The escape hatches were frozen. Anyone trying to get out would have found that, and pushed up. They'd have got him in. But he froze to death, so I think we can all relax.'

Finn looked up at the sky and they all watched a shooting star flare.

Aput barked.

'But stay vigilant. Any issues with that?' asked Maze.

Finn shook his head. 'Going home's not an option, given the plane just left. So I guess we stay vigilant. Let's look at the map,' he said, leading them to one of two large caterpillar-tracked vehicles parked by the iceway. The cab had room for a chart table and six seats. There was a hand-drawn outline of the camp on a geodesic grid.

Finn had dropped his hood, to reveal surfer's dyed blond hair. Falcon thought he was thirty-five, but conceded he'd pass for ten years younger out in the waves.

The cab felt like civilisation, with its plush seats, heating, the oddly beguiling aroma of new plastic and metal. The dashboard would not have looked out of place in Apollo 11.

'This is my kind of place,' said Finn, relighting the ramshackle roll-up. 'I live on a beach but I climb mountains for real fun – Southern Alps. Miles of wilderness, no people, no land predators.' He pointed outside. 'Just like that, but smaller. Difference here is we're a hundred and two feet above sea level, and you could go in any direction a hundred miles and that wouldn't change more than six feet. Sometimes you can see for ever. Sometimes you can't see your feet. So don't go for a stroll on your own.

'Back home we get calls from Mountain Rescue – a dozen a year. We go up, find the deceased, do an autopsy in situ. Or we get them out – helicopter, skidoo, whatever it takes. Then we do an autopsy back at the university. I'm a pathologist with the Christchurch police – part-time. We get a murder a year, in a bad year.

'So this is familiar, but different. We're gonna do our best. A fresh storm's coming – and that means we'll have a period of bad weather. We might have to cover the pit, go back, wait for the next window. If we get closed down we might not see the plane again, so we'll have to take the cats back to McMurdo. We'll return – but it might be weeks, months. If it looks bad we might have to call it off for the year.'

Maze ruffled the dog's coat.

'We've been here a week,' said Finn. 'RES – good work, Doc – gave us a plot on the tent, then metal detectors narrowed it down to the pit. We have three bodies in a collapsed Cook tent – here.' He pressed a finger down on a crisp square at the centre of the map. 'We're trying to gently melt them out of the ice. Jamesway A is food, heat, a few chairs. Jamesway B is the morgue and it holds all the artefacts recovered. We're working round the clock so you'll find us in there – flat out, unless we're down in the pit. Jamesway C is gear for the excavation, pumps, diggers – so no right of way. Keep clear. Keep out.

'I got your note on Lawrence Oates. We'll try tomorrow. We've marked a trail south along your line of lobster pots, Doc. A geodesic curve – see . . .' On the map a line of dots swung across the barrier.

'We know precisely how far back they struck their last camp, and where Oates walked. The lobster-pot line is marked with beacons. I presume this is Aput?'

The dog, wedged in the gear pit, looked up at her name.

'Chances?' he asked Maze.

'If Oates's body is thirty foot down, then slim. Cadaver dogs have sniffed out ancient human remains in Iraq, Tibet, Mexico so that ain't a big deal. Problem is this place is inert – you'll have seen that when our three friends in the pit emerged from the ice. So that limits the gases released. Then there's the flat landscape, high winds. There's nowhere for a scent to linger, or impregnate itself in wood, or soil. It's a long shot on a good day.

'Having said that, she got a whiff of Jack Ward from a hundred yards and he hadn't been dead for five hours.'

Finn, nodded, patting Aput's head. 'OK. Let's get going . . .'

They jumped down onto the ice. Falcon felt his throat contract as he took a breath of refrigerated air.

'You're both in Berth Six,' said Finn. 'There's a bunk bed, not much else. Don't wander about – the pit's thirty foot deep and you won't bounce. For the record I've been sworn in as a special constable. I represent the full majesty of the state. Which just means what I say goes. Anybody got a gun?' he said, zipping up his thermal jacket.

Maze slowly raised his hand. 'How many men you got here?' he asked Finn.

'Eight of us – two women, six men. Four of us from Christchurch, four from Scott Base to keep us alive – grunts, I guess, but they know their business.'

'All Kiwis?'

'Yup.'

'Mind if I keep the gun?'

'No. You think one of 'em's a plant?'

'No. But if one of 'em is, I'd look pretty stupid with an empty gun holster.'

They heard a bell ring.

'That's chow. We should go. It's not a restaurant. It's hot now, cold in five minutes. We're waiting on a radio call at three a.m. – we need to know exhumation and reburial permits have been issued in Auckland. Then we can bring them up. That's six hours. Eat now, then sleep. Grab your bags.'

They trudged towards the tents. Falcon looked at his boots making tracks and, as always, he thought of Cherry at Lamer, the line of their footprints leading back to the house, and Barton at the dining-room windows.

A group of men watched their approach, out on the ice, standing in a circle, heads back, most of them smoking. One raised a mitten in welcome. The nicotine was on the breeze and he could hear Maze sucking it into his lungs.

Falcon looked up: nightrise was to the south, and more stars were appearing, not in ones and twos, but in clusters and nebulae, in Gothic twisted galaxies. The sky looked like the bowl of a pipe, as the air is drawn through, so that a few pinpoints flare, then blaze.

By the time they reached the perimeter of the camp, marked by red flags, it looked as if the sky was on fire.

Falcon headed for the galley, following his nose, leaving Maze looking up at the sky, crunching a mint.

There were double zipped doors to the Jamesway, and a pair of industrial hot-air blowers inside, which made the whole structure shimmer. A man calling himself Auck, in NZ Navy overalls, dished up bacon sandwiches, coffee and biscuits, then fled. Falcon stood by one of the blow-heaters, eating, sipping coffee, alone. It was the strangest place he'd ever been, and it left him hungry.

Walking away, towards the berths, he stopped for a cigarette, thankful of the silence after the cacophony of the aircraft. The Barrier was dark, pressing up against his eyes, snuffing out the line of beacons, which led south in pursuit of *A Very Gallant Gentleman*.

Then he heard what sounded like a gunshot – not a pistol or a hunting rifle, but a howitzer perhaps, a field gun, which he imagined recoiling, a sudden white puff of smoke visible. No shell landed, but the echoes began, bouncing off the Jamesways, the cats, the generator.

Maze appeared, the dog at his heels. 'No need to duck, Doc. It's the sea-ice shifting to the south, cracking, splintering. It runs ahead of the storm. Once it starts, the echoes take over. The beakers call it cannonading. This is just the start.'

41

A thunderclap made him sit bolt upright, and he began to count the seconds, waiting for a flash of lightning, as if he was in some parallel universe where the sound ran ahead of the white electric light. It was typical of this alien land that he felt the laws of nature would be subverted, reversed. Then he felt movement, the subtle lifting up, the settling down, and realised it wasn't the storm but the ice again, the single howitzer shell now replaced by a distant bombardment. Shock-waves ran through the ice, mirroring the deep pulsing of the sea beneath. The echoes circled.

On his feet, pulling on the thermal jacket, the balaclava, the mitts, he thought of the dead men in the pit, and how they'd been held in this frozen noisy purgatory between air and water, and had had to listen to the Barrier's strange mechanics over the decades, as it rippled and juddered above the sea, interspersed with the long months of hush – the Barrier's deep winter silence, uninterrupted for them by the sound in their ears of warm blood coursing.

Outside, the Milky Way was a twisted bedsheet across the sky. His watch read 4 a.m. Jamesway B was lit within and he could see no shadows moving. He was about to walk past, when he glanced in through the unzipped double plastic doors. There was a rudimentary surgical suite, a single arc lamp poised, aluminium buckets, a warm air heater keeping the temperature around freezing. Small motes of ice fell in the still air.

There was a single gurney table, which wasn't empty.

The sea-ice cannonading reached a crescendo, then fell away.

The body was yellow, as if it had been stored in a smoke-house. Falcon's first impression, and the one that lasted, was how substantial it was – how fleshy. Water was melting from it, a constant drip, spilling over in a rhythmic waterfall, a parody of a heartbeat. The back of the head faced him, and he could see the skull cap had been removed and returned, a circle of rust-red sutures defining the ring, almost lost in the hair, which was shorn, but still brown in the stubble.

It was the presence of death, and it put him on his knees. His heartbeat, like the Barrier shudder, sent shock-waves around his body. The void circled like the sound of thunder, but he held it back, and felt the spectre of New Cross diminish, overshadowed by the reality of this one heroic death. Forcing himself to stand he held on to a metal table, crowded with surgical tools. He couldn't stop himself noting the detail: the specimen glass jars with their obscene samples of tissue, organ, bone, fingernail and hair. This parody of a human being – reduced to its constituent parts – was his creation. He'd found the tent, he'd taken up Cherry's quest. But could he ever have thought it would end here? Only the truth would be worth this.

He stood over the table, desperate to see the body restored.

It was Birdie Bowers, the nose still aquiline. The skin looked supple, if weathered, tanned, leathery. The eyes had fallen back, but not beyond sight, and the lips were parted but still full. There was nothing of the real ugliness of death, the distortion, the inhuman angles of shattered bones. A small sheet had been laid across the body to preserve a sense of privacy – and now he was close Falcon could see that a narrow handkerchief had been placed over the face but had slipped away – perhaps dislodged by the shuffling of the ice.

He draped it back over the eyes.

The chest – broad, muscled, but bony – was disfigured by a Y-shaped incision that had allowed them to remove the front of the ribcage for access to the vital organs. On the table there was a clipboard with a standard outline of a male body, upon which had been drawn the various scars and wounds noted on the corpse: lacerations across the shoulders where the harness for man-hauling would have cut deep, the fingers and hands a maze of cuts and grazes.

He couldn't look at the feet. He sensed their deformation, the obscene swelling, the discolouration. Frostbite and gangrene, dead flesh. He thought of the pain and the courage of carrying on, until the relief of the final tent, death and sleep intertwined, indistinguishable.

Another clipboard hung from the table. There was a check list, ticks by various symptoms.

The heading read: SCURVY.

Weakness (SEE DIARY)
Irritable and sad (DIARY)
Joints distorted ✓
Swollen gums ✓
Red and blue spots NONE
Bruises easily ✓

A free-hand note added: *No signs of adipocere (grave wax) – indicates exhaustion, starvation, utilisation of body fats. Scurvy – positive, early stage. Low body fat would leave victim prone to hypothermia. Preliminary chemical analysis indicates no abnormal lead content in digestive tissue.*

The end of the Jamesway had been cordoned off with yellow and black crime tape. Beyond it, laid out on a plastic sheet, were items retrieved from the tent: a sleeping-bag, a paraffin lantern, a message cylinder, a food box, a pair of boots, a tobacco pouch, a few books, a sextant, a set of tin plates, a brass box for matches, an oil stove, a tin pan, a sketchpad. Each one carried a numbered metal tag.

'Thin pickings,' said a voice, and turning round he found Finn, cradling a coffee cup.

'I'm looking for something,' said Falcon.

'Use these,' said the Kiwi, handing over surgical gloves. 'Looks like the guys who found them pretty much cleared the tent out in 1912. Plus, they'd already dumped a lot to cut down the weight of the sledge. Some personal effects went back for family – diaries, photographs, letters, watches, rings, that kind of thing. But you'll know all that – you're the expert.'

Falcon stepped over the tape and picked up one of the boots and – as he'd expected – found the BB in pencil on the inside of the finnesko.

'They're Bowers's,' said Falcon. 'I'm looking for a single boot. The men who discovered the dead went to locate Oates. They found one boot – discarded for weight is the thinking. He'd tucked a note inside one of his boots – he says so in his diary. I need to find it.'

'Maybe they took it as a souvenir back to England, back to the family?'

Falcon shook his head. 'They took Oates's diary, his sleeping-bag – but there's no sign of the boot.'

'Could be under one of the bodies,' said Finn. 'It's a tight squeeze – three men. God knows what it was like with five. I guess the body heat was a plus. This is important?'

Falcon shrugged. 'And this is everything?'

'Still got to move the other two, so who knows? But you should see this . . .'

Finn took him to one of the tables where there was a metal box full of oil. He slipped on a pair of the gloves and used a pair of surgical tongs to lift a gun clear of the liquid, which dripped thickly, revealing the weapon's original grey sheen.

'A Webley Mark IV – pretty much standard issue, I guess, in 1910. It was in a poor state, grubby with various fats and residue. The expedition members used them to kill the dogs, the ponies, when they were done for, or they needed the meat. You're the expert, like I say, but I think we assumed Scott's final party would have dumped its guns because there was nothing left to kill. The oil's a special preparation – it won't attack any organic residues, such as blood or tissue. We'll analyse it back at McMurdo. But my guess is it's picked up some animal remains. There was plenty of soot and bullet spatter. It was in working condition, just about.'

'Where was it?'

Finn showed him a sketch of the tent, the three bodies, the entrance tunnel, clearly marked.

'It's item fourteen,' he said. 'It lay by Scott's hand.'

'That's not possible,' said Falcon, kindly.

'I know.'

Atch, in charge of the party who had found the dead, described the scene in the tent when he'd first entered it that spring afternoon in 1912. Cherry had been next in and he had described the scene as well. If there'd been a gun in plain sight they'd hardly both have failed to mention it in their reports. And Finn was right – the guns were useless after the bloodbath at Shambles Camp, where they'd killed the last ponies and sent the dogs back with Meares and Girev.

One pistol might have been kept to hasten the end for an injured or dying man. But Oates for one was sure that that option was not at hand. Had he been misled? Had Scott considered self-destruction in those final minutes?

Falcon looked closely at Bowers's head, although he was unable to stand within the dead man's personal space, which seemed to exert its force even in death. 'There's no sign of a gunshot wound?'

'None,' said Finn. 'Can't say for certain with the rest, but no signs yet.'

Falcon went over to the tray of oil, his mind turning over the questions: whose gun was it, and how had it simply appeared in the tent? It must have been left after the finding of the dead, and before the collapsing of the tent. And why leave a pistol? Why was there suddenly no need for a gun?

'Can I?' he asked.

Finn handed him the tongs. 'It can take six to twelve hours for the oil to remove all the scud.'

Falcon let the pistol drip. 'I can see initials – here on the base of the handle.'

Finn came close, taking out a camera from his jacket, focusing. 'CHM,' he said.

'Cecil Henry Meares,' said Falcon, the foreign secretary's special agent, and the man who had recruited the two Russians.

'Again, impossible,' said Falcon. 'By the time they found the tent Meares was already on the ship back to London.'

42

He stood on the edge, the grave a bright square of light suspended within the rim of ice. Flexible pipes led from Jamesway C, pumping water down, pumping water up, steam leaking from joints. The pit was the size of half a tennis court. The ramp led down, but disappeared into a layer of water vapour, so that the floor was lost in a thick mist. Occasionally a man's head would appear, then his body by degrees, as he climbed the ramp. Within the fog, four arc lamps blazed, their light muffled, dissipated. Electric cables snaked away to the unseen generator, the rattle of which seemed precarious, like a faltering heart.

The cannonading had faded away to the south.

A man ascended the ramp, paused, and peeled back a balaclava. 'We need help,' he said to Finn, who began to descend, beckoning Falcon to follow. The mist was warm, cloying, and settled immediately on Falcon's face, as he took careful steps down the ribbed slope. Within a few paces he was embedded in the white vapour, but gradually the scene was revealed: at the centre was the green tent, the material cut into petals and peeled back to expose the interior, which had been compressed by the snow and ice that had settled above. Here the three bodies had lain, as they had lain, for more than half a century, slowly encased within the ice.

Falcon edged closer. There was a pane of milky ice between the air and the two men left in their graves. Falcon thought he could see light glinting off an eye. He watched as water, steaming, flooded across, then immediately collected in a narrow gutter dug around the tent. The carapace of ice was melting away, like condensation on a cold window, retreating.

Wilson and Scott were slowly revealed as they had been when Cherry last turned his back on them and crept out of the tent. The hood on Wilson's sleeping-bag was pulled up over his face, but Scott's face was open to the sky now, his keen eyes only slightly shadowed, the jaw in a rictus of pain, as if this was the moment when he'd dared death to take him, pulling open his jacket, letting the cold reach his heart.

There was a camera flash, then a series, as two of the scientists moved in to record the scene. Falcon felt the intrusion, the loss of privacy, the sense of trespass.

They began to work around Scott's body, using small tubes to spread water over the face, and along the sides of the sleeping-bag.

'The trick is to go slowly,' said Finn, 'which is tough when we have so little time. The bodies are thawed, but there's a crust of ice. The water starts out hot but by the time we apply it it's just a few degrees warmer than the ice. It's been three hours – we're close now.'

Scott lay on a kind of plinth of ice. Falcon was amazed by the natural appearance of the skin – yellowed certainly, slightly marble-like in its translucence, but there was nothing of the mummified husk he'd expected to find.

'There he is,' said Finn, his face a few inches from Scott's. The last film of ice was melting away. On his knees, using a small metal hose, he directed a trickle of water at his neck, hair and fingers.

Falcon watched the skin around the eyes, and the narrow mouth, expecting it to flex at any moment, stiff and embalmed, but alive.

For an hour more they worked silently, Falcon at the feet, Finn at the head, others ablating the ice under the edges of the body.

Finally, Finn stood. 'Lend a hand,' he said. 'There's only one way to do this.'

Falcon had expected a mechanical winch, or even a delicate manoeuvre with one of the gurneys, but they did it by hand: two on either side for the upper body, bending smoothly at the hips, as the torso came free. The sleeping-bag shrugged itself down to Scott's waist. Now two more, on each side, took his legs, and they had him upright, and Falcon could feel the heft of him, a strong man, thinned by starvation. He could sense the bones just beneath the skin. What was extraordinary was the suppleness of the body, the way the arms fell loose, and as they moved it sideways towards a stretcher, the head lolled to one side, and then rested on Falcon's shoulder, the face a few inches away, close enough for breath to mingle, if both had been alive. He thought then that Scott had made a legend out of the lives and deaths of real men, and that in some ways this had obscured their humanity, their weaknesses, their frailty at the end. There was nothing wrong with pity.

At the top of the ramp they transferred Scott's body to a gurney, putting him down on his side, preparing to slide him across, and over to his back. But Finn was on the far side from Falcon and called a halt. 'Hold it. There's something here.'

It had become clear from an inventory of Bowers's pockets that the rescue party had searched the bodies in 1912 and removed personal effects to take back for the families, but Finn had a hand in a small pocket inside Scott's jacket. He held up a centre punch, the inscription catching the light: MV *BJÖRN*.

A picture was taken, evidence that Scott's narrative was true. Again, Falcon wondered if they had too easily dismissed the German connection. Was it really credible that it had been left behind to mislead? What if the Kaiser had had an agent within Scott's expedition?

They returned to the pit for Wilson's body, which felt too slight, so that when the bag finally fell away they simply lifted him up, like a child. The three men left impressions in the ice – and on the groundsheet. The place felt ransacked, barren, an empty tomb. As they carried Wilson up the ramp, Falcon walked at the rear, the tail end of a funeral march, rising up to the white Barrier.

Finn was waiting at the top.

'Bad news. We've had the latest meteorological data from Beardmore – on the edge of the plateau. The storm's eight hours away, strengthening. Wind speed at ten thousand feet is eighty m.p.h. – but it'll sweep down and accelerate. We're looking at 120 to 140 m.p.h. Hence our visitors.' He nodded towards Jamesway A where the cook was throwing out scraps for a scrabble of skuas and petrels, fighting with their sharp hooked beaks for food.

'They've been scooped up by the winds. They're half a continent away from home. We're closer, but not that much. So here's the plan. We'll complete the autopsies, bury the beacons and the three men. We can cover the whole site with tarpaulin, but we'll leave the pit – it'll fill with blown snow. It's too late for the plane, so we'll take the traverse. If it's bad we'll lie up. Won't be nice – but there it is.

'Our time's up so Oates should wait. I've told Maze – he wants to go now, skidoo, follow the lobster pots. But he can't go alone. It's your call. I can't see a lot of benefit to it. But I won't stand in your way. You've got six hours – I'd need your word you wouldn't be later than that. We can't wait.'

He gave Falcon a set of keys without waiting for an answer.

'Skidoo number two – over there. Maze knows how to handle it. Don't be late. I mean it. We'll go without you.'

43

The skidoo was two-man, adapted to carry dogs in a rear trailer, which could take the beacons as well on the return journey. A two-stroke engine gave them 20 m.p.h. so the wind chill wouldn't kill them, but it was raw, brutal, ahead of the storm front barrelling down off the centre of the continent. Dawn had yet to break, but moonlight flooded the white plain. To the west a pyramid line of peaks marked the Western Mountains, each one a rugged cape jutting out into a sea that hadn't seen a wave since the dawn of man. Behind them they left Erebus, the distant volcanic peak smudged by a drifting line of ash.

Against the whining note of the engine it was impossible to talk. Falcon thought about Oates. He was the only soldier of them all, and the only one who'd seen serious military action. There was something laudable about Oates – not the Victorian heroism but something earthy and practical, almost anti-intellectual. He'd struggled at school, and with exams, and wished only to be with his horses, or on his boat. Being a soldier was a trade he took seriously. Did the rest consider adventure a game, the chance to write a legend? Oates was a professional – famously a hero without heroism. The atmosphere in the tent at the end must have been poisonous. Scott left the legend, and Dollman painted the gallant gentleman. (Although it was Atch and Cherry who coined the phrase – for the note they'd left in the cairn when they'd given up the search for his body.) And what of his crime? The eleven-year-old girl he'd raped, and the child he'd never acknowledged? Did he really walk to his death without a thought for them?

And what of Taffy's sketch? Did Oates think Taffy was mad? The babble of plots and sabotage and secret symbols must have seemed fantastic. When hope finally died, and there was no sign of the heralded rescue party, the baying dogs, he'd probably thought only of what lay beyond death – an end to pain and struggle. Why consider the fate of a scrap of paper? But then there was the last line of his diary: he'd sent a message home with Uncle Bill. Had there been comfort in those words?

Falcon peered over Maze's shoulder: the trail ahead was marked by the red blinking beacons marking each mile. This was Falcon's string of lobster pots, so he could just see the gentle curve, drifting west, swinging away in an elegant tangent from the straight line they had once formed. Everything was clear, lucid, because the air was entirely still – a harbinger of the storm to come.

Above, the sky told the truth: the stars were lost beyond a slight gauze of mist, colder air slipping over that below, an outrider of the gale. The moon, full and aspirin white, blazed through, but as if from underwater. And looking ahead Falcon thought the blackness beyond the horizon in the south looked folded, substantial, as if the night was weighed down by the turbulent, snow-filled air.

Maze pulled a quick ski-turn and came to a halt beside a blue flashing beacon. When he cut the engine the silence flooded in, surrounding them. The Barrier itself was asleep, the deeps still. Even on the surface not a grain of ice tumbled.

Falcon was startled when Maze spoke.

'This is it: twenty-one miles south of the tent.'

Aput, released, began circling them, the gentle impact of her soft paws crisp and light. They worked systematically, in a grid pattern, using the blue beacon as a centre point. There was no sign in either direction of the cairns – the waymarks – for the snow of decades had wiped the slate clean, the wind flattening, the ice absorbing. After an hour Falcon found his eyesight faltering, his brain yearning for features – anything that his wandering imagination could cling to in this vast theatre of nothing. Tiny details, their own footprints, took on fabulous forms: a distant city, a yawning chasm, a desert caravan, a string of ponies. That was how close madness lay: his mind had begun to construct an alternative world.

Maze lit a cigarette and they stood together watching the dog, which had come to her own halt.

'I think Oates has gone,' said Falcon. 'From the surface, certainly. He'll be beneath our feet, swimming in ice. I think his lonely walk is going to be his only glory. No Surrender Oates has given up. One day, a hundred years after Scott and the rest, he'll spill out of the ice into the ocean.'

'Born again,' said Maze, but his eyes were still out on the plain, searching.

'Where's Aput?' said Falcon, scouring the horizon.

'Relax – she's there.' Maze pointed with his cigarette, but there was something new in his voice, a note of hope.

She was two hundred yards away, lying flat on the surface.

'She's found something,' said Maze.

Closer, they saw that she was at the edge of a feature – no more than a shadow – on the icefield. They'd seen sastrugi on the journey since leaving SWB, the parallel ridges of ice and snow, some three feet high, but most almost invisible. But this seemed to be one *sastrugas*, and as they approached on foot it seemed to alter shape, at one point a bank, and then, from a different angle, a narrow hill.

They walked in time, their footfalls chiming, listening to the snuffling of the dog, which was manic, excited.

'It's a crescent,' said Falcon, in wonder, as they reached the low bank. It was about three foot tall, but turned in a perfectly formed moon-like curve, with tapering ends, which fell from the ridge stylishly to the ice.

Aput was absolutely still, head half down, but eyes ahead. Then she barked once, jumping up, heading for the heart of the crescent, her nose down on the ice, tail wagging furiously.

'What is it?' asked Falcon, his foot on the crescent bank.

'Clue's in the compass,' said Maze. 'The back of the crescent – the outward curve – faces where?'

Falcon had confessed his obsession with the cardinal points, so this was a test. 'South,' he said. 'The wind did this?'

'No. But the wind kept it like this. One of the geologists at Old Pole gave me the lowdown. He said to look out for them. It's a pony bank. They put them a distance from the tents, tied the beasts up, and hoped they'd hunker down in the lee overnight.'

'But Scott had no ponies on the way home.'

'Right – this was built on the outward journey. We're only a hundred and twenty miles from Cape Evans, so they'd have had twenty ponies, plus the dogs. This would have been a large encampment, the whole expedition, just starting out, leaving behind One Ton.

'My guess is it was bigger – much bigger. Somehow it's survived – maybe the wind remakes it or compacts the ice. It's rare, just one bank. The sastrugi lie in patterns, which shuffle and change. This is permanent. '

He had an ice pick in his belt, which he took out and swung at the face of the bank to the sound of metal on glass, and hardly a mark left to see.

'It's immortal,' said Falcon.

The dog had begun circling within the crescent, silent now after that one exultant bark. Then she lay down, paws out in front, head up, and began to growl rhythmically.

'That's it,' said Maze. 'She's got a scent. We need warm water.'

He jogged back to the skidoo and started the engine, the caterpillar tracks throwing out splinters of ice, the skis vibrating like divining rods, as he brought her to rest beside Falcon. They'd gaffer-taped a large bottle of water between the gear box and the engine. He took it out, checked it was hot, and replaced it with another from the trailer, keeping the engine running.

The area the dog had targeted was halfway down the bank. They both had picks and crowbars, so they began to chip away at the water-softened ice. They worked quickly, but Falcon kept glancing behind, towards the south, where the blackness massed on the horizon seemed to be creeping closer. Just once he saw something: an internal flash, diffuse lightning, rippling slightly as it ran eastwards.

'Storm's close,' he said.

Maze had an unlit cigar in his mouth and was hacking at the ice. 'We'll dig for thirty minutes. Then we go.'

The dog was nervous, inching forward, then back, the growl now internalised, like a groan. Intermittently the tension seemed too much for her, so that she'd let out a whimper and cower, as if expecting a blow.

They were so focused on the spot they'd chosen they didn't watch the warm puddle of water at the base of the bank. It was Falcon, glancing back south, who caught something in the corner of his eye.

'There. What's that?'

It was black, and rounded, still within a translucent layer of ice. They both got close before Falcon saw it for what it was. 'It's the toe of a sock, a heavy woollen material.' Even then, out on the ice, he'd thought it through: a sock, so no boots, just as Scott had written.

Falcon worked away with the hot water and within a minute they could see – through the poorly darned material – the flesh of the foot. He sat back on his haunches and slipped off his hood.

'There's no time,' said Maze. 'Let's work. Pray later.' He lifted his pickaxe. 'How tall was Oates?' he asked.

'Five nine – here,' said Falcon, handing over a tape measure.

They worked separately, Falcon at the foot, Maze where the head should have lain.

After three minutes working around the foot Falcon looked up and there was a glimpse of a face, just one eye visible, the wide forehead, the trim hair. A mask of opaque ice covered the rest, but then Maze lifted it clear. And there lay The Soldier. He'd never looked happy; all the photographs Falcon had seen, even the family pictures at Gestingthorpe, showed a man slightly removed from emotion, steady and focused on the long road. This was the closest he'd seen to a smile, the thin – slightly cruel – lips, buckled, the head back, as if exultant in the final moment.

'The death of pain,' said Falcon.

They worked on for ten minutes. 'He's holding something to his heart,' said Maze.

The outline of the body was now visible. They could just see the edge of a piece of paper held in his mitten.

'Get the paper,' said Falcon, his heart racing with hope. Had he died holding the crucial clue?

'I'll uncover the other foot. We need to be sure.'

Within a minute Falcon had exposed the left foot – and no boot. He'd said he'd walk out without them and he had, unable to face the pain in his rotting feet.

There was only one hope now. He watched Maze gently free the piece of paper and hold it up. Falcon felt the moment of elation die.

It wasn't a note at all, but a small photograph. Falcon took off his mitt and held it in his living hands. The ice cleared with the heat of his blood: it was a young girl – perhaps ten years old, standing in a studio before a backdrop of Roman ruins, cypress trees, a temple. There was something in the frank open face that spoke of The Soldier. A seriousness, a soul concealed.

On the back it said: 'Kit. Birthday 1909.'

Falcon thought the image unbearable: Oates struggling to walk away from the tent in the falling snow, until he came across the old pony wall. There was a storm, it was minus 40°C: a living freezer. He'd lain down to die against the bank of the wall, a picture of his daughter held to his heart.

Maze got out his camera to record the scene, and sank a radio beacon in the bank, trying to cover Oates's face with snow, and returned the photograph.

And one last treasure: the Scott Polar had asked the families if they wished to send something south – a final gift to be left with the dead if they were found. The items had arrived by airmail at McMurdo just in time – each in a padded envelope. Falcon ripped open the one marked simply 'Laurie'. It was a miniature wooden carving of a yacht, sails furled. Holding it close to his eye he managed to read her etched name: *Saunterer*.

He set it in the ice at the foot of the crescent beside the body, adrift on an endless white sea. Then they spilt some water around the hull and saw the ice forming.

'It might ride out the storm,' said Falcon.

They fled, the air around them beginning to weave in tangled gusts as the storm neared. Falcon looked back at the crescent bank from the skidoo. It was a small miracle, but perhaps Lawrence Oates deserved it. For half a century his body had become part of the crescent, an icy landmark, floating, edging, staying above the crushing snow. And his last act was preserved: not the shambling sad figure of Dollman's picture, but something more complex. In the privacy of death he'd allowed himself the truth. There was guilt here, and loss. But what of that last message he'd entrusted to Wilson? Had there been – at last – a message to his mother instructing her to take responsibility for the child? That would be a tragedy, to add to all the others.

44

In the dark of Berth Six at SWB Falcon slept fitfully. Finn said the cats were a 'rough ride' on the traverse, and they'd be travelling for twenty hours to McMurdo, with the storm harrying, so he'd better rest while he could. His head was full of half-dreams: Oates within the curve of his icy tomb, peering at the picture of Kit, Scott's head falling to his shoulder, Birdie's body with its Y-shaped incision, the specimen jars with their fluids and misshapen organs. And Cherry, his face lit by the fire in the library at Lamer, the notebook on his knee, a glass of whisky in his hand.

Before sleep took him he'd considered Finn's brief summary of the preliminary autopsy results: the underlying causes of death were led by starvation, this being a function of short rations, the long distance set between depots, and an acute shortfall of calories. The food was also low on fat content, but long on protein. Loss of existing body fat, burnt to meet the shortfall, had led to hypothermia, and thence to frostbite, also a lack of energy, and the wasting of muscle once the fat was gone. And there was scurvy – at least in its very early stages. The extent of the frostbite coincided with Scott's temperature readings, suggesting that conditions on the Barrier that autumn season were much colder than those recorded by earlier expeditions.

Those were the medical causes of death. But Falcon knew that the *prime* cause was sabotage: with adequate oil, and more food, they'd have made One Ton.

He heard Maze getting up, and the skittering of the dog.

A flashlight came on. 'I'm going to get fresh air,' said Maze. 'I'll be a while.'

Falcon, half asleep, felt Aput's nose sniffing along the edge of the bunk, and then the dog was called away. Falcon would remember later that he distinctly heard the striking of a match and, while tumbling back into a dream, caught the whiff of an expensive cigar.

But he couldn't sleep for long, so he slid out of the berth, got dressed, and walked out onto the ice. Before he had to quit the base he had duties to perform – and it was best done quickly. The wind was blustery, buffeting. The aurora was playing in the sky – although even it seemed cowed by the threat of the approaching storm, which was out there, rolling in, the first shimmer of ice crystals on the surface, creating a mist just a few centimetres high. The base looked deserted, everyone resting before the ordeal ahead.

Falcon's first duty was to leave gifts on the graves in the pit. He had the three small padded envelopes ready in his thermal jacket.

He was shocked when he reached the edge, because looking down he saw the bodies had been returned, but not covered. It seemed that nature would provide the shroud. They lay in their preordained niches, like three medieval knights in a forgotten crypt. Photographs had been used to arrange the bodies precisely as they had been found, and a thin glaze of ice was already sealing their skin, a sprinkler set to one side providing a freezing mist. The 'grave goods' removed would go back to Christchurch for analysis – including the Webley, and the centre punch.

The ramp took him down into the pit.

He stood at the foot of the grave.

The first envelope, when opened, was for Scott. The family had chosen a book. The Owner had been a great reader, and had meticulously assembled libraries on the *Terra Nova,* and at Cape Evans, and ordered catalogues to be kept. Scientific tomes, stories of exploration – but novels too, and verse.

Inside the package was a slim volume of illustrated poetry: *The Rime of the Ancient Mariner.*

He laid it on Scott's chest. There was an echo here, from the past, calling out: something about the illustration on the cover, of a ship approaching down an icy cavern, took him back to Pepys Road, so he buried the image quickly and opened the next envelope. This was for Bowers. The family had supplied a simple blue sew-on badge, the letters in gold thread: HMS *FOX*. Falcon recalled the armoured cruiser had been his first ship in the Gulf, and the Far East – on which he'd gone to sleep, according to a letter home, to the 'sound of men killing each other'. It hadn't kept him awake long. It was his coming-of-age.

He placed the badge on Bowers's chest.

Finally, for Wilson, a small wooden box containing water-colour paints: sixteen shades, in two rows of eight, with a groove for two brushes and a small metal dish for water. The box was engraved with the college arms of Gonville & Caius.

A camp chair had been set aside and Falcon drew it up to sit at their feet. His eye kept scanning the scene. The three men, their grave gifts.

A shadow passed over the pit and looking up he saw a bird, struggling to hold its position. It was small, snow-white, with black eyes and grey feet. He felt the Master's presence, and knew what he had to do next.

He stood. 'It wasn't Cherry's fault. I'm sure he'd want me to say that because he couldn't himself when he was here. He did his best. He followed orders. It wasn't enough, and he was sorry for that. I think that haunted him down the years.

'He wanted justice too, to name the killers, to tell the truth. But we might have failed in that, although the game's not run its course. I'm sorry. We both tried.'

He considered the grave and its gifts. The shadow of the bird had gone.

He wanted to say sorry, sorry for being late.

His mouth, suddenly dry, was the first danger signal. Then came the slight light-headedness, the sudden 'freezing' of the heart, the thudding beat. The world of ice and darkness retreated. The day – that *day* – began to crowd in on him, but it was not the same day. Here he was, walking down Pepys Road, a memory he'd lost, if he'd ever retained it at all. St Catherine's, on Telegraph Hill, had a chiming clock, which regulated the day for the children who played on the streets. It struck the hour – so he *had* left the house on time at eleven. But the V2 would not strike until 12.26 p.m. Why had it taken him so long to get to the post office and the sweet shop?

It was extraordinary being in this child's mind because it was a head without the rest of his life inside it – the V2 was just in the future (although probably being winched to the launch position at that very moment). Cherry and Lamer were in the future and in the past. Sofya was in the future. It broke his old heart to feel how happy he was in the past: he'd been sent on an errand and given threepence to spend – if he spent it quickly they could all go to the park and not waste the day slumbering.

He felt happy, not about the future or the past, but in the moment. He felt the innocent joy of being alive as he began to run down Pepys Road. He felt wonderfully sure of where he was, and where he was going. This was what his father called Falcon's 'manor' – these were his streets, full of his friends, and now that he was out of the house almost anything might happen. Once released, adventures could begin.

At the foot of the street, at New Cross Gate, the pavements outside the White Hart were crowded with men drinking. Ahead, he saw the sooty smoke of a train passing under the road at the station, first to the north, then the south, so he knew it was for Bromley and the coast. There were shops on the far side of the railway bridge, so he slowed down, looking in the windows. He had to dodge and weave because grown-ups rarely saw him: so, he kept his head down, watching shoes and boots.

'Falcon! Falcon! Come back, lad.'

It was Uncle Pat, who owned the second-hand-book shop. He was sitting outside on a chair, as he often did. He was the same age as Falcon's father, but this didn't count because he'd been a soldier, and he'd been shot in the back, and this had left him an invalid, so he often looked ancient, as if he might die at any moment, slipping away quietly on his chair. Talking to Uncle Pat was a task he tried to avoid, because the bookseller often felt faint, and would ask for a glass of water, which he'd set aside, as if the sight of it saved his life, not the drinking of it. When he came to the flat his father would help him up the stairs, and his mother would make strong tea, steeped in sugar.

'Sit here, Falcon. Watch the shop – Rosa's out. I've something you can take back for your mum. It's a present for your dad. Hide it as soon as you get home. If he asks where you've been make something up. Tell him a white lie – anything.'

'What's a white lie?' asked Falcon. He'd had no idea lies had colours. Already the black and red varieties were circling in his head.

'A lie that does no harm. Sometimes the truth is inconvenient, or breaks a trust, or is hurtful to someone else. The white lie just keeps everyone happy.'

He went inside the shop, leaving the door open.

Mr Noonan – Pat – was their closest friend, even closer than family. One day, according to legend, he'd come to the house – before Falcon was born – and said he was off to Spain to fight the Fascists, who were in league with the Nazis. He'd asked his dad to come too. (This was his mother's story, and she could not pass this point without crying, although she always laughed at herself at the same time.) His father had a good job, and she was pregnant with Falcon, so his dad said no. Pat had no wife or family. So he set off for Spain.

Sometimes Pat drank whisky with his father in front of the fire. So he knew what had happened. There had been a battle near a river called the Jarama. Pat was in an International Brigade, with the other British volunteers. It was a big battle, and Pat had helped defend a hill, but a lot of his friends had died. It was always the same fact: there were 600 of them at dusk but only 225 were alive at dawn. They called it Suicide Hill. It was over when Pat was shot by a sniper. He had a girlfriend in the army – they let women fight: they were called *miliciana*. She was called Rosa, and she took him home to a place called Taragona, where there was a hospital on the cliffs. When he could walk, Pat brought her back to New Cross, and they were married in a strange church in Greenwich, which was full of painted statues. Rosa looked after Pat, ran the shop, and did a lot, which made her angry most of the time. When she came to the flat – which was rare – she drank a bottle of beer and fell asleep by the kitchen fire.

Falcon sat on the chair in the street as he'd been told, watching the traffic go by, thinking this diversion for a book was making him late. But he had no choice. Pat was more than a friend: he was a 'comrade'. When the Labour Party met in the Methodist Hall, Falcon helped his father put out pamphlets and agendas and then he sat at the back. Sometimes Pat spoke about the war. On Falcon's birthday Pat had given him a badge, marked 'XV IB' and said XV was the Roman way of saying 15th – and that was the brigade which had fought on Suicide Hill. His father said that at the end of the war there was a general election back home and they wanted Pat to stand – but Pat said Falcon's dad would be better, because he was a South London boy, and had the gift of the gab and, besides, everyone knew Pat was a *Mick*, even though he didn't have an accent any more. And he was married to a 'wop', and anyway he didn't expect to live that long. But Falcon's dad turned that adventure down too.

He heard the clock chiming on the town hall. It was eleven thirty.

He wanted to get home in time for the park so he went inside to find Uncle Pat. As he closed the door the noise of New Cross died away: a tram bell ringing by the White Hart, the reedy fairground music from Deptford Park, the hooves of a dray horse, impossibly slow, like a failing heart. The silence inside was full of old paper, and dusty floorboards. There were three floors, connected by a metal spiral staircase. His father said that monthly meetings of the local Fabian Society took place in the back office, but Falcon had forgotten what the society stood for, or why. The Noonans lived in the basement.

Then he heard a thud. It was followed by a slow avalanche, which sounded like books sliding to the floor.

'Uncle Pat?' called Falcon.

There was no reply so he climbed up the stairs, past the first floor, then up to the top, and he saw Uncle Pat lying on the floor, looking at him, quite calmly.

Falcon didn't know what to do, so he began to turn and go down, because he wanted to get a grown-up.

'Stay,' said Uncle Pat. His right arm was flung out, and he flexed the fingers, as if beckoning him over. By his feet lay a book, presumably the one he'd gone to fetch and wrap for his father. Briefly, Falcon was distracted by the cover, which was an old-fashioned engraving, with hachures and the play of shadow and light. But then Pat's hand came up, so he took it, and felt the sudden claw-like grip. Pat's mouth was open, and crushed slightly against the wooden floorboards, so that saliva was spilling out. His eyes looked odd, faraway and out of focus. His face was fluid, and moving, and Falcon was shocked when he realised he was trying to smile.

'Your dad says you've a good mind – a memory. I want to give you a message, and then I want you to get help.'

His lips were blue, and his eyes seemed to have sunk back behind layers of glassy water. The old hand, which had gripped so tight, slid down to Falcon's fingers, and entwined, gently.

'Rosa's gone out and she'll be back at six,' he said.

'Is the message for her?'

'Yes. You're a go-between, Falcon. A messenger.'

Then something happened inside Pat's body, which made it jack-knife, so that he clutched his chest.

Suddenly he drew in a breath, a rattle of air and spit, and when his eyes came open Falcon was appalled to see how frightened he was, terrified by something he couldn't see.

'Tell her this,' he said.

Falcon listened to every word. Memory was his super-power, which was a game they played at school, passing round the American comics. Memorising what he saw was easy because there were shapes and patterns. Memorising what he heard was more difficult until he'd discovered that he could see the words in his head briefly, flitting by in phrases, sentences, paragraphs of the mind. It was one reason he was good at school.

It wasn't a long message. At the end Pat paused, took a grating breath, and said: 'Now go.'

Falcon found a man in the shop on the ground floor looking at a big book about the Roman Empire. He told him what had happened and the man said he'd run to the fire station – just opposite – and they'd call an ambulance.

'Stay with him,' he said. 'Good lad.'

Falcon had to go back. Pat had moved, somehow rolling over, and into a ball. Falcon sat down and told him help was on the way and that the fire brigade would be in charge. In the dusty silence he could hear Pat's breath – like a cat's, whistling, thin and uneven.

He didn't know what to do. When Edie was sick their mother always touched her, and told her soothing stories. He edged closer until his knee knocked Pat's foot. There was a noise then, vocal but lost.

Falcon felt a hot bolt of panic because he couldn't think of anything else to say.

He heard heavy steps on the stairs.

'Is he your dad?' said a fireman, kneeling down.

'No. He's Pat.'

'Go downstairs and keep an eye open for the ambulance.'

Two men – hardly grown-ups – were already on the ground floor unfurling a stretcher. They didn't seem to be in a hurry. He told them Mrs Noonan was out until six. A minute later they brought Pat down, strapped to the stretcher. The man who ran the paper shop next door came and locked up the bookshop. They all watched the ambulance setting off east, towards Greenwich. There was a small crowd and a few of the men took off their caps.

Then Falcon was on his own, and the town-hall clock was chiming again, and as it was twelve fifteen, he ran to the post office.

Which was where the old memory began again.

But somehow it had lost its charge, its vivid detail, so that rather than living through the explosion, he felt he could watch it, from the future. Running up Pepys Road he felt the old excitement – the urge to tell – but when he opened the door and saw them on the bed he just started to cry.

Which was when he opened his eyes. Snow was falling, and while the wind blew over the pit, the air was still beside the grave.

Falcon felt lighter, even joyful, but in a dull way, which suggested it was a state of being that might last. The missing piece of the past had recovered his sense of himself.

Before him lay Bowers, Scott and Wilson, already beneath half an inch of ice, which seemed to gather the arc light's savage glare and transform it into a glow, as if the heat was required to make the ice, to seal the tomb. Soon they would be gone.

Falcon stood up. 'It wasn't my fault,' he said, and something connected inside him, binding together a child and a man.

Someone cut the power to the arc lamps.

In the darkness he felt no fear, quite certain that he would never have to relive the moment again: the opening of the door, the sense of loss and being left behind, the urge to say he was sorry.

He heard the engines firing up on the two snow cats.

The spell broken he climbed the ramp by torchlight, braced for the wind.

Everything was ready. The berths and the Jamesways had been left to help mark the spot from the air. As soon as he entered number six he saw Aput, her leather lead casually looped over the metal post at the corner of Falcon's bunk. It was enough of itself, because Frank never went anywhere without the dog. And it was a goodbye letter too: 'She's yours now.'

He heard again his friend's last words, the echo of Oates's farewell: 'I'm going to get fresh air. I'll be a while.'

He knelt down by the dog, released the lead, and took her outside.

The Barrier was deserted, a clean sheet.

'I'm sorry, Aput,' he said. The dog panted, struggling with what she couldn't see.

45

It was a privilege to be given the key, and to be left alone. They'd taken dogs and a sledge over the sea-ice, then a small inflatable, working their way out through the 'brash' – the soup of melting ice, dotted with the small floes or 'growlers' – until they reached the 'pancake' ice, a thin veneer of crystals, like tracing paper. Penguins shuffled in thousands as they went past, and he thought of Cherry's description in *The Worst Journey* – 'their breasts like mirrors, reflecting the northern light'. Wilson, ever creative, had sung to them, luring them close enough to sketch.

Falcon felt they looked more like witnesses, edging forward in a line to see how the story would end.

Erebus looked down, black smoke leaking from the cone, her slopes white, shrouded in the mist that had descended when the storm had finally blown itself out after eight days. They'd spent three days on the traverse, creeping north, the cats buffeted, the snow pressing against the streaming windows. The wind had been a wild animal – the bear of the south.

His guide to Cape Evans – a young SeaBee called Cooper – had set him ashore on the black lava spit on which the hut stood and said he'd be back in two hours, setting off to take supplies to the fishing huts – metal containers adapted to sit over bore-holes in the ice. McMurdo was in lockdown: a comms blackout had been ordered to keep news of the finding of the dead from the wider world until decisions had been made in Washington, London and Christchurch.

Getting permission for the short trip had been tortuous. But Cooper shared a secret: the lost US marshal – Maze – had

left precise instructions for what he'd listed on the command
sheet as an 'authorised recce', ferrying Dr Grey out to Cape
Evans. The adventure had been given a blue stamp from
Maze's office, PRIORITY 1, which had helped cut red tape.
Falcon knew then that the promise – to take him to Cape
Evans – had been made with the knowledge it would be kept
posthumously. Which added lustre to the journey.

Falcon slipped the key into the padlock and pushed open
the outer door into the porch, designed to keep the winter
wind from blowing in at minus 40°C. The inner door was
bolted, but oiled, and without a fuss he found himself looking down the length of the hut.

He felt the ghosts stirring, looking up, filling their pipes,
weary at the long wait for redemption. All must hope for the
truth at last, except the guilty one, for without it they were
all condemned. They should have guessed that this would
be their purgatory, a wooden hut in the shadow of a volcano
named for Erebus – the land where the dead waited to cross
the River Styx to the afterlife.

'There's a traitor among you,' he said. The wood seemed
to soak up the accusation.

It's come to this, he thought. *We'll never know the truth
unless the dead speak.*

He let Aput off the lead and she sat down, front legs forward, hair bristling.

He'd studied the hut many times back in his cubbyhole
office at the Scott Polar. It didn't look preserved because
the driest place on earth had left it untouched by the passage of years. He was standing in the past: there were shouts
outside, the men playing football, the stove crackling. He
could smell the food, touch the drying clothes, hear the
clocks tick. It was the *Mary Celeste* of the snows.

The hut was split into two from side to side by a packing-case
wall. The first part – about a third of the length – was for the

enlisted men: they had their own mess-deck table, and the galley, a store and their bunks. An open gap led into the main hut, dominated by the great wardroom table around which they'd all gathered for celebrations: feasts of lamb and seal, redcurrant jelly, asparagus and chocolate, cigars and brandy. The officers' berths, and those of the scientists, lined the walls. The stove was at the back, surrounded by the cubbyhole laboratories for geology, biology and meteorology – the instruments and glassware left in mid-experiment. Ponting's darkroom took up the far end. Falcon thought of his pictures of the great midwinter feast: the men florid with food and drink, Union Flags draped, Scott at the head, every inch The Owner.

Aput growled, sinking her head lower.

The ghosts were still here. There was no doubt of that. There was a mirror at the end of the hut, by the photographic lab. It was in the corner of his eye, but he wouldn't look, in case he saw them over his shoulder.

He sat, motionless, and listened to them going about their daily routines that long dark winter, trying to fill the time, trying to blot out the thought of Amundsen – spotted by the *Terra Nova* at the nearby Bay of Whales – with a pack of dogs; trying not to think they were doomed to come second.

The officers had desk lamps powered by the oil generator, throwing light over charts (Lieutenant Evans's preserve), or the careful notes on experiments, all part of *Universitas Antarctica*. Or Meares mending pony harnesses, or Ponting arranging tableaux for the camera. Or the geologist clacking his rock samples, sketching formations a million years old. At five precisely the pianola would play, and there would be chess or dominoes – but never cards, although cigarettes were used for bets. And there were three lectures a week, mostly dreary, although Atch's account of the progress of scurvy had brought rigid silence. And Scott would work away at his desk.

Planning was a narcotic, and he never stopped, which turned it into over-planning.

And sometimes the door would open. Twice a day the instruments had to be checked – the wind, the temperature up on the slope – three separate stations: Algernon, Clarence and Bertram. Or perhaps the door had just burst open, and here are Cherry, Bowers and Wilson, back from their jaunt to find penguin eggs. A silence then, because only they can't see what the journey has done to them. The trauma is on each face, a look that would become commonplace in the decades to come: the thousand-yard stare of the men along the Western Front.

Cherry: he was here in so many guises. Editor of the *South Polar Times*, working at the wardroom table, helping the botanists with their experiments, playing cards, or running up to the meteorological stations, or down to the sea to check the ice. Busy, cheerful – and that was another nickname: Cheery. Which was sad, because after the winter journey the smile was a façade hiding the black dog of depression.

After food – the great event of every day – there would be time to write letters home, ready to send ahead of the ship when they got to Lyttelton. And there'd be 'kag' – endless discussions about everything, politics (Keegan was always ready to discuss the Irish question) or, a favourite, propositions such as if you ordered a pint of bitter at the Ritz would the waiter be surprised? There were no fights – according to the diaries. And there was the watch to keep, when they were all in the hut, but what was there to watch for? No bears, no Eskimos, no fur trappers, no ships under foreign flag. Just the darkness, just Nature, brewing its next storm.

The enemy was within all along.

'But who?' he asked, out loud.

In the far corner, behind a screen, he found Scott's bunk and his desk, and a precious window for when the light returned. Ponting's photographs had fixed the moment here: it was winter 1911 for ever, and Scott was writing, his head to one side, as if considering another deft phrase.

Opposite – but in the same enclosed space – were two more bunks: one for Lieutenant Evans, the nominal deputy, and one for Wilson, the *de facto* deputy, Scott's confidant and mentor. There was a slim volume of Browning on Scott's bunk, *A Tale of Two Cities* on a shelf above Evans's. A table beside Wilson's held sheets of paper, a few sketches in watercolour. Evans's corner was shipshape – anonymous. Wilson's was crowded with his landscape studies – subtle, heartfelt, even lyrical. Lieutenant Evans was the only suspect here – perhaps the prime suspect. But death, and the passage of time, had covered his tracks.

Falcon moved to the next cubicle, known with schoolboy humour as the 'tenements' due to the chaotic energy and industry generated in such a small space. In the first top bunk lay Cecil Meares, the dashing adventurer, the secret spy. Could they really suspect his loyalty? The pistol left in the tent was a baffling detail. Below him lay Atch, the surgeon, co-opted as leader when Scott never came home. The middle bunk of the tenements was Oates's – the space below a store full of pony tack, harnesses and skis. The pitched roof, where it met the wall, would have been only a foot above his head, and Falcon could see he'd used chalk to draw on the wood: a horse – a fine horse, not a pony, but perhaps one of the thoroughbreds he'd seen racing at the Curragh when he'd been stationed in Ireland. The horse was caught in profile, the legs in perfect motion, that mysterious combination of hooves on the ground, leaving the ground, and touching the ground. Above the pony was a sketch of a yacht at sea under sail. The grave gift had been perfect.

The chalk sketch gave Falcon an idea. He went back to Scott's bunk, but there wasn't a blemish on the woodwork beside the single bed. Lieutenant Evans, anonymous again, but Wilson's was a revelation. The watercolours had faded, but there were dim outlines in oil on the wooden packing case that made up the wall: a landscape of England, gentle hills and a church steeple, and then a penguin – an Adélie – and a white bird, neat, with black eyes. He touched the image, and whispered, 'Snow petrel,' recognising the seabird he'd seen hanging over the grave out on the Barrier, which he'd spotted later on a chart hanging in the mess room at McMurdo. Its whiteness was perfection.

He went back to the tenements and the final bunks: Bowers on top, Cherry beneath. The roof plank above Birdie's pillow was a maze of numbers – sledging totals perhaps, or a tally of stores. Like Scott he was an inveterate planner, and never idle. The mattresses were straw inside canvas and Cherry's looked plump, so Falcon did what he'd known he would do the moment he'd opened the door: he swung himself in and lay still for a moment. A photograph was pinned to the boards above, almost faded to a smooth grey but saved by the shadows of the hut. It was the ice-house, in the dell at Lamer. The child was Cherry, the woman – hatless, laughing – probably his mother. The scene was drenched in sunlight, a blanket on the lawn crowded with a picnic. There were other figures – children, almost certainly siblings, all younger – but their patience had broken and they'd not been able to stand still for the photographer. They were blurred, fleeting sprites caught on film. But Cherry's gaze was steady. What had he thought each night when he looked back into the eyes of his five-year-old self?

Who had *he* suspected as they'd waited for the ship to take them home?

Falcon left the tenements and moved back to the mess deck. On the same side as the tenements, and without a window, there were single deck cots for the enlisted men: Taffy Evans next to Crean, next to Keegan, Forde and Gwynne; a

Welshman, three Irishmen and a Cornishman. If Lieutenant Evans was the culprit, what of Crean and Gwynne? Were they accomplices, or could he have operated alone? He was in command – he could easily have contrived to set out duties for the others while he sabotaged the stores. But he'd been ill – and scurvy had nearly killed him before the end. Or had that been an elaborate subterfuge? Or a lie – if Crean and Gwynne were part of a plot?

And, last, the Russians. Judging by Ponting's photographs, Omelchenko – the pony man – had spent most of his time in the stables, hunched round the blubber stove with the rest, sooty-faced. He had been responsible for choosing the ponies – did he really have no choice but the 'old crocks' lamented by Oates, or did they leave behind the best animals? What better way to hobble Scott's ambitions than with lame beasts? Above his berth the wood was bare. He was a curiously peripheral character. He'd left early too, on the ship with Meares. Was there a hint of the guilty fleeing the scene?

Girev's cot, below, was without a mattress so that through the slats Falcon could see dog harnesses underneath, and a few bones, wrapped in paper. Falcon lay on the planks, stretched out, his feet meeting the bottom bar. Above his head the Russian had written the names of the dogs – not those bequeathed by the school children who'd sponsored the animals but the Russian names that had quickly supplanted them. It had been a small victory over imperialism, embraced by Scott's men, who'd preferred to learn the tricky tongue-twisters, like Dhol, and Chukha, Hitol and Puchel. Falcon wondered how he'd felt when Scott or Wilson – or another of the officers – took the animals a few yards away to put a bullet into their heads. Dog meat for dogs.

He went back to Atch's corner and sat down.

His boot hit a wooden box under the bunk, which he pulled out. It was full of discarded gear – a hat, assorted clothes, and some wooden goggles which he picked up and tried on, and noticed the inscribed initials: RS, so Scott's. And then, slipped in at the side, a piece of stiff card on which was one of Wilson's watercolours – a portrait, just a few lines, possibly of Taffy Evans. He picked out a cap, in black hessian, which he thought he recognised from pictures of Birdie Bowers, and inside, there they were, the initials BB. Atch – the nicest man surely, other than Cherry – might have been sentimental as well. Did he mean to take the mementos home to the relatives – or were they for his own comfort?

Falcon's time there was passing, so he unpacked his knapsack on the wardroom table, took out a sandwich, a flask and his Olympic Pen, and started taking pictures: some oil cans by the door (no holes visible), Wilson's watercolour dream of England, the bookshelves in Scott's corner, and finally a set of pennants – long slim flags flown from the sledges as they set off south, a typically medieval flourish. Scott's held a motto – Ready Aye Ready – and the cross of St George.

Finally, he stood at the door, looking back down the length of the hut.

The urge to take something with him – a memento, a souvenir – was almost overwhelming. But he'd promised he'd respect the hut for what it was: a memorial of itself. He thought of the box under Atch's bunk: the intimate belongings of the dead. Perhaps he, too, had been overcome by the notion that it was disrespectful to rob a tomb. Atch had been in command of the rescue party that had found the bodies: perhaps the artefacts in the box were not just their belongings, but their *last* belongings.

He couldn't dismiss the thought, so he went back to Atch's bunk, pulling out the box and turning it upside down. He ran his hands through a pile of scarves, jumpers and mitts . . . and there it was, a single finnesko boot.

His heart contracted, his breath held, as he looked inside and found the initials: LO. Had Atch kept the boot they'd found, looking for the dead? He thrust his hand deep inside, his fingers exploring, but there was nothing, just the sennegrass in the toe-end.

He hadn't dared to hope for better.

He pulled out a clump of the grass to double check and was about to set it aside when he saw a scrap of paper at the heart of it. Gently, fingers shaking, he pulled the sedge-like leaves apart until he had the note in his hand – neatly folded in four. As he opened it his hair bristled, standing up on his hands and arms. It wasn't a sensation, or imagination: *he was being watched.*

He felt them all crowding round – Cherry, too. For the first time the true shape of the symbol Taffy Evans had drawn that day at the foot of the Beardmore Glacier nearly six decades earlier was revealed.

He'd stopped breathing, and had to take a hurried, ragged lungful of cold air.

He stared at the icon, willing recognition to bring it shape and meaning.

THREE

NORTH AGAIN

46

Two weeks later

As they circled the open coffin, anti-clockwise as tradition dictated, Yevgeny Zamyatin spoke in the ear of his daughter Maria.

'Child, do not place the flowers yet. There are fifteen blooms, woman. How did this happen?'

They were beneath the dome depicting Pantokratoros – the Christ – so his whisper seemed to gain in volume, circling above their heads. Maria, one hand to her mouth, opened her hand to reveal the crushed head of the wilted sixteenth. She bowed to the dead, clutched the flowers to her chest, and fled into the shadows beyond the cheap, false, flickering lights of the electric candelabrum.

She was a widow of great resource, so Zamyatin knew she would simply snap off the head of an offending flower and return after a moment of prayer: tradition dictated *even* numbers for the dead, *odd* for birthdays. A mistake would be the one thing everyone remembered, that and the name of the woman who had been so negligent of custom. She had been a good wife in her time, and a resourceful cook, and Zamyatin would spend his last years under her roof, but they were bound by tradition, and she could be forgetful. Zamyatin, who had been born before the revolutions, had lived a life as rigid as death itself, as lifeless as the face of the young man in the coffin.

He tried to imprint an image of Maxim's precise facial expression on his mind so that in his letter to Sofya he could describe her brother that she might take from this the sense that he had been given by God a good death. Zamyatin felt this truly because the boy's spirit had gone. He was an empty shell – this they all felt, for only the ghosts of the troubled remain on earth for the full forty days. Maxim was free, circling no doubt in the dome above, his body alone left to endure the cramped attentions of the casket in which he lay.

Zamyatin took his chance to fall into line behind Wassily Repin, who knew the family, and had worked at the Lubyanka for three decades. Retired now, he laboured assiduously in his attic flat, where the skylights allowed him to attend to his life's work: the iconography of revolution. The book had been in the making for thirty years. Repin lived in a world of tricolour cockades, Menshevik white fists, Liberty Bells, the black lions of slaves, the thin crescent and star of Islam. His library of books had buckled the floor in the winter of 'fifty-two, and Zamyatin had helped him move each volume – at the insistence of the landlord – down the eight flights of stairs, to a dry wood store in the yard, which shared a vent with the boiler house.

Zamyatin had been Repin's superior in the records department at the Lubyanka, but they had known each other a lifetime, and rank only mattered when strangers were present.

'No marks on the face,' said Repin, contemplating Maxim's waxy cheeks.

'He looks like a child,' said Zamyatin.

Maxim's wife and children approached the coffin, clutching each other, the boy disturbed by the grief of adults.

'A natural death, a good death, he died in his time,' whispered Repin. 'No sign of the widow's family,' he added, a statement not a question.

There were perhaps just twenty mourners. Maxim's arrest three years earlier had been an embarrassment. Now Sofya's sudden disappearance with the traitor Valentinov had tarnished irrevocably the family name. Old friends, even family, would keep their distance.

'Her father is a Party man and they cannot afford misunderstandings. Sofya's situation . . .' Zamyatin bowed his head at this euphemism. 'This has had repercussions. Shelepin has been moved to Perm. They see it as a failure of control from the centre. I told internal security we would be here – it is always best to be open. They want a list of the mourners.'

Sofya's disappearance was no mystery to Zamyatin. Her letters came to Maria's flat on Tretyakov Street. Dr Grey, Sofya's beloved, was – it appeared – at the American base in Antarctica, waiting for a ship to take him to the Falkland Islands. Security was lax: Grey felt able to write to her explaining that he'd made an extraordinary discovery on the ice, one he wished for now to keep secret – even from Washington and London. He had found a clue to the identity of Scott's killer. It was a sign, a riddle, and he needed help to decipher its meaning. Was Wassily Repin, Zemyatin's old comrade, still obsessed with the world of symbols?

Carefully folded within Sofya's letter was her own copy of this very symbol: three lines, one straight, one sinuous, one curved. Zemyatin had his copy in his waistcoat pocket. He rested a fat finger on it now, waiting for his moment.

Maria placed the fourteen lilies carefully in the coffin. It was the last gift, and Maxim's face was almost lost beneath the blooms.

They all stood stoically in the nave to listen to Psalm 118.

Then pallbearers closed the coffin and began to prepare for the burial. The widow sat with her children, whispering, kissing their heads and hands.

Zamyatin, limping, asked Wassily for his arm, and for the support of the stacidia – the standing chairs that lined the narthex beyond the Royal Doors. The outer gates were thrown open, as was the custom at this point, and they could see snow falling, which was a blessing because it shrouded the litter, and the broken glass.

They rested together, Zamyatin and Repin, waiting for the bearers to bring the boy through. Voices rose in a rhythmic chant, and their noses drew in the sickly incense.

Repin, dropped his chin as if in prayer but Zamyatin knew his friend had never found solace in God.

He coughed and covered his mouth with his hand, within which was the scrap of paper. 'Those books of yours, Wassily. Have they survived the winter?'

'Every page is dry,' said Repin, chin still down.

'Good. If you have time . . .' He passed over the copy.

His friend was nearly eighty but his fingers were adept, fluent, and he had the little paper package open in a heartbeat.

Zamyatin nodded, looking at his feet. 'At first we thought of the Sickle and the Plough – yes? A symbol of the working man – here, in Germany too, for all revolutionaries.'

Repin was already shaking his head. 'No. It is not familiar, Zheny. The letter D perhaps, or T in some scripts. Intriguing . . .'

'You have the time?'

'No. But I'll try. I've been summoned from retirement one last time, Zheny. The director wants a report on the symbols of Ireland. The British have sent their army to the northern province to quell the chaos – a civil war, the cities are in flames. A religious war, Zheny, who would have thought this of the cold-hearted British? The army of the Irish Republic has moved to the border. Perhaps there will be a war of nations. I doubt it. The Irish are shy of the battlefield, like all weak peoples. I understand that we wish to train the rebels and send them money and guns. This will be the future – the balaclava, the bomb. We've done this in the past, and it did us little good, but there we are. It is a place riven by images – rival Gods, clashing tribes. I must become an expert in the Red Hand and the Green Fist.'

He glanced again at the curious symbol. 'But yes. I will look for you. It will be in a book – that is a certainty. It is important?'

'It is sensitive, Wassily. Do not mention it to anyone else. A private matter – but of academic interest.'

Repin was no fool. Carefully, he folded the piece of paper and placed it in his wallet.

They joined the end of the procession. Maxim's friends from university had spread sticks on the path to stop bad spirits following the coffin and taking their friend to hell.

Zamyatin and Repin held on to each other, their sticks skittering on the ice.

At the grave the priest said the words they all expected, like a charm.

In his turn Zamyatin took the filigree silver holder and its tiny cup and poured the vodka into the grave. Then they all took handfuls of grit and snow and threw them into the shadows. This, for Zamyatin, was the sound of old age.

Within a minute they were alone and Repin had lit a cigarette.

'And now a glass for us, Wassily – at Luka's. Who knows? In this winter of ours, it might be our last.'

47

Two weeks later

Falcon had the phone to his ear, but the tone of it ringing had gone on for nearly a minute, so he opened the window to hear again the wall of sound: a quarter of a million sea-birds calling *ewa ewa*, which, the Hercules' pilot had warned him, was the islanders' word for cacophony. The stench of guano made him gag, and he pulled the window closed. In the comparative silence he heard the phone pick up.

A voice said, 'You've to take it now,' but the accent was heavy, rural, a backwater somewhere. He heard the visceral thud of the phone being knocked against wood. The line was crystal clear: he could hear a fire crackling, a dog barking once and being shushed, then the sound of conversation, and a glass being set down.

'Falcon?' As she said his name he heard a door close and the acoustic was transformed: a smaller space, but with a brittle echo, off stone perhaps, and tiles.

'Sofya?'

'Yes, me.' It was the first time they'd spoken in nearly six weeks. On the Falklands they'd swapped telegrams, another air letter.

'Where are you?' he asked. 'It's safe to talk – no one's listening.'

'You first,' she said, and he knew from the tone that she was saving good news.

'I'm in a place called the Devil's Ashpit – it's pretty much cinder, a mountain of it, with a view over the Atlantic. I'm on the east coast of Ascension Island – I landed an hour ago at Wideawake. A flight to Washington in ten days – or I may just get a cabin on the post boat from Cape Town to Portsmouth.'

He was in a long, narrow room, a single prefabricated building, computers along one wall, open windows opposite. The air was sweltering, the noise of the birds ceaseless, waxing, waning, like a wave. The ocean itself was grey and limitless. 'Your turn.'

She laughed. 'I'm in the South Pole Inn,' she said. 'County Kerry. I do not believe this phone can work. You have to wind it up to get the local exchange. I'm in a corridor outside the bar. I have Guinness – a half.'

'Tom Crean's pub?'

'Yes. Twenty years dead, but still *his* pub.'

'I miss you,' he said, which came from nowhere, like a long-forgotten name.

'Why are you there?' he added.

'I sent the symbol to Zheny. This is still our secret, yes?'

'Yes. I've told nobody – yet. I think they want to suppress the truth, Sof. We're better on our own.'

'Good. He gave it to old Repin – he knew Father, too, from the university, but mostly from Luka's bar at the corner of our street. As a child I despised him. He hated the sound of children. But Repin studies symbols. He worked at the Lubyanka for thirty years.

'Repin is busy, despite his age, because the Kremlin watches Ireland. This is our great luck, because here he finds the symbol, but not in his books, in the files at the Lubyanka. I will send details, but there is a letter, from 1925, handwritten, I have seen this – a photocopy. It was from a man called Pa Murray, a member of the IRA, Falcon. But Murray goes back much further. The IRA has roots – they were called the Irish Republican Brotherhood. These men organise the uprising of 1916. They were much admired in

Russia – they started a revolution, inspired our own. We are proud of them. Lenin was proud of them. Their revolution failed, but the fuse had been lit.'

'What's the letter about? Why does it contain the symbol?' he asked.

'You are sure it is safe to talk?' she said.

'The line's good,' said Falcon. 'It's NASA's. I'm at their tracking station. For Apollo. Anders – he's the radio man here – said he never listens to lovers, and I can see him now, outside smoking, taking Aput for a walk on the clifftop.'

'Aput? I thought America—'

'No. The Yanks have pulled strings. A working dog – the paperwork is done. She comes home with me. And no quarantine, not from the Great White.'

There was a short silence. 'So we're lovers?' she asked.

'Yes. And lovers share secrets.'

'Murray comes to Moscow to see Stalin. There is a file. The Kremlin is paying then five hundred English pounds a year to banish the imperialists, or at least to distract the British. They do neither. The debriefing note – I have it here, a copy – states that the men of the IRB have "energy, daring, flair, illogicality, a tendency to disunity and splits, lack of organisation, courage and naivety". In short, starry-eyed rebels. They could be Russians.

'Murray wanted more money – and guns. But Stalin was not impressed. He complained that they had yet to murder a single bishop. And they'd spent the sea journey to St Petersburg gossiping openly about uprisings and Russian backing. So they cut the money. The letter Repin found was written later by Murray, and pleads for another chance – but the signature carries a flourish – a mark made up of three lines.

'It is the symbol. Repin went back to his books. Before the First World War it was the Republicans' own, a signature for all – yes? – as are the two strokes of the Christian fish. It is the outline of the Irish harp. Zamyatin says in his letter: "Tell your man to look to the Irish."'

'Why are you laughing?' asked Falcon.

'It's on my half-pint glass, Falcon. The Irish harp.'

Falcon imagined her, in black, balanced on one suede shoe, leaning against a whitewashed wall in a stone-flagged corridor, the archaic phone in one hand, the half of black stout in the other.

Trailing the telephone cable, he walked back to the window, which gave a view of the Green Mountain – covered with exotic trees, bamboo and banana – and beside it the Red Mountain, a volcanic cone of incinerated dust that made him think of white Erebus.

'Is Crean our man?' he said, unable to wait, thrilled that she'd taken up the search on her own.

'No,' she said. 'My heart says no. But it is not the end. Something else has begun.'

The evening sun had touched the South Atlantic so one of the technicians servicing the computers gave him a can of Miller High Life.

'Tell me everything,' he said.

'Annascaul is a "township" – yes? Just the pub, a few houses, like a Russian village on the road east. It knows all secrets, Falcon. Many people remember Tom. People here now, in the bar by the fire, knew him like a brother.'

'His grave is close to the pub. He is the spirit of the place. A proud Irishman, yes, but no more. There are others, Falcon. Proud to be rebels, some even yearn to fight in the North. But never Tom. When he finally came home for good he had the life he'd always wanted. A quiet life. A wife, children, and his pub with its view of green fields and grey rocks. Yes, he has sympathies. He joins a great demonstration when a hunger striker dies. The British raid the pub and find nothing but his Navy uniform.

'A life of contradictions. His brother is a policeman for the British. The Republicans shoot him dead. He remains silent. Perhaps, say the old men, he wishes to step out from the shadow of Scott. Is he wary of his fellow patriots? Perhaps. Scott is forgotten. He is forgotten. He dies quietly, and is missed.'

In the background Falcon heard muffled voices, a laugh. 'Can you still speak?'

'Yes. They bring me another drink. I do not ask, this just happens. A moment.' Falcon heard a match strike. 'Things run deep here,' she said. 'I do not know enough. But I know when I hear truth. They say he was not a bitter man, not an angry man. He felt the cause. I am sure he hoped for freedom. But he did nothing.'

The computers in the room began to whirl, deciphering incoming radio signals.

'But, yes, I did find something,' she said. 'Crean was a popular man but none of his shipmates from *Terra Nova* ever visited – except one. Gwynne, the third man in this last party – yes? And Gwynne has a story to tell them all over the whiskey by the fire.'

'The Cornishman?' prompted Falcon.

'Yes. He sat by the same fire I have sat by and he sing the songs they love. But how does he know the words, Falcon? His father, Treve Gwynne, was a fisherman from a place called Sennen, a cove, with a harbour, near your Land's End. But the boat sometimes goes to Ireland to miss Atlantic storms.

'Treve marries a woman from Dublin, and brings her home. He is a hard man. The boy dotes on his mother who is soft and loving. He lives in the Cornish cove until he is sixteen. Then one day his father does not sail home. The three bodies come back on the tide, a month later.

'His mother takes him to Ireland, to Dublin, to a great family of Catholic patriots, and two of his uncles, Falcon, are of this Irish Republican Brotherhood.'

Falcon heard her drawing on the cigarette.

'He becomes a patriot too. He has the fervour of the convert. He joins the Brotherhood. But he must live and he wants his own ship but has no savings, so he joins the Royal Navy, seemingly for the same reasons as Crean – for the money, for the life, and he knows the sea because it is in his blood. He goes with Scott, is part of the last returning party *and* part of the rescue party. He was there, Falcon, when they found the bodies.

'In Dublin he uses his back pay to buy a boat – the *Josephine*. He marries and starts a family and at night he makes plans with the rest for revolution. He is in the city for the great Rising of Easter – he plays his part. He tells them all here in Annascaul brave stories of barricades, and flags, and the proclamation of the Republic.'

'But he'd be dead now, Sofya. So we'll never know,' said Falcon.

'Yes. Dead. This year, Falcon. Only this year.

'Gwynne has a son, Liam. The station master here – a man called O'Neil – was a friend of Crean's. There are no secrets. O'Neil is an IRA man – he all but said it. This son is a big man – he means a rebel leader. He has gone north to Belfast, where they fight again. They fight now, Falcon. O'Neil says the son will know the truth.'

Schmidt the radio man was walking back across the clifftops, the dog lolloping free at his side.

'Sofya, I have to go. This must be our secret. If Whitehall hears of an Irish connection they'll close us down. The truth will never be told. But Belfast – can we find him? The city's in flames.'

'I will try. O'Neil said he'd smooth the path.'

'Could it be Gwynne?' he asked.

'Yes,' said Sofya. 'After Gwynne's death this son, Liam, comes south just this last spring. He visits the South Pole

Inn. He brings a gift for the pub, for Crean's family. The inn is full of the things of the past, yes? They say memorabilia. Scott's men had long flags made for the sledges – like knights in armour. This one was Gwynne's, from the expedition. It was green, Falcon, with a single gold-threaded emblem of the Irish harp. It hangs over the fire.'

48

It was a stillborn day in Cambridge, the light already bleeding away into a grey sky, the market-stall awnings dripping beaded curtains of icy rain. In contrast the window of Thomas Cook boasted a six-foot-wide Technicolor picture of the beach at Iraklion, on the north coast of Crete, the tables set in a foot of blue Aegean. Inside, behind the counter, a blackboard advertised cut-price all-inclusive packages to the Algarve and the Costa Brava.

Falcon gave his name and was handed an envelope containing his rail tickets to Liverpool, the boat to Larne with an overnight cabin, and his hotel details. He still had his sea legs, but he'd made himself walk out to the VW to check that all was well and pack a fresh knapsack. His train left in two hours. Tomorrow, as long as the boat sailed in poor weather, he'd see Sofya. Belfast was a battleground: the newspapers' front pages that morning had pictured a riotous mob besieging an armoured car, but the promise of the rendezvous still made him smile.

By the time he got to the small, triangular park opposite Isaac Newton's old rooms at Trinity, the time was right. A plaque said 'All Saints' Church – 13th Century. Demolished 1865.' There was a slim, stylish Victorian memorial cross, and some flowerbeds blackened by frost. He patted Aput, sure that even she couldn't pick up the scent of the dead in a churchyard six hundred years old.

A busker outside Heffer's bookshop sang a Donovan single, 'Candyman', which made him think of his stash of dope. He'd left it untouched, taped to the wheel arch of the VW.

The post boat had taken fifteen days to reach home. He'd spent most of the voyage in his cabin – shades of Cherry again – working on a long explanatory note for Century House, which included an outline of the evidence found on the Barrier, but nothing about Taffy's symbol. That was reserved for a separate document, for which he had very different plans.

Lady Strood walked confidently under the metal arch over the gateway to the old churchyard.

'Dr Grey – Falcon.' She smiled. 'Welcome home. Bravo.'

She had on a stylish full-length wool coat in black and a sable fur hat, which made her look like a Moscow tourist. He wondered if she ever ventured into public without the protective carapace of a new identity. She looked energised, perhaps remembering the icy winters of a Berlin childhood.

She sat beside him. 'What will you do? A holiday?'

'I might drive up to the Norfolk coast. I need to think about publishing our findings. Dr Finn, the pathologist, has agreed to co-author. Or does Her Majesty's Government have other ideas?'

A tight smile, and she looked up at a flagpole, over Trinity's gate, which was making the odd clattering noise reserved for the masts of ships. 'The truth must out,' she said. 'The view in Whitehall is that the discoveries on the Barrier – the tent, Scott, then Oates – can't remain secret for long and we feel that there is no need to postpone an announcement. We felt the Scott Polar was the ideal venue. Dates are being discussed. However . . .' She rearranged the coat, turning the collar up against the icy air.

'Ah,' said Falcon. 'I thought we had an understanding.'

'Downing Street has taken a view,' she said. 'It's felt there should be no reference – at this stage – to sabotage, or the secret notebook. Finding the dead is an international coup. The pictures, when released, will go round the world. Why overshadow it at this stage with what is still, frankly, an unfinished story?'

Falcon had picked up a fresh supply of Ducados when they'd stopped at La Gomera in the Canary Islands, so he made an elaborate ceremony of lighting up, jettisoning the match on the third throw. He wondered if it was an occupational hazard for people like Lady Strood that they lost sight of the need for the truth to be timely. Secrecy became addictive.

'But that's not the real reason,' he said.

'No. It's just bad timing,' she said. 'Half the Civil Service is in Brussels. It's Wilson's fixation. The Cabinet is keen to have something to say about economic growth – especially with an election mooted. De Gaulle's departure has opened the door to a fresh application. Can we step through? The Common Market's a precarious structure, balanced by a fundamental quid pro quo: the French want to protect their farms, and the Germans want to protect their factories. We were seen as inimical to both – but minds change. There is widespread unease on the Continent about the Americans' clear lead in technology. Britain's entry is being seen as a way of kick-starting a European counter-challenge. The French and Germans are with us. The Irish – great power-brokers, like so many small nations – are pleading our case. The mood music is positive. We don't want to spoil that – do we?'

If she only knew, thought Falcon.

'But when?' he asked, affecting curiosity, yet knowing the answer.

'The current thinking is 1987, seventy-five years after the men died.'

Eighteen years to wait: childishly, he thought it sounded like a lifetime.

'You'll appreciate the problem,' said Lady Strood. 'Yes, we have proof Scott's story is true. But being unable to name the guilty men brings Germany back into the frame, as it were, even if we then rule them out. Although there's always that intriguing note from Filchner– that's out in 1975. Who knows what he will say? Another good reason to hang fire. It's a tricky time, you see.'

'It's always a tricky time,' said Falcon. 'I could go ahead – you said so yourself. A telephone call to Paris, or New York.'

'It would do great harm to the national interest,' she said. 'I'm sorry, but the view is a prosecution might be brought. To discourage others. To make it clear we – that is the government – did not want this made public.'

'I see,' he said. He wondered how many national secrets never emerged from the filing cabinets of Whitehall.

'History is a wide horizon,' said Lady Strood, trying to win back lost moral ground. 'In the grand scheme of things does it matter, a few more years? I've always loved this place,' she said, looking round at the small park. 'The church they pulled down was actually called All-Saints-in-the-Jewry. This was the ghetto, you see, this tiny triangle. And then the Jews were banished, their place usurped. But now we are back. England was a haven to me. It's a long game, history.'

Some dry icy snow began to fall.

She moved on to outline arrangements already broached with the Scott Polar for an event to announce the finding of the dead.

'We think a date in about a month would be good. The Kiwis are back at the site. Oates's body has been examined, and it's been suggested that he could be buried with the rest. A nice touch, which the family is considering. Come the day you'd be the only academic voice. Can you produce your paper by then?'

'Yes. *Nature*, I think. I've made discreet contact with an editor. It'll be fairly limited: an outline of how we found them, the development of RES, and then I'll fold in the autopsy results from Christchurch.'

'Excellent,' said Lady Strood, examining her gloves, then pulling them off, exercising arthritic hands. She had an amber ring on her wedding finger; it was struggling to reflect any light at all.

A black cloud was overhead, the snow thickening.

'One final piece of news,' said Lady Strood. 'Your assailant at Old Pole, Jeff Ward. Our friends at the Pentagon believe he's a KGB operative. The Lubyanka is somewhat embarrassed by the incident.'

Looking beyond Lady Strood, who had begun a long digression on Cold War politics, he could see the four-square tower of St John's Chapel. In its far shadow a narrow stone alley led down to the river, often cluttered with bicycles. There was a second-hand-book shop, and beside it a single black doorway marked 8.

Earlier, he'd knocked smartly, and heard an electric buzz free the lock.

One of the senior fellows at Caius had recommended Golding, Trot & Whistler, solicitors, of Portugal Place. They were discreet, efficient – and, most importantly, unlike many partnerships, set to thrive for many years. Mr Trot's son was already an articled clerk, as was Whistler's.

He'd made three new copies of Scott's diary and Oates's memoir, adding his explanatory note on the Irish harp, and what they knew from Ireland about Gwynne. He'd addressed three envelopes to the head offices of the *Guardian*, the *Washington Post* and the *Irish Times*. The original of Scott's diary was still in its box of seals' teeth in the artefact store at the Scott Polar.

His instructions were simple. The firm would hold his last will and testament. On the occasion of his death the three envelopes were to be posted, first class, air mail. Plump, padded, gravid. He'd handed the packages over to Mr Golding, who'd slipped them into the office safe, a little ceremony that took Falcon back to the library at Lamer, and Cherry's sleight of hand on the night Bones was born.

He told Golding he was travelling and might wish to update the final note at intervals. 'It's just unfinished business,' Falcon had said, shaking hands.

He was in no doubt that the government would delay publication for as long as possible. Ireland would become a key ally, and Washington was the principal broker for peace in the North. It might be decades – more – before the truth saw the light of day. This way at least death brought certainty.

Lady Strood must have sensed she'd stretched his patience. She stood, and he shook her cold hand, then watched her walk away, exhibiting the spy's ultimate skill: within a moment she was part of the crowd, lost in a flurry of snow.

49

Belfast

The Crown was tropical, hot and damp, the stained-glass windows obscured by condensation, touched by the ghost-like fall of snowflakes. The gilded interior flickered in sympathy with a series of coke fires, the acrid smell of which permeated the stout. Falcon counted fifteen pints on the iron, glass-top tables – only one of bitter, the rest pitch-black. He noted the subtle tell-tale difference with the 'mainland': each of these pints had been lovingly poured, the head removed with the sideways swish of a knife, then carefully topped-up, until the delineation between black and white was sharp. In a Cambridge pub they would have been still milky, if clearing, like a rising snowstorm on the Barrier.

The door opened and briefly he caught sight of the Europa Hotel, the glass sixties box-like design already an irresistible invitation to the IRA. The pub door closed slowly, inhibited by a metal dampener, so he saw a British Army armoured car sweep past, a soldier head-and-shoulders out of the manhole, a Union Flag torn away in the wet snow.

Aput raised her head to sniff the world outside, then edged closer to the coke fire.

The sound of the military engine was distinctive, and it made Falcon's pint vibrate on the glass table, so he picked it up and took an inch off the top, for a moment examining the Irish harp etched on the glass. A garrulous barman on the ferry had told him the symbol had been on the glasses for nearly a century – but if he wanted to see the 'real McCoy' he'd to get himself to Dublin to see the Trinity College harp, a fourteenth-century treasure, a 'marvel' he must see if he went to 'the South'.

The door was still closing with a series of judders, and Sofya must have slipped through fleet-footed, because she appeared in front of him, in a dark full-length coat and black beret, which she took off immediately, shaking the snow-flakes to the wooden floor.

They embraced, retreating only a few inches to examine each other's faces. Falcon felt a lot of things – an increasingly thrilling experience, which made him feel less lonely, and more connected, embedded even, in the lives of others.

Aput, excluded, barked rhythmically until Sofya held her head for a moment in both hands by way of introduction.

'Let's take a booth,' said Falcon, leading the way into one of the bar's many snugs, in which there was one table and a banquette, so they sat side by side, at rest but touching.

Sofya threaded her arm through his, as if they'd been together a lifetime. 'It's too cold,' she said.

'Baikonur in winter?' asked Falcon.

The barman appeared with a half-pint for Sofya.

'It's the damp,' she said, and handed the drink back, asking for a pint. 'The city. I had no idea,' she said. 'It is 1930. We are in the past. I saw a child with no shoes – on the icy pavement. The women working, the men on the doorsteps of bars. And the checkpoints, the soldiers. I feel at home – it is not a good feeling.'

Falcon put a pebble on the table: it was black and smooth. 'I stole it from McMurdo, the US base – well, from Observation Hill, which overlooks it. Just a penguin's gift.'

She took it and let it lie in her closed hand. 'It's a gift, Falcon, that's all that matters. I thought you never gave gifts.' She sipped her drink, looking ahead. 'You've changed. The eyes look out not in. The past is finished now, and you are to blame for nothing,' she said emphatically, as if delivering a verdict.

He'd written her a letter at a fine desk in the Governor's House at Port Stanley, about the lost hour of his life.

Sofya studied his face: looking into each eye in turn, the crow's feet at the corners. 'A new person – or a person remade,' she said. 'No ghosts?'

'No. Just Cherry. And he's part of me.'

Falcon thought about the room he'd got them in the Europa Hotel. It had a view of snowy rounded hills and the lough, a double bed, a trouser-press, and a single armchair. He thought how warm it would be under the covers. He hailed the barman and ordered two pints of Black Velvet – champagne and Guinness – and a bowl of water for Aput.

'Celebration?' asked the barman.

'Yes. Celebration,' said Sofya.

They talked and drank for an hour, the pub filling, the heat thickening with cigarette smoke and the pungent sulphurous edge of the coke fires.

Finally, Sofya got out a city map.

'You've found Liam Gwynne? He'll talk?' asked Falcon.

Since he'd returned to the UK they'd had two snatched telephone calls. They'd agreed again to keep the Irish harp a secret, given the chaotic security situation in Northern Ireland, the pressure on London to allow UN peacekeepers onto the streets, and the watchful eye of Washington.

'There's an intermediary, a go-between, for the first meeting,' said Sofya. 'They said they have to be sure. The situation is . . .' she shrugged '. . . explosive. The British pay for spies, infiltrate, it is difficult to find trust here. Liam is a marked man. The IRA is trying to win hearts again. So . . .' she took out a notebook '. . . at three tomorrow. Gibney's Bar – off the Falls Road.'

She placed a finger on the map. 'We're to wait outside and meet Father John. If we pass whatever test is set we will see the son.'

Falcon sipped his pint, looking around the bar, examining some of the other customers.

'You think someone follows?' asked Sofya.

'It's just a feeling.'

'There was someone on the boat.'

'Moscow?' asked Falcon.

'I doubt this. I am a minor functionary. I didn't exist before I went. But it is a paranoid state. I can't promise there's no shadow. I went up on the deck to watch the lights of Liverpool. We were passing the river front, an old woman tells me what to see – the Royal Liver Building, a clipper, the new cathedral lit up. But this man at the rail he looks the other way, across the muddy river, to a flat line of lights – chimneys and docks. This is not right.'

'Young, old, smart, tall?'

'Tall. A coat over a suit. Perhaps in the middle age. But with the energy of the young. He pretended to read a news-paper in the wind. I hid on the boat, under my coat in a seat, and I wait until women come aboard to clean. I walk away through the dock gates. It was dawn. Half a mile later I hear shoes running. I stand aside in an alleyway and he goes past.'

'A runner?'

'Yes. The breath was easy.'

Had Lady Strood guessed he'd told her less than the truth? Had Parkis been ordered to step back into his life? Sofya's description was so reminiscent of the legal clerk's willing enthusiasm that Falcon could see his face now, eager to please, attentive. But what skills did a legal clerk bring to such a mission? He knew Falcon by sight, certainly, and there was a sense of trust between them.

'It could be MI6,' he said. 'Tomorrow we need to shake them off if they're on our tail.'

The door opened to reveal an urban blizzard, the pave-ments running with icy water, the streetlights blurred.

'One more piece of the jigsaw,' said Falcon. 'Meares's gun. Why was it left in the tent? The file had an address for his widow, in British Columbia, so I got the number, and rang from the Scott Polar. She's still alive, bright as a button. I asked a few questions but she said the people to talk to were at the museum in Victoria – they'd got all his letters and gear.

'I rang and said I'd been cataloguing artefacts at the Scott Polar and I'd found Meares's pistol. They said they already had it – he'd kept a box of stuff from the *Terra Nova*. I told them the one I had was marked CHM.'

Sofya had ordered whiskeys, so they sipped in tandem.

'The archivist rang me back – apologetic. She said they were sure the pistol was his but they'd just checked the item in the museum. It wasn't her area of expertise, otherwise she would have known. The pistol was etched with the letters JG. I've checked the crew manifest, Sof – John (known as Jack) – Gwynne was the only man with those initials. Christchurch say their pistol – the one found in the tent – is in working order. The one in Canada is faulty – the hammer was jammed. Without fitting a replacement part it would never fire again.'

Sofya sipped her whiskey. 'They swapped guns?'

'Yes. Meares didn't need a gun. He was on the boat home. My guess is Jack Gwynne left the gun in the tent when the rescue party found the dead. Two questions for his son Liam: why did he need a gun, and why did he leave it in the tent? Make that three questions. Don't forget, Meares was an Irishman – was he in on the plot?'

50

The Falls Road was a mire, snow and slush and dirt, the shop awnings dripping icicles. Soldiers in capes stood at corners, their rifles dipped, radios crackling. A few streets on the Lower Falls had been demolished to make way for flats, but most of the old Victorian houses still stood, in blood-red bricks, two-up, two-down, backyards separated across a flagged alleyway, rubbish-strewn, patrolled by cats. Children ran free in the gutters.

They zigzagged through alleyways and streets, and Falcon – looking back at the corners – was sure they'd either not been followed or had shaken off their tail. They'd found a café and sat over mugs of tea – and, to be doubly sure, they'd chosen their moment to exit through the back door, across a yard, leaving a pile of coins on the table.

The stipulated bar was on Salisbury Street, its name framed by the street number: 67 GIBNEY 67. Half-hearted snow fell so that the whole street looked to Falcon as if it existed behind tracing paper.

They were still early so they had a cigarette, trying to shake off a bad night's sleep. The Europa's fire alarms had gone off twice, prompted by telephone bomb threats, so they'd stood in the snow as the Army searched the rooms. At one point they felt the faraway shock-wave as a bomb went off somewhere else in the city centre. They'd stood, shivering, under the tram wires, which shorted intermittently, casting the scene in a vivid light, which brought back to Falcon a memory of the pit they'd dug to reach the tent.

One of the children milling outside the bar must have been on lookout, because the priest found them. He came out of the public bar smoking a cigarette with yellow fingers.

'Father John?' asked Falcon. Aput greeted him with a low-level growl.

The priest was tall and wide, the black cassock dusted with ash. 'Nobody mentioned a woman,' he said.

'She's just in from Annascaul,' said Falcon. He'd taken Cherry's line on religion, deciding there were better diversions, so a city steeped in it, two virulent varieties, left him wary, but he was determined not to be intimidated.

The priest's head was bare, revealing curly russet hair, and small eyes.

'We're together,' added Falcon, and offered cigarettes as the priest opened an umbrella, which he held over his own head.

'There's been a car bomb – down Divis. The place will be crawling. It's at your own risk. I have to be somewhere else. We need to talk before you meet Liam. Come on.'

St Peter's Cathedral, its two distant spires narrow against the sky, was a mile away, just seen through the falling snow as they set out through the maze of backstreets.

The sound of a bomb – the dull crump – brought everything to a stop. They stood, waiting, on a patch of waste ground in which stood a burnt-out car. There was an echo, a siren, the sound of a single window smashing nearby, then the priest was walking again. All the pubs they passed were boarded up or behind windows dripping with condensation. It was just after three o'clock.

Falcon had been to conferences in Belfast – at Queen's – and had always known the city was a tinderbox. But that summer the spark was Derry, and the riots had brought the British Army to the Province, and inevitably the bombs to Belfast.

The waiter who'd brought them breakfast in their room said he'd been told the Irish Government might send troops in to defend Catholics. 'That'll be war then,' he'd added cheerfully, waiting for a tip.

That morning's *Belfast Telegraph* had said the bitter fighting had caught the IRA by surprise, that Catholics felt abandoned and afraid, some ready to flee south. On street corners Falcon had seen the graffito: 'IRA = I Ran Away'. The situation was desperate, and 'peace lines' were being built, wire and concrete strung across the city, separating warring tribes.

A police station lay ahead – a three-storey concrete bastion rising up above a pet shop and a bookie's. Armed soldiers manned a gun emplacement on the street corner. A child let a dog on a string urinate on the sandbags.

Hurrying on, they spilt out suddenly into a square, the cathedral rising up before them, black-sooted, each of the twin spires lost now in the falling snow.

Inside, beyond the heavy copper doors, the interior was laced with incense, mixed with a thin damp mist, which had crept in from the slushy street. The scent of candles, which burnt in military rows, was cloying.

Father John took Falcon's arm, a moment of connection. 'I've to take confession. There'll be the usual suspects – come in last, when the pew's empty. Why is your woman here? They must have told her at Annascaul you'd to be alone.'

Sofya had taken a seat and covered her head with a silk scarf like the other women, the dog at her feet on the kneeler.

'We're together,' repeated Falcon. 'I'm sorry – I can't leave her. This is us. Why? Is there a problem?'

'No one likes surprises,' said the priest, turning away, slipping into one of three confessional boxes in the side aisle. It was in dark wood, with a green damask curtain across the doorway. A line of women filled a pew, waiting their turn.

A choir was singing on a scratchy tape, and a group of pilgrims making a tour of the stations of the cross, their prayers ragged but rhythmic. Falcon sat beside one of the great iron radiators, which vibrated noisily, pumping out damp heat that rose into the high, ark-like roof and bled away.

Sofya held a rosary in one hand: gold links, with jet beads, and a silver cross in the Orthodox style. It struck Falcon that she was more at home in this building than he could ever have been.

The light on the top of the confessional box blinked to green. A woman came out, dabbing her eyes, and set off for the altar rail where most of the penitents knelt, mumbling their prayers.

Falcon thought about Jack Gwynne. *If* he was their man, how had he sabotaged the depots? He'd been one of a party of three – the last returning party – trudging north, back to the ship. Lieutenant Evans could be set aside – unless all three were part of a plot, which was an unlikely scenario if Gwynne was the ring-leader. Suffering from scurvy, barely conscious, lying finally on a sledge, Lieutenant Evans was a blind witness. Had the two Irishmen worked together, or had Gwynne contrived to strike alone? Taking extra rations was easy, but spiking the fuel cans, hiding boxes of food, and finally torching the Northern Barrier depot were brazen acts. Which brought them back to Crean, despite Sofya's verdict: had he been persuaded to stand aside, to let his fellow countryman strike a blow for Ireland? Had he been given a choice? Or was his silence kept under duress. Was the quiet man of Annascaul mute by the orders of others?

The last woman came out of the confessional, jaunty, her sins put away, and set off for the candles at the altar rail.

Falcon slipped into the box, pulling the curtain across behind him. The air was heavy with polish and nicotine, but no hint of whiskey or beer.

Father John let the silence stretch out. 'You say, "Forgive me, Father, for I have sinned."'

'I think I'm here to listen,' said Falcon, taking off his glasses and slipping them into his jacket. 'O'Neil, the IRA man at Annascaul, told Sofya we should talk to Gwynne's son Liam. That suggests to me there is something to tell. Which is why I'm here. I don't have a confession to make.'

'Do you not have a burden?'

He could see the priest now through the patterned mesh of black material – an assemblage of glimpses, the head back perhaps, one hand covering his eyes. It occurred to Falcon that listening to sins must be a penance of itself. 'I had a burden,' he said. He felt suddenly lighter, even elated. He'd told Sofya everything he'd felt on the Barrier, at the foot of the three graves, but saying this out loud to a stranger seemed to widen the horizon of the future.

He felt a strange, thrilling excitement, an urge to speak. 'I thought I was responsible for the death of my family in the war – in London. I was late, they waited, and a rocket fell. Only I survived.'

'How long did you carry this burden?' said the priest.

'I was five then. I found out the truth a few weeks ago. I was late home because of a white lie, not my own. I'm innocent even of that. I did a good deed. I held the hand of an old man as he died.'

There was a sound, a shifting, and Falcon saw that the priest had his head against the mesh, his eyes closed.

'That's great, isn't it?' he said. 'The world must be a different place.'

Falcon nodded.

There was a narrow gap at the foot of the mesh where it reached a shelf. A slip of paper came through, and on it an address.

'We had to be sure you weren't followed,' said the priest. 'You were shadowed from the Europa Hotel, but you lost them well enough. You have no shadows now.'

Falcon heard the priest shuffle his wooden chair closer to the screen.

'Liam's out of the city. The British have spies and they're rounding men up. It's a cottage just over the border. They'll meet you there. It's not far – an hour, a little more. It's bandit country, so don't skulk, just stay in plain sight. I'll take you to the car.'

He placed his hand on the mesh. 'Don't take the woman to the house. Leave her at the bothy just beyond the border. She'll be safe enough. They're not expecting her, and they're living on their wits. Why take chances?'

'The son will be there?' countered Falcon.

'Yes. Liam will be there. They've been running men over the border to bring guns. We need guns. We need men who'll use them. Our people are being driven from their homes. When Liam comes back he'll not be empty-handed.'

There was a silence, and Falcon was convinced that for the first time in this life he had acquired Cherry's great gift: he could hear the snow falling on the roof of the great church.

The priest's voice came closer. 'I have to ask you if you wish to change your mind. You can walk away. I have that with authority from Liam. Both of you can go home. But I can't ask again. No one will ask again.'

It took a moment for Falcon to reassemble the jigsaw behind the mesh: Father John was praying, his hands clasped to his forehead, bent forward.

'I'll go on,' said Falcon. 'We'll go on. If the son has a story to tell.'

'Yes, he's a tale to tell. But before you go there's a story he won't tell you, but it's the story you must know.'

51

Their driver – introduced as 'Bates' by Father John – searched them before they got into the car, then took the N3 out of the city at a steady speed south, past two police towers, bristling with soldiers. There were no road-blocks (although, Bates said, they were stopping everything at the border). In Armagh he'd parked by the clock tower, and got them cans of beer and pies from a butcher's shop. Three soldiers, strung across the high street, patrolled with guns and radios. Falcon guessed Bates was armed because he wore his coat buttoned up, sat awkwardly behind the wheel, and his eyes – which Falcon watched in the rear-view mirror – never stopped moving. He chewed gum, so a muscle in his jaw was always flexing, like a cow with the cud.

They pulled off the N3 five miles short of the border, near Middletown, and took a by-road towards Barter Farm. Bandit country was more water than land: lakes, ponds, meres and black rivers, as if all the sweet rain of Ireland was bubbling up to obscure the hated line of the border. It lay ahead in a jigsaw of half-light made up of trees, hedges and telegraph poles, stone barns and shelters. The dog lay across their laps on the back seat, while they had to keep clearing away the condensation on the windows to look out at the snow, which was turning colder, settling as they got closer to the Republic.

The contrast with Antarctica was stark. The air on the Barrier had been pin-sharp, cold and arid, the blizzards murderous but brief. Here the sky sagged with the damp, a buckled quilt of black and grey, the dark green of the land glimpsed through the snow in the hedgerows and the wind-blown corners of the fields. There was forest too, in patches on the hills, and white brooks filled the gullies and rills.

The farmer was at a five-bar gate, a woman dressed in a man's full-length green coat, and a wide hat. She took a cigarette from Bates but didn't look at Falcon or Sofya. 'They said he'd be alone,' she said.

'The priest was happy,' said Bates, getting out of the car, checking his watch. Then to Falcon: 'Your woman's to keep her chin down. They fly over, the Brits. Do what the farmer says. They send out patrols from Tydavnet, but we've some luck too – there's a field hospital set up ten miles east, so they're watching that. You'll get by all right. The boys'll meet you on the other side at the bothy.'

The farmer came back with gear and a bottle of Jamesons, which was passed around. Falcon said no, but Sofya took a swig and didn't choke, then lit a cigarette, the flare harsh in the thickening gloom. The snow was colder, a cloud of hot breath rising as the farmer led the cows out of their shed. Falcon gave up on his glasses and slipped them into an inside pocket.

A low mist was creeping up out of a brook, and they heard gunshots, but the farmer spat in the mud and said it was hunters after rabbit.

Bates checked his watch. 'Go on, go now,' he said, jettisoning the cigarette, slipping into the car and driving off down the track too fast, so that the back end skidded in and out of the deep ruts in the mud.

They walked just behind the herd, up a valley with shallow sweeping sides, which were white and unblemished, except for a line of pylons. Aput walked ahead, unmoved by the strangers or the cows. The other dogs kept their distance, as if she didn't exist.

The border itself was a gate, decorated with barbed wire and a sign:

COUNTY OF MONAGHAN
REPORT ALL CROSSINGS:
Garda Siochana nah Éireann.
Tydavnet. 908829.

There was a post with a phone box on top.

The farmer undid a padlock and swung the gate wide for the cattle, which ambled off up the track. She followed, with a crook, lighting a cigarette, but told them to branch off east, down the footpath.

'Keep to that until you reach the bothy,' she called. 'They'll come for you.'

For ten minutes Aput led the way. They were in a wood of pine, the snow teeming between the trees, feather light. Their own footsteps made all the noise they could hear: twigs breaking, the watery splash of their boots on the sodden peat.

'I think we've passed it,' said Falcon.

'No – there,' said Sofya, pointing ahead. Down the path they could just see the rough masonry wall of a ruined building.

Following instructions, they took cover inside. The walls were a foot thick, and stone, the roof sturdy – but there was no glass in the windows, and the straw was damp.

They'd been told not to make a fire, just wait, and the patrol would get to them soon after seven. They had an hour, so Falcon told Sofya the story Father John had given him in the confessional: the real story of Jack Gwynne. There was time, and there was a sense in which this was the perfect place – a room, a cell. And Father John had said he must leave Sofya here at the bothy: the story could stand as a parting gift.

'I'm not sure what this tells us,' said Falcon, standing at the door, watching their footsteps disappear as the snow gathered. 'But I guess it tells us why. It's not proof of anything, but it offers a motive. Which is good – that there's a personal story. I guess all wars are like that, thousands, millions of personal slights, amalgamated, woven into one. It would have been a shame if it had just been for Ireland – not that she doesn't deserve her martyrs, and she's got enough.'

They heard a helicopter then, frighteningly close, shaking the roof timbers, so Falcon stepped back from the door as a searchlight caught nearby trees, and then was gone. A moment later the downdraught shook the forest, the snow falling in avalanches.

'This is the story of Jack Gwynne,' he said. 'An Irishman by choice from the age of sixteen. His father's buried back in Penzance. His mother's family are proud Irish patriots – rebels – a long line of martyrs and bombers, speechmakers and organisers. Young Jack leaves Cornwall, joins the Brotherhood, with the rest – and he's trusted because he's now his mother's son.

'One night he's in a working men's club in north Dublin, and the speaker's Tom Clarke. He's a legend to all. He got caught carrying dynamite in London – a whole gang of them were going to plant a bomb. Betrayed by spies he's picked up with the rest, and ends up at the Old Bailey. He gets life in solitary confinement and enforced silence. He will hear no words, speak no words.

'He's given one book a year, chosen at random. He walks the exercise yard alone, watched from above. His guards are mute. On one occasion – at Chatham – he kept the madness at bay by working out how many bricks there were in the prison, and how much they weighed in total. He started using his memory to try to save his sanity. He tried to calculate and categorise his memories – all of them, everything he'd ever seen, heard, touched, smelt. After a few years he felt he'd exhausted the past. There was nothing left to remember. He'd made a library of the past in his own head and he'd read every book.

'In some ways he had no past. He'd used it up. But he still had a fortune in time. It's my idea of hell, Sof.'

Outside the snow fell.

'Clarke said later to the family that it *was* hell. Not a metaphor – a reality. An exquisite torture, to have a mind – a great mind – but to have nothing to focus it upon. Just the four stone walls. The high window, a scrap of sky, the flagged floor, the one book, already read, re-read, memorised. Death would be a sweet thing.

'His case was a scandal, the subject of public outrage in Ireland. In the end they had to give him pencil and paper, access to a library. He translated the Bible into Irish, then into shorthand, having taught himself the skill from a book. Back in Dublin there were more calls for his release. Protests. When they eventually let him free, after fifteen years, he was the only one of the Irish prisoners not to be taken directly to a mental asylum. He went home to Dublin, married a proud Fenian called Kathleen Daly and set up a tobacconist's shop, working tirelessly in secret for the Brotherhood.'

Outside they heard a gunshot, then a crackle of more.

'Hunters,' said Falcon, but he wasn't sure.

'This is the man Jack Gwynne heard speak in Dublin that night in 1910. After he'd been cheered to the rafters, Clarke asked if any patriot in the audience would swear an oath, there and then, to take revenge one day on his behalf for what the British had done to him. To deliver hell, in payment for hell. To strike a blow for Ireland. Jack Gwynne is first on his feet. He swears the oath. And the place goes mad – they clap and stamp their feet, and Tom Clarke comes over and embraces him, and that's the greatest moment of young Jack's life. Right there.

'A month later he volunteered to go south with Scott.'

Sofya was at the window watching the snow fall. 'What happened to Clarke?' she said.

'He was in the GPO in Dublin at the Easter Rising – his name is first on the proclamation of the Republic. Some people say he's the first President of Ireland by force of arms. They shot him with the rest at Kilmainham Gaol – a miscalculation that led to this.' He held his hands out in the shadows. 'To the Republic, to the North, to the war. To this night.'

There was a footfall and a man stood in the doorway: the snow, and all the light there was, fell behind him. He was young, maybe twenty-five, whippet-like, but to Falcon he had weary, dead eyes.

'I'm Noble,' he said. 'You've to follow me. Not the woman.'

For the first time Falcon felt in his bones that he'd made a mistake in coming to the border country.

Aput growled, but Sofya hushed her.

Falcon had already made a decision, ruled by his heart. 'She comes, or we both go back.'

52

The garda report on Jack Gwynne was perfunctory. He'd died on 30 May the previous year in Castletown Berehaven in Kerry, a quiet fishing port in the far west. (Falcon saw his error then – if too late: when he'd checked on the crew of the *Terra Nova* he should have asked for precise dates of death. Gwynne had perished less than two weeks after Mr Parkis had appeared at Fen Ditton with Scott's diary.) The garda said Gwynne had taken a room in McCarthy's Hotel on the town square, facing the long sea lough. (A map was stapled to the report.) He'd met four old comrades from his days in the IRA, the successor to the Irish Republican Brotherhood, which they'd all joined in their youth.

The report – two sides of A4 in erratic type – came with a newspaper clipping from the *Kerryman* showing three police-men on the quayside looking down into the black water of the lough. A trawler, its gear up, floated in the background. Two women on the harbour wall watched the scene, one pointing, the other with a hand over her mouth as if stifling a scream. A caption read: 'The morning after: the grisly scene at Castletown Berehaven'.

After their food and drink the IRA men had struggled up the narrow stairs of McCarthy's to bed – all except Gwynne, who said he wanted to get some air. He was last seen on the quayside, by one of McCarthy's barmen, smoking methodi-cally, watching the stars wheel overhead. The next morning his body – cut into several pieces – was found floating on the tide, nudging the quay. The head – which had been severed by the same propeller that had done the rest of the damage – was not found. The *Go Girl!* – registered in Bantry – had come in at dawn, drawing the floating body into its screw, which had sliced it cleanly, before someone spotted blood, and the engine was shut down.

A coroner's court was convened in McCarthy's saloon. The verdict was accidental death, the body identified by the son of the deceased, Liam Gwynne, thanks to a scar on the palm of the right hand – a memento of Antarctica, where he'd let slip a fish knife flensing a seal. It was suggested that Gwynne, the worse for drink, had stumbled into the Atlantic and drowned. The *Irish Times* felt the verdict warranted a single paragraph on page five: 'Antarctic hero dies in tragic accident'. Gwynne, a widower, was to be buried in Goldenbridge Cemetery, Dublin, next to his wife.

Falcon put the garda report on the stone floor. He'd struggled to read it by the flickering light of candles, and a fire, in what was the only room of an old croft at a place their guide Noble had called the Echo Field.

There was an old man at the fireside, while Sofya sat in the shadows, cradling a tumbler of colourless spirit.

'Reports of my death . . .' said the old man, smiling, repositioning the heavy plastic-framed glasses on the bridge of his nose. He had a remarkably small round head, and what hair he had was white and rimmed a bald patch, but his eyes dominated: dark and set deep in the shadows of a strong brow. He looked like a fighter, old bones pressing up through tanned skin. It was this juxtaposition of age – he had to be in his early eighties – with a lingering power that unsettled. He hadn't got up when they arrived with Noble, but Falcon could see his limbs were long levers, ideal for hauling fish or an Antarctic sledge.

Jack Gwynne laughed silently to himself, shaking his head.

'Who died in the harbour?' asked Falcon, tapping his foot on the cutting from the *Kerryman*.

'An informer. From up Warren Point. He was shot here on the Echo Field – that's the routine. Then they took the body down west. They – the IRA Army Council – wanted me out of the way, you see, a dead man. If the truth was coming out they needed me to be history. The crew of the *Go Girl!* were in on it too. I was a potential embarrassment. That was it. I always thought it was an English disease. The Irish aren't embarrassed about much. Have you seen the state of Dublin recently?' He spat in the fire.

'How did they know the truth was coming out?' asked Falcon.

'The Brits can't keep a secret. And we're back in bed with the Russians. And we knew what was in the diary. Christ – I told the Brotherhood the truth of it in 1912. I told Tom Clarke – I'm proud of it, for pity's sake. They thought I'd made it all up. But I killed 'em, all right. Scott and the rest. But there was no proof to hand.

'And now here you are. Something brought you to Ireland. Something you found out on the ice. More letters, probably – another diary?' He waited a beat for an answer.

Falcon just stared into the flames, aware that the long-anticipated moment of confession had come and gone. 'I killed 'em,' he'd said, three words plain and surely true. Falcon felt the odd calm that always comes with the end of a journey. This man had murdered a legend, and thereby created another.

'What now?' asked Falcon.

Gwynne laughed. 'Liam's along later. There're decisions to be made. The top men from the two commands, North and South, they're meeting at Dundalk.'

Outside they heard an owl in the woods.

After leaving the bothy they'd emerged from the pines and seen before them a wide peat bog, running away to the horizon. The croft stood next to a small bungalow. Falcon had seen the sign made of twisted iron on the wall: 'Majorca' in a fluid script.

They'd be given food – a nameless stew, with potatoes. Gwynne had introduced the cook as Flaherty when she'd brought the pot in from the bungalow, which was low and mean, with damp disfiguring the stucco walls.

But Falcon knew her as Oriana, whom he'd last seen at the Fitzwilliam, caught in a gilded mirror. She had no first name here, but she did have a gun – a black pistol, held in a holster at her hip. She called the bungalow the 'guardhouse', elevating her role from the purely domestic to the military.

But after she'd set down the stew pot she'd knelt on the stone floor and worked her hand roughly around Aput's ears, clicking her tongue. Her hair caught the light, and he recalled now the soft lilt of her accent that day in the Scott Polar.

'You shouldn't have brought the woman. It's no place,' she said. The accent was broader, Kerry perhaps. There was a sly smile of agreement from Gwynne, and Falcon felt the icy fear of the outsider.

So there were three IRA soldiers: Gwynne, Noble and Flaherty. But young Liam Gwynne was on his way to join them. Outnumbered certainly, and they were armed, although Gwynne seemed semi-detached, belligerent, unstable.

'It's called the Echo Field for the gunshots,' said Gwynne, cruelly. 'You'll have guessed that: two or three, more on a crisp winter's night. Then the crows, for a few minutes, a fox barking – then silence.'

'They kill people here?' asked Sofya, and Falcon was oddly appalled by the calmness of her voice. It occurred to him that she was assessing the situation, making judgements on the risks they faced.

'They do,' said Gwynne, taking another spoonful of the thick liquor of the stew. 'We do,' he added, after a moment's thought. 'There's been business done today already. Scores settled.'

Using the spoon for emphasis, and twisting in his chair, he held Sofya's gaze. 'The Russians are sending guns, and a boat. They say you're missing – maybe with the Brits. That you know about Scott. You shouldn't have come.'

He turned to Falcon. 'You should have listened to Father John. And you should have handed over the diary when you had a chance. The Russians were frit because they thought Scott had named Girev or Omelchenko. My lot were frit he might have named me. It was a bloody mess. They sent Flaherty here and the rest to Cambridge, but you moved too fast.'

'Big mistake,' said Flaherty, letting her hand linger in the dog's hair. But her voice had betrayed her, nerves making the two words shimmer. Noble came in from the snow, and they traded Irish, fluent and rich, before she fled, slamming the door.

Aput growled. 'The dog knows,' said Falcon. 'She's trained to find bodies – hidden bodies, in ice and snow. I doubt peat is much of a challenge.'

'There's always a fresh grave,' said Gwynne, looking into the fire. 'Our man in the village cuts the peat here. The nearest house is a mile south – and he's one of us. Well, he is if he knows what's good for him.'

'That's enough, Jack,' said Noble.

Gwynne refilled his pipe and they sat and smoked, and Falcon thought that even if they let Sofya walk away, he'd been a fool for coming south.

He thought his only hope was to get them to turn on each other.

'You've read the diary?' he asked Gwynne.

'No. But there'll be no surprises. If he'd named me – and the Brotherhood – we'd have known by now. It's you we have to fear. You found something in that Godforsaken place that brought you here.'

He relit a pipe and the bowl crackled and spat.

'You're the problem, Dr Grey. You and me both. She's an opportunity. A bargaining chip. We're liabilities.'

'What's going to happen?' said Falcon.

'That's a subject of discussion at a higher level,' said Noble.

The peat collapsed in the fire, sending up a shower of sparks.

Falcon's options were narrowing but he felt that if he kept talking he could play for time. He didn't like the slow, plodding pace of the soldiers. They were the little men – even Noble – waiting for orders from above.

'How did you do it?' he asked Gwynne. 'The oil, the food, the fire. Was Crean in it too? And Lieutenant Evans – a bitter man. The three of you, was it?'

'Why should I tell you?' he asked, the bony skull thrust forward, the thin lips drawn back to reveal small, child-like teeth.

Falcon shrugged. 'It's a question I have to ask. I was brought up at a place called Lamer – a country house north of London. Cherry-Garrard was my guardian. That's why the diary came to me. He wanted people to know Scott was murdered. He wanted them to know by whom – that was my job.'

Gwynne's head was down, but he nodded at that.

'He was a good man,' he said. 'Better than the rest, although that's no great thing. That was a regret – that he took so much of the blame. But then it was his choice to go. He *paid* to go, for Christ's sake.'

Gwynne set aside the pipe, which had gone out, and began to roll cigarettes, setting them out on the hearth.

There was the sound of a car braking on gravel, and Noble left them.

Gwynne gave the first of the cigarettes to Falcon. 'The problem with men like Crean is that to them Ireland's an idea, not a country for men to live in. He'd talk a good game – and he'd sing all night. And talk some more – all the Irishmen talked. God, we'd have put the Greeks to shame with our debating. Oates too – he'd been a soldier at the Curragh, he'd argue the toss of it with the rest. And Keegan – and Meares, for that matter. All Irish.

'In Cardiff, before the ship left, I told Crean straight we should strike a blow for freedom when we could. Scott was a stuffed shirt. The whole thing was a colonial expedition – we might as well have been native porters trundling their port and cigars and their gramophone records across the ice. He said I wasn't to speak of it again. If I did, he'd tell an officer and I'd be dropped like a hot stone. And no pay.

'So I was on my own. There was a bit of below-deck hot air about spiking the motor sledges, burning the pony hay, that kind of nonsense. But they didn't have the spine for it.

'I had to wait on the moment. I'd promised Tom Clarke I'd deliver them to hell. I wanted Scott dead – in the tent for ever. In a cell of ice. I couldn't stop 'em going south – but I could make damn sure he never came back.

'It fell right into me lap. Last returning party. Just three of us – and Scott and the rest next through for each depot. I acted alone. Crean never knew nothing. Evans was chewed up with hatred for Scott, but he was no traitor. The rest was easy.'

He ran his tongue along the edge of the second roll-up and gave it to Sofya, who came out of the shadows to take it, followed by the dog, which lay down in a crescent shape in front of the hearth.

'We had our roles, see? Evans was dying. Crean wanted to save his life – another medal in it for him, and a few more cheers for the hero. That was his game. He was the wet-nurse, at his officer's beck and call. They looked after the gear, the tent, the cooker, the harnesses, the sledge. My job was the commissariat – food and fuel. Mostly I just took extra under their noses cos they didn't know what was in the boxes, or the cans. I told 'em the men who'd gone through had left plenty behind, that they'd cut themselves short rations, left more for us – and for Scott. Evans didn't think twice: he ate for two.

'First thing, after breakfast, I'd leave 'em in the tent. Crean had to get him dressed, up on his feet, and everything packed. I had the run of the depots. Later – by the middle of the Barrier – I thought I'd better make sure they were good and dead so I hid a few boxes, and punched holes in the fuel cans – that was a close call there coz Crean heard me and came out to see what was up. I kept me cool. He wasn't the brightest spark, Tom, but loyal like a dog.

'By the time we got to the lower Barrier we was hauling Evans. He just sat there on the sledge, the snow settling on him. One day we tried relaying – we picked up a spare sledge at a cairn and tried dragging him a mile, then coming back for the second sledge and the gear to split the weight. But Evans was in a bad way – and he didn't want Tom to go. I reckon he thought we were gonna leave him out there and run for home. We gave up so I got sent back to get the food off the second sledge. Sent back alone. There was snow falling, and it was a mile, and I thought I'll not get another chance: I lit the fuel, piled up the food boxes, and left it burning.'

Gwynne's body was folded forward, face to the fire, which had flared up, so that it shifted and guttered with the flames. It was extraordinary that this man had been there on the ice, watching those flames, thinking five men would die.

Gwynne licked his plate. Sofya stood up, collected them all and put them on the table in the shadows. Then she lit her cigarette with a glowing stick from the embers.

'I was in the rescue party,' said Gwynne, still lost in the past. 'When we found them – the final tent – and all the diaries, I thought the game was up. Taffy was the danger, you see, because I'd tried to get him on board one night.

Drew the sign for them all, said we weren't alone, that men were fighting for their countries, for freedom. Taffy's like all the men of South Wales, loves the hills, loves chapel, likes to hear the language but can hardly speak it, and he won't fight for freedom. He took fright, which was tricky, coz he loved spillin' the beans, did Taffy. I told him to keep it buttoned or I'd get the lads to do for his kids. One word, he'd be coming home to a funeral.

'But what if he'd told 'em – told Scott? They'd read it in the diary. I sat splicing rope thinking, Any moment now Mr Atkinson would ask for a word. Then it would be the brig on the ship, a volley of bullets at Portsmouth, or Tilbury. Or a volley of bullets right then, right there.

'I was in a funk, all right. But there was nothing in the offical diary. Scott blamed nobody – especially not himself. It was the cold, the ice, the ponies – everything but the truth. I was safe.'

'How do I know you're telling the truth?' asked Falcon.

'You found the tent?'

Falcon nodded.

'I was detailed with the rest to collapse it – I was the last person inside. I'd bought a gun, just in case, which was against orders. I got it off Meares – he was off home on the ship and mine was useless. Only officers had the right, see? If things went bad I'd have used it for my own head.

'If I'd been found with it there'd have been questions. I didn't want questions. I wanted to fade away. And I didn't need the gun. It's tricky just slinging stuff, in case someone spots you, coz we're cheek by jowl. I couldn't take the risk, so I left it there.

'I thought: If they ever come back for the bodies they'll find it. I wanted to put the cat among the pigeons so I put it by Scott's hand – so people would think he'd wanted to do for himself but couldn't pull the trigger. A coward in the end. I told him that to his dead face,' said Gwynne.

Falcon nodded. 'We found something else at one of the depots. A centre punch we reckon the saboteur had used on the fuel cans. It was engraved MV *Bjorn*. That's why they suspected the Germans. How do you explain that?'

Gwynne shook his head, as if trying to dislodge the memory. 'I got it in Cardiff when the Krauts came to see us off, Filchner and his crew. We swapped stuff – keepsakes. I gave one of the stokers a knife I'd lifted out of the galley, *Terra Nova* engraved on the handle. I dropped it that time Tom Crean came out of the tent of a sudden. I'd just put a neat hole in the last oil can, so I walked away.'

A creature – a fox, perhaps – barked once in the pine woods and Aput answered.

'They mean to suppress it – the truth?' said Falcon.

'That's it, you got it there. That's the trouble. I did what I did but I didn't want it to stay a secret. I told the Brotherhood we should claim responsibility – say we'd cut down the imperialists. But they said lie low. There were plans being made. They wanted everyone to stay quiet, wait for the signal. I waited four years. I got a gun and we trained out at Kildare. On the day, the Easter Monday, I was in the Shelbourne Hotel, and we had the Brits pinned down on St Stephen's Green. We shot 'em up. But the rest was chaos. They didn't get a grip on the docks, or the railway, or the telephones for that matter. Still, it was the spark.'

They heard voices outside, a sudden burst of Irish, then laughter.

Gwynne's eyes narrowed. 'But they don't want the truth even now, what with half the British Army up the road.'

'I want the truth told too,' said Falcon.

'That's why they're going to kill us both,' said Gwynne.

53

Flaherty came in through the door, snow teeming around her, and for a second they didn't see the man with her, who wore an overcoat down to his boots, a black IRA armband, with his collar up, and a crumpled fishing hat.

The one-time cook stood to the side to let the newcomer have centre stage. There was something ceremonial about the way she set her boots at precisely the width of her shoulders, her hands behind her back.

The man – who Falcon judged to be Liam Gwynne – was in his thirties, the resemblance to his father striking: the small head, the brow, the long bones, although the eyes were softer, appraising his prisoners.

'My name's Captain Liam Gwynne, of the Belfast Brigade,' he said, casting the hat on the table. He looked at his watch, as if following a pre-set timetable to the minute.

Flaherty, studying her boots, seemed to sway uncertainly, and avoided Falcon's eyes.

'So you're the man, Dr Grey,' he said, rolling his shoulders to relieve joints stiff with the icy cold. 'Nothing stands up without you – you found the evidence, you've read the diary but you know more than that. And you've not told London. There's your mistake. They've an eye on you, but not close enough.

'Who were you going to tell? The papers, is it? Paris maybe – no.' He clicked his fingers. 'New York. They'd have it on the streets before the Brits knew it was coming. Or the TV. Headlines round the world, all right. A desperate fine story it is.'

His father handed him a roll-up but left him to light it him-self. The body language between the two was brisk and cold. Meanwhile Flaherty stood her ground, eyes down on those country boots.

'At Dundalk just now there's a man, chief of intelli-gence, knows what Century House knows – about the tent, about the bodies. He's a smart fella, our man. Elo-quent. He went misty-eyed with it – said it was like the archaeologist who dug up a grave in Greece and took the gold mask from the face of the dead. He sent a telegram to the King – that's what our man said. "This day I have gazed upon the face of Agamemnon." Did you gaze upon the face of Captain Scott, Dr Grey?'

'I did,' said Falcon.

'You'd be telling everyone what you saw, then. But that's not our problem. Our problem is that you know they were murdered, and who killed them. And they'll listen to you. The press, MPs, TV. Senators. Even your man in the White House. We can't have it, you see – not now. There's another battle beginning in the long struggle. There'll be a new IRA. Soon. We've got the Army on our island and we want them gone. Your story sees the light of day they'll be here another fifty years. London can't lose face, not to Scott's murderers. And we need money – the Irish in England, the Irish in the States. We can't carry it, the burden, of killing Scott. We might as well bomb Balmoral.'

He threw his cigarette, half smoked, into the fire, and put a hand on his father's shoulder. 'We'll take you home, Pa. A debrief on the journey. We need to know what was said.'

So that had been his role: while they ate their stew, and smoked his cigarettes, he was to find out what Falcon had discovered on the Barrier.

Outside, thinly, they heard a telephone ring once, presum-ably in the 'guardhouse'.

Everything stopped. Gwynne poked the fire and they heard a door slam.

Noble appeared, snow falling heavily now beyond him, his face flushed. 'That was Carney at the Horse and Groom. He says two cars took the old road ten minutes ago. Dublin plates. He says they stopped for petrol – Carney says they're garda for sure and—'

Captain Gwynne held up his hand for silence. 'We'll talk about this in the house.'

He grabbed his hat, holding it in one hand while he produced a single sheet of paper from his overcoat pocket. Falcon's blood cooled because he knew then that this was judicial, which seemed to rob the room of its foetid heat.

Captain Gwynne let a few seconds of silence stretch out: 'The Southern Command, under the Army Council, has this day at Dundalk issued this warrant for the summary execution of Dr Falcon Grey. Can he step forward.'

'What happens to Sofya?' said Falcon, standing.

The word 'execution' seemed to have a half-life, echoing in the room, diminishing slowly. The little military pageant was tawdry, its rushed procedure without dignity, but he knew that in this damp corner of Ireland what this man said was justice.

'No questions,' said the captain. His voice was soft and educated, his body relaxed, the limbs fluid. Falcon hadn't met his eyes yet, which were dancing round the room, like the firelight.

'Do you have anything to say?'

'Yes. What happens to Sofya?'

'I'll take that as no comment. That's the business done. Say your goodbyes. Flaherty will be back to carry out the sentence. The woman goes with us to Dublin. We've no choice with you. You could have stayed away. It's your choice.'

Flaherty shuffled her feet unsteadily.

'This makes no sense, son,' said Gwynne, from his chair by the fire.

'Stay out of it,' said the captain. 'You're lucky to walk away. You're a dead man anyway. A death certificate and all. You've got a few years yet – enjoy them. I've vouched for your silence, do you hear? You go running to anyone with your story I'll pay the price. You know what that means. You want the grandchildren to see that, do you? Their father on sticks with a bullet through each knee?'

Gwynne shook his head, and turned to the fire, using the poker again to riddle the coke.

'What's happening to Sofya?' insisted Falcon, stepping forward.

Flaherty, jumpy, had the gun out before they heard the footfall, the barrel wavering. Given that until now she'd acted as the cook, it seemed to Falcon that she had been given this task to prove herself worthy of promotion.

'Steady now. They can say goodbye,' said Captain Gwynne, smiling, pushing the declaration of the court into his coat pocket. 'You've got a minute,' he said to Falcon, putting on his fishing hat and leading the others out into the snow, closing the door almost gently.

For the first time Falcon noticed a clock ticking in the shadows.

Outside they heard voices raised, then a car engine firing into life.

They held each other. 'They're watching us through the window,' said Sofya, putting her chin on his shoulder, her cheek against his neck: 'I've got a knife,' she said. 'From the old man's plate. I'll wait until they take you away. I'll try to get Noble with the knife. Then I'll open the door – let the light out, and the dog. If I can get the gun I'll try to come to you – but, if you can, strike when you see the light.'

'What with?' he whispered.

She pressed a second knife into his hand, then held his head.

'Last night, in the Europa,' said Falcon, 'when we came back, after the bomb alert, I saw the bed, your clothes, mine, the tangle, and I thought, I'll see that again, every night maybe, for years. Even when we're old, it'll look the same to me, feel the same.'

'It's not over,' said Sofya. 'If they shoot you, they will shoot me next. Maybe not now – they might take me with them if the police are close – but soon. You must strike first, Falcon. I am a hostage because they want you to go quietly. But they've got their orders, and they'll be from the Lubyanka. The girl – Flaherty – she is not looking at me, not once. So it's her job. But she is unhappy. Ashamed. She knows she is to kill a woman, and I do not think she has done this before – or even thought of this. But she'll kill you. Do not hope otherwise. Act. I will not be taken back to Moscow. Or bartered with London. When you see the light, kill her. She's a soldier too. Do it for all of us.' She put his hand on her stomach. 'All of us. It's three months. I feel it is a girl.'

Falcon felt the weight of the news, the way it changed the light in the room.

If they'd had one more minute they'd have found a name, but Noble opened the door and they caught sight of Flaherty, drinking from a hip-flask.

'Time,' said Noble. 'It's not a long walk.'

54

Flaherty was in a hurry, her coat half on, spooked perhaps by the report of cars on the old road. She made Falcon take the path ahead through a stand of thorn trees to a rough gate, which hung off its hinges. She had to heave it aside, whistling, and Falcon recognised 'The Rising Of The Moon'. Beyond lay the snowfield, almost featureless now in the gloom, gently emitting its pale, anonymous light. A trench ran away from them, glistening like coal, flooded with meltwater, beside it a line of planks. From the pit a sickly mist was rising, as if the earth was smouldering. Falcon thought of Hell, and the shadow of Erebus.

'Walk on the duckboards,' said Flaherty, and Falcon thought she'd lost the tremulous quality of nerves from her voice.

The moon *was* rising – had she known? It was just visible now on the far horizon, through the falling snow. In silhouette it revealed a few standing stones, like old teeth in an empty jaw. Falcon stopped and looked back: he was leaving footprints across the white plain. He thought of Scott and his men, and the certain knowledge they'd had of death approaching with every step. Death was here too, because Flaherty was keeping her distance, so the knife was useless. Scott had had time to contemplate oblivion, fashion it for others, belittle it. But Falcon's life was measured in seconds. Everything he had he would lose in the next minute.

Ahead, with its own moon-shadow, a single broken fence post stood beside the trench.

'Wait by the marker,' she said, and something about her voice made Falcon look back again, and he saw that his guard had stopped, put a cigarette between her lips, and held a lighter to the tip, its blue flame lazy in the windless night. She'd put the torch under her arm to free her hands and the beam fell into the trench. Two bodies, woven together by their arms and legs, lay in the shallow water, their feet bare, with just their shirts and trousers – checks and cords, belts, everyday clothes, but no coats or jackets. One had his face down in the water, but the other was looking right at the flashlight: a young man, with fair hair, and glasses – one lens smashed, bloodied.

'Do you know their names?' Falcon asked, catching her looking down at the victims. He felt the knife in his pocket.

'RUC – from Derry. It's not my business.'

'She – Sofya – thinks you've to shoot her next,' said Falcon.

She licked her lips, and held the gun stiffly at her side, the better to hide her nerves: she squared her shoulders, dropped her chin, and Falcon heard the breath leaving her.

She took a step towards him. This was the way with executions, speed ahead of thought.

Behind her the darkness was broken by the crisp outline of the cottage door opening, a rectangle of light, which took Falcon's eye beyond his executioner, who turned, following the wide-eyed stare, her boots skidding on the muddy boards.

He owed it to Sofya, and his child, so he pulled the knife, and thought of Scott opening his jacket at the last, daring the cold to stop his heart. He took one step, two steps, three, the knife in his fist.

There was a flash of blue-white light at the cottage, and the first gunshot, then its echo. A car's lights swept the Echo Field, then another close behind.

Flaherty's torch beam picked out two electric green eyes on the path. Falcon expected a shot but the cook hesitated, and then the dog was on her, jaws around her arm.

She twisted back towards Falcon and there was a second shot, but no light, and the gun fell, as her hand went to her chest and – balanced for a fleeting moment – she said, in a matter-of-fact, nerveless voice, 'I'm hit', registering the fact, no more.

Then she fell into the pit, the greatcoat flapping once like a flag, and Falcon knew she was dead before she splashed into the water and the mud. Aput stood on the edge of the pit, teeth bared.

Falcon heard a footstep on the wooden boards and turned to find a man behind him, perhaps twenty yards away, a thin trail of smoke leaking from a gun in his right hand, which he held out, away from his body.

It wasn't a stranger, but he couldn't see who it was. For a second, he thought it was Cherry, an angel after all, back from Erebus, and the land of the dead, to play his part in the final scene.

Then the man spoke: 'The cottage,' he said. 'We've men there now. It's safe.'

It wasn't Cherry after all, because the voice held echoes, but not of Lamer's stately pleasure grounds. This man broke into a fluid run, and it was the release of suppressed energy, the smooth, clean-limbed action, that gave away his identity. It was Parkis, who'd started it all, walking down the towpath on that day in May at Fen Ditton with a gift from Cherry: a leather satchel from his dull office at Lincoln's Inn, and Scott's secret diary.

Postscript

Six months later

One small duty remained, and then the past was his at last: luggage for the future.

He was early and had sought out the shade in the Goldsmiths Tavern. There were two men at the bar drinking Guinness. The barman was drinking tea, and took his time decanting a half of stout, which Falcon took to a table by the door, wedged open by a cleaner working a mop over the parquet flooring. Outside there was a splash of sunshine, bleaching out the colours, and the constant to-and-fro of strangers. The barman turned up the radio: Harold Wilson had called a general election. The world was going forwards but Falcon was going back, one last time.

He checked the time: across the New Cross Road stood the bookshop, and he'd rung a week earlier and spoken to a man who said the owner, Rosa Ramos, was out, but she was in every day after noon.

One of the drinkers put 'The Rising Of The Moon' on the jukebox, which reminded him of Parkis, running along the duckboards beside the peat trench, leading the way back to the cottage, Sofya standing in the doorway, Noble's gun in her hand, Captain Liam Gwynne lying in the snow, a bullet hole in his back. The cottage door open, and Noble sitting by the coke fire, holding both hands to his stomach, and a blood-soaked shirt. And the garda everywhere, two of them frog-marching Jack Gwynne to a car.

Parkis ordered the driver to take it slow as they drove away an hour later on the old road. Travelling north through snow-choked lanes, he'd told them how lucky they'd been. Century House had kept an eye on Sofya after her defection. She'd been seen buying tickets for Ireland and he'd been dispatched, with a fellow officer, to follow. Once the Pentagon had sent Century House a verbatim typescript of her conversation with Falcon from Ascension Island – all communications were recorded, even between lovers – MI6 called in the help of Irish intelligence, D-J2, based at Phoenix Park.

They'd been an hour behind them, which had nearly been too much.

The radio marked noon with three beeps: two short, one long.

The bookshop had a plate-glass window behind which the latest publications were artfully arranged. A girl in a black-and-white striped miniskirt was on her knees, adjusting a spotlight. The ground floor – up the six steps – was a coffee shop, with a gleaming Italian machine, glass cups and saucers. Students – mainly – sat in battered chairs or flicked idly through plastic boxes of second-hand LPs.

As he opened the door a bell rang and Falcon caught the unmistakable hint of hash on the air, but the once-irresistible urge to smoke was gone.

He asked a young man in flared jeans if he could speak to the owner.

'Upstairs,' he said.

With the last step the memory returned – not a jarring flash of the past, but a measured reveal, like a book opening. It was from this spot that he'd seen the old man lying on the floorboards and taken his hand.

'Rosa Ramos?' he said.

A woman tidying a shelf turned.

He'd planned to ask after a book – *The Worst Journey*, perhaps – and start a conversation but now, face to face, he couldn't stop the unburdening, which wasn't desperate but joyful, as if he'd come with a present.

'I'm sorry – my name's Grey, Falcon Grey. I used to live up the street. I was here, right here, on the day the rocket fell. Mr Noonan collapsed. I'm sorry to bring back bad memories. I stayed with him. I was only four – but he wouldn't let go of my hand.'

She took a step back, and he thought he saw the intervening years, the loneliness perhaps, the bleak loss of the survivor.

'You're the little boy who left the book,' she said. 'I thought you'd be back.' And there was the smile again, full voltage, and some part of him struggled to understand how sadness – grief – can become joy.

'I – my family . . . They died, you see, that day,' he said.

'We all knew your family – it was dreadful. I am sorry,' she said.

'It's all right now. I'm just here because he gave me a message for you, Mr Noonan – Uncle Pat – and it's never been delivered and . . . It's difficult to explain but until recently I didn't remember it – any of it. The explosion and finding them dead, it wiped things out – lots of things. But now I remember it all. I have a good memory – he knew that. My dad told him.'

Falcon let the past speak. 'Tell her I love her. Tell her I'm sorry I've stolen our old age – our old age together. I don't want to die – tell her that, because she's always said I'm planning to leave early. Tell her I'm sorry I didn't say this more often. I should have left her in her own land, but I stole her. I'm sorry. She wanted children most of all. All she got was books. Tell her to marry again. Now go.'

Falcon nodded, marking the end of the message. 'I didn't want you to think he hadn't thought of you. I'm sorry I'm so late. But the memory wasn't mine to give.'

'I know these words,' she said.

'Rosa?' The voice came from the floor below, followed by an unsteady step on the metal staircase.

An old man appeared, rising, eyes large behind thick spectacles.

'You see, Falcon, he didn't die. You saved him. You held his hand and then you got help, even though you thought it was hopeless. But it wasn't.'

She touched the old man's shoulder. 'Patrick, this is him, the Greys' boy who left his book behind.'

Mr Noonan had come to a stop, but he seemed to sway, holding onto the banister.

'He won't take a stick,' she said.

'Good God! Is it you? For a long time I thought you were dead,' he said to Falcon. 'Nobody was left to ask. I went to the brewery where your father worked and they said you'd been taken in by an aunt. I'm sorry – I distracted you that day. It's haunted me that I asked you to tell a lie to your parents, even a white one.' He smiled at a memory. 'The book, Rosa,' he said. 'It's in the third drawer of the desk.'

'I'll get it – wait,' she said, and they heard her rapid steps descend.

Mr Noonan took off his glasses. 'It takes courage to come back – thank you for that.'

There was an awkward silence. 'You've your mother's eyes exactly,' he said.

'I didn't know that,' said Falcon.

Rosa appeared, breathless, holding a book. It was *the* book, of course, meant for his father, but left behind the day the V2 fell from the sky. *The Rime of the Ancient Mariner*. It had been the key that had unlocked the past as he'd laid a copy on Scott's chest in the tent on the Barrier. But for the book the truth might never have been told. He'd studied the cover as he'd held the old man's hand that day in 1944.

He saw now that the artist had signed the etching: Gustav Doré. It showed an old-fashioned ship with masts but no sails, becalmed between cliffs of ice. It was night-time, but in the distance, looking down the great chasm, a full moon was rising. There was nobody on the ship that Falcon could see, but icicles hung from the rigging, and above it all a white bird floated in the air.

Acknowledgments

Cherry: A Life of Apsley Cherry-Garrard, Sara Wheeler's spell-binding biography, provided the spark for *The White Lie.* Its last line: 'He was buried in St Helen's Churchyard, with his secrets' was an invitation to imagine what those secrets might be. The other key was an academic article in the *Polar Record* by Prof. Chris Turney. *Why Didn't They Ask Evans?* This brought speculation about Scott's fate to the fore and named a principal suspect. Fittingly, Prof Turney's title was a deliberate echo of the 1933 novel by Agatha Christie, of the same name. Turney's *1912 – The Year the World Discovered Antarctica* was also essential reading.

And, of course, I relied on Cherry-Garrard's own master-piece, *The Worst Journey in the World.*

More generally I must mention Francis Spufford's wonder-ful examination of the magnetic attraction of the South Pole. *I May Be Some Time.* It places the reader inside Scott's mind in the final hours of his life – an unforgettable experience. Roland Huntford's *The Last Place on Earth,* is unbeatable for drama, while David Crane's *Scott of the Antarctic* offers a rare bal-anced view. Sue Limb and Patrick Cordingley's *Captain Oates* is a revelation, and like *Cherry* points to the fictional way ahead

In my story (spoiler alert) Scott and his men are recovered from their icy tomb, a series of scenes in which I drew heavily on Owen Beattie and John Geiger's terrific *Frozen in Time* – a true account of the exhumation of one of the doomed mem-bers of the long-lost Franklin Expedition.

Finally, Scott's own diaries are everyone's basic text. With-out them there would be no legend.

For my modern space adventure I am indebted to Deborah Cadbury's *The Space Race,* and *Epic Rivalry: The Inside Story of the Soviet and American Space Race,* by Von Hardesty and Gene Eisman. James Harford's panoramic biography of the Soviet Union's rocket genius, *Korolev,* and Michael Neufeld's *Von Braun* provided the raw material for fictional versions of these two great protagonists of the Space Race.

Experts at the Scott Polar Research Institute, Cambridge, were generous and unfailing in providing help for this project. I must mention in particular Prof. Gareth Rees, and Dr Bryan Lintott, who provided astute advice on how my fictional hero might try to find the bodies of Scott and his men. I must also thank Dudley Vaughan, a US Navy SeeBee who actually worked at the 'Old Pole' and was unstinting in providing answers to my many questions, and access to his own most atmospheric photographs.

For armchair travellers I would recommend the revelatory *Sakhalin Island,* a non-fiction work by Anton Chekhov, which takes the reader on an epic Russian overland journey into internal exile. On Ireland in the 1960s I turned to *Making Sense of the Troubles,* by David McKittrick, and David McVea. Inspiration also came from Helen Litton's empathetic *Thomas Clarke* – part of the '16 Lives' series on the rebels executed after the Easter Rising.

Closer to home I am beyond grateful to my wife, historian and writer Midge Gillies, for unfailing support in the project and practical help with editing, plot and character. Many years ago, when *The White Lie* was a hopeful project, I received a lot of sound advice and encouragement from publisher and writer Roland White, and my then agent Faith Evans. My current agent, Teresa Chris has harnessed her love of Cherry's *The Worst Journey* to haul this new, fictional, version of the Scott story all the way to the Pole. My editor at Hodder & Stoughton, Jo Dickinson, has – by good judgment and inspired editing – helped create a single, compelling, storyline. And I'm grateful to Mike Weighton for reading the proofs with such a keen eye.

And finally, I must thank my daughter Rosa, yet again, for pointing out at a very early age that you should always look for the moon, even in daylight.

Out in paperback now,

THE SILENT CHILD

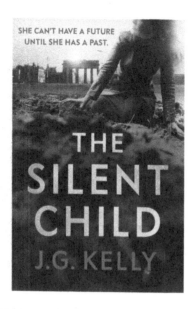

SHE CAN'T HAVE A FUTURE UNTIL SHE HAS A PAST.

1944

Leo Stern arrives at the Nazi camp at Borek with his wife Irena and his two daughters. The Sterns are spared from the gas chamber when they witness a murder. But in a place that humanity has deserted, Leo is forced to make unimaginable choices to try to keep his family alive.

1961

For seventeen years, Hanna has been unable to remember her identity and how she was separated from her family at the end of the war, until the discovery of a letter among her late uncle's possessions reveals her real name - **Hanna Stern** - and leads her to Berlin in search of her lost past.

Helped by former lover Peter, Hanna begins to piece together the shocking final days of Borek. But Hanna isn't the only one with an interest in the camp, and lurking in the shadows is someone who would prefer Hanna's history to remain silent.

Read on for an extract . . .

HODDER

PROLOGUE

Long Fen, Cambridgeshire, December 1945

Hanna sat alone on the back seat of the polished black car, her battered suitcase on her lap, the world outside only dimly seen through the misted windows. The engine, cooling, made an odd ticking sound, but otherwise there was silence, until she heard crows calling. She cleared a porthole in the condensation with her glove. The landscape was entirely flat, but upside down: the sky grey and sooty, while the snow-covered fields seemed to pulse with a gentle current of inner light. Her breath kept obscuring the scene, so that she had repeatedly to wipe the glass clear, each time noting another visual detail: a lone willow, a string of telegraph poles running to the horizon, a stretch of water-filled ditch, the surface glazed with ice as if by cataracts.

Setting the case carefully down she slid across the leather seat and cleared a circle in the window on the opposite side of the car. Mr Hasard, the driver, was smoking by a mail-box mounted on a metal post. When they'd come to a halt after the journey north from London, he'd wound down his window and sounded the horn, and Hanna had counted out the triple echo. He'd done it again before switching off the engine and getting out, his shoes making a brittle crunch in the snow.

'They'll be here soon,' he'd said, although who 'they' were had not been clear. Hanna was inured to these moments, when the adult world seemed to require only that she sat quietly and waited politely for the future to unfold.

She watched Mr Hasard throw the cigarette away with an impatient gesture, stamping his feet, looking towards a house in the distance that stood half a mile away, at the end of a rutted track.

Hanna read the sign that hung from an iron arm on the mailbox:

SWAN HOUSE
MAZUREK

Mr Hasard came back to the car, threw open the door, and pressed down on the horn, the cigarette hanging from his mouth.

'We'll have you warm and safe soon,' he said, checking his watch.

When he'd come to the chateau in Poland to fetch her – the car was black again, but smaller, battered and dusty – he'd taken her hand and said he was 'Mr Hasard-with-one-S', and that he was her *provisional guardian*. His duty was to collect Hanna and take her to Paris where 'further decisions' would be made about her future.

They had driven for three days, skirting towns where it was possible, but where they couldn't, edging through streets full of rubble, past sullen crowds gathered around bonfires against the cold. The fires carried ash up into the sky, and Hanna watched the rising smoke, craning her neck to see the clouds, while everyone else seemed hypnotised by the flames.

When Hanna wasn't asleep on the back seat she sat next to Mr Hasard, who asked her gentle questions she couldn't answer. There was something wrong with Hanna's memory. The last year, which she'd spent in the caretaker's cottage on the estate, was vivid: from the swans on the frozen lake at Christmas to the rabbits running from the last stook of hay at harvest time. But back beyond these images there was nothing. The first six years of her life were lost, and when she was urged to see into that darkness she had to look away, although she never cried.

They reached Paris, a pale city, where all the buildings had been arranged in squares, and around parks, or along wooded streets, and all the fountains were dry, and full of snow. The apartment was on rue Delambre and had so many mirrors, and tall windows, Hanna felt constantly unsure if she was looking at the real world of rooftops and drifting smoke, or its reflection. The rooms were bare, but the plaster was ornate, and depicted swans, just like the ceilings at the chateau. Mr Hasard came each day and explained that he was waiting for what he always called 'instructions'. A tutor visited in the afternoons to teach Hanna English and French, but she still thought in German, although some of the few words she said out loud, and unbidden, were Yiddish – words she was urged to forget.

A woman called Suzanne looked after her and cooked her meals, and was always there, beside her bed, when she woke up pooled in sweat, rigid with nightmares she couldn't remember. In the dusty park by the apartment, Suzanne told her that the doctor, who had examined her twice in the yellow day room, thought she'd had a great shock, which had upset her so much that the past was lost, but that it might be found, if they were patient and kind. Hanna asked for a sketch-book and pencils, and Mr Hasard admired her work, although it revealed nothing of the past.

Finally, after three months, instructions did arrive in Paris, and now here she was, after a journey of trains and boats, somewhere north of a city called Cambridge, in England, on what Mr Hasard called a 'fen' – a frozen landscape of fields and poplars, which reminded her of Poland, as if her journey had described a great but pointless circle.

She heard brittle footsteps on ice, and then voices close to the car, and through the porthole that she'd cleared she saw that two elderly people had arrived and were shaking hands with Mr Hasard. The three adults, dimly seen as a single shadow, came to the side of the car. The door opened, and Hanna had to jump down, clutching her case.

Mr Hasard performed a slight bow towards an old man. 'Hanna, this is Count Mazurek.'

'Welcome to Swan House, Hanna,' said the old man, in what Hanna recognised as English, which he spoke very slowly.

'You can call me Uncle Marcin. This is my wife.' It wasn't an old man's voice, Hanna thought, and she saw that his hair – which was swept back off a broad face, was only streaked with grey. He had a peasant's great hands – like those of the estate workers back in Poland – and broad shoulders, and a round head that hung forward, as if its weight was too much.

He took her hand gently in what Hanna felt was a sign of welcome.

But his wife, who was bird-like and still, stood back watching them both.

'She remembers nothing?' said the count to Mr Hasard.

'No. As I said in my letter, she can recall nothing before the estate at Łabędzie,' he said, slipping on a pair of driving gloves. He opened the boot of the car, retrieved a large flat brown paper parcel, and gave it to the woman, who clutched it to her chest.

'But she *can* speak?' asked the count, looking at Hanna, and then Mr Hasard, a smile widening.

'Oh yes. When spoken to.'

They all looked at Hanna, who looked at them back.

Mr Hasard touched the rim of his hat. 'I must get the ferry, and the roads are bad. The car has to be back by nightfall.'

A minute later, after a conversation Hanna did not understand involving 'expenses' and an 'invoice', Mr Hasard shook her hand and then they all stood back and watched the shiny black car drive away, until it seemed to tip over the distant horizon.

Marcin took Hanna's suitcase, and they set out on the rough, icy track to the house. He told Hanna that they too had once lived in the great chateau at Łabędzie and that his wife was a *countess*, but Hanna could call her Aunt Lydia. They had fled Poland when the Germans invaded in the first days of the war so that the count could continue the battle in the sky. Their grown-up daughter Natasza had been left behind, trapped in a city called Warsaw, where she had bravely helped hide Jewish children like Hanna away from the Nazis who wanted to kill them. Finally, she'd escaped with Hanna to the family estate, and hidden her safely away again. But Natasza had been killed helping others reach freedom.

All this, the most important words Hanna had ever heard, came from the mouths of these two strangers out on this wide fen, under a tin-lid sky, on a still-born day, already close to dusk. Hanna felt she should mark the moment, so she stopped walking and turned to face the countess. 'I'm sorry I don't remember,' she said.

'In time,' said Aunt Lydia, smiling with her lips, but not her eyes, which never seemed to meet Hanna's.

The house had a brick façade – flat and foursquare, with blank windows – and a central door with two pillars that held up a little roof, which tilted giddily to the left. It looked like the house was falling over very slowly. Smoke dribbled from a chimney in a black lazy line.

The front door swung open to reveal a bare hallway, with worn wallpaper, and floorboards. The house smelt of cabbage and polish. In a kitchen with a stone floor Aunt Lydia gave her a glass of milk and boiled her an egg, which Hanna ate with bread and butter in front of a coal fire. Lydia also gave her a cup of black tea that tasted of herbs, which Hanna sipped, staring into the flames. She felt that if she kept very still, and silent, and remained well-behaved, things she wanted to happen would keep happening; she'd be left alone in a room of her own, and then she could open her suitcase and take out her sketch-book and pencils.

Lydia announced that Hanna was tired and should go to bed.

'It's gone bedtime for little girls,' she said, but Hanna felt this remark wasn't for her at all, but someone in the past.

They climbed up uneven wooden steps to the second floor, and then to an attic, which comprised several rooms off a wide corridor. Lydia showed her into one, at the front of the house, with a sloping ceiling and a single window. Marcin pulled back a heavy curtain to show Hanna that snowflakes were touching the glass.

The bed was big enough for two grown-ups and was made of iron, and Lydia had to help Hanna turn back a wedge of blankets so that she could slip beneath. Her suitcase was set on a wooden chest while Marcin fetched a glass and a jug of water. Finally, the old man stood at the door, his hand on the light switch, smiling shyly before letting the darkness flood out from the corners of the room to press against Hanna's eyes.

She heard them say goodnight.

Sleepless an hour later, she burrowed her way from underneath the covers, drew back the curtains, and looked out over the strange flat country, disguised by snow, but now under the light of a familiar moon, by which she opened her sketch-book and drew the first line, describing the pale horizon.